What

Survives

of Us

Kathy Miner

7/15
amazon

Min

About the Author:

Kathy Miner lives in Colorado Springs, CO, with her family and critters. She welcomes comments, questions and conversation about her book, and can be contacted via email at kathyminerwriter@gmail.com, or you can visit her website at www.kathy-miner.com.

Acknowledgments

This is a work of fiction. All characters, locales and events are fictitious or are used fictitiously, and are the product of the author's imagination. Any resemblance to actual events, locales, business establishments or persons, living or dead, is entirely coincidental and not intended by the author. However, care was taken to present plausible scenarios, and several books were instrumental in supporting this endeavor:

HOW TO SURVIVE THE END OF THE WORLD AS WE KNOW IT, by James Wesley, Rawles.

Diseases in History: Plague, by Kevin Cunningham.

Outdoor Survival Guide, by Randy Gerke.

The Forager's Harvest: A Guide to Identifying, Harvesting, and Preparing Edible Wild Plants, by Samuel Thayer.

Discover your Psychic Type: Developing and Using Your Natural Intuition, by Sherrie Dillard.

The last book in particular provided a map in an uncharted land, for which the author was grateful.

For the most up-to-date information on superbugs and the threat of plague, one must turn to the internet and use great caution. The most credible, and easily the most terrifying site the author accessed was the Center for Disease Control and Prevention website at http://www.cdc.gov/.

As with all works of the imagination, any exaggerations, inaccuracies, inconsistencies or outright errors are the fault of the author.

Dedication

You can tell a first-time author by the length of the dedication, and I will be no exception. Writing is, first and last, a solitary endeavor. In between first and last, though, countless people encourage, collaborate, brainstorm, nag, commiserate, harangue, enable and finally, celebrate.

I have been supported in spectacular fashion by a fleet of patient and brilliant friends, many of whom proofread and offered advice. Until they write books of their own, they'll never know how grateful I am. Cheryl Rose, Laura Martin and Candice Moriarty – my fellow warrior moms in the world of Autism, your insights and corrections were deeply appreciated, as is your continued friendship. Tammy Themel, you are the smartest person I know. When you said you liked my book, I cried with joy. Annette Milligan, you may be a gifted artist and a talented proofreader, but you're an even better friend. I can't possibly thank you enough for the hours you spent at my kitchen table designing this cover. Kim Bender, my sister-in-love, I thank you for your corrections and comments, but most of all for your encouragement and love. Nan Anders, you caught an error not one other person did, and I'm so glad you enjoyed the book, even though it's not your usual cup of tea. And Cody Crosby, my beloved nephew and youngest proofreader, your insights were invaluable. Who could have guessed, when I was changing your diapers, that I'd benefit from your thoughtful and analytical reading skills one day.

Phyl and Max Miner, mom and dad, you have supported me through absolutely everything, and *never*, not even *once*, have you told me I was nuts, even when you *had* to be thinking it. Your love is the solid rock I've built my whole life on. Mom, your curiosity and life-long love of learning are qualities I have always admired and tried to emulate; I keep choosing to be just like you as I grow up. Dad, you are and always have been a place of calm and peaceful reason for me to return to, and your good opinion of this book meant the world to me.

Jesse, Casey and Kaya Reynolds, my babies, you are the air in my lungs and the beat of my heart. Without you three, I wouldn't have enough depth to write copy for the back of a cereal box. Jess, you are pure golden joy, as I've told you all your life, and the fantastic person you are is flat-out tickles me. Casey, my wounded cub and my greatest teacher, you keep inviting me into the Unknown, and I am so grateful for that, for you. Kaya, my Mach 5, high-octane, full-speed-ahead daughter, you are delight and laughter and sweetness. I can't wait to see how the three of you will change the world.

Rob Anders, my love, without you this book would never have made it past that weird, "I dreamed about this character, and her name was Naomi..." stage. You yanked me out from behind every excuse I propped up, brushed aside my "Oh, so busy!" laments and said, "Yeah? So? Are you a writer or not?" You ticked me off so much I started writing, and that is a debt I can't imagine repaying. Your support has been rock-solid, your belief in me honest and constant, and your love has enriched this whole family beyond words.

Finally, Kristy Zeluff, beloved sister, half my soul. You are my beginning and my end, and you deserve an entire dedication page all to yourself. By rights, I should list you as co-author – how many different versions of Chapter 13 did you read? It wasn't until I sat down to write this dedication, and tried to put into words how integral you have been to every step of this process, from first nebulous ideas to final draft, that I realized the truth of it: I wrote this book for you.

ONE
Colorado: The First Day

Naomi saw her first corpse in the Safeway on Nevada Avenue. She had stopped in to pick up some salad greens and a gallon of milk for dinner, as well as ingredients for her famous (if she did say so herself) ginger snap cookies. The weathermen were forecasting snow, not unusual for mid-March, and the way the clouds were piling up over Cheyenne Mountain, Naomi figured they'd gotten it right this time. Cookies would be cozy, along with the pot roast she'd had slow-cooking all day.

Unfortunately, predictions of snow always made for long lines at the grocery store. The line at the self-check stretched halfway to the back of the store; it seemed half of Colorado Springs had chosen this store at this time to stock up on storm supplies. Naomi shifted gently from foot to foot, easing the ache in her knees brought on by the change in the weather and the 40 pounds she really should try to lose one of these days. She let her gaze go unfocused and let her mind drift for the moment, resting the relentless hurry of her brain - a trick she'd learned at a self-help seminar or some such.

She had shuffled nearly to the front of the line in this delicious, peaceful state when a flurry of movement and startled exclamations yanked her back to awareness. Up by the registers, someone had collapsed. A cluster of people blocked Naomi's sight until a man wearing a red Safeway employee vest shot to his feet so quickly, he staggered. His eyes were comically wide – Naomi heard a few people around her laugh reflexively – then he threw his arm across his mouth and nose and walked away swiftly, straight out the front doors of the store.

Naomi blinked. *How odd,* she thought, and the first tingle of warning slid gently down her spine like cool fingers. She looked back at the fallen figure – a woman, she could see now – and that warning repeated, a cold burning.

She didn't hesitate. Calmly, she stepped out of line, and set the basket she was carrying on the nearest shelf. Her walk was swift but unhurried as she followed the Safeway employee out the front of the store. Not until she was locked in her vehicle with engine running and heat blasting did she process what she had seen.

That woman had been dead. Naomi squeezed her eyes shut, but the image was still there – a young woman, her hair dark with moisture or sweat, stringing across her forehead and stuck to her cheeks. Her skin grayish and strangely mottled, like Naomi had never seen before. Her lips blue, cracked and swollen, parted over straight white teeth.

And her eyes. Naomi crossed her arms, clutched her elbows with her hands and squeezed, trying to steady the shaking that had started in her legs and moved up through her torso. Her staring eyes, bloodshot, light-less, empty. Naomi had never seen empty eyes before.

"Just calm down," she muttered to herself. "Just get home. You're okay." She took several deep breaths and eased her vehicle out of the parking lot, hyper-focused on the mundane tasks of driving. Rearview mirror. Reverse. Brake. Shift. Gas. She could hear sirens approaching rapidly, and she didn't want to be here when the emergency vehicles arrived.

She didn't want to question why she had abandoned her groceries and walked out – such a rude and graceless gesture, she despised finding other people's castoffs in the grocery store, really, was it such an effort to return that unwanted item to its proper place? Most of all, she didn't want to think about the dead woman, or the way her face looked, like it was already rotting. Naomi shuddered.

She had been to funerals, of course. She had seen preserved, molded and made-up bodies from a distance, but always from a distance. Naomi had never been able to explain the cold terror, the sense of terrible wrongness she felt at such events. Those horrible corpses, so like and so terribly unlike a sleeping human.

This wasn't quite the same feeling, though. The woman's corpse had been awful, but not *wrong*. She tried to sort it out as she drove home, but couldn't fit words around what she was feeling. Those that kept coming made no sense: Dread. Danger.

Snowflakes were swirling fast and thick against her windshield by the time she pulled in her driveway, and what little dusk Colorado Springs experienced was gone. Her headlights cut through the dark to illuminate her garage door as it rose; in the house, lights glowed, and the familiarity of it all brought tears to her eyes. Home, heart, everything.

Scott's car was already in the garage – home early because of the weather. He'd called mid-afternoon to say he'd pick Macy up from her after-school program, and she predicted she'd find them both curled up with a book by the wood-burning stove in the keeping room; Naomi maintained a strict "no electronic media on a weeknight" rule for Macy, even on Fridays, and Scott had always and ever followed the house rules in support of his children. Naomi gathered her purse and the shopping bags she'd collected on her afternoon errands, and headed into the house.

The scent of pot roast was rich in the air as she stepped inside. Persephone was waiting for her just as she always was, soft, golden, butterfly ears perked forward, small head cocked to the side. Her body quivered, but she stayed seated, as she'd been taught, until Naomi set her bags down on the bench in the mudroom and hung up her purse and coat. Naomi held her arms out and the little dog leaped.

"There's my good girl, what a sweet girl, yes, I missed you, too," she crooned, and closed her eyes, enjoying the dog's soft, warm fur and comforting weight against her chest. Persephone snuffled under her chin, gifting Naomi with tiny, enthusiastic licks along her jaw. Naomi laughed and hugged her lovingly before she set the dog down, feeling tension drop away from her shoulders and back. There. She was home. Her world was right once more.

છ

"Check it out – how weird is that?"

Grace looked up from her homework as her little brother gestured at the TV. Benji was watching the evening news for his social studies current events assignment, and the TV was tuned to a local channel. On the screen, a fire truck, ambulance, and half a dozen cop cars were sitting in front of a Safeway store, lights flashing. "What happened? Did somebody rob the store?"

"Nuh-uh. This woman just dropped dead. Now they won't let anyone leave the store because they think she might have a communication disease."

"'Communicable,'" Grace corrected. "Where is this – Colorado Springs?"

"Yep," Benji answered. "Southgate area, they said. Where's that at?"

"Down south, not far from the World Arena – you know, where we saw 'Walking with Dinosaurs' with Dad?"

They passed through Colorado Springs once a month on their way to visit their dad, his new wife and their brand new baby half-brother in Woodland Park, and sometimes went on the weekends to shop or catch a movie with their mom and step-dad. Lately, Grace had been visiting even more frequently on dates with her boyfriend, William. There wasn't much to do in dinky little Limon. She tried to think of what else would be nearby that Benji would recognize. "It's not far from the zoo, just a little north and east, I think."

"Okay." He frowned in concentration as he wrote carefully in his notebook. "Will you spell 'communicable,' please?"

Grace smiled. "Sure thing, buddy." He was so cute, with his polite, studious, serious ways. As little brothers went he was bearable, though she suspected he had been in the bushes with his buddy Nate the other night, spying on her and William when he brought her home. Some blackmail might be in the works. "Did they say what disease they thought she had?"

Benji read from his notes in his best "Announcer Bunny" voice, not that he'd ever let his friends know he still watched *In Between the Lions* on PBS. He was in 7th grade for pity's sake – way too old for a show that taught kids to read. "Authorities refuse to speculate as to the nature of the woman's illness," he read from his notes, "But we will keep viewers informed as this story breaks." He paused, wrote something down, then continued in his normal voice. "They think she was a soldier from Fort Carson, and that she was really young. Some people inside the store called the news station and talked to the reporters before the police took their phones away."

"Huh. The police took their phones?" That struck Grace as extreme. "Bet they weren't too happy about that." She returned her attention to her own homework, but a part of her mind had locked onto the story, the facts clicking into place with too few pieces to complete a picture. She'd follow up, she decided, later this evening, either online or on the late news. Grace couldn't resist either puzzles or mysteries, and this story seemed like both.

ॐ

Brian Nelson flopped down on the bleachers beside Jack Kiel – Pastor Jack to the kids – and lifted his t-shirt to wipe his dripping face. The raised shirt revealed a regretful expanse of white belly spreading over the top of his basketball shorts. He tugged the shirt back down and wheezed in air. "Darn altitude. Can't catch my wind."

Jack didn't smile, and figured that would count in his favor when the Day of Reckoning came. Brian had moved to Colorado at least 20 years ago. "Yeah. It takes getting used to, that's for sure."

"Oh, shut up." Brian's reply was easy and without heat. "I'm fat and out of shape. Even lies of omission are a sin."

Jack laughed, and together they watched Jack's youth group kids – including Brian's oldest son – hustle the basketball up and down the court. It would be Jack's turn to substitute next, when one of the players needed a break or a drink of water. Or a minute to flirt with the group of teenaged girls watching the action, Jack thought, and smiled. Some things never changed.

"Small group this week," Brian commented after a few minutes. "Where's Ava and the kids from the Springs?"

"She got called into work, last minute," Jack answered.

Ava Beckett was a Colorado Springs police officer who attended their Woodland Park church with her husband, also a cop, every week. They were both Safety Resource Officers in Springs-area high schools, and had organized a group of kids to come up the pass to play basketball every Friday night with Jack's youth group kids. It had proven to be an interesting experience; most of Jack's kids were from sheltered, middle-class families, and the kids Ava brought all fell into the "at-risk" category. Watching the two groups learn to mingle and understand each other, and to develop tentative, fledgling friendships had been immensely rewarding.

"That would stink," Brian commented. "One of the advantages of being an accountant, I guess. Other than April 15th, I don't get called in for emergencies. Did she say what was going on?"

"Some kind of quarantine situation," Jack answered, "I guess there was a death at a grocery store in the Springs, and they don't know what the woman died of. The health department took one look and called in the CDC. Ava says they're bringing in cots and bedding for the people still in the store, keeping them over night. She's working crowd control – I guess a lot of family members have gathered, and they're angry and scared."

"I would be too, I imagine. Probably just another case of West Nile," Brian predicted, then nodded at the action on the floor. "Getting a little hot out there."

He was right, Jack thought – elbows were being applied just a little too liberally. "Hey!" He shouted. Shoes shrilled on the floorboards as the action stopped, and ten faces swiveled his way, several of them more flushed than they ought to be. "Don't make me come out there and whup up on ya'll! Keep the elbows tight, boys!"

Perfect time for a pastor to sub in, he decided, watching them scuff and grumble. He stood and peeled out of his sweatshirt. Unlike Brian, his thirties hadn't brought weight problems with them, a fact he owed at least as much to good genetics and these Friday night basketball games as to his eating habits. "Alright, you babies, which one of you wants to get a drink of water and sweet-talk the ladies?"

He jogged onto the court, serenaded by a chorus of giggles from the girls, and slapped the kid with the reddest face on the shoulder. "James, why don't you take a break and give an old man a chance to play?"

~

Naomi dropped the last dish in the drainer and hung her soggy towel on the oven bar to dry. Dinner done, dishes done, and a luxurious Friday night stretched out in front of her. For the most part, she had managed to hold her sense of unease at bay; she hadn't mentioned the dead woman in Safeway to Scott, and she didn't intend to. She wasn't in the habit of keeping secrets from her husband, but she couldn't see how any good would come out of talking about it. Just a lot of baseless speculation, she had decided. No need to let that into her cozy world this evening.

Scott had headed out to putter at his workbench in the garage, but not before he'd slid his hand slowly and lovingly down her spine and dropped a kiss on the nape of her neck. Naomi smiled. He was consistent, maybe even predictable, but the upside of that was anticipation. Twenty-three years, and that slow smile of his could still rev her up.

Macy had a 4-H project spread out on the kitchen table, and was humming softly to herself as she worked. Her hair seemed to glow in the soft light, a shade exactly between her father's red and her mother's blonde, the purest strawberry Naomi had ever seen. She'd once asked a stylist if she could match it – Naomi's blonde had been maintained in salons for years now – but the stylist had shaken her head. "That color is a gift from the gods," she'd said. "You'd end up with orange or pink. Better just enjoy it on your daughter."

And Naomi did, smoothing her hand over her daughter's shining head, as she had done thousands of times before. Macy was in her second year of sewing, and was piecing together a simple quilt from scraps Naomi had given her. Naomi sat down beside her, and Macy handed her a piece.

"This one?"

Naomi smiled, and fingered the Black Watch plaid. "A shirt I made for daddy when we were first married. The sleeves weren't quite long enough, but he wore it anyway. He just rolled the sleeves up, even in the dead of winter, and he never said a thing."

Macy smiled. "That's just like daddy." She handed her another scrap, a tiny mint-green gingham check. "This one?"

"A little jumper I made for Piper, when she was just tiny. I made one in every color of gingham they had." She reached across the table, selected pink, yellow, blue. "I called her my rainbow baby."

Macy took the piece back, rubbed it between her finger and thumb, then held it to her cheek. "I miss her. I wish she would come home more often."

"I miss her too, punkin." In so many ways, Naomi thought. She missed those easy baby years, when she'd been the bright center of Piper's world, instead of a source of discomfort, strain and disappointment. Her oldest daughter was finishing up her junior year at the University of Northern Colorado – not all that far away, but she didn't choose to visit home very frequently.

Piper had been almost twelve when Macy was born, a surprise tag-a-long. She had adored her baby sister on sight, and that adoration continued to be mutual – Macy was convinced her older sister hung the moon. Naomi always thought of Macy as the magical glue that held her family together. Her birth had come along just as Piper decided her mother was an embarrassing throw-back to the 1950's, possessed no discernible ambition beyond being "Suzy Homemaker" and rescuing stray animals, and therefore was a failure as a modern woman and role model for her daughter.

When she gave voice to her criticisms, she came up hard against her beloved father's disapproval. Scott rarely stepped in to discipline the girls, but he'd made it perfectly clear that he would brook no disrespect for Naomi. Piper might not have given a rip for her mother's feelings, but her father's good opinion meant the world to her. She had never spoken of it again, but her disdain for Naomi and the choices she'd made was clear.

Naomi had tried to bridge the gap, of course. She'd reached out, read books, attended seminars, but nothing she'd learned or tried had worked. In the end, she'd reached the conclusion that time was the only healer. When Piper knew herself better, when she understood her own value as a woman, she'd be more accepting of the choices her mother had made.

"I have an idea." Naomi looked at the clock, and calculated. They might just catch her before her Friday night social life revved up. "Let's Skype her. We should find out what her plans are for Easter."

Macy's smile dazzled. "I'll get the laptop!"

Ten minutes later, that same dazzling smile shone on Piper's face via the computer monitor. "Hey, bitty bean! Are you rebelling at last, breaking the weeknight 'no electronics' rule? Better not let Mama Bear catch you – she'll put you on pooper-scooper detail for sure."

Naomi leaned over Macy's shoulder and smiled warmly in spite of the pinch to her heart. "It was Mama

Bear's idea," she said lightly. "We missed you. Are you getting ready to go out?"

Piper grimaced. "Sort of. Study group at the pub. Hopefully we'll get something done before too many 'adult beverages' have been consumed."

"Well. Good luck with that." Naomi straightened. "I'll let you girls chat for a bit. Macy, don't disconnect until I've talked to her, please."

She puttered around the kitchen, listening to Macy talk about her life, about the things that shaped the world of a 10-year-old: 4-H, the horse camp she was desperate to attend this coming summer, school. And she savored the patience and warmth in Piper's voice as she responded to her little sister; oh, these girls, they were her whole wide world, the breath in her lungs.

"Mama," Macy hopped up from her spot at the table, and gestured to the computer. "She has to get going. Better ask her about Easter." To the screen: "Please come home for Easter, Piper, we could do eggs, it would be so fun."

Naomi took Macy's place. "So, do you have plans for that weekend? Easter's on the 8th this year."

As she spoke, Ares strutted into the kitchen, stretched, sat down on his pudgy kitty behind and yowled for his supper. Piper laughed. "Sounds like you're still starving Ares to death, poor boy."

Naomi scooped him up and snuggled him, the only human afforded that privilege. Ares was a rescue, like all their animals, and even though he'd been with them for years, he would permit no one but Naomi to touch him.

"Easter?" she prompted. She was tempted, oh so tempted, to play the "Macy would love to see you" card.

"I'm not sure, mom. I'll see how my big project is going and let you know." Piper was majoring in Sociology, and loved everything about her course of study. People fascinated her. "Hey, big excitement down your way tonight, huh?"

"What do you mean?" But Naomi knew. She knew. A cold fist of fear tightened in her chest.

"That Safeway we always shop at, on Nevada – you didn't hear about that woman dying, and the officials quarantining the place? Oh, yeah." Piper's lips twitched in a sneer she didn't bother to hide. "No media on a weeknight."

"They quarantined the store?" Naomi didn't realize she had clutched Ares to her chest until he let out a snarky meow and struggled to get down. "Why? Did they say why?"

"I told you – a woman died. Must have been some kind of terrible disease – they've called in the CDC and CNN says they've got the National Guard on alert just in case."

"In case what? Why would they need the National Guard?" Lord, should she have stayed? Had she brought home some sort of contagion, endangered her family? She was nearly panting, and could hear hysteria pushing through in her voice. Piper frowned, and Macy looked up from across the table, small face wrinkled in concern.

"What's wrong, Mama?"

"Yeah, geez, take it easy, mom. I'm sure they'll get the whole nasty mess all cleaned up before double coupon Tuesday."

Naomi took a big breath, held it for a moment, then exhaled the hurt Piper's snotty tone had lodged in her heart. She tilted her head to the side, and examined her daughter's delicate face, that darling, tilted nose Piper hated – too cutsey – the waterfall of fine, straight blonde hair she'd inherited from her mother – hot pink streaks this week, Naomi rather liked them – and her father's green as moss eyes.

"You're so pretty." Piper hadn't tolerated compliments on her beauty since she was 15, claiming she intended to use her brains, not her looks, to achieve her goals. For once, Naomi didn't care about inciting her daughter's wrath. "I know you don't like it when I say that, but you are. And as beautiful as you are, you're 100 times as smart. I love you, honey."

Macy, bless her sensitive little heart, chose that exact moment to drape herself over her mother's shoulders and beam at her sister. "I think you're pretty too, Piper." Her smile took on a crafty slant. "Will you bring me a present? When you come for Easter? Pleeeaaaaase?"

Piper's face was soft. "We'll see, bitty bean. I'll do my best." Her face stayed tender as she met her mother's eyes, and Naomi's chest ached with warmth, delight, love at the rare softness from her daughter. "I love you too, mom. Have a good night."

In the years that would follow, Naomi would take this moment out and cradle it close, savoring it as a perfect moment, a gift, something she recognized as precious even as it was happening. Her baby girl, gentle little arms wrapped around her neck, soft silky cheek pressed to hers. And a warm smile from her beautiful warrior daughter, a young woman so full of strength and power, eager to take her place in a world about to change forever.

TWO
Colorado: The Next Day

Naomi followed the scent of coffee into the kitchen the next morning, and found Scott leaning on the counter, frowning. He was watching the tiny TV he had mounted under the counter for her a few years back, and she felt again that awful sense of knowing what was coming before he spoke. Instead of getting herself a cup of coffee, she sat down at the kitchen table, suddenly cold.

"Look at this, hon." He gestured with his coffee mug. "It's all over the news, local and national. That Safeway you shop at all the time has been quarantined." He shook his head, took a sip. "That's too close to home. You could have been there, just as easy as those other people."

He moved to the sink, rinsing his cup and putting it neatly in the dish drainer. Before she realized she was going to speak, Naomi was blurting. "I was there. Yesterday. I saw her."

Scott turned around, his frown deepening, not yet registering the full impact of her words. "What? You were – what did you just say?"

"I said I was there. At the store. I saw the woman who died." Naomi took a huge breath, trying to steady her shaking voice. Crying was not going to help, but tears sprang to her eyes anyway. "I was in line, at the self-check. I saw her fall. Well no, I didn't, but I saw people gathered around her. Then one of them moved away, and I saw her, and I put my things down and walked out of the store. The police and fire trucks were just getting there as I left."

Scott moved until he was crouched right in front of her. He stilled her wringing hands with his big, warm calloused palms. His eyes, normally so warm and gentle, were sharp and intense. "How close did you get to her?"

"I don't know - you know I can't judge distance. She was up by the cashier's station. I was still in line and there were a few people ahead of me." She bent her head and pressed her forehead to their clasped hands, giving voice to the fear that had woken her repeatedly throughout the night. "What if what they're saying is true? What if she had some sort of disease, and I brought it home to you and Macy? Oh my God, Scott!"

"Honey, you've got to get a hold of yourself. Macy'll be up any time, and you don't want her to see you like this." He waited until she sat up, then cupped her face in his warm hands and wiped her cheeks with his thumbs matter-of-factly. Naomi's tears had always come easily, and Scott had stopped being fazed by them years ago. "There. You probably didn't come any closer than 30 or 40 feet. Do you remember hearing her, or anybody, coughing?"

Naomi closed her eyes, putting herself back in the store. She remembered hearing a newborn's cry – so distinctive – and noting, as she often did, how the catchy music probably made people linger as they shopped, so they could sing along. And yes. Someone coughing violently. She opened her eyes and gazed at Scott, unable to voice the confirmation.

"Okay." Scott took a deep breath, and smoothed his hand along the side of her face. She felt a spike of worry from him, as if it had stabbed her in the chest. "It's okay, honey. It is what it is. I really don't think you got close enough to her for it to matter."

He straightened, then gazed out the window over the kitchen sink for a few moments, tapping his fingers on the table. Then he nodded. "I've got an errand to run." He leaned to give her a quick kiss, and a reassuring squeeze on the shoulder. Her rock. "Be back in a couple of hours."

ॐ

As it turned out, Grace never had a chance to follow up on her mystery story. She slept late Saturday morning, after a too-long-but-worth-it conversation with William on the phone, and then had to hustle out the door to make it to school to catch the track bus. Normally, she would have caught a ride with William and his younger brother Quinn – the three of them were right in a row in school, with William a senior, Grace a junior, and Quinn a lowly sophomore – but she had promised her mother she'd drop Benji at the library. The tiny local branch had brought in a program on robotics, and Benji was beside himself with geeky glee. He talked non-stop all the way there about servos and touch sensors, oblivious to the fact that Grace didn't have the faintest idea what he was talking about.

"Nerd." She scrubbed his head with her knuckles as she pulled up in front of the library. "Just don't forget me when your robot minions rule the world."

He grinned, thanked her for the ride in his meticulously polite way, and was off like a shot. Grace drove the rest of the way to the high school, parked, and jogged towards the waiting bus. Hopefully William had saved her a seat across the aisle from him – in bigger schools, boys and girls often rode on separate buses, but Limon had only fielded 23 kids on the team this year, not enough to justify the gas and expense of an extra bus. Instead, coach had the boys and girls sit on opposite sides, which always struck Grace as silly and frankly naïve, considering what some of these kids had been doing the night before. She and William weren't the only dating couple on the team, though they might be the only ones not having sex.

She'd been upfront with him from their first date on; Grace didn't intend to raise a baby until she was good and ready, and no way was she taking the chance. William had been a good sport about it, probably because she didn't object to some wandering hands. Secretly, though, she wondered what everyone got so lathered up about. It felt good when William kissed her, and wonderful when he nuzzled and nipped at her neck, but she was nowhere near losing control. Her girlfriends talked about getting carried away - "We just couldn't stop!" - and Grace just didn't get that. To her ordered and logical mind, the risks just didn't outweigh the thrill.

She bounded onto the bus, and spotted William immediately, sitting behind his little brother. Well, okay, maybe not "little" – Quinn wasn't quite as tall as his older brother, but where William was lean, Quinn was bulky, in a way that turned all the girls' heads when he took his warm-ups off. He was also as shy as his older brother was confident; Grace knew he struggled with some sort of learning disability, though William insisted Quinn was brilliant, in his own way. His protectiveness and pride in his brother were some of the things she liked best about him. And then there was that smile.

"Hey, gorgeous." His eyes were so, so blue. Grace felt just a little swoony when he smiled at her, and those blue eyes lit up. "I was afraid you'd miss the bus."

Grace smiled back and plopped down in the seat he had, indeed, saved for her. "Not a chance. Mornin', Quinn."

Quinn mumbled an inaudible reply and ducked his head, his ears flushing a rosy pink. William always made a point of speaking to Benji when he saw him, and Grace did the same with Quinn and their four younger brothers, who were all in elementary school. Grace had known the Harris family her whole life – their ranch bordered Grace's mom's property to the north – and she'd heard her mother speculating that Mrs. Harris had started trying for that girl she wanted so badly when she had raised William and

Quinn up old enough to help with the livestock. Now that she'd spent time with the family, she didn't agree – Mrs. Harris adored all six of her boys, though she did speak with great anticipation of a little granddaughter one day.

"Did you hear about that quarantine thing they've got going on in the Springs?" William asked.

The puzzle, with all its empty pieces, flared to life in Grace's brain. She leaned forward, interest sharp. "I did, last night. Benji was writing about it for school, and I meant to follow up and check the news this morning. What are they saying?"

"Nothing, that's the thing. They aren't letting anybody out, and the only people going in now are wearing hazmat suits. They even kept the first responders – the firemen and police. And nobody on the inside has a phone or has been allowed contact with their families."

Click, click, click. Grace didn't like the picture her puzzle was forming. "Benji said they thought the dead woman was a soldier from Fort Carson – have they said anything about that?"

"Not that I know of," William paused, then grimaced. "My mom says she doesn't want us to go into the Springs tonight. You know, after we get back from the meet."

Grace blinked. "Wow. She really thinks it's that big a deal?"

"She's trying to be all cool about it, but I can tell she's scared. So..." He paused again, and gave her that heart-stuttering smile. "If you want to come over for dinner, we could go for a ride after. Bet we could even talk mom into popping popcorn and making cocoa when we get back."

Grace grinned. After the divorce, her mother had sold both hers and Grace's quarter horses, saying they couldn't keep up with the feed any longer. Grace had understood, but oh, the misery was still sharp in her heart. She loved to ride, and William knew her well. "That sounds perfect. Way better than a movie. It's a date."

ॐ

Pastor Jack prided himself on being open-minded. As a rule, he wasn't interested in criticizing other religions or labeling their beliefs as wrong; Evangelism, he believed, was best accomplished by living a Godly life, and doing so in such a joyful way that people not of your faith would seek you out, asking for the Secret of your Joy.

Nor was he interested in dwelling on Satan. People, he believed, had enough excuses for their poor behavior; the Devil made me do it had been worn as thin and flimsy as tissue paper. From his personal, professional and spiritual perspectives, it was time for humanity to take full responsibility for its actions and decisions – enough with the blaming, either of mankind's innately sinful nature, or of Satan and his demons.

"Get over it," he would say to the youth he worked with. "Satan tempts everybody – that's just a cop-out. You choose your path. You decide who to be."

These perspectives, of course, had brought him more than his fair share of criticism in seminary. Too much of the World, many had said. Heretical, a few had accused. But Jack didn't dwell on the disapproval of others. His work *was* in the World, after all. He was successful working with youth because they sensed what was in his heart: He truly wasn't interested in judging them – that belonged to the Lord. As Mother Teresa had said, judging people left you no time to love them, and Jack lived every single day by this simple, powerful mantra.

With one exception.

Layla Karela. She was three people ahead of him in the checkout line at City Market this bright and beautiful Saturday morning, and Jack caught himself keeping his face averted, praying she wouldn't spot him. She always wanted to chat about this or that kid, and the effort of maintaining a baseline politeness while conversing with her gave Jack a teeth-grinding headache every darn time.

Layla taught English and directed the drama program at the local high school, and there was a lot of overlap between his youth group kids and the kids she worked with every day. Jack had been hearing the kids talk about Ms. Karela for years, and he knew from them that she was a popular teacher, fun in class but committed to excellence and meticulously fair. Parents talked about her, too – she was involved, dedicated, professional – all the things a community could wish for in a teacher of their youth, with the exception of the fact that she was a practicing Witch.

And she didn't even have the courtesy to be subtle about it. Jack shuffled ahead in the line, keeping his head down but straining to listen to her conversation with the checker just the same. Everyone was buzzing about the quarantine in Colorado Springs, but not Layla, oh no. She was talking about the upcoming metaphysical fair in Colorado Springs – she would be reading Tarot there as usual, he learned, and barely repressed a shiver of revulsion. She and her ilk came close to making him reconsider his doctrine of non-judgment.

They disgusted him, with their ridiculous costumes, their cards and crystals and fripperies and geegaws, their talk of past lives, Chakras and Spirits. All that hoo-ha, of course, appealed enormously to the kids he worked with – always and forever, teens would be drawn to the danger, the mystery, the edge. And that, Jack told himself, was what made their practices unforgivable: The corruption of the kids he loved and counseled, the peril to their very souls. He knew all too well just how real that peril was.

The checker wished Layla a good morning, promising to look her up at the fair for a reading – Jack made a mental note to add the poor girl to his prayer list – and the line crept forward. By the time Jack was leaving the store with his groceries, he had put the near-encounter with Layla out of his mind and moved on to a mental list of the tasks he hoped to accomplish that day. This, of course, made Layla's unexpected presence in the parking lot all the more unpleasant.

She was leaning on the bumper of her junker jeep, face lifted to the sun, eyes closed. Tiny multi-colored beads sparkled in the long strands of her dark hair – he had noticed that she wore it long and loose when she wasn't working, up and sleek when she was – and a tiny smile lifted the corners of her mouth. Jack wasn't sure how old she was – a couple years his senior, if he had to guess – but she looked younger than usual like this, her face open, relaxed and filled with quiet joy. She was parked right beside him. Of course.

Jack resigned himself to the grinding headache as he popped open his trunk and started loading in his groceries. "Good morning, Layla. Car trouble?"

She blinked her eyes open and focused on him. Her chest lifted in a peaceful sigh before she answered. "Yep. Battery's dead. I called a friend, but he's tied up and it's going to be a while." She closed her eyes and lifted her face once more. "I don't mind, though. What a beautiful gift from the Universe this morning, especially after the snow last night – some quiet time to just enjoy the sun."

Since her eyes were closed, Jack didn't refrain from rolling his. "Sure." He finished loading up, shut his trunk, and took his cart to the corral while his conscience gave him all manner of Hell.

He drove right by her little vine-covered cottage – even her house was clichéd - on his way home. Literally, right by. Man, sometimes being a Christian sucked.

"Layla, I can give you a ride home – you could put away your groceries and come back with your friend later to get your jeep."

Those eyes blinked open again. She had the darkest eyes he had ever seen, black, shining and liquid, like a lake at night. She smiled. "That is so thoughtful of you, Jack. I'll take your offer, thanks."

She loaded her groceries into his back seat, and within moments, he was trapped in the car with her. She smelled like some weird perfume – probably incense, which would explain his intensifying headache – and she chimed every time she moved. Bangle bracelets laddered up both arms, multiple ankle bracelets on one ankle, earrings that brushed her shoulders. How did she think with all that jingling?

"I've been meaning to give you a call," Layla said, as they pulled out of the parking lot. "I've got a student who's new to town, and he's having a hard time with the adjustment. Family moved here from Chicago, so he's got that city edge on him and the kids really aren't warming up. Tenth grader, loves basketball, thinks we're all a hopeless bunch of hicks." She smiled. "Which we are. Anyway, I wondered if you could ask one of your Friday night kids to reach out. They'd have to be ready for the re-buff – he has his shields up but good."

It was things like this that made his head pound. If she would just be shallow and selfish, he wouldn't feel so conflicted about loathing her. "I'll ask Trevor. And maybe Jason. They've both lived in bigger cities – they may connect better."

"Thank you. He's been on my mind – wrote a pretty anguished paper about leaving his life behind that had nothing to do with the writing prompt. I tried to talk to him – thought maybe he was reaching out, a lot of kids do through writing assignments – but he gave me the stiff arm." She sighed. "The curse and privilege of teaching English, I guess. We learn a lot about the kids through their writing, but they won't always let us help them."

"That must be difficult," Jack said stiffly. Just a few more blocks. He resisted the urge to fudge, even a little bit, on the speed limit. In contrast to his jaw-clenching tension, she seemed completely relaxed, long-fingered hands lying gracefully in her lap.

"It is, at times," Layla agreed. She turned to look at him just as he was home-free, pulling into her driveway. "Jack, why do you dislike me so much?"

Unbelievable. Jack gazed straight ahead, feeling her eyes on him. Penance, that's what this was, for his unkind thoughts, as deserving as she was of them. He turned his head to look at her, keeping his face still, neutral. "What makes you think I dislike you?"

Layla snorted and rolled her eyes. "Please. I teach teenagers. So do you, so you know what I mean. It rolls off you in waves."

"I'm a Christian pastor," he answered stiffly. "I should think the reason for my disapproval would be obvious." Lord, he sounded stuffy. This was one of the things that ticked him off about her the most – the way she made him feel square and unnatural, like a stick-in-the-mud fuddy duddy.

"No," she said thoughtfully, after a moment. "That's the thing. It's not obvious." She shifted onto her hip, twisting her body to face him more fully, her face open and earnest. "The kids talk about you, you know. They talk about how accepting you are, how you teach tolerance and compassion. Frankly, I liked you for a year before I even met you. I think what you're doing, what you teach the kids, is a good thing." Another pause. "Did I offend you in some way?"

"Of course you did! Everything about you offends me!"

His voice was loud, abrasive, edgy, even to his own ears. He shut his eyes for a moment, struggling to moderate his response to her. He wasn't used to losing control of an interaction like this; normally, he could sense just how to talk to someone, just when to pause, when to sit back, when to touch someone's forearm. But with Layla, there was no rhythm to the interaction – just a lot of disconnected near-misses and frustration.

He opened his eyes and found her watching him patiently, a frown drawing a vertical line between her eyebrows. He took a deep breath, reached for calm reason, and hit her with both barrels. "Exodus 22:18. "Thou shall not suffer a witch to live."

It was satisfying, so very satisfying, to see her mouth drop open. She goggled at him for a moment, then her spine snapped ram-rod straight, and battle lit her eyes.

"I am so disappointed, hearing that from you. I thought you were broader-minded than that."

Whatever satisfaction he had briefly enjoyed sizzled away under the stinging heat of her words. He used all the subterfuge he possessed to hide that fact from her. "Your disappointment is irrelevant to me. The fact of the matter is, your 'religious practices' are an offense to God and to Christians."

"Really. That's strange – I've got it on good authority you don't feel that way about Jews, or Muslims, or Buddhists. What makes my spirituality any different?" She didn't give him a chance to answer. Her face was fierce in its animation – he felt a moment of pity for any students that had to face down Ms. Karela when her temper awoke. "And you're pretty selective with your Bible verses there, aren't you? What about, 'Thou shall not kill?' Or, 'Judge not lest ye be judged?'"

Jack's eyes narrowed. "Even the Devil uses scripture for his own purposes."

"The Devil!" He would swear, later, that her hair lifted around her head, writhing and crackling. "For your information, pal, the word 'witch' was not used in the original Hebrew or Greek versions of that verse – King James added it to his translation to support his persecution of wise women and female herbalists, and scholars aren't even sure what the term meant when it was originally used in Exodus. So applying an Old Testament law – which was meant for an ancient Jewish tribe, by the way – to a modern spiritual practice is dangerous and backward thinking!"

Now she was on his turf. Here, at least, his footing felt sure. "The Bible is the inspired word of God, and as such, is as relevant to us today as it was to the ancients. And your information is skewed; the original Hebrew uses the word 'm'khashepah' to describe the person who should be killed, which is defined as 'a woman who uses spoken spells to harm others.' The original Greek word, 'venefica,' can be translated as 'female poisoner,' which is, in my opinion, an even more appropriate description of what you people do."

"Oh, really. Really." Flushed face, accelerated breathing, repetition of meaningless phrases. Yeah, he had her now. "Why don't you illuminate me? What exactly is it you think 'my people' do?"

"You seduce young, vulnerable minds. You steal them away from Truth with sparkles and glitter and empty promises of something other-worldly, something mysterious. You make your service to Satan look glamorous, which is unforgiveable." He pointed a finger at her nose, filled with righteous, protective wrath. "Unforgiveable."

"Satan again! Jack!" She shook her head, her expression a mixture of anger and bemusement. "I don't even believe in the Satan you Christians are so afraid of! Look, I can't speak for all neo-Pagans, Wiccans, Witches or otherwise, but there's no Devil in the Craft I practice."

"Your lack of belief doesn't make Satan less real. It just makes you more susceptible to his influence, an easier tool to wield." He overrode her gasp of outrage and forged on. He had her on the run, and he was not about to give up the advantage. "You were right about one thing. I don't disparage other religions. I've studied them, and I believe they are seeking the Divine, even if I don't always agree with their practices. But I won't recognize or validate what you do – what you seek is profane."

For an eternity of seconds, she just stared at him. Her stunned silence was a triumph he savored, basking in the afterglow of righteousness well spent. Then, she laughed.

"So let me get this straight – you think I'm a mindless tool of Satan, that my spiritual practices are an abomination, and that my only purpose is to recruit more evil minions to serve the Great Pretender. Does that about cover it?"

There was a trap here, he could feel it. But he wasn't about to start back-tracking now. In for a penny, in for a pound. "That's a fair summation."

"Huh. That's interesting, considering you don't know anything about me or my spiritual practices, which I consider to be very private, by the way." He started to interject, but she held up her hand. "No, now you've spoken your piece and it's obvious you've been wanting to for quite some time. It's also obvious that you've done your homework – that was really good, that information about the original Hebrew and Greek – and you certainly caught me unprepared. That won't happen again. Because you know what?"

She paused, gathered her groceries, popped open the car door and slid out. Then she bent down to grin at him. "Game on, Jack. Thanks for the ride."

ക

While Scott was gone, Naomi distracted herself with the feeding of "Naomi's Ark" as Scott called her collection of animals – little Persephone and Zeus, the aging lab that was Scott's constant shadow; Ares and his two subordinate kitties, Athena and Artemis; and finally Poseidon, the blue Macaw she'd rescued just a few months before Macy was born. Macy would take care of her little family of mice and the fish when she got up; unlike Piper, she had inherited her mother's love of animals.

If Naomi had her way, the menagerie would include some backyard chickens and maybe even a miniature goat or two, but Scott had put his foot down. For a while, she had fostered animals in the process of being re-homed, which was how they'd ended up with Zeus and Artemis. Once they were in her home, she couldn't bear to give them up. Now, she volunteered her time at public awareness events for Dream Power Animal Rescue, and Scott had begged her to please, please refrain from holding the featured animals, which was how she'd fallen in love with Persephone. The little mixed-breed dog was ridiculously cute, with her sturdy, terrier-like body, her silky, golden fur, and her cascading, Papillon-like ears. Persephone had curled up in her arms, trusting, warm and sweet, almost like a newborn baby, and that had been that.

Caring for the animals calmed her, as always. By the time Macy shuffled into the kitchen, her rosy golden hair a snarled halo around her sleepy head, Naomi had started a batch of homemade cinnamon rolls and had a pot of ham and bean soup simmering on the stove. She got Macy some breakfast, then smiled when Persephone snapped to attention and raced to the back door. A few seconds later, she heard the faint rumble of the garage door opening; Scott was home.

She left Macy eating breakfast and joined him in the garage. He'd backed his truck partway in, and was unloading case after case of bottled water. She peered past his shoulder, noting that the back of his truck was packed almost to the roof of the cap with not only water but canned and dry goods as well. Scott straightened, and their eyes met for a moment. Met and held. Then he shrugged, and started unloading again.

"It was time to re-supply and rotate anyway," he said, and to Naomi's ear, his casual tone sounded just a little forced. "I had this on the list to do over spring break, but now's as good a time as any."

Scott was what he called a "prepper" – not a hard-core survivalist, per-se, but he believed in having emergency supplies on hand, in the event of a catastrophe. He had lost family in the wake of hurricane Katrina – an elderly aunt and uncle who had died in their own home of dehydration and heat stroke – and to this day, the ease with which their deaths could have been prevented haunted him. Ever since, Scott had stocked and maintained a storage space with several month's worth of bottled water and non-perishable food, as well as other emergency supplies. He rotated the supplies regularly and donated what they hadn't used to a local food bank. The dual-purpose plan was quintessential Scott: It was a way to both protect his family and give back to the community.

And while Naomi had never shared his "prepare for the worst, hope for the best" mentality, his preparedness was a comfort to her now. "Maybe I'll run over to Natural Grocers this afternoon," she said, her tone as carefully casual as his had been. "I could stock up on some necessities. Some oil of oregano, some garlic caps, a bottle of colloidal silver."

"Re-supply your 'arsenal.' Good idea." Scott had always supported her natural remedies for their family's illnesses. "And fill your car up while you're out, okay?"

"Okay." She paused, then spoke in a rush. "Oh, this is silly, right? I mean, we're just over-reacting. We are. We'll laugh about this in a few days, won't we?"

Scott straightened, and again, their eyes met and held. "Maybe. A lot of people would say so, that's for sure." He held his hand out to her, and she took it, lacing her fingers through his. "But I'd rather live feeling silly than die saying 'dang it.'" He smiled when Naomi giggled. "See? We're laughing already."

THREE
Everywhere: The Days That Followed

Five days later, everyone quarantined in the Safeway store was sick. Within ten days, they were dead, all of them, though it would be some time before officials confirmed this fact. People, presumably medical or CDC personnel, were filmed by news crews entering and exiting the building encased in hazmat suits.

Desperate families pressed the perimeter line relentlessly, some of them even camping out in tents. They mobbed any vehicle that crossed the yellow line, demanding information about their loved ones, but none of the officials involved were talking. Six days after the quarantine started, police had to use riot gear and tear gas to repel a group that tried to walk through the line.

And all the while, the whole world watched. News crews from all over the United States and a growing number of foreign countries formed a third perimeter around the police line and the families, vans bristling with lights, power chords snaking everywhere. Round the clock, they broadcast very little news and a great deal of fear back to their home viewers. Officials might not be talking, but the media had found numerous experts on communicable disease willing to speculate.

A biological weapon, some of them posited. Highly contagious and deadly, they all agreed, as evidenced by the official response. None of them could come up with a reason – other than the direst of scenarios – the families would not be allowed any kind of contact with their loved ones. Reporters alternated their interviews between sober, grim-faced PhDs, doctors and former CDC employees, and terrified husbands, wives, parents and children of the victims.

Finally, eleven days after the start of the quarantine, the official announcements began.

Bubonic Plague. One of the paramedics had seen the disease before, and suspecting the highly contagious pneumonic form, had immediately set the quarantine in motion. The plague was not unheard of in the western United States – several cases were reported each year, with fatalities occurring only if the victims did not receive antibiotic treatment in time – but as it turned out, this was Bubonic Plague with a caveat.

The first victim, a soldier recently returned from active duty in Pakistan, was unaware she was carrying a sleeping superbug: bacteria enhanced by a mutation of the NDM-1 gene. Known to only a few virologists in the world, the mutation had only recently been identified; antibiotics that could combat NDM-2 weren't even in the pipeline. Like its predecessor, NDM-2 was both prolific and promiscuous, transferring itself easily among many types of bacteria via microbial mating.

World-wide, NDM-2 had already infiltrated dozens of bacterial species, gifting even easily-treated infections with its special talent: antibiotic resistance. Even the most powerful drugs of last resort were useless against it. A day spent shooting prairie dogs with friends, a flea bite she'd been all but unaware of, and NDM-2 had been introduced to the Black Death by Private First Class Emma Turner.

It was untreatable.

There was no vaccine.

It was 99-100% fatal.

Furthermore, the desperate attempt at containment had failed; officials on Fort Carson had confirmed twelve additional cases, and three fatalities. Memorial Hospital had isolated nine cases, Penrose Hospital seven more.

Symptoms were scrolled along the bottom of every cable and satellite TV station, and droned endlessly on the radio: fever, weakness, swollen lymph nodes, nausea and headache were among the earliest signs, followed by rapidly developing pneumonia. The time from exposure to death varied; some succumbed in three days, others fought on longer. Thus far, no one had lived more than ten days.

While the people in the Safeway store sickened and died, the CDC and FEMA had been quietly mobilizing the National Guard. When the official announcements began, the Colorado Springs Airport had already been closed, and every major route out of the city had been blocked by troops. On the advice of the world's top virologists and molecular geneticists, Colorado Springs was transformed into a modern-day Eyam, though the quarantine was not voluntary.

The plan sounded simple: Residents were instructed to stay home. Skeleton crews of employees were being organized at Colorado Springs Utilities, hospitals, police and fire stations, protected by the Universal Precautions used in the medical field. If residents needed food or medical supplies, there was an emergency contact number they could call. If they tried to leave the city, they would be turned back. No exceptions.

Over and over, local and national TV stations ran an address to the city of Colorado Springs by the Mayor, her face worn into lines of worry and fatigue, her eyes shadowed by the terrible decisions she had been forced to make. She spoke earnestly, persuasively, bluntly.

"We are ground zero. If this disease escapes our city, it will result in a pandemic of Biblical proportions. The facts you have been given are not exaggerated. I know what many of you are thinking; every year, we're warned about this or that superbug, about the swine flu or H1N1, but this isn't hype. For years, experts have been saying that it's just a matter of time. Well, that time has come.

"All of us are scared, and many of us are desperate to leave, perhaps to join family somewhere far away and safe. Believe me – there's nothing I wouldn't give to be sitting at my parents' kitchen table in Walnut, Iowa, with all of my family safe and sound, right about now."

The mayor leaned forward and paused, her face intense. "But I need you to know this: If we carry this disease out of Colorado Springs, nowhere will be safe. Nowhere. Which brings me to my most difficult point..."

The mayor paused again, swallowing repeatedly. When she finally spoke, her voice was steady, but the grief in her eyes was magnified by tears. "If you or your loved ones get sick, do not go to the hospital. Do not go to your doctor. There is no medicine for this disease, no treatment. We cannot help you." Her voice broke, and again, she fought for control. "For the sake of our community, for the sake of humanity, we must do everything possible to keep this plague contained. My prayers, and the prayers of the world, are with us all."

In the years that would follow, historians would note the heroic attempt at containment by the people of Colorado Springs. With few exceptions, people followed the official dictates to the letter. And for almost a week, the city was preternaturally quiet. All local TV and radio stations had been shut down; the residents of Colorado Springs received news of themselves from sources on the outside.

Reports varied wildly on the progress of the disease, since officials remained largely uninvolved, but hospitals received a steady trickle of people too terrified to stare down the Black Death alone. Two weeks after Emma Turner died, the death count had risen to several hundred, with no way of knowing how many people had died at home, but hope soared that the disease had been contained.

Then, an explosion. Cities all over the state of Colorado reported outbreaks. It was never determined whether infected residents had managed to evade the blockades, or whether the disease had traveled the way people do, casually and routinely from place to place. Before a more extensive quarantine could be discussed, states across the nation began to report in, and the news worsened by the hour: By the end of day 19, the pandemic was official. The first foreign nation to report an outbreak was Great Britain, followed closely by Australia and China, and after that, there was no stopping it.

The President of the United States gave his last address to the nation on the 28th day of the plague. He had developed a fever that morning, he said candidly, and before his illness progressed, he had a few things to say. Though he had not been a popular president, and his administration had accomplished little of note, he would be remembered by the surviving generations for the words he gave his people as he faced his own death on international television.

"Some of you will survive," he began, without salutation or preamble. "Some of you are immune, and a very lucky few will survive the plague. Less than 1% of the population, they're telling me, but enough of you will make it through this to continue the human race. When you go on, when life resumes, it will be tempting to assign some blame for the millions who have already died, and the billions who will likely die in the days ahead."

The president paused, and shook his head wearily. "Don't waste too much time on that. We already know we did this to ourselves. Overuse of antibiotics created the superbug. Our immune systems are shot and the majority of us are overweight and half-sick already, thanks in part to food processed to last longer than we will. Drugs for every symptom you can think of, not enough exercise, too many conveniences and corners cut. We set ourselves up, and now we're falling. I know this, and you know it, too."

Another pause. Then, the president squared his shoulders, all trace of illness or fatigue dropping away. "Analyze it enough to understand it, and move on. Do you understand me? Learn what you need to from our mistakes, then go on and *be better*. Be stronger, smarter, more honest, more brave. When the ugly scramble to survive ends, pick up the pieces, forgive yourselves for anything you needed to do, and rebuild humanity using the very best that is in each of you. Let that be your monument to those of us that don't survive. Make your very lives a monument."

FOUR
The Survivors: Colorado

The second corpse Naomi saw was her husband. Scott died on the 17th day of the plague, 10 days after the start of the city quarantine, and before she had even figured out how to keep breathing, Macy was sick. For Naomi, the world shrank to her daughter's small body, to the next rattling breath, and the next, to the rhythms of fever and chill, sponge and cover, and the constant coaxing of broth, water and herbal tinctures down a small, unresponsive throat.

They had lost contact with Piper right after the plague broke the boundaries of the city. Scott had been trying to arrange for her to join his sister and brother-in-law in Michigan, but plane tickets couldn't be bought at any price, and he didn't want her driving cross-country alone. Failing that, he had tried to convince her to head for their cabin on Carrol Lakes just outside of Woodland Park. If worse came to worst, he told her, they would join her there as soon as they could leave the city. Piper, being Piper, had stalled. She didn't want to leave her studies, didn't want to leave her friends, and most of all, didn't want to admit the situation could be that serious.

The last time they spoke, Piper had mentioned a friend whose family lived in the mountains, but the call had dropped before she had given them a name or an address, and Naomi hadn't been able to reach her since. Service had been spotty at best – the lines were simply overwhelmed by a frantic world trying to connect with loved ones.

Piper didn't even know her father was dead. Naomi tried her number hundreds of times a day, whenever her hands weren't soothing Macy, preparing medicines, or caring for the few animals she had left. Just hours before he had died, she and Scott had argued terribly over the pets.

"Naomi, for God's sake, *think* for once instead of just feeling!" He had to pause to cough and cough and cough, then to catch his breath. "I know you love them. I know they depend on you. But so does Macy, and you've got to take care of yourself, too! Your heart is too soft – you're not going to survive this, if you don't lighten the load!"

She hadn't been able to answer him, throat locked closed with grief and hurt, stricken into silence by the harsh words from her tender husband. They were the last coherent words he spoke to her. Shortly after, he had drifted into a fevered world of muttered nonsense, interspersed with moments of terrifying clarity. She would give anything to forget some of the things he had said.

"Piper!" His eyes had flown open. "No, oh no, I'm so sorry!" His eyes were lucid but filled with horror when they met hers. She reached out to soothe, but he gripped her hand so hard her knuckles grated together. "So broken, Naomi, she'll be so broken. She'll need you so much, but she'll push you away. Don't let her! She'll die of the shame if you don't help her. Promise me you'll help her - promise me!"

Naomi had nodded, beyond fear, beyond despair. Still clutching her hand, Scott eased back on his pillows, but his eyes darted frantically, watching something she could not see. His face crumpled, and he sobbed a single terrible sob. His head rolled on the pillow, his lucid gaze met hers again, and he smiled with tears filling his eyes. "Macy will be okay, Naomi. I promise. She'll be okay."

A cold like Naomi had never experienced had radiated from her core at his words. She had leaned to kiss his forehead, murmuring nonsensical words of comfort, to hide the shudders that wracked her. When she leaned back, his eyes were closed, his face peaceful. He died less than an hour later.

In a numb twilight, Naomi had smoothed and straightened the covers around him, checked on a sleeping Macy, then had started complying with his last request. Macy's mice were released in the yard, the fish dumped on the compost. Then she released Poseidon from his cage and carried him outside on her leather-protected forearm.

Her body almost betrayed her then, and she had to stand for several minutes, swallowing, swallowing the sobs back down, face turned away from the big Macaw while he shifted and muttered on her arm, unsettled by her behavior. When she had regained enough control to look at him, he turned his head nearly upside down – what Scott used to call his "charmingly inquisitive act" – and asked, "S'up?"

Naomi had given up her battle against the grief then. She launched Poseidon into the air - he flew to the nearest tree and roosted there, screeching his dismay, while she ran into the house, hands over her ears. She couldn't handle any more loss, just couldn't. In the morning, she would assess how much food remained for the other animals, and make the necessary plans. But she hadn't made it that far, waking in the middle of the night instead to Macy's moans as she shook and burned with fever.

The days had blurred together since then, as Naomi tried everything she could think of to save her daughter. She read every book she had on herbs – even ended up throwing one across the room because it could tell her how to make a lovely potpourri, but not how to help her daughter breathe. Before they lost the internet, she had scoured websites for information, finally stumbling across a master tonic recipe which seemed to help, along with some poultices. This morning, for the first time, Macy appeared to be sleeping easily.

Naomi couldn't count the number of times she had smoothed her hand over Macy's heated face, and she did it again now as the morning sun streamed in the window. Definitely cooler. She sat back in her chair, and just watched the rise and fall of Macy's chest for long, long minutes – still a whistling wheeze, but the deadly rattle had retreated.

She didn't think about hope – didn't even let the word enter her head – but her shoulders dropped a fraction as a tiny bit of tension eased. Her fingers slid through Piper's number on the cell that rarely left her hand; she didn't need to lift it to her ear to hear the "all circuits are busy" message. She closed her eyes, and rubbed her hand over her heart. She could feel her daughter there, alive, she just knew it. She placed the cell phone on Macy's bedside table, and for the first time since Scott had sickened, she took a huge, gulping, shuddering breath.

The room around her looked like a cyclone had hit it. She had been sponging off in the bathroom across the hall and just dropping her dirty clothes wherever they landed; likewise with Macy's soiled pajamas and bed sheets. Every surface was cluttered with bottles and books, basins of water, used poultices and mugs of broth. In the corner of the room, curled up on one of her discarded sweatshirts, Persephone watched her with liquid eyes. And on one of the upper shelves of the bookcase, Ares was doing his best sphinx imitation, tail swishing, green eyes slitted.

"Hey, guys." Naomi's voice crackled – she hadn't spoken above a murmur in weeks. "Are you okay? Are you hungry?"

She held out her arms to Persephone, and the little dog shot across the room to huddle in her arms. Her small, sturdy body shook with tremors of anxiety and joy, and Naomi closed her eyes, burying her nose in the soft fur – familiar, warm, musty scent of dog. "Come on. While she's sleeping, let's go see about some breakfast."

The kitchen was as bad as Macy's room, dirty dishes teetering on every counter and littering the top of the table. Whenever she had thought to, Naomi had thrown down food and water for the animals, but she had no earthly idea who had been eating what. One of the cats had thrown up a hair ball by the sliding glass door, which made her frown – usually Zeus gobbled them up before she could get to them, easily his most disgusting habit. His food dish was still full, too. Before she even started looking for him, she knew.

Other than caring for Macy, Naomi had taken the time to do only one thing: Tend to Scott's body. There was no one to call, no one to ask for help. So she had stolen moments to wash him, to say goodbye to the body she had loved and slept beside, to kiss his beloved strong hands, and finally to wrap him in his favorite afghan. She didn't have the strength to carry him down the stairs, to dig a grave and bury him, so she had ended up wrapping him in plastic tarps, which she had sealed with duct tape. She had laughed and cried as she'd completed that last step – Scott had enjoyed a life-long love affair with duct tape, and she swore she could feel his amusement at her desperate innovation.

She found Zeus just where she knew she would, curled up against Scott's body in their bed, his head resting on Scott's chest. She smoothed her hand over his cold, silky ears, and sobbed. "Oh, Zeus. Thank you for going with him. He'll be so happy for the company. What a good dog."

ℬ

Grace worked for two days, trying to dig graves for her family. Finally, exhausted, with bleeding hands, she made herself stop. She had barely made it 3 feet down, even though she'd dug in the garden where the soil was soft. She needed a Plan B.

The plague had hit Limon in the first wave: Mrs. Dunwoody, the organist at the Methodist church, had collapsed in the middle of a Sunday morning service. Grace couldn't believe people had been stupid enough to help her – had they not been listening to the news? If it had been up to Grace, Mrs. Dunwoody would have died where she lay instead of infecting half the church, including Grace's grandfather.

Her mother had sickened next, her stepfather and Benji the very next day. She knew she wasn't supposed to call for help, but she had tried anyway. Nobody answered at the local medical clinic or the police station. She finally reached a man at the fire department, who had promised to send someone, but no one ever came. On the morning of the 5th day, Grace woke to find Benji and her stepfather already gone. Her mother had lingered for a few more hours.

"Dead." Grace said the word aloud to the huge, prairie sky. "They're dead. Mom is dead. Wayne is dead.

Benji..." Her voice broke, her breath hitched. Sweet baby brother. "Benji is dead."

She could not permit herself to start crying. To start might mean never stopping. She kept making herself repeat the facts, deal with the reality. She hadn't suffered so much as a sniffle – she assumed that meant she was one of the less-than 1% that was immune. It also meant she had a duty. Grace wasn't a spiritual person – she didn't know how she felt about God or any other idea of deity – but she understood her responsibility to humanity. The president's speech had riveted her, and his words were lodged deep in her heart. She had survived, and it was her job to go on, to help rebuild.

She leaned her shovel against the house, and stretched with her hands fisted in the small of her back. She had run out of food completely this morning after rationing for days, and she could feel her body weakening. They had lost phone service some time during her family's illness – she wasn't sure when – so the most logical thing to do was get in the car and go see what she could find.

She hadn't heard from William in well over a week, and this was one fact she could not force herself to dwell on. The last time they talked, one of his little brothers had been sick. She had promised to call the next day, but kept getting a busy signal. She hadn't even tried since.

Their ranch was the closest – it was logical to start there. Grace went back in the house, showered and changed her clothes. Even as she fussed with her appearance, she recognized the stall tactics in her behavior. William wouldn't care if her hair was dirty and her clothes covered with grime – he would just be happy to see her. She took several deep breaths, then made herself leave the bathroom. She found the keys to her mother's truck hanging by the door and headed out.

The roads were deserted. Grace crept along at a snail's pace, disoriented, a little dizzy, inexplicably terrified to be outside. She lifted her hand to her head – was she getting a fever? Her forehead was cool and dry, but she was breathing too quickly. Panic, she realized, and forced down a deep breath, muttering calming nonsense to herself. "Take it easy. You're fine. Everything's okay. Just keep swimming."

But no amount of positive self-talk could unknot her stomach muscles as she turned into the Harris family's driveway. She scrutinized the house as she crawled along – nothing looked out of place, but something felt off. She parked the truck by the back door, shut off the engine, then hopped out before she lost her nerve.

"Hello?" The screen door slammed behind her as she entered the mud room, making her jump. "Hello, is anyone home? Mrs. Harris? William?"

She stepped into the kitchen, and recognized the chaos of illness: Dishes everywhere, though it looked like someone had made a start on cleaning up. The sink was filled with soapy water and soaking dishes, and a single spot had been cleared at the kitchen table. She lifted her head, sniffed, and winced. Faintly, she could smell sickness – improvised bed pans for people too sick to reach the bathroom, soiled sheets.

A creak sounded behind her and she whirled. Her heart jolted painfully; a man loomed in the deep shadows of the mudroom with a baseball bat poised over his shoulder. "No! Please – it's just me! It's Grace!"

The man made a strangled sound and lowered the bat. "Grace?"

He stepped out of the shadows, and the looming man transformed into Quinn, just Quinn, just a sophomore punk. He blinked over and over, staring, confused. He swayed, and put a hand on the door jamb to steady himself. "Grace? Are you really here?"

He was about to fall over, she realized. "I'm really here." She walked over to him, took the bat and led him to the cleared spot at the table. He just stood there until she pushed him into the chair. "Are you alright?"

He gazed up at her with glassy eyes, and she reached out automatically to feel his forehead. Cool. "How long has it been since you've eaten? Or slept?"

"I don't know. Slept a little this morning, I think. Not hungry." His gaze dropped to his hands, avoiding hers.

"Well, you've got to eat something." She bustled into the pantry, grabbed peanut butter and graham crackers off the shelf. Quinn kept staring at his hands while she found a plate, smeared some peanut butter on the crackers then set them in front of him. "Here. You need protein. Get started." There was orange juice in the fridge, and she poured him a tall glass. "Drink this first – your blood sugar is probably low, which might be making you feel nauseous."

He obeyed her without raising his eyes, taking a long swallow of the juice, then starting on the crackers. She watched his slow, robotic movements for a while, listening for any other sounds in the house. Then, without speaking, she went to answer the question she couldn't ask.

All of them. Mr. and Mrs. Harris, the four little boys, and William. All of them, dead in their beds. She stood in William's bedroom doorway, staring at his still face, and felt her brain split in two.

Part of her analyzed what she was seeing; she had just cared for her own family, and she could see Quinn's Herculean efforts in the clean bedclothes, the washed faces, the neat rooms. He must have worked around the clock. No wonder he was on the verge of collapse.

And the other part of her brain howled. Howled like a terrified, mortally wounded animal.

Grace shut William's door and returned to the kitchen, where she found Quinn still staring. He had finished the crackers and juice, and there were crumbs at the corner of his mouth. Without speaking a word, Grace rinsed out a washcloth and matter-of-factly wiped his hands and face. Then she helped him up and walked him into the living room. Without being told, he curled up on the couch. He was asleep before Grace had finished unlacing and removing his boots. She draped an afghan over him, then sat and watched him sleep.

In so many ways, he was still a little boy. His face was soft with youth, cheeks rounded with good health and brown with sunshine, sandy hair cut haphazardly. Even his powerful arms seemed innocent and childlike, clutching a pillow to his chest.

The non-animal part of her brain catalogued these observations and coldly considered her options. Having a dependent lessened her chances of survival. Quinn had already spoken more words to her today than in all the other times she'd been around him put together. She didn't really know him, didn't know what he was capable of, didn't know what assets he would bring to an alliance.

Then she remembered the baseball bat and the meticulous care he had taken of his dying family. Tears flooded her eyes, surprising her, and she ruthlessly blinked them back. To start was never to stop. Decision made, Grace headed to the kitchen to make herself something to eat and to start assessing their resources.

ॐ

Sometimes it was dark in Jack's world, and sometimes everything spun in a kaleidoscope of colors that split his skull. So hot, so cold. He shifted restlessly, trying to draw in a deep breath of air, and gasped at the agony, daggers sliding between his ribs, freezing the muscles of his diaphragm with pain. A firm hand lifted the back of his head, a rim pressed to his lips, and the tiny sip of cool liquid was like manna in the desert.

"He's not going to make it if he can't draw more air." The feminine voice was harried, a voice he vaguely recognized but didn't have the energy to identify.

Another woman's voice answered, one straight out of his own personal Hell. "Tell me what to do for him."

Jack's eyes flew open. She was standing above him, beautiful evil Jezebel, her arms raised to hold her disheveled hair off her neck. That dark hair rose while he watched, writhed and slithered around her head, shiny black cobras. He gasped and slammed his eyes shut, then his body was seized in the most violent fit of coughing he had ever experienced.

"Get him up – get him upright!" Arms lifting, sitting him up. He leaned forward, hacking, hacking, hacking until a liquid mass filled his throat and mouth. He tasted copper, gagged, spat, spat again, then collapsed back. The world was hazed red with pain. Someone was sitting behind him, supporting him in a sitting position, and he leaned into the embrace, beyond caring who it belonged to.

"I'll get some pillows – hold him there." A few quiet moments, then they were moving him again, more pain, the warm, soft body sliding out from behind him to be replaced by pillows that held him almost upright.

Harried voice spoke again, more compassionately this time. "Keep him sitting up as much as possible, and do anything you can do to keep him breathing deeply. Steam might help, a menthol rub, maybe a poultice – try onions, if you have them. Keep him hydrated – get as much liquid in him as possible. And...watch him."

His siren's voice sounded right beside his ear, luring him towards treacherous shores. He wanted to turn towards it and he wanted to lunge away. "Watch him? What do you mean, watch him?"

Harried voice snapped defensively now. "I can't explain it, okay? If you watch them, it just helps. You asked how you could help him, and I'm telling you."

"Okay. Alright. I'll watch him – that makes sense." Soothing, apologetic, respectful. She played that just right, he thought. Just like I would have. "I can't thank you enough for coming. You must be overwhelmed."

"You have no idea. I haven't seen Dr. Derber in days, and I haven't been able to reach him on his cell." The silence between the women was absolute for a few moments. "I need to swing by his house. See what's...what."

"Blessings on you, and on the work you're doing. I'm asking for angel's wings to wrap around you, to comfort and support you."

Jack almost worked up the energy to sneer at that, but not quite.

"Yeah. Angel's wings." Harried's voice was wry. "I'd trade an army of angels for one more medical professional. Do your best to keep him among the living, okay? We're going to need him on the other side of this mess."

ॐ

Twenty-one days. Naomi counted again, then again. She was sitting on the deck, soaking in sunshine, with Macy's old baby monitor plastered to her ear. Over the hiss and pop of static, she could hear every deep, clear breath Macy took. Clear. *Clear.*

She had lost track of dates when Scott got sick, and if you'd held a gun to her head, she couldn't have even approximated a guess. Weeks? How many? But as Macy had slowly, slowly improved, Naomi had finally dared to hope. She wanted to count days.

All the TV channels were broadcasting "No Signal," and it took over an hour of painstaking searching and holding the radio in strange positions to finally get a channel in clear enough to hear. She jury-rigged an antenna of wire and aluminum foil, then carried the radio out to the deck with her desk calendar.

She listened for a while, disappointed to realize what she had picked up was a repeating public-service announcement rather than a live broadcast. The man's voice droned through a list of instructions on what to do if you were stricken with the plague, then summarized the disease's progress world-wide. As of the current broadcast, the United States had lost contact with Great Britain and several other European countries. Germany was reporting 99-100% fatality rates, as was China. India had gone silent. Finally, he concluded.

"You are listening to this announcement on the Emergency Broadcast System. The date is," he paused, and a female, computerized voice took over, giving the current year, followed by "April 28."

Naomi was startled. Had it really been that long? She crossed the days off on the calendar as she counted. Twenty-two days since Scott had died. Twenty-one days since Macy got sick. The significance of that number made her heart pound. According to the reports they had heard, Macy had survived eleven days longer than any other plague victim. Macy had *survived*.

She tipped her head back to stare at the sky. So blue, so clear. And quiet. She had never known such quiet. Naomi felt her awareness expand to encompass the outside world for the first time in weeks. No distant rush of traffic, no sirens, nothing.

Her focus had been complete: Macy's breath, Macy's temperature, liquid in, waste out, bathe her, tend her, soothe her. She had hardly spared the animals a glance, aware of only one other thing: the link to Piper she felt in her chest. She felt it there now, a fullness, next to the gaping emptiness that was Scott, next to the fierce death-grip she had on Macy. She laughed a little, sadly, at the thought. Truly, she had a new understanding of that expression now. She had spent the last 21 days standing between her daughter and Death.

She closed her eyes, and felt her oldest daughter, her warrior girl, vibrating with life, there in her heart. She was alive. She would stake her own life on it. "Piper," she whispered. "Piper, my girl, my fierce girl. I'll find you. Somehow, I'm going to find you."

FIVE
Piper: Walden, CO

There were times, Piper would swear, she could feel her mother's presence. It was the strangest thing. Distracting. And given her current circumstances, being distracted was dangerous.

Piper forced her back up straighter against the wall she was leaning on and lifted her chin. Thinking about her family was not an option; homesickness knocked the wind right out of her, and looking vulnerable was dangerous as well. Cool confidence, she reminded herself, as she watched people trickle into the mess hall for lunch. You are strong and capable. Polite, but remote. Untouchable. She hadn't figured out all the nuances of the social hierarchy here yet, but she was crystal clear on one fact: There would be no easy resolution to the problems and tensions plaguing this group.

She and Noah had arrived here three weeks ago. They had been some of the last kids to leave UNC's campus; Piper didn't have a concrete plan, and Noah didn't want to leave until she did. When she lost contact with her family and it became obvious the plague was going to spread, Noah offered an option she preferred to heading to her family's cabin alone.

"My dad and my brother, they're, well, they're..." He had trailed off, rubbed the back of his neck, then continued in an embarrassed rush. "They're survivalists, okay? They have a compound in the mountains, just outside of Walden. We can go there and see what's going to happen, wait this thing out."

The information gave her pause, but turning down his offer under the current circumstances would be the height of stupidity. "I would appreciate that, truly," she had said. "I can meet my folks at Carrol Lakes later, if it comes to that. And my dad's a prepper, so I doubt your dad or your brother will seem all that strange to me."

"Uh..." Noah's face had pinched, then flushed dull red. "Please don't tell either one of them that. They have some pretty strong opinions about their lifestyle. They think anyone who doesn't live like they do, or doesn't prepare to the extent they have, are morons. 'Arm Chair Survivalists' and 'Mall Ninjas,' they call them. It's why I don't go home much."

They had packed up and headed out the day after the announcement that the plague had become a pandemic. Piper had racked her brain for a way to get a message to her folks about where she was going, and eventually just ended up leaving the information written on the mirrors in her dorm room with a permanent marker. Noah had balked at leaving the exact address – there was more survivalist in him than he wanted to admit – but had agreed to the general information "South-east of

Walden." How that would lead her folks to her, Piper had no earthly clue, but at the time it hadn't been worth arguing over. She would join them in Colorado Springs if this blew over, or they would join her at the cabin if it didn't.

It had taken them two days to make the 130-plus mile trip, what with Noah's determination to not arrive empty-handed. He had insisted on stopping at every single grocery or drug store en-route, even the tiniest hole-in-the-wall dives – there wasn't much food left by then, but he had cleaned out anything left on the shelves, even feminine sanitary supplies.

"For trade," he had told her without a trace of embarrassment. "After the plague burns itself out."

Noah's brother Levi had met them at the entrance of what had once been a campground, and was now a compound housing one family – Noah's sister Jenny, her husband and their three kids – and a half dozen individuals hand-selected and invited by their father to be a part of the group. Levi stayed well back from their vehicle as he informed them they wouldn't be allowed in until he was sure they weren't carrying the plague. He had obviously been less than pleased to see Piper, as well.

"Did you clear this with Dad?" His words were directed at Noah, but his eyes never left Piper's face. Cold, cold eyes. Holding his gaze had been both uncomfortable and difficult, but she made herself do it anyway. She knew when she was being measured.

"No. I haven't been able to reach him – cell service has been pretty much non-existent. That's why I brought

Piper – her folks are in Colorado Springs, and she hasn't been able to connect."

Finally, Levi's gaze moved to his brother. "So you haven't talked to Dad since when?"

"Monday morning. As soon as they announced the plague had left the Springs, nobody could get through to anybody." Noah must have read something in his brother's demeanor, because his eyes narrowed. "Why? What aren't you telling me?"

"Dad's sick." Levi didn't stall or try to soften the announcement. "He started running a fever Tuesday night. We thought we got everyone out of town and locked down in time, but we didn't. Jenny's youngest has it, too – little Karleigh." Levi dropped his head then, so Piper wasn't sure whether she'd seen a flash of emotion or not.

"How bad is it? I mean Jesus, Levi, he's tough as hell. I can't imagine..."

"It's bad. Jenny's taking care of them both, with Ruth and a few others spelling her. Ruth's got us wearing masks and gloves, the works. So far, no one else has any symptoms, but we have to wait and see. We should know in 2 or 3 days. They're saying the incubation on this thing is anywhere from 1 to 6 days, but Sanders thinks we should give it at least two weeks."

"Brody Sanders? He's here?" When Levi nodded, Noah blew out a breath, his face tight with tension. "And he's what – in charge while Dad is sick?"

"Something like that." Levi's eyes were cold, cold again. "For the time being, anyway."

"Fantastic." Noah muttered under his breath. "Alright, so as of right now, we're quarantined. Where are we staying?"

"That depends. Do you need one bed or two?"

It took a minute for the implication to sink in, then Noah blushed scarlet and Piper leaned to speak to Levi for the first time. "Two beds." No embellishment or elaboration necessary.

Levi's eyes shifted back and forth between them for a moment, then he frowned and shook his head. "This is trouble Noah. It would be better if she were already spoken for. Think about that while you guys are twiddling your thumbs for the next 14 days." He pointed down the right fork in the two-track. "Head down to cabin six. You'll have to pump your water and there's no electricity, but there's a wood-burning stove and plenty of wood stacked outside. Outhouse is right behind the cabin. Do you need food?"

Noah's face was still burnished with embarrassment. "We're good for a day or two."

"We'll drop off supplies on the edge of the clearing tomorrow, along with a walkie-talkie. If either of you get sick, let us know. I'll keep you posted on Dad."

And without so much as a goodbye or another glance in Piper's direction, he turned and walked up the left fork in the two-track. Piper watched him go, then turned to look at Noah.

"'Spoken for?'" She didn't need to ask if Levi had been serious.

"I'm sorry." He wouldn't look at her, focusing instead on bumping along the rugged two-track. They passed several cabins, numbered in reverse order: Eight, seven, then six. Noah pulled up close to the door, then shut the engine off and stared at the steering wheel for a moment. The cooling engine ticked in the silence.

"Piper, I'm sorry. Best-case scenario, this is just a short-term situation. We'll get you connected with your folks, and figure out how to get you to them." He looked at her finally, and his grim expression made the hair on the back of her neck prickle. "But just in case that's not how it works out, I should fill you in on the group dynamics. I'm not sure who all is here, but I'm pretty sure they're not your kind of people."

Piper frowned. "Meaning what, exactly? That I'm a snob?"

"No." Noah gave her an impatient look. "That's not what I meant, and you know it. They're not my kind of people, either. Look, let's unload and settle in. We've got two weeks to fill, and explaining this could take most of 'em."

The next day, following the delivery of their promised supplies, Noah had used the walkie-talkie to both check on his father and ask Levi for a complete list of the compound's current inhabitants. Noah's father was still alive, but reading that list had returned the grim look to his face.

"Except for Jenny and her husband, all of these people are military or former military. Army and Marines, mostly, three of them special forces. And besides Jenny, there's only one other woman – Ruth Mitchell. She's a medic, did tours in Iraq, Afghanistan, Syria and Pakistan. She put in 30 years before she got out. I know her pretty well – she's alright. But some of these guys..." His voice trailed off and he shook his head wearily. "I'm not sure what Dad was thinking. This is a real testosterone fest - so many alpha males living together is bound to cause problems."

"Is that why Levi said it would be better if I were 'spoken for?'"

"Yeah." Noah looked miserable. "Look, we can still hope this will just be short term. Have you tried your folks lately?"

"No signal. And my cell is just about dead." Piper went for a reassuring tone, not sure if she was trying to comfort Noah or herself. "I grew up in Colorado Springs, Noah – Fort Carson, Peterson Air Force Base, NORAD, the Air Force Academy. It's not like I haven't been around people in the military."

"I know. But you knew them from a civilian perspective, in non-combat conditions. This is different. We may not think of this as a war, but you can damn sure bet they do."

"True. So." Piper took a deep breath. "Let's talk about the contingency plan, then. Say I'm going to be here a while. Should we present ourselves as a couple?"

Noah looked up swiftly, analyzing. Softly, he asked, "In name only?"

"Yes." She would not insult him with an apology.

Noah masked whatever he was feeling so completely, she couldn't read even a hint. The trait made him a hell of a poker player. "That might work in the short term, but not for any length of time. It's too easy to tell when a couple is intimate, when they're fighting, stuff like that." He grinned suddenly. "Remember?"

Piper laughed. "In our dorm, freshmen year! We used to bet on who was hooking up and who was holding out. I had forgotten all about that."

Noah snorted with disdain. "Of course you forgot – I won the contest, and you never paid up."

"You did not win! We couldn't get confirmation on half of them, and even if one of your boys blabbed, there was no guarantee it wasn't just big talk!"

"You are one sore loser, Piper Allen. C'mon, admit it – I was better than you at reading the situation."

Piper cocked her head to the side as she remembered another detail. "You used to say it was because you watched your older brother. You could always tell when he had scored with one of his girlfriends."

Noah winced. "I probably should have kept that to myself. Could get awkward. But seriously," he sighed. "Pretending to be a couple is a bad idea. Some of these guys just don't respect social norms and boundaries. If they thought they had a chance with you, they'd push me to defend you. I can hold my own in a bar fight, but these guys are trained in hand-to-hand. I don't want to go there."

"I don't blame you, but I do need to point out that I'm completely capable of defending myself." Piper raised her eyebrows. "You've been in a bar fight?"

"Growing up with Levi was a bar fight, day in and day out," Noah said ruefully. "He wanted to be sure his little brother could protect himself, or so he said. And yes, I've been in exactly one bar fight."

"Did you win?"

"I don't want to talk about it."

"Which means you lost." Piper smirked until Noah looked up. His face was dark with regret.

"No, I won. It made me sick to my stomach. It's not like the movies - it's ugly. And embarrassing." Noah stared into a middle space, gaze unfocused. "Levi used to tell me I wasn't a fighter by nature, so I had to watch out. If I get pushed over that line, I lose control of myself. I don't even remember a lot of the fight – my friends told me later that I pounded on the guy until his face was just mushy pulp. The cops broke it up, but I don't remember that either."

"I'm sorry. It sounds awful." Piper reached out to squeeze his shoulder, and laughed a little. "I guess we're opposites in that respect – my mom says I was born to brawl. When I was little, she had to bribe the neighborhood kids with cookies to get them to play with me. I was always slugging someone."

"Yeah, not me. If I never have to be in a physical fight again, I'll be happy." He paused, searching for words. "I felt like I lost myself – like I had been taken over by someone I didn't like and couldn't control. My friends were all like, "Dude, that was awesome!' and I just wanted to hide somewhere and puke."

"I really am sorry, Noah. I shouldn't have teased you."

Noah shrugged. "It's okay. But if you don't mind, I'd rather change the subject."

And so they had. As predicted, Noah had spent much of their two week confinement talking through the rest of the list. In addition to Ruth the medic, there were two arms experts, one of whom was Levi, two field survival specialists, a communications specialist, and a mechanic. Everyone had a specific role to play, and most of them had cross-over training in other skills – Levi and Tyler Kelly, the mechanic, were also the group's cooks, and Noah, she was surprised to learn, had been trained as an EMT – his father intended him to serve as backup for Ruth. Finally, there was Brody Sanders, who was a tactician like Noah's father.

"Sanders is the son of a guy my dad served with in the Marines," Noah explained. "He's only a few years older than Levi, so early 30's, but he's totally old-school. He's fourth-generation Marines. His dad lived in Walden until he died from cancer a few years back – he was one of dad's best friends. Dad felt like it was his duty to look after Sanders, but neither Levi nor I like him much."

"Why not? Were you jealous of your dad's attention?"

"No, nothing like that. It's like I said – Sanders is old school. He fancies himself a real hard-ass, and in a way, he is – he thinks qualities like compassion and mercy are weaknesses. And he can justify anything. I'm pretty sure he's the only man on Earth I'm afraid of."

That surprised her. "You're not scared of your dad? Or Levi?"

"No, not at all. I wouldn't want to face either one of them in a fight, but if I did, at least I know they'd fight fair. Even if you beat Sanders fair and square, you could never turn your back on him again. He'd put a knife between your ribs and you'd never see it coming."

On the 5th day of their isolation, Noah's father died. Levi came to the clearing to tell them, his face lined but controlled. He looked a decade older than the first time Piper had seen him.

"He fought hard, Noah. It gave him a lot of comfort to know you were here, even if he couldn't see you."

Piper rested a hand on Noah's shoulder. His face was locked tight, but he couldn't hide the misery or the sheen of tears in his eyes when he looked at her. He rested a hand over hers for a moment, then turned back to his brother.

"And Karleigh? How is she?"

Again, Levi didn't hesitate with harsh truth. "She's not going to make it. Lucas is sick, too." This time, Piper didn't have to guess at what Levi was feeling – it was all over his face. He was grieving for his niece and nephew and didn't feel a need to hide it.

"Jesus, they're just babies. Karleigh is what – three? And Lucas will be nine next month, is that right?"

"If he makes it. It's bad, Noah. Jenny is crazy. We can hardly get her to eat or sleep. She made Aaron take Caden to one of the remote cabins – they're both fine so far, but Aaron is just totally out of it. That little Karleigh, she's the apple of his eye. I took Max out to stay with them until it's over, one way or the other – he's got a comforting way about him, and he'll make sure they both eat and rest."

Noah's hands clenched into fists. "How much longer do we have to stay here? We haven't had contact with anyone but each other for six days, and neither one of us is sick. We should be doing something to help."

"I told Sanders you'd feel that way, but he says two weeks. Before Dad died, he asked me to abide by Sanders' decisions. For now, that's what I'm going to do." Grief flashed on Levi's face again. "And Noah, I'm sorry, but we can't wait to bury him."

"I understand." It was all Noah could get out before he turned his back on both of them and stood there for a moment, hands on his hips. His shoulders shook once, and he walked swiftly back to the cabin without a word to either of them.

Piper turned back to Levi, and their eyes held as they measured each other without the buffer of Noah. When Levi spoke, his voice was low and gravely with emotion.

"It's harder for him. Noah. He and Dad didn't see eye to eye, and Noah puts a lot of stock in agreement and getting along. He's a peace-keeper, always has been. It's going to eat at him, that he and Dad couldn't talk before he died."

"Yes, it will." Piper rubbed a hand over her heart, feeling the mother-bond she could never quite sever, no matter how disgusted she got with her Martha-Stewart-wanna-be mom. She would give anything – anything at all – to feel her mother's plump arms around her right this minute. "I understand exactly how he feels. I'll do what I can to help."

"Are you sleeping together?"

"None of your business."

"So, no." Levi shook his head. "You're trouble, Piper. When you join the group, you're going to want to tread careful. You're too young and too pretty."

His words were not a compliment, and Piper didn't take them that way. "Noah has been filling me in. I'll watch my step."

"You're going to need to do more than that. Lay off the make-up. And do you have baggier clothes?"

Piper felt heat creep along her hairline. In spite of her best efforts, he was getting under her skin. "I'm not wearing make-up." She held her arms out, and looked down at her baggy UNC sweatshirt and utilitarian jeans. "And what would you suggest? A snowmobile suit?"

"If you have one." He didn't laugh, and there wasn't even a hint of humor in his eyes. "Wear a pair of Noah's jeans. And a baseball cap. Josh is in contact with a ham operator in the Springs – we'll see if he can get any information about your parents, and we'll figure out how to get you to them as quickly as possible."

Piper had had just about enough. "Wow. I apologize sincerely for neglecting to bring my burka. Any other orders you want to bark at me before I head inside to ritually disfigure myself for the good of the group?"

Levi didn't even acknowledge her sarcasm. "Yes. When you and Noah join us, don't make eye contact and keep your head down. Don't speak to any of the men unless it would be rude not to. Answer briefly, then walk away. Don't engage in conversation with them, don't laugh, don't smile. Any of those actions will be taken as an invitation to pursue." His eyes narrowed. "Unless you want to be pursued?"

"Hmm, let me think." Piper tapped her chin with her index finger. "Do I want to be pursued by a group of backwoods military knuckle-draggers? So I can – what – fulfill my life's ambition of being a womanly little bed-warmer, maybe with some campfire cooking and cabin-floor-scrubbing thrown in for funsies? Golly, tempting as that sounds, I'm going to have to give it a 'Hell no.' Wait!" She held her hand out to him excitedly. "Unless you throw in latrine duty. I just can't say 'no' to latrine duty!"

"Shit."

Levi hung his head, and for a moment, Piper thought she was going to receive a well-deserved apology. She was decidedly wrong.

"Look. I get that you're real smart, and you're pretty quick with that wit. Noah has been talking about you for almost three years, whenever he bothers to come home. You're both into that sociology shit, studying different cultures and mores and what-not. Well, now you get to find out if you're life-smart, not just book-smart. You break the rules at UNC, you get a little paddy-slap, maybe a call to mommy and daddy. You break the rules here, and you are out the door. I won't have Noah put himself in harm's way trying to protect you, and I won't tolerate the danger to what's left of my family if you get this group all stirred up."

She would be good and god-damned if she'd let this guy run her over. Guest or not, there were some basic rights she was not going to cede. "So you're the big boss of the group now? What about Brody Sanders? Given your attitude, I can see why your father left him in charge."

Levi's face went still and blank – it appeared the Ramsey brothers shared a talent for poker-faces. "Like I said, you're quick. And you're not afraid to take a shot when you see it. You think I'm some kind of Neanderthal, some kind of chauvinist jackass, but I'm trying to help you. You can either figure out the new rules and abide by them, or I'll personally toss you out on your clever little ass. Are we clear?"

"Crystal." She hissed the word at him. Spinning on her heel, she marched said ass back to the cabin, feeling his eyes on her the whole way. At the door, she turned to stare him down. She was surprised to find not anger but despair and resignation written plainly on his face.

"Christ." He heaved a deep sigh. "We are so fucked."

With that, he turned and headed back the way he'd come. They hadn't spoken a single word since. Noah, being Noah, had noticed the strain between them whenever Levi visited the clearing, but he didn't ask and Piper didn't fill him in.

The remainder of the two weeks had crawled by, punctuated by the deaths of little Karleigh and her brother Lucas a few days later. Levi reported that their sister was wild with grief; she had joined her husband and surviving son in the most remote of the cabins, and he wasn't sure when the bereaved family would be returning to the group. Max, one of the field survival specialists, was still with them, making sure they stayed fed and safe.

Jenny and her family still weren't back when Noah and Piper's quarantine ended. Within 24 hours of joining the group, Piper determined she had a problem. Rather, she had four of them. As it turned out, the chauvinist jackass Neanderthal had been right.

Ethan Torres and Adam Peterson, field survival specialist and sniper respectively, were openly vying for her attention. It took her almost a week to remember which name went with which man because they were always together, always flanking her whenever she left the kitchen, where she had been put to work washing dishes and helping with food prep, or when she sat down to eat. Josh Bennett, the communications specialist, was slightly more subtle, but only slightly; he updated her hourly on the news from Colorado Springs, whether there was news or not.

Worst of all, though, was Brody Sanders.

He never spoke to her and he never stopped watching her. The feeling of his eyes on her had become distressingly familiar, and she was pretty sure he had started following her to and from the cabin she still shared with Noah – either that, or she had crossed the line into full-blown paranoia.

To a certain extent, Piper had taken Levi's advice. She had kept quiet and kept her head down while she studied the group, trying to learn the lay of the land. She had always prided herself on her adaptability, on her ability to get along with many different types of people and social groups, but this collection of steroid-fueled good ol' boys was beyond her capabilities to adapt to. Worse, she didn't even want to.

If she had to pretend to be amused by one more juvenile, risqué joke, or listen to one more exaggerated story of battlefield ass-kickin', or bite back one more grammatical correction – *"You 'don't got none?' Are you serious? Don't you mean you 'ain't got any?'"* – she was going to suffer some kind of aneurism, she was sure of it. There was a limit to how far she was willing to contort herself to fit in. And she had just about reached it.

SIX
Naomi and Macy: Colorado Springs, CO

Leave, Scott had told her. Take Macy and get to the cabin. Leave the city, avoid people, don't draw attention to the fact that you have food and water. Over and over he had repeated the same instructions. Towards the end, his ramblings had taken on a desperate edge; he had known, Naomi was certain, that he wouldn't be with them. She couldn't count the number of times he had made her promise – "Say it, Naomi, say you'll go, say you'll take her and get to safety, promise me!" – which made her failure to act all that much more painful now.

Naomi leaned her head on the front door and shut her eyes. "Open it," she whispered to herself. "Just open it. Just start small."

She put her hand on the door knob and went light-headed with terror. *Danger.* Danger everywhere outside that door. She could feel it, as surely as she felt her heart booming against her ribs. She stepped back, and looked down at Persephone, who was looking up at her patiently. The little dog scooched over until she was resting against Naomi's leg, a gesture of support rather than of demand.

Naomi reached down and scooped her up, and together they headed for the sheltered back deck, where Macy was resting in the early May sunshine.

She had fallen asleep, Naomi saw as she stepped outside, halfway through a stitch on her embroidery sampler. Naomi lifted the embroidery hoop free of Macy's hands, tiny, white and spider-like in the wake of her illness, and completed the stitch before setting the sampler aside. She tucked Macy's blankets more snuggly around her, then sat down on the other lounge chair to watch her baby sleep and think through her options.

She didn't want to go. This was home, security, safety. They had enough food to last several more months, and summer was coming – she could garden to supplement their canned and dried stores. Power and water were her biggest concerns – the lights had been flickering for days, sometimes going out for hours at a time, and every morning, she heaved a huge sigh of relief when the tap responded and the toilet flushed. The failure of both systems was simply a matter of time. She had a back-up generator, but Scott had warned her about the dangers of using it, how the noise might draw attention she didn't want.

It was tempting, so, so tempting, to plan to hunker down here. To ride it out until the plague had run its course and the world began to recover. Scott knew her homebody self well, knew she'd feel that way – hence his demands for repeated promises to leave. Staying in the city, he had insisted, was far too dangerous. Looters, gangs, rioting and fires, secondary diseases from the lack of sanitation and unburied bodies – over and over, he'd listed those dangers.

Naomi hadn't had contact with anyone other than Scott or Macy for over a month, and hadn't heard any current news in almost that long. She had stopped trying Piper's cell, though she kept the phone nearby, just in case. She had no earthly idea what was going on out there. Yesterday, she heard what sounded like distant gunshots, but how could she know for sure? In the early days of their marriage, she and Scott had lived down by Fort Carson – she had heard automatic weapons firing on the practice range just about every day, and had become used to the sound. The city was so quiet now – was she hearing training exercises from Fort Carson again? Even as the thought crossed her mind, she recognized the desperate rationalization in it.

She needed information. In the absence of TV, radio and internet, there was only one way to get it. She needed to go out there. Out the front door.

She stood up and put Persephone on a stay, leaving her to watch over Macy's sleep. The little dog was more reliable than a monitor for letting Naomi know when Macy needed her, racing to find Naomi when Macy wanted help getting to the bathroom or a drink of juice – Naomi wasn't sure what she'd do without her at this point. She more than earned what little food she consumed, and in spite of her promise to Scott about the pets, Persephone would be staying.

Of the other animals, Ares was the only one left. When the weather warmed up, she had released all three cats into the back yard. She had put out food for a few days, then every other day. Cats, she knew, were brilliant at learning to fend for themselves. Artemis had vanished almost immediately, and she had only seen Athena a few times before she, too, disappeared. Naomi had no way of knowing whether the cats had headed for richer hunting grounds or had become prey themselves, but her heart was peaceful over it. She could not bear seeing an animal neglected or abused by humans, but the natural cycle of life and death was a different matter.

Ares, though, had been coming and going with regularity. Sometimes, she only knew he'd been there by the gifts he left on the deck – dead squirrels, chipmunks and birds. Some nights, he yowled to be let in at the door, which invariably signaled a change in the weather. She had started watching the sky, noticing the direction and strength of the wind, and she was getting pretty good at predicting when he'd show up.

Tonight probably wouldn't be one of those nights, she mused, as she retraced her steps to the front door. The day was soft and clear, a gentle spring day in the Rockies, without even a hint of clouds building over Cheyenne Mountain. A perfect afternoon. Just right for a short walk around the neighborhood, to see what was what. She reached for the front door again.

Danger. Naomi stood there, hand resting on the door knob, torn between frustration and fear. If she couldn't even open her front door and step out onto the stoop, what hope was there, long-term, for her and Macy?

"Get over it," she ordered herself in a soft mutter. "Stop being such a coward. Open the damn door."

She sucked in a deep breath, and twisted the knob with sweaty fingers.

The front lawn was overgrown in patches, and brown where winter-kill hadn't been treated. Naomi stepped across the threshold and broadened her perspective to the neighboring houses, and the houses across the street. The signs of trouble were like repeated slaps. She should have expected to see them, but they shocked her just the same.

Across the street, the Sullivan's front door was wide open. She could see boxes and suitcases stacked just inside the door, but leaves and trash had blown in to rest against them. The door had been open at least a few days, maybe longer. Naomi stepped onto the front sidewalk and took a few steps, reaching towards the Sullivans' home with all her senses. It felt still, completely still.

When she reached the end of her driveway, she stopped, examining each house from where she stood. Garage doors stood open that were usually closed. One house had all the front windows boarded up with plywood. And was that...a body? Naomi strained to see, and forced herself to move closer, shuffling sideways down the street, ready to run in an instant.

It was a body, a woman – she knew the family by sight, but didn't know their names. She was curled on the ground between what had to be graves, two mounds of dirt scratched in the front yard – her children? A mottled gray arm was flung over one of the mounds, as if embracing a sleeping child, and Naomi could see where the woman had hemorrhaged, coughing her life out just as Scott had done.

For a long moment, she stood there, waiting to feel something. Shouldn't she? Wasn't she supposed to feel shock, sorrow, horror? There was a woman dead in her front yard, her body slowly dissolving back into the earth, a woman she had known well enough to wave at when they passed in the street. Had she spent all her grief on Scott, that she had nothing to give this quiet corpse?

She moved to the middle of the street and scanned both directions, looking for any signs of life. From her vantage point, she could see about 20 homes. Down the street, a cat scooted across the asphalt and disappeared into the weeds. Other than the soft, rise-and-fall shush of the wind and the occasional call of a bird, the world was absolutely silent. Naomi glanced back at her house and decided to check one block deeper into the neighborhood. She didn't want to be gone longer than a few minutes.

Hunching her shoulders, she crept along the side of the road, wincing at the loud crunch of gravel under the sandals she'd slipped on. Silly, pretty, strappy sandals adorned with beachy blue and green beads. Stupid shoes for this task – she had to start thinking such things through. She didn't know what was worse – the houses where nothing looked amiss, or the discrepancies that signaled trouble: a minivan with all the doors flung wide, just sitting in a driveway; another home with two bodies in the front yard, tangled together in death like lovers; several vehicles parked in driveways with a driver slumped motionless behind the wheel.

And every time the breeze lifted, it brought with it the scent of rot. She knew, of course, what the source of the smell was, but she didn't want to dwell on it.

As soon as she had been able to leave Macy for any length of time, she had moved all her belongings out of the bedroom she'd shared with Scott, and had sealed the door shut with layer after layer of plastic and tape. When Macy could leave her bed, they'd had a ceremony, there in the hall, in front of the bedroom door. She had calligraphied his name on the wall beside the door, as well as the dates of his birth and his death, and Macy had used some of her precious strength to embellish her father's memorial with glitter and stickers. Scott's remains would have to rest in his unorthodox tomb for the foreseeable future, and Naomi knew he was one of the lucky ones. So many, so very many dead, and no one to care for them.

The breeze also stirred the trash, which was everywhere in what had once been a pristine neighborhood. Animals, she guessed. There hadn't been any trash pick-up since the start of the quarantine, and animals would certainly have been drawn by the smell. Maybe pets, who had escaped from their homes or been set loose, like Artemis and Athena. Dogs would have the worst of it, she pondered as she trudged along. Cats retained their hunting instincts no matter how domesticated. Dogs, for the most part, were more dependent on humans, and would have to overcome more conditioning to kill for food.

As if she'd conjured him, she heard a low whuff from the doorway of the house she was passing. Sitting on the front porch, still and watchful, was one of the largest

Rottweilers she had ever seen. When her gaze met his, he whuffed again, ears alert. She stopped walking, and he cocked his head to the side, studying her.

Anxiety. Not hers, his. It rolled off him – that, and *hunger*. Naomi blinked, startled. She had always been good at reading an animal's body language, especially dogs. It was a knack she'd simply always had, and that knack had been further honed by her years of work with rescued animals. But this was more than reading posture, gaze and ear position – it felt like his thoughts had touched hers.

She wasn't scared of him, not for an instant. She kept her body turned to the side – to face him fully might telegraph a challenge – and he rose to his feet. For pity's sake, even lean as he was, he had to weigh 150 pounds. He turned, looked over his shoulder at her, trotted through the open door, then turned to look at her again.

Naomi surprised herself with a rusty chuckle – it had been a long time since she had felt amusement of any kind. The big guy was exhibiting what she had always called "Timmy's in the well!" behavior – he so obviously wanted her to follow him, it was as if he could speak.

"I'm coming, boy. That's a good boy – I'll follow you."

She paused in the doorway, seriously doubting the wisdom of what she was doing. The door had been gnawed and dug open – the dog's strength and determination to be free awed her. Surprising, then, that he hadn't taken off. She heard the click of his claws on the hardwood ahead of her, and crept farther into the dim house.

She smelled them before she saw them. The man was lying on the couch, the woman slumped on the floor beside him. Both dead, and had been for some time. Naomi lifted the neck of her t-shirt over her nose and breathed through her mouth. The dog stood by them, anxious, vigilant, and whined softly. *Help.* His eyes were liquid with sorrow.

Naomi shook her head. "I'm sorry, boy. I can't do anything for them."

The dog's ears pricked at her voice, and he whined again. He padded away from the couple, leading her up a half-flight of stairs to what appeared to be bedrooms. He bypassed the first, entered the second. From her vantage point, Naomi could see soft lavender paint on the walls. She edged closer, glimpsed the corner of a white crib with frilly white bedding, and flattened herself against the wall. No. No, she could not go in there. Could not.

The dog re-emerged and stared at her until she met his gaze, then tried his "follow me" behavior again. Walk away, look back, whine. *Help.* His distress was a pressure in her brain. She shook her head. "I can't," she choked, as if he could understand her. "Please, I can't."

He whined again, softly, and disappeared into the bedroom. Naomi shut her eyes and tilted her head back against the wall. She had to get out of here, had to get back to Macy. But what if the baby in that room was still alive?

She didn't give herself time to think or agonize, just pushed away from the wall and swung into the room. The dog was sitting beside the crib, vigilant once more. Naomi smelled blood and corruption, and she knew, even before she saw the tiny, chubby arm, out-flung and discolored, saw the slitted, staring eyes. She reached into the crib and pulled the soft, fluffy afghan over the baby's face, tucking it gently around her still form. Then she looked at the dog.

"You're a good dog. Good boy."

She turned to leave, and he followed her. As she walked back through the house, she saw further evidence of his desperation – he had clawed open all the cupboard doors as well as the refrigerator, looking for food, even as he had staunchly guarded the decomposing corpses of his little family.

She hurried back home, anxious to make sure Macy was okay, with the dog right on her heels the whole way. She stepped through her front door and he followed then sat, as if looking for direction.

"Well, I guess this is your new home, big guy. We'll check on our girls then get you some food. And you're going to need a name."

She ignored Scott's voice, scolding in her head, as she bustled out to the deck. Macy was still sleeping, but Persephone shot off the lounge chair when she spotted the strange dog, quivering with excitement and anxiety. The two sniffed and sniffed, rigidly at first, then with growing enthusiasm and warmth. Finally, the big Rottweiler settled down with a sigh and laid his head on his paws. Persephone curled up next to him – her whole body wasn't even as big as his head. Naomi left them like that and went to find the newcomer some food.

She scrubbed and scrubbed her hands and arms in the kitchen sink. By now, she was fairly certain she wasn't going to get the plague, and Macy had already survived it, but she couldn't be too careful. She tried, and failed, to forget the cold rigidity of the baby's corpse when she had tucked the afghan around it, so unlike the warm resilience of a living, sleeping baby. Poor, poor tiny girl – gone before she had lived.

Naomi was not a spiritual person. She took her children to church with regularity because that's what her parents had done, and made sure they attended Sunday school and vacation bible school. If people asked, she said she was Christian, because that was the way she was raised. But in all honesty, it didn't interest her as it did some, didn't consume her as it did others. Religion had never made her feel much at all.

Until now. Now, she was pissed.

"You listen to me, God," she muttered as she scrubbed. "That baby! Why did you let her even be born, just to take her back so soon? Seems to me you let her down. Seems to me you've been letting a lot of people down."

Naomi scrubbed harder for a few minutes, then stopped. She stared out the window over her kitchen sink, where she could see the top of Cheyenne Mountain over the neighbor's roof. She ran her eyes along the familiar ridgeline and imagined herself there, among the pines, hearing only the wind. Then she firmed her mouth and spoke again.

"Okay, God, I want you to know I'm grateful that you let Macy stay. I don't know why you had to take Scott, but I know some people lost a lot more, and I'm grateful for Macy. And I'm grateful for Piper – I know she's still alive. I can feel her. But here's the deal: You need to do right by that baby girl. You need to make sure you take her soul to you, or you give her another chance, whatever it is that happens. She never had a chance to ride a pony, or play dress-up, or fall in love." Naomi shook her head. "Not fair. It's just not fair, God. If I can't believe you're fair on some level, I don't know what I can believe."

Naomi dried her hands, then got Zeus' old feed dish from the cupboard and scooped some of his food into it. It wasn't ideal – Zeus' food was formulated for older dogs with joint problems – but it would have to do. She carried the bowl out to the deck, where the sun was starting to slide towards the top of the mountains. Both dogs lifted their heads when she stepped outside, and the big Rottie shot to his feet as soon as he scented the food. Naomi sat down cross-legged on the deck and started feeding him, handful by handful, so he wouldn't bolt the food and be sick. His whole body shook, but he took the food from her hand as delicately as Persephone would have.

"You need a name," she mused. She examined his collar for a name tag while he chewed, but found only his license and rabies tags. "I've been on a Greek gods kick – that's what Scott called it." Pain tightened across her chest, and she breathed deep, trying to warm and loosen the constriction around her heart. She missed his gentle teasing, so much. "We lost him, just like you lost your people. We're all just trying to survive, see?"

She fed him the last handful of food, then let him snuff around the bowl for a minute. When he finally accepted the food was gone, he heaved an enormous sigh and settled down next to her, watching her with ancient eyes. After a minute or so, he scooted closer, so that his nose was resting against her hand. Another minute, and she felt a tiny, grateful lick touch her palm.

"What a sweet, sweet boy you are. Brave and true." She considered. "'Hercules' is too cliché, don't you think? And 'Apollo' isn't right – I'm pretty sure he was a blonde."

Persephone trotted over to settle against the big dog's side as if she'd known him her whole life, and just like that, Naomi knew his name. "You're 'Hades.' Now, don't look at me like that – he's not the god of the dead, he's the ruler of the underworld – there's a big difference. He's Persephone's consort, and even though he kidnapped her, I like to think they grew to love each other. He could be cruel, it's true, and he was stern, but he was also fair and just."

Naomi smoothed both hands over Hades' head, learning the silkiness of his ears, the sturdiness of his skull, the bulky muscle of his neck and shoulders. His eyes slid shut under her stroking and she felt his anxiety ease, as surely as she'd eased his hunger – he had been as starved for affection and comfort as he had been for food. Beside her, Macy stirred, and Hades lifted his head.

Macy's eyes fluttered open. She stretched, yawned with a soft, humming sound, then went still when she spotted the big Rottweiller. Before Naomi could say a word, Macy's face bloomed into a glorious smile. She beamed at Naomi with shining eyes.

"I knew he'd come! I dreamed him!" She reached out a hand, and Hades shuffled on his stomach over to her. He pressed his head into her caress with a soft, joyous whine.

Naomi felt the hair on the back of her neck tingle and lift. She was seeing...a reunion. Not a first-time meeting. "You dreamed about him?" She was proud of her casual tone. "When?"

"When I was really sick," Macy answered matter-of-factly. "He said he was coming to us, that I needed to stay. That you needed me to stay."

"He talked to you?" Naomi couldn't tell if she sounded casual any more, and didn't much care. Something was moving underneath the surface of this exchange, something she just wasn't ready to deal with.

"Of course he didn't talk to me, not like people do," Macy scoffed. "You know what I mean. When you feel what animals feel, you just *know*. Like you knew how he felt when you saw him with his other family. You knew he was worried about them, and you knew you didn't need to be afraid of him."

"Macy," Naomi whispered, all pretext of "casual" forgotten. "How did you know about that? I didn't tell you that. You weren't there."

"I dreamed that, too." Seeing the distress on her mother's face, she leaned over and patted her on the shoulder. "It's okay, Mama. I dreamed a lot of weird things when I was sick." Her face slid into a crafty grin, and Naomi nearly wept with joy at seeing it. "I dreamed you were so happy I lived, you bought me my very own horse - a beautiful, pure white Arabian!"

Naomi's tears escaped her, leaving her sobbing and laughing at the same time. The ploy was so Piper-like – it made her miss her oldest daughter, the pain a deep slice across her heart, even as she reveled in the living, breathing humor of her baby. "Did you really? What else did you dream, you little opportunist?"

Macy's face went still, her eyes growing distant, and Naomi was instantly sorry she had asked. "I dreamed of Piper. She's alive, Mama, but she's in danger. It's going to take you a long time to find her – a very long time. But you can't give up, no matter what. You can't stop looking for her. She's going to need you to help her fix her heart."

"What else?" Naomi whispered. She desperately didn't want to know, but to not ask felt like the most cowardly course. She couldn't take it. "What else do I need to know, baby?"

"Daddy. I dream of him all the time. He stays close, for...later..."

Cold, cold to her bones, cold slicing to her very marrow. Terror made her angry, and she struggled to keep the bite of it out of her voice. "Macy. Love. Daddy is gone. We talked about this."

Macy reached out and gentled her with a soft palm against her cheek, comforting her a second time. "I know, Mama. It's okay. Hey, is there any soup? I think I could eat some..."

Clever girl, Naomi thought, watching as her daughter ruffled Hades' ears, then gave Persephone a stroke for fairness. Knows just how to distract her mother. Macy's appetite still hadn't returned, and she desperately needed to put some weight back on. She was frail to the point of fragile, and though she did her best to eat the nutritious dishes her mother fixed her, eating exhausted her.

"I'll get some. Do you want to eat out here?"

"Yeah, that would be good. I'll just stay here and get to know Hades. Thanks, Mama."

Naomi paused in the doorway, watching as Persephone hopped up to curl against Macy's side, and Hades rested his head on the lounge chair, eyes closed, while Macy stroked his ears. Then she went to heat up a cup of the rich chicken noodle soup she had fixed yesterday. Not until she was headed out with a tray, attractively arranged with crackers and some canned fruit, did her footsteps falter.

Macy had known Hades' name.

SEVEN
Grace and Quinn: Limon, CO

Grace found Quinn where she usually found him these days: tending to the plants he was forever adding to his family's gravesite. She stifled a sigh of impatience and stood watching him for a moment, wondering for the countless time what was wrong with her, that she couldn't grieve like Quinn was grieving.

It had taken them four days to bury both her family and his, using a system Quinn devised of soaking the earth, then loosening it with a pickaxe and a pitchfork, and finally shoveling enough soil away to create ragged holes. Grace had smoothed the sides as best she could, then used old blankets and mattress pads to line the graves. She had not shed a single tear as she wrapped her mother tightly in the sheets she had died in, then her stepfather, then little Benji. Quinn helped her lay the bodies carefully in the grave, Benji snuggled between their mom and Wayne, then she had carefully tucked a quilt over all three of them. She had only faltered when it was time to throw the first shovelful of dirt; Quinn, sensing her distress, had gestured for her to go back in the house.

"Get what you want to take back to the ranch," he said, his voice hoarse from disuse. "I'll finish."

It was the coward's way and she knew it, but she took it anyway. She lingered inside, wandering from room to room, picking things up and setting them down without even looking at them. She stuffed some clothes and her riding boots into Wayne's big duffel bag, haphazardly grabbed toiletries from the bathroom, then just gave up and sat on the couch until she didn't hear Quinn's shovel hitting dirt any more.

She heard him come in the back door, then check the tap in the kitchen for water. The power had been flickering on and off for days, more off than on, but he got lucky – the tap sputtered then gushed. Silence, during which she assumed he was drinking, splashing, probably washing up, and all the while she just sat and stared, drifting in a limbo where there was no feeling, no loss, no loneliness, no sorrow, no fear.

He appeared in the doorway, t-shirt filthy, face shining clean, and just looked at her. This was his way, she was learning – he didn't speak unless he had to, but simply gazed at her in a steady, wide-open way that didn't allow for subterfuge. Somehow, she knew she could more readily lie to herself than to him.

Grace stood up, fussing with her bag so she wouldn't have to meet his gaze. "Thank you," she said brusquely, as if he had scraped the ice off the windshield of her car, or brought in the groceries. "Let's head back to your house and we'll...finish up there."

"Don't you want a marker?"

It took her a moment to process what he meant. "Like a cross or something?"

He nodded, and her mind went perfectly blank. It was terrifying. What symbol, to sum up the lives of her family? She thought her mother might like a cross, but not Wayne, he never went to church, and Benji only went to Sunday School when their mother dragged him – if he worshipped anything, it was technology, robots especially–

"Grace?"

She was breathing too fast – she just couldn't make one more decision, couldn't take one more step into the unknown – how was she supposed to make this choice? It was her responsibility to make sure her family wasn't forgotten, to mark that spot for future generations to know that three human beings were resting there, three people who had been loved –

"Grace, it's okay. I'll take care of it. It's okay."

Quinn moved to her side and took her elbow, like he was helping his elderly aunt cross the street. He steered her towards the front door, murmuring soft and soothing sounds so low she couldn't make out the words, just the tone. She didn't realize she was crying until he handed her a wad of tissues and told her gently to "Blow."

By the time he had driven them back to the Harris ranch, she had wrestled her grief back into its box. No time for that luxury right now, she told herself sternly. To start crying was to never stop. She rolled down the window as they pulled into the driveway and lifted her face to the soft May sunshine, focusing her mind on the next task that needed doing.

Quinn showed no such restraint as he prepared his family for burial, breaking down so often, Grace offered to complete the task for him. He refused with heart-breaking politeness, choking out a barely audible, "No, thank you," as his big hands tenderly washed his mother's face, straightened his little brother's pajamas, and carefully arranged William's track medals around his neck.

While he worked, Grace prepared the grave as she had for her own family, lining it with blankets. Then Quinn carried all seven of his family members to the communal grave, keeping his mother for last. He clutched her body for a long, long time, sobbing without shame or self-consciousness, his deep, broken voice keening like a child for his Mama.

Grace stood behind him silently for a while, and just rested her hand on his shoulder. She didn't have his easy way of comforting, but she had to do something for him. In the barn, the horses were restless – she could hear them blowing and stamping in their stalls, and every once in a while, one would shrill out an anxious whinny, a chorus with Quinn's grief.

Finally, he had nestled his mother beside his father and his brothers, and had covered their bodies with dirt a painstaking handful at a time, standing in the grave with them, reaching out for the dirt piled nearby. Silently, Grace had facilitated his task, pushing dirt closer with a shovel until their bodies were no longer visible and Quinn was up to his shins in dirt. They had worked together to fill in the rest of the grave shovelful by careful shovelful, and it comforted Grace enormously to know for certain

Quinn had taken just this sort of tender care of her own family.

They hadn't spoken a word to each other for the rest of that day, nor the next, working together in an easy silence that allowed them both the space they needed to adjust to the new shape of the world, a world without parents to buffer or shelter, without siblings to share the road.

That had been over a week ago, and once again, they had decisions to make. The food was all but gone. They were running low on feed for the horses, and Quinn had long since released the cattle to forage on their own. The power had been out for days, and Grace knew they couldn't count on it returning any time soon, if ever. They had a back-up generator they ran for a few hours every day, but their fuel supply wasn't infinite. All of these concerns crowded and clamored in Grace's head as she watched Quinn's big, grubby hands press the soil around the columbines he had moved from his mother's flower beds to the small garden that now flourished on his family's grave.

At the center was a small blue spruce he'd transplanted, then surrounded with graduated rings of shrubbery and perennial flowers he'd moved from all over the ranch. Quinn's mom had possessed quite the green thumb, Grace remembered, and Quinn had clearly inherited her gift. He had been working on the garden whenever the necessities of living didn't demand his attention, and though he didn't speak of it, Grace could see the comfort and peace he gained from the activity. She thought of her family's barren grave and flinched. Shame made her tone sharper than she intended it to be.

"Quinn. We need to talk." When he looked up, she added, "About leaving."

Quinn went still for a moment, then brushed his hands off and stood up. He surveyed his work, then turned and headed for the house. Grace followed him into the kitchen, watching silently while he washed his hands and got a drink of water. He was thinner than he'd been before the plague, his hair starting to look shaggy and unkempt. She touched her own hair, scraped back in a messy ponytail, and couldn't remember the last time she'd looked in a mirror. Finally, Quinn sat down at the kitchen table, meeting her eyes with his wide-open gaze in silent invitation for her to speak.

"We're pretty much out of food," she began, "So even if we decide to stay, we're going to have to go to town to see what we can find. I know your mom always had a huge garden, but even if we had seeds it would be what – a couple months? – before we could harvest anything to eat."

Quinn nodded his agreement thus far, so she continued. "We should find out who else made it, too – there have to be some more survivors in Limon. That'll help us make our decision. If we decide not to stay here, I have another idea."

She paused. She didn't trust her decision-making skills when she yearned so deeply for the course of action she was about to suggest. Her emotions were clouding her analysis, and she wasn't sure how to counteract that effect. "We could head for Woodland Park, and see if my Dad made it. My Grandpa was really sick – we should check in there, but I don't think he would have made it. I don't have any other family close by – some cousins in Kansas. What about you – do you have other family close by?"

Quinn's voice was always deeper than she expected it to be. "My mom's sister and her husband live in Limon, and my cousins. My grandma is in a nursing home in Colorado Springs. If we leave to go to Woodland, maybe we could stop in and see if..." He trailed off.

"Of course," Grace agreed, and wondered how long their conversations would consist of words left unsaid, of sentences started and not finished. "In the meantime, let's head into town and see what's going on."

They decided to take Quinn's dad's new pick-up, which had the fullest gas tank. Quinn drove with a confidence that told Grace he'd probably been driving on his family's ranch for years. As they skimmed along the deserted road, Grace fiddled with the radio, trying to find any signal at all. Every time they passed another homestead, they slowed the truck, looking for signs of life. Twice, they passed vehicles that had gone off the road with drivers slumped behind the wheel.

Quinn stopped at the stoplight at Highway 24 automatically and looked both ways. The businesses here all catered to the travelers on I-70, and the evidence of trouble was ample – one of the gas stations was burned out, and the Denny's, McDonald's and Country Pride Restaurant all had their windows broken.

"People looking for food, you suppose?" Grace asked, and Quinn nodded. They idled there for a moment. Then Grace spoke again. "Do you think it's safe to go on?"

Quinn shrugged. "We don't have much choice."

He started off again, creeping across Highway 24 and continuing down Main Street into town. Not until they were just passing the Dollar General did they see another living soul.

The woman scared a shriek out of Grace and made Quinn jerk the wheel in reaction. She came out of nowhere, screaming and waving frantically for them to stop. Quinn hit the brakes, but both of them reached for the auto-door-lock simultaneously. Their eyes met for a moment, in perfect communication of their mutual trepidation. The woman skidded to a stop by the passenger window, wringing her hands, her face haggard and wild.

Quinn said softly, "Just put your window down a little bit."

Grace complied. "Can we help you?"

"Yes, thank God, thank God! I need you to help me get my kids to Colorado Springs, to the hospital – they're both sick, and I can't reach anyone – no one is even picking up at 9-1-1!"

Quinn and Grace exchanged another look. Grace spoke again, hesitantly. "Ma'am, do they have the plague? Because-"

The woman lunged at the window, her face twisting and twitching. "It's not the plague! They'll be fine, if I can just get them to a doctor! Wait here – I'll be right back with them!"

The woman scuttled away, and Grace looked at Quinn in anguish. "What do we do? I think she's nuts or something! Do we help her? Should we just keep going?"

Quinn's hands were wringing the steering wheel. "I don't know," he said. "I don't know what to do."

The woman reappeared, and what she carried made both Quinn and Grace suck in a breath: a little boy, in blood-stained footie pajamas. She shifted his limp body to her shoulder, and his head lolled to the side, his face bluish grey, his eyes slitted and dry-looking. She reached for the passenger door, jerking it frantically when Grace didn't unlock the door.

"Here! I need you to take him, then I'll go get the baby! They just need a doctor – they'll be fine! Please! Please, you have to help me, please!"

Grace groped for Quinn's hand - she couldn't stop staring at the little boy's face, so much more dead-looking than her family, or Quinn's. He gripped her hand hard, so hard it hurt.

"Turn your face away, Gracie, just close your eyes," he said hoarsely. Then he raised his voice, speaking to the woman. "Ma'am, we're sorry. Your little boy is dead. We can't help you."

She lunged at the window again, spit flying as she raged. Her face was flushed red-hot, her eyes and nose streaming. "No! Don't you dare say that! He's just sleeping – he'll be fine! You have to help me, god damn it! He's going to be fine!"

She started to claw at the crack in the window, and Grace's nerve broke. She released her seatbelt and threw herself across the bench seat until she slammed into Quinn, trying to get away from those scrabbling fingers and the kind of grief that stole sanity. Quinn started easing the truck forward, picking up speed as the woman fell behind. Grace watched the woman chase them, gripping Quinn's rigid arm with both hands. The woman stopped running, dropping to her knees in the middle of the street, just as Quinn rounded a corner on two tires. She was lost to their view, but Grace knew she'd remember that woman's face to her dying breath, the disfigurement of despair as she clutched her son's corpse to her heart.

"Holy shit holy shit holy shit!" Grace's teeth were chattering in reaction, her stomach quivering, a fine shaking sending tremors through her arms and legs. By contrast, Quinn was absolutely rigid, knuckles bone-white on the steering wheel, his face locked in an expression of horror.

"What do we do? Should we go home? What if they're all like her?" Grace's mind was spinning – she couldn't get a lock on this possible new reality – it was too awful. It had never occurred to her that other survivors might be a threat. What if she and Quinn were the only sane ones left?

"I don't know, Gracie, I don't know." He drove in silence for a few minutes, aimlessly turning up and down the streets they'd both known all their lives, scanning for another potential threat. Finally, he shook himself. "Let's head for my aunt's house. See what's happening there. We'll just take this one step at a time."

Quinn's aunt lived by the elementary school. Quinn pulled up in front of the house and put the truck in park, but didn't shut it off. "Slide over behind the wheel. I'll go in and check. If there's any trouble, just lay on the horn or get out of here. If we get separated, I'll meet you back home."

"I'm not leaving you, Quinn." She really didn't know what pushed the words out of her with such vehemence. She felt responsible for him, that was part of it. William would have wanted her to watch out for him. And he carried his own load – he certainly hadn't been a burden. She could have wished he had William's brains, but he was who he was. And there was no way in hell she was leaving him. "You have five minutes. If you don't come out or signal to me, I'm driving this truck through the front window."

Quinn ducked his head at her words, but didn't say anything. After a moment, he slid out from behind the wheel, then waited while Grace took his place and adjusted the seat for her shorter legs. He shut the door, then pointed at the door lock thru the window. Grace obeyed, then watched him walk slowly towards the back door and let himself in.

Grace checked the clock on the dashboard and settled in to wait. Just over four minutes had passed when Quinn reappeared. He was carrying a grocery bag, and his cheeks were shiny with tears. Grace unlocked the doors, and he slid into the passenger seat.

"All of them?" Grace asked, even though she already knew the answer. Even though all she really wanted to know was what he had in the bag.

Quinn nodded.

"I'm sorry." She didn't feel sorry, not really, but she knew she was supposed to say the words. What was wrong with her? She counted to 30, hoped that was enough of a respectful silence, then asked, "What did you find?"

Quinn wiped his face on his sleeve, and blew his nose on a napkin he found in the glove box. "Some beans. A little bit of rice. There was a lot of food in the freezer, but most of it was warm, and I don't know how long their power has been out."

"Good call, leaving it behind. Food poisoning would suck." She paused again. "Are you ready to go? Is there anything else you need to...do here?"

Quinn shook his head. "No, they're too far gone to bury. They're all together in Aunt Sue and Uncle Brad's room. I just shut the door." He paused, then opened the grocery sack between his feet and pulled out a framed picture. "I took this – thought I'd put it on my family's grave, so they're all together."

Grace looked at the smiling family, recognized Quinn's aunt as the woman who had helped her set up a checking account at the bank, recognized his young cousin as a friend of Benji's, and shut her eyes. These people were gone, consciousness fled, everything that had made them unique – personalities, likes, talents – dissolved into nothing, while the bodies that had harbored them rotted in this house. How could this be happening? Where was all the energy, all the spirit and humanness and *life* going?

"Quinn?" Grace whispered, "Do you believe in...Heaven?"

Quinn was quiet so long, she thought he wasn't going to answer. She watched his face as he stared straight ahead, tears once more tracking silently down his cheeks. Finally, he heaved a deep, shuddering breath.

"I guess not 'Heaven,' like Christians believe. It never made much sense to me that you had to believe a certain way so you could go hang out on a cloud and play the harp forever – either that, or burn in hell." He glanced at her sideways, embarrassed. "That sounds like a little kid. I don't say what I'm thinking very well. It's why I don't talk much."

"It's okay. You said it just fine." Grace hesitated. "So you think when we die, we're just gone? Just like we were never here, unless we build a bridge or write a piece of music or something?"

"No, not at all." Again, he slid his shy glance sideways at her. "I think we go on forever. That the best part of us – our souls, I guess – returns to God. And then you talk it over with God and decide what you'll do next. Like maybe you want to be a horse, or a flower, or the wind. Or maybe you want to be a man instead of a woman, so you can be a father instead of a mother – I don't know. Maybe whatever you need to learn. Maybe you talk it over with God, and decide, and then you go live that life."

Fascinating. She never would have guessed. "So you believe in reincarnation."

"I guess. If that's what it's called." He looked embarrassed again. "My mom would freak – she made us do the whole Sunday School thing, so don't say anything to her-" He broke off, and his face went white as bone. He stared at her, and she could see his loss, alive and fresh, in his eyes. She looked away so she wouldn't have to feel it, too.

"Let's get going. I think I have a plan." She watched him out of the corner of her eye, waited until he had wiped his face again, then went on brusquely. "One of us should drive along the street, and the other one should go in the houses one by one, to see if there's any food. That way we can get away quick if we have to. Do you want to drive or go in?"

He wouldn't meet her gaze. "Isn't that stealing or something?"

Grace blinked. It hadn't even occurred to her that what she was proposing was technically illegal. She, who had never cheated on a test or snuck out after curfew or gotten a speeding ticket in her life. "I guess it is. Should we just try Bella's Market, or the gas stations?"

"No. They'll be cleaned out for sure – my dad tried Bella's not too long after the plague hit, and he said there wasn't one thing left on the shelves."

Grace wrestled down a spurt of frustration with him. The least he could do was come up with an idea, instead of shooting all hers down. "What, then? Just go back home?"

"No." Quinn looked up and down the street, and resignation settled on his face, in lines worn by care and grief. She could see the old man he would become, there in his 16 year-old face. "You're right. If all these people are dead, they don't need their stuff anymore. Maybe they'd even want to give it to us, to help us stay alive."

"Whatever keeps you keepin' on," Grace muttered, then grimaced. Just because his moral code was still intact and hers seemed to have deserted her was no reason to get frustrated with him. "Do you want to drive or run in?"

"I'll run. You drive."

They worked their way down both sides of the street, zig-zagging back and forth. After the third house, Quinn's face was set in rigid lines, but he didn't voice a complaint or ask to trade jobs, so they kept on the way they were. He wasn't finding much – a little flour here, some macaroni there, but he rarely came out completely empty-handed. At one house, he was gone so long, Grace was about to go in after him. Finally, he came around the side of the house with a rusty-red chicken tucked under one arm, his shirt bulging with what could only be eggs. Grace hopped out and ran around to open the truck door for him.

"Backyard henhouse," he said, as he set the chicken on the passenger seat. She rustled her feathers and hopped into the back seat at Quinn's urging, making low, anxious cooing sounds. Grace helped transfer the eggs he had found to the various containers, nestling them in flour, rice and beans so they wouldn't jostle together and break. "She was the only hen left, but there were a bunch of eggs. If there wasn't a rooster around, they should still be good to eat."

"Protein," Grace breathed, mouth suddenly filled with saliva. "Is this enough for now? Should we head home?"

"I guess we could." Quinn looked up and down the street again. "We just saw that one lady. There have to be some other people alive."

"Probably." Grace thought for a moment. "They might be hiding. Or they may have gathered somewhere."

"Maybe they left," Quinn said. "I-70 is right on the other side of town."

"Where would they go? The plague was everywhere, last I heard. All over the world."

"To find family, like you want to do."

They stood there, in the middle of the deserted street, with the truck purring beside them and the chicken still rustling and softly clucking its concern in the back seat. Grace could feel the oncoming wave of all the decisions waiting to be made, and struggled not to let them swamp her. For now, they just needed to take the next step.

"Let's finish this street, then try some of the stores and restaurants in town. We should take as much as we can while we're here – more trips into town will waste gas."

Quinn nodded his agreement, and they continued. In addition to food, Quinn started to come back with other useful items – toilet paper, a first aid kit, over-the-counter medicines. Grace scanned the area endlessly, her muscles tight and ready to react in an instant, so much so that a throbbing headache had started at the base of her skull by the time they finished the long residential street. Quinn, too, looked exhausted, leaning back in his seat and closing his eyes, his face taut and gray with strain.

"Let's just drive through town," Grace suggested. "If the stores look cleaned out, we'll just forget it and go home."

Quinn nodded without opening his eyes, and Grace kept glancing at him as she drove. Finally, she asked. "Was it really bad?"

"Yeah." Still, with closed eyes. "I don't want to talk about it."

"Okay." She drove on, part of her mind focused on scanning the streets and the store fronts – most of them sporting broken windows – part of her mind occupied with plans and contingencies. She was so distracted, she didn't see the men standing in the middle of the road, both of them holding shotguns, until it was almost too late to stop.

"Holy shit! Quinn! Look!"

Quinn's eyes shot open and he lurched forward, hands on the dashboard, scanning quickly. "It's Mr. Weaver. He owns the True Value. And I think that's his son – he coached William's little league team one year."

In unison, both men raised their shotguns. The elder Mr. Weaver called out.

"Aren't you one of the Harris boys?"

"Be ready to stomp on it," Quinn hissed low. "This feels bad. Look at their eyes." He raised his voice, nodding. "Yes, sir. I'm Quinn Harris."

The younger man stepped forward, shotgun still raised. "We're going to ask you to turn over all the goods you've stolen. Looting is a crime."

Quinn's face twitched; in it, Grace could see a lifetime of obeying his elders warring with the need to adapt to a new world. "Yes sir, it is, but we took only from those who no longer needed it. And only what we need to survive. Food and such. We didn't touch any valuables or money."

The two men exchanged a long look. Quinn reached out and gripped Grace's leg. "Be ready," he whispered through stiff lips. "If they squint when they look back at us, they're going to shoot. Floor it and swerve to your left around them."

No sooner had he finished speaking than the two men returned their attention to the truck, and Grace saw exactly what Quinn had warned her about, as if the world had dropped into slow motion. Their bodies tightened in preparation for the recoil, both men's cheeks tucked in tight to site down their weapons, and without another thought, Grace jammed the gas pedal to the floor and jerked the wheel to the left.

In an instant, the world became a deafening boom, flying glass, and a freaked-out chicken squawking and flapping in terror. Quinn had dropped down to the floorboards, the windshield in front of him shattered, the glass in front of Grace webbed with fine lines.

In the chaos, Grace's mind was an island of cool logic, cataloging facts: by telling her to go to the left, Quinn had directed the gunfire to his side of the truck; her tires were spinning ineffectually, so she lifted her foot slightly off the gas pedal, until she felt them catch and the truck lurched forward; the men had been caught by surprise, and for the moment at least, had lowered their weapons; Quinn had ducked, but he was twisted around, looking up at her, and he didn't appear to be hurt; the chicken was going berserk and would probably die of a heart attack in the next few minutes.

That last fact made her snort with wild laughter, and she added another fact to her collection: she might be a tiny bit hysterical.

"Stay down!" she barked, when Quinn would have lifted his head. She flew past the two men, then watched them in the rearview mirror until they raised their guns again. She held the truck steady, and ducked when she heard the double-boom. The rear window exploded, the chicken let out what sounded like a scream and launched itself out the back window, flapping and fluttering wildly as it hit the back of the truck, then tumbled to the tarmac.

Quinn sat up, his eyes running over her frantically. "Are you hurt? Did they hit you?"

"No–you?"

"I'm fine."

Grace kept their speed high but not reckless for several minutes, squinting against the wind whipping into the wide-open cab of the truck. Then, she surprised herself with a hiccup of laughter. "Can't say the same for the chicken, I'm afraid."

Quinn just stared at her for a moment, incredulous. Then he, too, gulped out a laugh. Then another. They were both whooping, tears streaming, by the time Grace pulled back in the driveway at the Harris ranch. She parked the truck and leaned against the steering wheel, wheezing. "That poor thing – I thought it was going to lay a dozen eggs back there!"

"Are you kidding me? That chicken was so scared, it'll never lay an egg again! Besides, they've probably already got it turning on the rotisserie over at the deli!"

The image set them both off again. Quinn quieted first. The troubled frown on his face shut Grace's laughter off like a switch had been thrown.

"What is it?"

"Why did they shoot like that?" He rubbed his chest. "Could you feel it? I knew they were going to shoot as soon as I saw them. I could...feel it. In my chest and in my gut. They felt like..." He shot her a sideways glance, as if he feared ridicule or disbelief. "They felt like predators. They didn't think of us as people. I could see it in their eyes." He looked down. "That sounds stupid."

"No, Quinn, it doesn't. I knew, too." Grace stared into space for a few moments, thinking back over the incident. The way her brain had slowed everything down so she could analyze all the pieces, her absolute surety that they would shoot. She had read about such phenomena among survivors of catastrophes or high-stress situations.

She glanced over at Quinn, reluctant to share the other negative hypothesis she had reached. But if they were going to make it, they needed to look at the reality they'd been dealt head-on. "Do you think that's why we didn't find any other survivors? Maybe they've been killing them, to hoard all the resources for themselves?"

"Yeah." Quinn didn't hesitate. "I thought of that, too." He looked over at her. "They'll come here. To take what we have. We need to go."

Grace was nodding before he finished speaking. "We'll get ready tomorrow and leave as soon as we can."

EIGHT
Jack and Layla: Woodland Park, CO

Someone was shuffling cards. Jack shifted, then stretched, trying to blink open his gummy eyes. He felt so very, very strange – weak, shaky, hungry and holy cow – so sore! He stopped moving and decided to just open his eyes...only to find himself in a gypsy caravan wagon. He blinked up at the rich, jewel colors of the canopy over his head, completely lost.

The sound of cards shuffling drew his attention again, and he turned his head. Oh, good Lord.

Layla was sitting at a delicate scroll-work table, in front of a window draped with antique lace and sparkling multi-colored beads. She had one leg drawn up, her bare foot tucked on the inside of her thigh. The window was open, and a warm breeze wafted in, stirring the lace, the beads, and Layla's hair. She frowned in concentration at the cards she was laying out in a pattern, then sat back, alternately gazing out the window and back down at the cards.

Jack would lay odds she wasn't playing solitaire. He pushed up on his elbows, struggling to sit up – if he was going to berate her for using those tool-of-the-Devil Tarot cards in his presence, he wasn't going to do it lying down – and instead ended up flat on his back, stars floating and darting in his vision, gasping as bands of pain tightened across his chest.

"Oh!" A clatter, and she was by his side. "You're awake!"

"I am," he gritted, blinking to clear his vision. "Where am I? What happened? I feel like someone beat the tar out of me."

Layla sat down beside him on the bed, casual and familiar, like she had every right. She reached out to feel his forehead. "You're at my house. Rowan helped me get you over here."

"Rowan?" He remembered a woman's voice, harried, impatient and compassionate all at the same time. "Rowan Lee, Dr. Derber's PA?"

"Yes. A bunch of the kids went to your house looking for you, and found you passed out on your kitchen floor. One of them thought to call me, and I called Rowan. We brought you here so I could look after you."

"Passed out? What?" It was hard not to panic; where his memory should be was just a reddish, hazy blur. "Did I fall? Was there some kind of accident?"

She gazed at him silently for a moment. "You don't remember."

"No! Why would I ask if I remembered?" His gaze darted around the room, looking for anything that would point him towards stable ground. Bohemian colors rioted everywhere – he should have known this was Layla's room the instant he opened his eyes. "And while I'm asking questions, why does my mouth taste like a goat's rear end?"

Layla smiled sadly and turned towards the bedside table, picking up a drinking glass with a straw in it. She slipped her hand under Jack's head and held the straw to his lips. "It's just water, but it'll help. If you feel up to it later, you can sit up and I'll bring you a toothbrush and a basin."

Bring him a toothbrush? Why wouldn't he just get up and go to the bathroom to brush his teeth? Jack sipped the water, watching her with narrowed eyes.

She took a deep breath. "You survived the plague, Jack. You're one of only three that Rowan knows about that survived. Do you remember the plague?"

If he hadn't already been lying down, this would have taken his legs out from under him. Memory flooded back. The tense waiting; comforting parishioners with friends and family in the Springs; waking night after night, gripped by a dreadful premonition, a terrible "knowing;" then, the news that it had spread...

"The Witts were sick," he blurted. "I remember. I visited them. Then..." He trailed off, and looked up at Layla, really looked at her for the first time.

She had aged a decade. Her face was lined with exhaustion and sorrow, and the loss in her dark eyes was fathoms deep. She reached out again and smoothed her hand over his forehead as if checking for fever, avoiding his gaze. Jack blinked, startled by the strength and chaos of the feelings he sensed from her. Joy and misery, in equal parts. He had no idea what to make of it.

"How long was I sick?"

"Over three weeks. We found you on April 10th. Today is the 4th of May. We weren't sure you'd make it until about a week ago." Layla smiled, and her eyes suddenly filled with tears. "And I wasn't sure you'd open your eyes and be snarky again until about five minutes ago. Excuse me."

She stood up abruptly and left the room. Jack watched her swift retreat, then stared at the patchwork canopy, processing, remembering, wondering. His parents in Wisconsin? They were elderly, and his dad especially was in poor health. Had they made it? Phone service had been problematic, he remembered, the lines overwhelmed. His youth group kids? The predictions of mortality rates had been so dire – surely the officials had exaggerated...

Layla came back in the room carrying a tray, which she set on the bedside table. "I brought some essential oil of peppermint – you can swish that around in your mouth until I find a toothbrush. And I brought some chicken broth – do you think you can eat?"

Jack's stomach answered with a tremendous growling rumble, and they both laughed. He rose on his elbows and Layla moved to help him, lifting under his arms, helping him slide back against the pillows she swiftly propped up behind him. The simple exercise left him gasping and chasing stars in his vision again.

"Why does it hurt so bad?" He choked. "My ribs?"

"You strained them coughing. We can wrap them if it'll make you more comfortable. Rowan didn't want to restrict your breathing in any way while you were recovering, so she just left them be."

"Okay." He nodded towards the chicken broth. "I'd like to try some of that – it smells good."

Just holding the warm mug made his arms shake with fatigue. He sipped, and closed his eyes as the fragrant, rich broth spread soothing warmth down his throat and into his stomach. "So good. Is that rosemary?" She nodded, and he sipped again. "You'd better get it over with, Layla. Just tell me. How bad is it?"

Layla stood up and walked to the window, arms wrapped around her middle, shoulders hunched. She had lost weight; her jeans hung loosely on her hips, and her spine and shoulder blades cut sharp bumps in the light t-shirt she wore. She turned to face him, and the dappled sunshine coming in the window didn't soften the terrible grief on her face.

"As bad as they said it would be. We haven't had any contact outside of Woodland Park for a while, but before the internet went down, there were millions reported dead, here in the U.S. and all over the world."

"Millions..." Jack's whole body went weak, and he fumbled to set the mug on the bedside table. Layla moved to help him, and sat down again, her hip resting against his thigh. She seemed perfectly comfortable touching him. "An exaggeration, surely..."

Layla shook her head and curled her hands with his, both comforting and seeking comfort. "No. By now, it's probably billions. Less than 1 in 100 people survived, Jack, and most of those were immune – we never got it. You recovered, but Rowan only knows of two more here in Woodland Park. A woman who made it here from the Springs before Highway 24 closed, and one of our kiddos – James. Other than that, everyone who got sick died, usually within a few days."

Jack tipped his head back and tried to take it in, tried to imagine it, tried...and couldn't. "This is a dream," he choked, "Isn't it? A really bad dream?"

"No." Layla's tone was gentle, but she wasn't going to allow him his fantasy. "At last count, there were just over 100 of us here in town. Rowan says there may be more – she's been traveling non-stop, you can't believe how tireless she's been – but I don't think so. We're both hoping, when the plague burns itself out, that some of us can go down and open up 24..."

"Why is it closed? What happened?"

"From what we hear, people tried to get out of the Springs in droves after the plague left the city, and some of them died behind the wheel. The vehicles started piling up, people tried to go around – you know how narrow it gets, though, just outside of Manitou Springs – and last we heard, the road was completely impassable. We thought people might try for Rampart Range Road or Old Stagecoach Road, but no one has shown up via those routes yet. We've had a lot of rain – they could be washed out by now, with no one maintaining them."

He was not going to start listing all the people he knew, so she could tell him "yes" or "no." He just couldn't face it yet. "What else?"

"Well, we still have water, but the power's out, so we've been rigging up generators. Rowan's brother Alder survived, too – he used to work at the Walmart in the hardware department, so he has a little know-how – and he's been helping to get the survivors grouped together and set up with the generators we do have."

"Police? Firemen? Other clergy?"

"None that we know of." She smiled sadly. "You're the only game in town, as far as authority figures go."

Jack closed his eyes. There was no way he could assimilate all this. He didn't want to. If he could just take one step back in time, all of this would go away, and they could go back to the way things were. To a time when plagues were third-world problems, when modern medicine could fix just about anything, and when the biggest problems he faced were confused, angry teenagers and a problematic relationship with the local Witch/English teacher.

Layla continued. "We haven't been able to reach your family – Alder went to your house and looked around until he found your address book, I hope that's okay – but we do think that immunity to the plague occurred along genetic lines, so you should be hopeful. About half the time, survivors are members of the same family – a mother and daughter, or brother and sister. Of course we don't have enough data to confirm that yet – Rowan plans to gather it, when she gets a chance, but she's the only one with any medical training left alive, so..." She trailed off, and Jack could feel her scrutiny. "What is it? Jack?"

He was panting. He pulled his hands away from hers and pushed up against the pillows, ignoring the tearing pain in his chest. "Was it the Rapture?" His deepest fear erupted out of him. He clutched the sheet over his chest, in the grip of the kind of terror he had never experienced, his body alternately flushing and chilling, shivering and going rigid. "Did the Rapture occur? Have I been left behind?"

Layla blinked at him. "The Rapture? As in from the book of Revelations?"

"Yes!" He reached out and clutched her arms with a strength he shouldn't have possessed. "Are there any other Christians left, or am I the only one? Was I too flawed? Did God deem me unworthy? Did the trumpet sound, the archangel shout?"

"Jack, you need to calm down-"

"I don't need to calm down! I need to know! Has the Tribulation begun?"

"Jack!" Layla grasped his shoulders and shook him, hard. "Shut up and listen to me! I know you're in shock, and having trouble taking this all in, but you can't go off like that! Not even here, in private! People are scared enough without all that bullshit!"

"'Bullshit,' is it? Not to some of us."

Jack narrowed his eyes as the worst of suspicions occurred to him. She wouldn't have. She couldn't have. His eyes flew around the room, and his suspicions grew.

There, on the bedside table: Crystals, clustered at the base of an aloe plant and a Gardenia in a pot, along with some acorns. His eyes flew upwards: A sprig of some herbs, wrapped in orange and gold ribbons, tied over his head – there were more in a garland over the bedroom door. And there, on her ridiculous, curly table by those God-forsaken cards: hundreds of charms wrapped around a vase with willow branches spraying out of it, a tiny pot of rosemary, and an incense burner.

"Why did I survive, Layla?" he rasped. "Tell me you didn't call in Satan, and sacrifice my immortal soul. Tell me you didn't bargain with the Devil to save my physical life at the price of my eternity with God!"

Layla shot off the bed and staggered back several steps, one hand flying to her throat. She opened her mouth, but no words came out. After a moment, she straightened her spine, and her chin lifted; dignity settled on her shoulders like a protective cloak, even as tears shone in her eyes.

"There is no Devil in the Craft I practice. I apologize for setting up elements I thought would help you. I did not weave a healing spell – that would require your permission." She reached up and began untying the bundle of herbs from above his head. "I'll remove these so they don't disturb you any more."

Jack watched her, eyes still narrowed suspiciously. Her apology seemed sincere, *felt* genuine, but Satan was gifted at misdirection. "What are those things?"

The bundle of herbs came free in her hands. "Thyme, for courage, and basil, for protection from the pain." She moved to the bedside table. "Aloe, for healing; gardenia, to bring comfort to one who is ill; acorns for strength; and clear quartz, the 'all-healer,' to guard against the loss of your vitality and to draw out your pain."

She started to leave the room, and Jack gestured to the table. "You forgot that stuff. Get rid of all of it."

Layla looked over at the table, sighed, then looked back at him. "No. Those are for me, and they stay. Incense of cypress, to lessen the grief of death. Willow, for sorrow. Rosemary, for rememberance. The charms are for people I've lost. People we've lost. Friends. Students. People who may not have any one else to remember them. If my altar makes you uncomfortable, look the other way."

She left then, with her ridiculous trappings and her dangerous notions. Jack did exactly as she suggested, turning away from her so-called "altar," rolling onto his side slowly and painfully. He couldn't believe how weak he was. He slid his hand along his side gingerly, exploring, and was shocked at how much weight he'd lost. He lifted up the covers and gazed in dismay at his scrawny legs, poking like sticks out of the bottom of his boxer briefs, and his concentration-camp ribcage. He let the covers fall and closed his eyes.

Over three weeks. The implications of that were just now setting in. She must have fed him somehow, kept him hydrated, or he wouldn't be here to ponder it. He squeezed his eyes shut tighter. Oh, Lord. She must have bathed him, too, and taken care of the most base of his bodily functions. A dull flush started at his hairline and traveled all the way down to his chest. No wonder she'd been so casual about touching him. "Mortification" didn't begin to cover it. To owe her this debt, her, of all people. He didn't know how to bear it.

Jack opened his eyes to stare up at the bright canopy, and felt his heart crack wide-open with despair. Tears rose and ran down his temples, in a river he doubted would ever end. "Blessed Father," he choked, "Am I forsaken? Did You take Your faithful home and leave me behind?"

He cried, for how long he didn't know, too weak and heart-sick to attempt to stem the flood. Then, exhausted, he slept. When he woke, the sun had shifted to the opposite window. He blinked swollen eyes open and stared at the golden light, alive and dancing with dust motes. It took him long minutes to recognize what the sun was illuminating.

His Bible. And the Crucifix that had hung above his bed. There, on the other bedside table, beside a framed picture of his family. He reached for the Bible, hissing against the pain in his side, and cradled the familiar, worn leather against his heart. An unfamiliar bookmark caught his attention, and he opened to Psalm 46:1-2 "God is our refuge and strength, an ever-present help in trouble. Therefore we will not fear, though the Earth give way and the mountains fall into the heart of the sea."

"I read to you." Layla's quiet voice sounded from the door. She was leaning on the doorjamb, watching him, her face in deep shadow and unknowable. "When you were sick. It seemed to calm you."

"I love the Psalms," he said, too undone and wrung out for subterfuge, or strategy, or righteousness.

"I do too," she said quietly. She didn't speak for several long moments, and Jack became aware of the total silence of the house. No rumbling refrigerator, no TV playing in the background, not a single sound related to electricity. "I don't reject all the teachings of Christianity, Jack. Just the one that says it's the only way to the Divine."

Jack shut his eyes. "I can't talk about it right now, Layla. I just don't have it in me."

"I'll let you rest."

"Wait!" His eyes flew open. "Layla, wait!" She turned, and he struggled to a sitting position, waving off her help. "I want to thank you. For everything. For keeping me alive, when so many died." He looked down at the Bible, now in his lap, and smoothed a shaking hand over the cover. "I've never been so scared in my whole life. I don't know what any of this means. I don't know if I'm even happy that I'm alive, the way things are now."

His throat closed up, and he struggled not to give in to tears again. He could feel the needs of the community already pressing on him, and at some point, he had to reclaim his strength and the leadership that went with it. He may as well start now.

"You're not alone in feeling that way," Layla said flatly. "We've lost five people to suicide. Their families didn't make it, and they decided not to go on. Three of them didn't even do violence to themselves – they just closed their eyes and never opened them again."

His heart ached for those lost souls, for more loss of precious life. "Can you get me their names? I'd like to pray for them."

"I can do that."

He had to find a way to build a bridge here, to help her understand. He owed her that much, at the very least. "Layla, I want you to know that it's not...you." He laughed weakly, then winced as his ribs sang. "That sounds like a break-up line. Let me try again. It's not you as a person I object to. It's what you believe, and what you espouse. I can't condone it. It contradicts what I believe to be true, right down to my bones."

"You tolerate Judaism. Islam. Buddhism. Even Native American Shamanism. The kids have told me about the speakers you brought in to youth group. Was all of that just an act for the kids, some kind of sideshow? For what purpose?"

She was firing up, and he was very nearly spent, struggling just to keep his eyes open. He pushed his slumping body back up on the pillows, and tried to form a coherent reply.

"Oh, for pity's sake." Her tone managed to convey exasperation and concern at the same time. She marched to his side, and helped him slide down between the covers, rearranging the pillows for him. "Sleep, before you pass out. We'll talk about this later, when you're stronger."

"Okay. Sorry." His voice was slurred. Unbelievable, how quickly and completely exhaustion rolled over him.

She tucked the covers around him, a gesture that flooded him with memories of his mother, of comfort, warmth, security, safety. Her hand smoothed across his brow again, balm and agitation, and tears started to leak from his closed eyes.

In that moment, he hated her. Hated her for her patience and gentle comfort, for her passion and fire, and for the confusion she made him feel.

She wiped his face matter-of-factly. "Maybe someday you can tell me why you hate the way I celebrate the Divine so much."

Jack was too tired to snort. Not in this lifetime. "I'd rather hear how you came to love the Psalms," he managed, before sleep took him under.

NINE
Piper: Walden, CO

"Come with me."

Piper looked up, startled. She had lingered in the mess hall after she finished dinner, writing in the journal she'd started to keep and savoring a mug of almost-hard cider. Someone, she figured, needed to document the changes the world was going through, even if her perspective was profoundly limited.

Brody Sanders stood in front of her table, staring down at her. Well, this was a first. He'd never spoken directly to her before.

"Excuse me?"

"Come with me," he repeated. No "please," no explanation. Just a command he clearly expected to be obeyed. He towered above her, wearing the only expression she'd ever seen him wear: stone. Hard face, hard eyes.

"Uhm, do you mind if I ask why?"

"We need to talk."

Piper narrowed her eyes. Something about this was starting to feel very, very off. "We can talk right here."

She pushed the chair opposite her out with her foot. Cordiality never hurt.

"We need to talk in private."

Piper leaned back and crossed her arms over her chest. No way. No way in hell. She glanced around, and discovered they were the only ones left in the mess hall. She could hear the rattle and clink of dishes being washed in the kitchen – that was usually her job, but this was one of her rare rotations off. She gestured to the empty hall around them with a hand she hoped didn't shake. "This is private enough, don't you think?"

Brody continued to stare for a few moments, then sat. His movements were economical, controlled, powerful. "You aren't Noah's woman."

So this was it. The showdown she'd been hoping wouldn't happen. She'd put off all three of her other suitors by hinting she was a lesbian. Up until this moment, her biggest problem had been their conspiracy to get her together with Ruth, who really was homosexual.

"I'm not anybody's woman." No subtlety, not with this guy. "I'm not interested in men sexually."

Brody's stare hadn't wavered since he approached her, and it didn't flicker now. "You're lying."

"Nope. Sorry to disappoint."

"It doesn't matter whether you are or you aren't." Brody reached across the table, and his hand circled her wrist. He didn't squeeze, didn't hurt. "I gave you time to choose. You didn't. So now I'm choosing."

Piper couldn't help herself; she jerked her arm reflexively, but his hand didn't budge. Neither did her wrist. "Let go of me."

"No."

Cold sweat slicked Piper's underarms and sides, but she was god-damned if she'd let him see her fear. "Look, let me be crystal clear, Sanders. I don't want to be your woman. I don't want to be anyone's woman. You can't 'choose' for me, and I don't know where you ever got the idea you could. Now let go of my wrist before I call for help. Somebody's still in the kitchen."

Sanders' hand disappeared under the table. It reappeared holding a semi-automatic pistol. He laid the gun on the table between them. "If you call for help, I'll shoot whoever comes."

Piper stared at him, incredulous. "You have got to be kidding me. Look, pal, I'm turning you down because I'm not into guys – it's nothing personal. You need to go find yourself a willing woman. And here's just a hint for you: next time, try wooing instead of threatening. Much more effective, I promise."

His stare was starting to feel reptilian. Had he even blinked yet? "You're the most expedient option. We've scouted Walden and the surrounding ranches, but there aren't many people left alive. Only a few women, and none of them are appropriate."

This was getting more surreal by the minute. "So, let me get this straight: You're not even really attracted to me – you're just looking to scratch an itch, and I'm your most 'appropriate option?'"

His eyes did flicker then, sliding down her body like a cold, oily caress. "You're not unattractive. And sex is a biological need."

She jerked her wrist again, got nowhere. "I'm speechless, Sanders. I had no idea you were such a sweet talker. You've made your pitch, I've turned you down, and I'm calling your bluff – you're not going to shoot anyone. Let me go. Now."

Sanders pulled her in closer, and leaned across the table. This close, she could see that his eyes were a deep, true blue. They might have been beautiful if there had been even a single spark of humor or warmth in them. "Listen carefully. I'm only going to explain this once, and if you don't grasp it, I'll give you an object lesson. I've made a choice, and you will abide by it. You came into this group with no skills and no value, and this is a way you can earn your keep. You should consider yourself lucky that I won't allow the others to use you."

This could not be happening. This was not the world as Piper knew it. "You're insane," she whispered. She couldn't muster confidence or strength in her tone any longer. "I'll tell the others, and they won't let you hurt me. They don't like you anyway."

"They don't like me, but they need me. Ramsey's dead, and I'm the only tactician. And if you tell them, I'll kill Jenny's boy."

Piper went light-headed. Jenny, her husband Aaron, and their only remaining child, Caden, had just rejoined the group a few days ago. Jenny was hanging onto sanity by a thread, and she couldn't bear to let Caden out of her sight. Her eyes clung to him no matter what she was doing, and it hurt to see how hard she was trying not to smother him. When he was near her, Jenny's hand rose and fell over and over, smoothing his hair, touching his arm, a soft rub of his back. Unlike most 11 year-old boys, Caden tolerated the embarrassing maternal affection, obviously sensing his mother's need.

Losing Caden would kill Jenny, there was no doubt in Piper's mind. She could not comprehend the casualness with which Sanders spoke of killing a child. Noah had mentioned that Sanders had seen too much combat, had lost touch with his humanity, but this...this was beyond anything she could have imagined. She couldn't think of a single thing to say.

His thumb moved against her wrist, and she was shocked to recognize it as a caress. "I'm not a monster. I just know how to apply pressure to get what I want. I won't be unkind to you."

"I'll leave." She blurted it out before she could think, but she couldn't gulp the words back now.

"No, you won't. If you do, I'll come after you. And I'll kill Noah."

"You can't just start killing people! You'll never get away with it – the rest of the group will turn on you!"

"Do you really think I can't make it look like an accident? Piper." It was the first time he had said her name, and it made her feel sick. "It's simple. If you don't capitulate, I will take them out one by one. I don't need any of them to survive, and it would mean more resources for me in the long run. If you try to run, I will bring you back, and I will retaliate."

Scrabbling, like a rat in a maze. Piper had never encountered a problem she couldn't think her way out of, and her brain felt like it was shorting and sparking as she frantically looked for a flaw in his plan. Tactician, indeed. She had not seen this coming, and she could not see a way out.

"If I could just have some time..." she began weakly, but he shook his head.

"You've had enough time. Your decision right now is whether you come with me, or whether whoever is in the kitchen slips and cracks their head open because they didn't see the puddle of water by the sink."

As if on cue, the kitchen door opened. She kept her eyes pinned to Sanders, and couldn't suppress a wince when a familiar voice called out.

"Piper? What are you still doing here?"

Levi. It was Levi. Shit, shit, shit – should she try to act? Try to take Sanders by surprise? Levi had been a soldier, too, surely he could...

He saw it in her eyes. His hand tightened on her wrist, just enough to warn her. He palmed the revolver and slid it into his lap. "Go ahead," he whispered. "Try it. I'd enjoy taking him out."

Piper opened her mouth, but her voice was strangled by terror. She cleared her throat and tried again. "Nothing. We're just, uh, talking."

Levi stopped beside their table. Sanders shifted his grip so that his fingers were laced gently with Piper's, and Levi's eyes fell on their joined hands. He frowned. "Well. This is...cozy."

Piper stared as hard as she could at Levi, willing him to read her mind, to see her need in her eyes. Under the table, Sanders shifted his foot so that it rested on top of hers. Then, he pressed. Hard.

Her eyes flew back to his and he shook his head, the movement so tiny, Levi didn't see it. He kept his eyes locked with hers, but spoke to Levi. "Yeah, it's cozy, and you're a third wheel. Beat it, Ramsey."

"Piper? Are you okay?"

"I'm fine." She forced the words out, hated how breathless she sounded. "We're just...getting to know each other. It's fine. I'm fine."

Levi was quiet and still, so still, Piper couldn't help looking at him again. He was frowning at her, his disapproval obvious. "Well. I guess there's no figuring the fickleness of women."

Idiot! Her mind screamed. Are you blind? Can't you see what's happening? Get over your god-damned preconceived notions about me and help!

Another warning press on her foot, and her eyes skittered back to Sanders. He smiled slightly, the expression even more intimidating than his usual stone-face. "No figuring. Do us a favor and let your brother know Piper will be staying with me tonight."

Another moment of un-godly tension in which Piper didn't dare look away from Sanders. He was a snake, about to strike. Then, Levi moved away.

"Tell him yourself. And turn the lights out when you leave."

When the outside door had sighed shut behind him, Piper tried to yank free again. Sanders tightened his fingers around hers so hard her knuckles cracked.

"No. He's watching through the window. Lean across the table and kiss me."

"No."

"Do it now, or he dies, and his brother in ten minutes."

When she still hesitated, Sanders let go of her hand and stood up. "Fine. Like I said, I'll enjoy ending him."

"No!" Piper jumped to her feet and acted. She slid around the table, stepped into his arms, and kissed him.

Sanders didn't hesitate either. His arms banded around her, one huge hand sliding to cup her buttocks, pressing her against the ridge of his erection. Piper felt gorge rise in her throat; this had turned him on? His lips were cool, slick and gentle against hers, and the gentleness made her angrier than she'd ever been in her life.

Mindful of Levi watching – she could feel his eyes – she broke the kiss as naturally as she could manage, and leaned back in Sanders' arms. She smiled sweetly up at him. "Let's get one thing straight, Sanders. I hate you. You are a pathetic abomination and-"

He slid his hand up to the nape of her neck, rubbed in what felt like a caress, then pressed on something that made her knees go out from under her. He caught her weight easily, lifting her against him, then nuzzled into her neck, making it look like they were carried away by passion. His mouth slid up the side of her neck to rest against her ear.

"You will never speak to me that way again," he whispered. "I can cause you more pain than you can imagine, and never leave a mark on you." To prove his point, he slid his hand higher, until his thumb was resting behind her ear. He pressed, and Piper's world went white-hot with pain.

She cried out, tried to arch away, but Sanders just hauled her closer. He lifted one of her legs around his waist and ground against her, biting and suckling at her throat like a vampire. Piper blinked frantically, trying to clear her vision, while his voice grated against her skin.

"You won't call me Sanders anymore, either. You call me Brody. Say it."

Piper squeezed her eyes shut and held her breath, trapping the sobs in her chest until she thought her lungs would burst. She wouldn't say it — he couldn't make her. And she wouldn't cry, wouldn't give him the satisfaction, she had her pride, damn it —

He moved his thumb behind her ear again, pressed, and pride disintegrated. When she could speak, she did. "Brody," she choked, among broken sobs, and hated herself even more than she hated him.

He actually smiled at her. "Good. Now let's go. We'll go to your cabin first so you can get your things and tell Noah you won't be back."

Her brain shut down. Overload. She couldn't process anymore. She walked through the woods beside him, docile as a lamb, and didn't fight his hand curled around her upper arm. She entered the cabin she'd been sharing with Noah, felt a moment of vague panic and gratitude that he wasn't there, and stuffed her things into a backpack. She left him a note, and had to read it over to discover what she had said: "Staying with Brody. Take care. Piper."

Brody took the backpack from her, and they walked to his cabin in silence. Piper had just enough brain function left to worry that she might be going into shock, to rage that she was wimping out, giving in, giving up, but mostly, she drifted. She was in a numb, muffled place, and she wasn't sure how to get out, or if she wanted to.

They reached his cabin, and Brody shut and latched the door behind them. He set her backpack down, and lit several oil lamps while Piper stood in the middle of the room, swaying slightly, staring at nothing. He moved to stand in front of her, then reached for the hem of her sweatshirt.

Piper roared out of her padded cell with an abruptness that caught them both by surprise.

She was swinging before she could think, and Brody caught her fist a scant inch from his nose. He twisted her arm down and behind her, but before he could yank her close, she dropped to the ground and twisted out of his grip. She kept right on spinning until she was crouched behind the table. Her eyes darted around the room, looking for anything she could use as a weapon, anyplace she could barricade and defend herself.

A low rumble of laughter from Brody sent ice down her spine. His chest was rising and falling swiftly, and his eyes were bright with something unholy. *My God,* he was *enjoying* this, she realized. He *wanted* her to fight, to resist – it excited him. Piper's mind struggled to analyze, to process this information to tactical advantage, but he didn't give her time.

Rather than go around the table, he simply shoved it to the side and walked straight at her. Piper tried to scramble around him to make for the door, but he caught her by her long ponytail and yanked her back. Piper screamed at the shock of pain, clutching her head, and ended up on her knees in front of him. He pulled on her hair until she was forced to look up at him.

His face was flushed and slack with lust, and he was nearly panting now. Still using her ponytail to control her, he rubbed her face against the bulge in his pants, moaning and rocking his hips against her. Then he hauled her to her feet and bent his head to kiss her.

"I can make it good for you," he rasped. "This doesn't have to be rape, Piper."

His mouth clamped onto hers, and once again, Piper felt gorge rise in her throat. This time though, she didn't try to stifle it, oh no. *It comes to this,* she had time to think, and vomited onto his face and chest.

Brody roared and shoved her backwards so hard she fell. Using her own momentum, Piper rolled until she was on her feet and sprinted for the door. He caught her by the back of her sweatshirt this time, and twisted until she was choking, clawing at the neckband.

"God damn it," he muttered. He hauled her to a corner of the cabin where a water jug and basin were set up next to a sink. Trapping her in the corner with his body, he let go of her sweatshirt. While she wheezed in air, he unbuttoned his shirt and peeled out of his t-shirt. He dropped the soiled clothing on the floor, then pointed at the basin.

"Clean up the mess you made," he gritted.

Piper stared up at him, desperately trying to calculate. His bare chest was about six inches from her nose, heaving with outrage. An animal-like musk rose off his skin; that, combined with the scent of her own vomit, made her stomach heave again. He grabbed her by the ponytail and shook her so hard she saw stars. It hurt too much to even scream – she couldn't get any air.

"You puke on me again and you will lick it up, do you understand?" He gave her another shake. "Answer me."

"Yes!" she gasped. He let her go, and she couldn't stop herself from reaching up to rub her head. My God, she had never imagined her own hair could be used as a weapon against her. Her scalp sang with pain. Keeping her eyes lowered, she turned slightly away to pour water into the basin, then took one of the washcloths from the stack. She wet it and wrung it out, her movements as slow as she dared to make them, her mind racing and calculating.

There had to be a way she could debilitate him, just for a moment, so she could get out the door. Why hadn't she run when she had the chance? Why hadn't she just asked Levi for help?

She shook her head, trying to order her thoughts. Berating herself for past failures wasn't going to get her out of this. She re-wet the washcloth, wrung it out, and pretended to drop it. Brody growled, and she flinched, scooping the washcloth out of the water with quaking hands. She was out of time.

Turning, she wiped his face, throat and chest clean with quick, economical movements. She wasn't rough, which would anger him, nor did she hesitate, which he might interpret as a caress. Finished, she turned and dropped the washcloth into the basin, then stood with her arms hanging at her sides, face lowered.

For a moment, he didn't seem to know what to make of her stillness. He slid his arms around her waist, and she went completely limp, as if she had fainted. She heard him grunt in surprise, then lean to put his shoulder against her stomach. He straightened with her draped over his shoulder and moved towards the bed in the opposite corner of the room.

Piper forced herself to let her body flop unresponsively. If he liked a fight, she'd give him the opposite. He lowered her to the bed, and she sprawled awkwardly, hair draped across her face, one arm twisted painfully underneath her. Still, she didn't stir. He straightened, and she could feel him looming above her, staring.

This was a desperate gamble, and she didn't have a back-up plan if it failed. Her brain logged that away as something to remedy in the future: she needed to be prepared, to have multiple contingency plans. Never, ever again would she fail because she hadn't thought a situation through.

After several long moments, she felt him tugging at her shoes. One by one, they dropped to the floor. It took every bit of concentration Piper possessed to keep her face slack and her limbs relaxed. This was the moment of truth; if there was any humanity in him, he would leave her like this, and wait until she regained consciousness to resume his amorous attentions.

His hands slid up her legs, lingered appreciatively on her thighs, then slid higher. His thumbs brushed the apex of her legs before they moved on to the snap of her jeans.

Gamble lost. She was dealing with a pervert who would strip and rape an unconscious woman. Piper's eyes snapped open, and she kicked as hard as she could at his face.

Her foot caught his cheekbone a glancing blow, but without her shoes, all it did was arouse him again. He caught both her ankles, yanked her legs apart, then landed on her with his full weight. Piper's air left her with a whoosh. He snagged her wrists and pinned them to the bed on either side of her head. When her struggles weakened, he braced himself on his forearms, still holding her wrists, and stared down at her.

Piper sucked in air and stared back. She was out of calculations, out of options. There was only one thing left for her to do: damage him as much as possible. She lifted her head, shifted her shoulders, and sank her teeth into his wrist as deeply as she could.

She never saw him swing, never saw the fist that exploded against the side of her head. Her ear popped excruciatingly, and the world spun with crazy colors. She was too dazed to stop him when he yanked her jeans and underwear off, then reached for the hem of her sweatshirt. She flailed at him weakly, thwarting his efforts, until he just fisted his hands in the neckline and tore it off her.

Piper curled into a ball and locked her arms around her knees, but he was relentless. Inch by painful inch, he pried apart her protective cocoon until he was once again sprawled on top of her. By now, she knew that fighting was only egging him on, only hurting her, but she could not stop. She would not make one thing about this easy for him.

"Piper," he grated. He had her wrists pinned again, and he rose up off her so he could look down at her naked body, her sweatshirt hanging shredded and open from her shoulders. He shifted so that he held both her wrists in one hand, then coasted his hand from her neck to her thighs, lingering and stroking. Everywhere he touched, it felt like worms were squirming against her skin, burrowing into her, rotting her.

"I don't want this to be rape," he whispered, staring into her eyes. "Stop fighting me. Let me make this good for you. I can make it so good."

End game. No way out. Piper closed her eyes, and felt tears stream out of the corners, tracking warm and wet down her temples. Taking a deep shuddering breath, she nodded. "Okay," she whispered. "Okay."

A deep, approving rumble shook his chest, and he nuzzled his face against hers. His mouth slid down her throat, and she turned her face towards him, nuzzling back, finding the edge of his jaw, then his throat, with her lips.

Then, with all the strength and rage in her, she lunged and latched her teeth onto his throat. She bit deep, deep, felt his blood spurt into her mouth, heard him roar.

His hand fastened around her throat, and still she hung on, determined to kill him or die trying. Finally, lack of oxygen broke her grip and she fell back against the pillows, clawing at his hand. Her vision darkened around the edges but he didn't relinquish the crush-hold he had on her throat. She could feel his other hand fumbling at his pants, hear his animal growls of lust and pain, but it was all starting to seem very far away.

She stopped struggling, her hands falling limply at her sides. Alright, she thought. So this is it. At least I died trying.

He released her then, and as her body sucked in breath after desperate breath, he shoved her legs apart and tore into her brutally. Piper's scream was long and anguished. Her last thought before she finally lost consciousness was that she would rather have died.

TEN
Naomi and Macy: Colorado Springs, CO

Naomi lunged into wakefulness, stifling a shriek and clawing at an invisible hand that had locked around her throat. In the bed beside her, Macy was shivering and whimpering in her sleep. Panting, Naomi scooped her close, tucking her small body into the curve of her own. On the floor beside the bed, both dogs stirred and lifted their heads. Hades rumbled with a low growl that ended on a whine. Naomi shushed him, then shut her eyes and concentrated on stilling her violently pounding heart. Macy stirred, and burrowed closer to her mother.

"Piper," she whispered. "Mama, it's Piper."

"I know," Naomi whispered back. Here, in the dark, they could talk about it, about the way Macy *knew* things now. "She's hurt. But she's still alive."

"Yes," Macy agreed. She cuddled her face into the curve of Naomi's shoulder, and Naomi felt warm tears against her skin. "Mama, it makes me so sad. I wish she didn't have to hurt."

Oh, God. Naomi cradled her close, kissing her soft, soft hair. "I know, baby. I know. I would give anything, do anything, to be able to take the hurt for her."

Macy rested her hand in the center of Naomi's chest, and Naomi felt a profound warmth radiate and spread. "Keep your heart touching hers. It's what will keep her alive."

Naomi mustered up her courage. "Macy? How do you know that? How are you so sure what will be? Do you have dreams?"

"Sometimes," Macy answered promptly, her sweet voice lilting in the dark. "Sometimes, I just know. It's just a feeling, but it's as sure as what I see, or what I touch. I know it's true, for sure."

Her words resonated with Naomi on an instinctive level. Something inside her had shifted and changed as well – she could *feel* the truth of things, *feel* what to do and not to do, and she was starting to trust those feelings as much as her other five senses.

"Do you think something happened to you, when you were sick? Do you think you..." her voice trailed off – she couldn't give voice to such an awful possibility.

Macy giggled a tiny giggle. "What, mama? Do you think I died and came back?"

"Don't say it out loud," Naomi admonished, and hugged her tighter.

Macy giggled again, harder. "Mama, it's not like saying 'Voldemort' – it's just words." She paused, and Naomi felt her shift into a more serious vein. "And it's not an awful end, it's not just nothing. It's like a curtain we can't see through, just like they say. We go on – it's just...different."

In this, Naomi was the child, Macy the teacher. "Did daddy go on?"

"Oh, yes! He hasn't moved all the way through the curtain yet – he comes and goes. You can do that sometimes, when there's great need." Macy paused. "He's here now."

The hair on the nape of Naomi's neck rose. She blinked frantically in the dark, looking for – what? A ghost? An other-worldly light? Ectoplasm? "Don't say things like that, Macy, it scares me half to death! I don't know what to think about the changes in you! Or the changes in me!"

Macy reached up in the dark, and stroked her cheek. Her touch felt like the brush of fairy wings. "We're all changing, mama. Everyone that's left. It's why we're still here."

Naomi closed her eyes, and let her daughter's touch comfort her. They were both quiet for long moments. Then, Naomi whispered, "Is daddy still here?"

"Yes. It makes him sad that he scares you now." Macy sniggered. "He says that he'd die before he would ever hurt you, but, well, it's a little too late for that now."

Naomi barked out a sound that was half-laugh, half-sob. "That sounds just like him! Smart alec!" She relaxed, and almost immediately, she could feel him there – his warmth, his comfort, his steady, sweet presence. "Tell him I miss him, honey. Tell him I miss him so much."

"He knows." Macy hesitated. "He says we have to leave soon, too. He says you promised."

Naomi grimaced. "I don't want to go. I think we can be safe here. I don't want to leave our home. What if Piper comes here looking for us?"

"He's right, mama. We can't stay. The soldiers will come."

"How do you know that for sure? There's half a city between us and Fort Carson, and Peterson's clear out on the plains."

"Mama." Exasperated. "I just *know,* remember?"

"Macy." Frustrated. "Do you know *everything*?"

Naomi hadn't meant the question seriously, but Macy took it that way. "Not everything, but I know lots. We have to go. They need you in Woodland Park."

"Woodland Park? What in the world?"

"Ugh, mom!" She sounded so much like Piper, Naomi's heart clutched. "You've just got to take my word for it, okay?"

"Well, yes ma'am."

They both fell silent, then, wrapped in each other's arms. Naomi felt Macy's little body relax, felt her ease back into sleep, felt her own mind begin to drift on half-awake currents. Just before her eyes slid shut, she would have sworn she felt the brush of Scott's kiss on her lips.

They woke to a chorus of growling dogs. Hades and Persephone were both facing the bedroom door, Persephone standing between Hades' front legs, her little head not even rising to his chest. Naomi sat up, blinking in the early morning light, and both dogs looked over at her.

Danger.

Naomi's heart rate kicked into high gear. She didn't question the strength or the accuracy of the message she had received in stereo. It hadn't been delivered via audible sound, per se, but was more a pair of transmitted impressions, one distinctly "Hades" in origin, the other clearly "Persephone." Both of them agitated.

She would have to sort that mystery out later. She rose and slid into blue jeans, stuffing her nightgown into the waistband. A distant banging sound, accompanied by a slight vibration in the house, made her go still for a moment. She looked down into Macy's wide-awake, frightened eyes.

"I want you to hide in the closet," Naomi whispered. "And I don't want you to come out, no matter what."

She helped Macy scramble into the closet, and tucked a blanket around her. "Persephone." She called the little dog over, then snapped her fingers and pointed to the floor beside Macy. "Down. Stay."

Persephone obeyed instantly, and Naomi sent a mental image to her as well: Comfort. Protect. As if she heard her, Persephone scooted closer to Macy, her eyes bright and alert, her delicate, butterfly ears belying the deadly protectiveness Naomi could feel radiating from her. She stroked the dog's tiny head, then her daughter's bright hair. "Persephone will stay with you. 'Though she be but little, she is fierce.' I'll be back in a minute."

She stood up, shoved her feet into shoes, grabbed a hooded sweatshirt to cover her flimsy nightgown, and she and Hades were out the door.

"Heel," she commanded, and he prowled silently along beside her, his big body taut with power and watchfulness. Underneath, she sensed the aggression he would unleash only as a last resort, and only if she asked it of him.

They slid to the front window and Naomi peeked out. A convoy of Humvees, all painted desert beige, stretched out in the street in front of the house. Across the street, she could see soldiers moving around in the Sullivan's home – to the best of her knowledge, there was no one left alive over there to protest.

Macy had said the soldiers would come; Naomi shivered, then hurried towards the kitchen. She didn't keep much food upstairs – Scott had warned and drilled and nagged about visible lights, cooking smells, and keeping the bulk of their resources hidden. The storeroom was concealed in the basement behind a pile of storage boxes, and Naomi vowed to never, ever again complain each time she had to shift them all, then shift them all back again when she had retrieved what she needed.

That the soldiers would eventually try her house, she had no doubt. She didn't want to give them a reason to look more closely – best to hide what food was visible, and–

She never made it to the kitchen. Without warning, the door to the garage popped open, making her jump and yelp involuntarily. Hades gave one hard bark, then moved in front of her, hackles up, growl rumbling. The soldier in the door raised an automatic weapon and pointed it straight at Hades' brave heart.

"Call your dog off or I'll shoot him, ma'am."

She stepped to Hades' side and rested a hand on his back. Hades stopped growling, but remained on high alert. "What do you want?"

"Ma'am, we have been authorized to search for and seize all food and fuel in this area."

"Authorized by whom?"

"The United States government, ma'am. Colorado Springs is under martial law now and for the foreseeable future."

Thank God Scott had warned her about this, too, or she'd be shaking out of her shoes right about now. She was shaking enough as it was. "Really. And what if we're still using that food and fuel?"

"Ma'am, under martial law, you will not be permitted to hoard food or fuel. We are escorting all surviving, non-infected civilians to the refugee camp on Fort Carson."

Naomi was quiet for a moment, scrutinizing him. Good grief, he was no older than Piper. Discomfort rolled off him in waves – he was not enjoying the task he had been assigned. "What about people who are recovering from the plague? My daughter shouldn't be moved until she's stronger."

She could track what he was thinking by the expressions on his face: Surprise, disbelief, wariness and pity. "Ma'am, very few people survived after being infected with the plague. We know of less than twenty between here and Denver. Are you sure it was the plague your daughter had?"

"Very sure. My husband died of it." It was the first time she had said the words out loud, stark and naked like that, and she was surprised by how badly they hurt. "Yes, my daughter survived, and no, I'm not delusional. I don't have her body tucked into bed in the other room, slowly decomposing."

His face blanched, and he looked down for a moment. "I'm glad to hear you say it, ma'am. We've seen that. More than once."

Okay, it was time to cut to the chase. "We aren't interested in moving to the refugee camp. We have other plans." She paused, locking eyes with him. "If I give you what food and fuel I have, will you move on and pretend you never found us?"

He dropped his head, unable to maintain eye contact. "Ma'am, I have a job to do. I have orders."

She waited until he peeked up again, his face miserable under his helmet. Really, after dealing with Piper all these years, it wasn't fair to him. She could read him like a book: gentle maternal authority should do the trick. "Son," she said softly. "Your orders come from a government that probably no longer exists. My daughter and I aren't 'civilians' – we're human beings, survivors, just like you. Please forgive me for asking, but did your family make it?"

He looked down again, but not before she saw tears shining. "I don't know, ma'am. They're in South Carolina. I haven't been able to reach them."

"Your parents?"

"Yes. And my wife. She's expecting our first in July."

His agony and desperate worry caught her like a kick in the chest, left her breathless. "I am so sorry. I truly am. I can't reach my oldest daughter, either. That's why we can't go to Fort Carson. If she doesn't find us here, she'll know where to look for us."

He stared at her for the longest time. A humvee roared to life out in the street, and she saw him come to a decision. "You need to lie low, ma'am, and you should get out of the city. You're lucky we found you first – word is there's some kind of super gang forming, based out of the downtown area. Looks like they've got military training and they're heavily armed. Rumor is they're holed up in the houses around Memorial Park, but if brass knows, they're not telling us. We've come across some of the homes they've looted, and it looks like they're either recruiting or killing survivors. You sure you have somewhere safe to go?"

Naomi nodded. "We do. I'll get us ready, and we'll get out as soon as we can."

"Good. Keep your food and fuel. We'll get by without it."

"Thank you." She pressed her hand over her heart. "Thank you so much."

He ducked his head. "You make me think of my mother, ma'am. She can give a guy the stink eye and make him do the right thing, too."

Naomi laughed, then said, "Wait." She put Hades on a stay, and hurried into the kitchen. She came back with a large baggie of cookies she'd baked – Macy's favorite, to try to tempt her appetite. "Can you hide these away somewhere, save them for yourself? Think of them as a care package from your mom?"

He took the bag from her, and tears filled his eyes again. "She bakes crummy cookies, just awful, but it's the thought that counts. Thank you, ma'am, I really do appreciate it."

She nodded. "Take care."

"And you."

He stepped back into the garage, and she followed, watching him exit out the side-door he'd jimmied open. He shut the door behind him, then disappeared from view.

Naomi watched from the front window, rigid with tension, until the convoy moved on about 15 minutes later. Then, she raced back to the bedroom. Macy was right where she'd left her, as was Persephone.

"It's okay, baby, it's alright." She scooped her up, held her close. "Are you okay?"

Macy squirmed to get down. "Gotta pee, mom! Really bad!"

Naomi laughed, giddy with relief, and swooped Macy into the bathroom. When she was finished, Naomi picked her up again and they headed downstairs to find some breakfast. She hadn't carried Macy for years, but she'd lost so much weight, and she tired so quickly, Naomi had gotten back in the habit again. The fact that Macy didn't complain about it told her there was still a need.

She deposited Macy in the kitchen, checked out the front window again, then went to fix breakfast. Granola, yogurt and canned fruit today, she decided. This was not a good time to risk the smell of scrambled eggs. As she worked, her euphoric mood dissipated.

She needed to get them ready to go, and how in God's name was she supposed to do that? What should she take? She looked around the kitchen, thought her way through the rest of the house. She and Scott had lived here since before Piper was born. How was she supposed to leave a lifetime behind, not knowing if it would be here when she got back?

All day, she packed. And unpacked. Piled, un-piled, sorted, cried secret tears she hid from Macy, started over, and then started over again. The photo albums? How could she leave them? How could she justify taking them? Her great grandmother's orange juice pitcher? How much of the bottled water? Which food? By mid-afternoon, she was exhausted, heart-broken and thoroughly pissed off.

She trudged out to the deck where Macy was resting and reading in the dappled shade with the dogs. Ares surprised her with a yowl as she stepped through the French doors; he was stretched along the top of the cushion on Macy's lounge chair, supreme ruler of all he surveyed. Persephone was sleeping, but Hades sported a fresh scratch on the tip of his nose, and his dark brown eyes were locked on the interloper.

Naomi scooped Ares up and collapsed into the chair next to Macy's. "Well, look who dropped in for a visit." Ares stretched in her lap, pressing into her caressing hands, his purr vibrating against her legs. His gray and black striped coat was scuffed in spots, and he felt leaner than before, but still fit and strong. "Looks like life is treating you decently."

"Good thing he came to visit today, since we're leaving tomorrow."

"If I ever get us packed." Naomi let her head drop back. "I can't believe how much stuff we have, and how much of it I want to take." She rolled her head and peered at her daughter. "I don't suppose you could look into your magic crystal ball and tell whether we'll ever be back here again? It would make deciding what to take and what to leave a little easier."

Macy looked away, and the movement struck Naomi as evasive. "I think you should plan on being able to come back. And you could hide stuff in the secret food room – stuff you want to take but that doesn't make sense. Like your jewelry and pictures and things."

"You," Macy had said. Not "we." Naomi stood up abruptly, dumping Ares to the ground. "That's a great idea," she said briskly. "We'll just take what we need to get to the cabin and get settled. The sentimental stuff can stay here until we can come back for it. Do you need anything, before I get back at it?"

Macy closed her eyes and shook her head. "No, I'm good. I'm just going to sleep for a little bit."

Naomi gave her cheek a soft stroke, but didn't linger. Spurred and energized by fears she absolutely would not give voice to, she moved through the house methodically and swiftly. Sentimental treasures, ferried to the basement to be stored in the secret room; supplies for the journey, stacked by the door to the garage.

She decided on five days worth of food and water, and concentrated on protein sources like nuts and canned meat. Food for the dogs. Clothing for both of them, including their winter wear – jackets, boots, mittens, scarves. It could snow any month of the year in Colorado, and they were heading for a higher elevation. Camping gear – area trail maps, back packs, sleeping bags, reflective blankets, fishing poles. Flashlights, candles, matches. All the over-the-counter medicine she had left in the house, plus her essential oils, herbs, tinctures and teas. Toiletries, handy wipes. Duct tape.

Just before dinner time, she got hung up again, this time on books. She stood in front of the floor-to-ceiling shelves in their home office, and agonized. Some were easy to select – *Edible Wild Plants and Useful Herbs*, from one of Piper's 4-H projects was an obvious choice, as was the *Outdoor Survival Guide* – the author lived in Montrose, and she and Scott had met him at a book signing. Scott had collected an entire shelf of books on prepping, including how-to's, and books on living off the land, and she needed to look through and decide what looked most useful.

After those selections, the real pain began. Years of interest, exploration and enjoyment were collected here. Books on crochet and quilting, making jewelry and rock-painting with kids. Old friends from her favorite authors – Nora Roberts, Barbara Kingsolver, Alice Hoffman. Classics she loved to re-read every few years – *To Kill a Mockingbird, Gone with the Wind,* Shakespeare's *Much Ado About Nothing.* How could she leave behind Harry Potter, Anne of Green Gables, or Laura Ingalls Wilder?

A rustle in the doorway made her turn. Macy was staring at the shelves, too, her face stricken. "Mama. Our books."

"I know, honey." She held her arm out, and Macy moved to stand in the curve of it. "I want to take every single one of them."

"Can we?"

"Nope." She squeezed Macy's shoulders, then steered her towards the door. "Let's get some dinner. We'll figure it out later."

She didn't return to the books until after she'd settled Macy into bed for the night. As before, the break from the task had clarified it; she marched into the office, collected only those books she felt were necessary or useful, and left all the rest behind. If she paused, even for a moment, to remember, to dwell, to think all this through, she wouldn't be able to take another step.

She blacked out the one window in the garage with cardboard, then packed the back of Scott's pickup using a tiny flashlight to illuminate the task. The animals would ride in the jump seat – Hades might be a little uncomfortable, but it would have to do. There was only one other item she needed for the front seat, and she'd been putting the task off all day.

Naomi checked on Macy, found her sleeping, and headed for the bedroom she used to share with Scott. She leaned her forehead on the sealed door and tried to steel herself. If only she had thought to do this before. She took a deep breath, then started slicing through the tape with a utility knife.

She pulled her sweatshirt up over her nose when the door cracked open, but to her immeasurable relief, found it wasn't necessary. She had wrapped Zeus' body in plastic and tucked it alongside Scott's, then covered them both with an quilt she'd made. Apparently, her make-do measures had sufficed; the smell of corruption was very faint. Nevertheless, she avoided looking at the bed, and walked swiftly to the closet.

The gun safe was tucked on Scott's side of the walk-in closet; she had already taken the key from the hook downstairs, and she fished it out of her pocket. Opening the safe, she took out the 12 gauge shotgun she used when they shot skeet, and Scott's .45 automatic pistol, then took their respective cases from the shelf above. She carried the firearms into the hall and set them on the floor. Another trip back to the safe, where she took all the ammunition they had on hand for the weapons she had selected, as well as Scott's hunting knife in its scabbard. She returned to the safe a third time and stood there, uncertain.

Should she take Scott's AR15 rifle or his shotgun? Piper's youth shotgun? What about the little .22 rifle? The weapons were all in good repair, and she was at least moderately familiar with them all. She and Scott still shot skeet regularly, though Scott had given up hunting years ago; one near miss from a drunken out-of-stater had been enough.

Naomi ran her fingers along the stock of his shotgun, comforted to know his fingers had touched it last. Her friends had always considered it a strange hobby for her animal-loving self, but she loved to shoot skeet. She was inexplicably good at it – the first time Scott took her, when they were dating, she had powdered the first 15 clay pigeons he'd thrown. Piper had inherited whatever strange alchemy gave her the talent, and Scott had grumped and griped about trying to compete with Annie Oakley and Atticus Finch.

She had no earthly idea what she might need, and didn't like to think about needing weapons of any kind, at all, ever. Skeet was one thing, but she could not comprehend pointing a weapon at a living creature and pulling the trigger. It wasn't that she was opposed to hunting; she just knew it wasn't in her to do.

She dithered around far longer than she should have, indecisive, and finally decided to leave the extra weapons behind. She would hide the key to the safe, and hope they were here when she returned. She carried everything downstairs, loaded the handgun and stowed it in the glovebox before she could second-guess herself, then packed the shotgun and the remaining ammunition in the back.

Her steps dragged as she headed back up the stairs for the umpteenth time this day, a fresh roll of duct tape in her hand. She had managed to avoid looking directly at the bed on every trip into the room, and Scott deserved better than that. She paused outside the door, paused for so long she wasn't sure how to start her feet moving again. On a deep breath and a stumble, she entered Scott's crypt.

All that anxiety, and the shape on the bed wasn't markedly different. She put her head to the side and allowed herself to really examine his corpse, really analyze it. Her husband's corpse. The body she had been familiar with her entire adult life, the body she'd made children with, now returning to its basic elements there, in the bed they'd shared for more than 20 years. His cells lived on in his daughters, along with his gentleness, his love of popcorn and books, his quirky sense of humor and his quiet, powerful intelligence.

There just wasn't anything to be afraid of. "I'm sorry I had to disturb you, love, but I promised you we would leave, and I needed a few things." She held up the duct tape and smiled, tears spilling over that ached and healed at the same time. "I don't know if or when we'll be back, so I'll re-seal the door. I love you so much, Scott, so much. I'll keep the girls safe, I promise."

It was after midnight by the time she finally snuggled into bed next to Macy. She didn't expect to sleep, and she didn't, getting up twice in the night to add items to the truck or re-arrange the load. Just before dawn, she gave up and returned to the truck again to dig out the backpacks. She really ought to pack them with emergency supplies, in case they had to abandon the truck in a hurry.

The thought made her snort. The truck was already packed with emergency supplies; she guessed that meant the backpacks represented end-of-the-road catastrophic supplies. Macy found her still at it an hour later, muttering and cussing under her breath as she tried to decide what should go in the packs and what she could walk away without.

"Mama? Do you want me to fix some breakfast?"

Naomi looked up. Macy was dressed in jeans, a t-shirt and a zip-up hoodie, and the clothes hung on her. She'd been wearing soft lounge pants or sweat pants since her illness, and Naomi hadn't realized just how frail she'd become. Her eyes were huge, her cheekbones too sharp, her little hand where it rested on Hades' back too delicate and white.

"No, honey, I'm just about done here. I'll come in and we'll do it up right with blueberry pancakes." She zipped the backpacks, set them in the back of the truck, and shut the cap. For better or worse, they were packed. "Is Ares still here?"

"He is. Can we take him with us?"

"If we can get him in the truck. He and Hades haven't quite figured it out yet, I'm afraid."

They went to the kitchen, and Naomi kept up a steady chatter while she mixed up pancakes, trying to keep Macy's mind off the fact that they were leaving, maybe for good. Macy chatted right back, talking excitedly about the craft supplies she'd packed, and Naomi was fairly certain she was trying to do the same thing.

After breakfast, Naomi washed up, made sure they both used the bathroom, and got the animals loaded. Then, without indulging in a last walk through the house, without so much as pausing on the threshold, she drove them away from Christmas Eves and Easter egg hunts, lazy summer days and cozy, crisp fall nights, away from Scott, away from home. She refused to even glance in the rearview mirror as they pulled out into the deserted street and headed towards Cresta Road.

It felt strange to be driving after so long. Macy was quiet beside her, gazing out the passenger side window, taking in the changes. Trash blew everywhere, and vehicles were abandoned alongside the road. They had to drive around a minivan that was angled across the street, driver's door open, a man's bloated body tumbled out to rest upside down on the pavement, legs still trapped inside.

"Macy," Naomi said quietly, "Climb in back with the animals and try not to look. You don't need these pictures in your head, honey."

Macy complied with clumsy haste, and Naomi could hear her sniffling. She wished she could stop to comfort her, but they needed to keep moving. The empty streets had the hair on Naomi's nape prickling; the city was so silent, she was afraid their truck could be heard for miles.

When they hit Highway 24, Naomi's heart hit her shoes. As far as she could see in both directions, vehicles were backed up, abandoned. She sat there, staring at the cars, trucks and SUVs, trying to take it in, trying to adapt, and failing completely.

She'd seen it so clearly – they would drive up Highway 24, make it to the cabin, hunker down and wait for Piper. Her simple plan – laughably simple, she could see that now – had kept her putting one foot in front of the other. Now, she felt as if her lifeline had been severed.

Had she really thought she could pull this off without Scott? Who was she kidding? She was an overweight, middle-aged, sheltered housewife. A Martha-Stewart-wanna-be who gave cookies to soldiers. It was a miracle she'd kept herself and Macy alive this long – if Scott hadn't been prepared, they would have starved to death by now. Naomi leaned her head on the steering wheel and tried to keep her breath from hitching into sobs.

A soft thump on the seat beside her made her turn her head. Ares had jumped from the back seat and was sitting, staring at her. When their eyes met, he meowed a loud, grating, obnoxious meow, then jumped to the dashboard and stared out at the vehicles blocking their path. He meowed again, even louder, and Naomi surprised herself with a snort of laughter.

Sympathy would certainly have dissolved her into tears. Ares' imperial impatience was just what she needed. "Alright then, your highness. As you command. Hang on, honey, this could get interesting."

She eased the truck forward, weaving between vehicles, getting out once to put an abandoned car in neutral and roll it out of the way. They made it across 24, and Naomi started revising her plan out loud, more for her sake than for Macy's.

"We'll head up through Old Colorado City and see if this breaks up after Manitou Springs. If it doesn't, we'll head for the Garden of the Gods and take Rampart Range Road." She swallowed hard, thinking about the sometimes precarious dirt road with its spectacular views and precipitous shoulders. "I've never driven it – Daddy always did – but we'll just take our time."

The main thoroughfare through Old Colorado City was clogged as well, and many of the tourist-attracting shops had clearly been looted, some of them burned. Naomi stuck to the side streets and wove them through the quaint residential neighborhoods, heading constantly west. She ended up on El Paso Boulevard, then slowed as they reached the point where the street once again intersected with Highway 24, crossing underneath it.

Still completely impassable. Naomi put the truck in park but left it running, considering her choices. Looked like her best option was to take Garden Drive and head for the Garden of the Gods. Rampart Range Road twisted up into the mountains just inside the park boundaries. She was reaching to put the truck in reverse when a thump and flash of movement on the passenger side of the truck made her shriek and jerk back against the driver's side door.

A woman was plastered to the window, staring in at Macy. Her face was filthy and scuffed, her hair matted and too dirty to reveal color. Incongruously, what looked like hefty diamond studs winked at her earlobes, and her perfect teeth were straight and white between her chapped, parted lips. She called over her shoulder, never taking her eyes from Macy.

"David? There's a little girl..." Her shaking hand rose to touch the window, stroking. "Oh, she's so beautiful. I want the little girl, David..."

"Get down on the floor, Macy!" Naomi lunged across the seat, popped open the glovebox, and grabbed Scott's handgun. She pointed it at the woman's face through the glass, astonished that her hand was rock steady. "Get away from us. Get away now!"

The woman glanced at the gun, grimaced, and backed up a step, then two, still craning to see Macy. Her hands wrung desperately against her chest. Naomi could see that her fingernails had once been carefully manicured, and an intricate wedding ring graced the fourth finger of her grimy left hand.

"David," she called again. "Don't hurt the little girl. I want her."

Naomi's gaze flew out the front windshield and all the air left her lungs. A half dozen men, armed with a motley assortment of weapons – two guns that she could see, a shovel, an axe, a baseball bat – were advancing slowly on the truck. Movement in the rear view mirror caught her eye; they were behind her, too. She'd driven right into an ambush.

She'd read a book once about fear, about the many and varied reactions people were prone to when faced with mortal danger. "Fight, flight or freeze," the author had said, just about summed it up. Naomi had always figured she'd be a freezer, one of those unfortunates who just locked up, couldn't move, couldn't act. How wrong she'd been.

It felt like she had all the time in the world. She set the gun down on the seat beside her, put the truck in drive and floored it. The men's faces were almost comical with surprise — they obviously hadn't expected her to act so quickly — and they dove this way and that as she bore down on them. One of the men fell, and she didn't even hesitate, barreling right over his legs, distantly hearing him scream.

She shot under Highway 24 and kept right on going. A shotgun boomed behind her, once, twice, and the truck jerked hard to the right. Naomi wrestled it back to the middle of the street and screeched through the curves in the road, intent only on putting some distance between them.

She didn't let up on the gas until the road she was on intersected with Manitou Avenue, which was congested with vehicles. This time, she didn't bother with finesse, ramming and screeching through until she was climbing up a steep hill into the warren-like residential area of Manitou Springs. She wove randomly down streets until she saw what she was looking for. She jerked the wheel and they careened up the steep driveway towards a house that wasn't visible from the street. Naomi drove right off the driveway, circled around behind the house, and shut the engine off. The silence was sudden and absolute.

Naomi spun around. "Baby, are you okay? Macy? Answer me!"

Macy was huddled on the floor behind the passenger seat, head down on her knees, arms over her head. She looked up at her mother's sharp command, and her face was bone white. Naomi sucked in a breath and reached to haul her daughter's shaking body into her lap.

"It's okay, we're okay, it's okay," she crooned, rocking them both, comforting them both. The dogs scrambled into the front seat and pressed as close as they could get, adding their shaking to the mix. Ares, however, seemed more irritated than frightened. He yowled angrily from the back seat, hissed at Hades for show, then settled down to groom his ruffled fur.

Naomi shushed Macy gently and rolled down the window. She listened, straining, and heard a distant, buzzing sound. A small motor – a dirt bike? A scooter? The sound ebbed and flowed, strengthened and faded – they were looking for her. Naomi transferred Macy to the passenger seat beside her.

"Stay here, honey. I'll be right back."

Hades slid out to shadow her, and they inspected the back of the truck. The window of the cab was broken, and the rear passenger side tire was shredded. The driver's side tire had taken a hit, too, and was slowly deflating. They wouldn't be going on in this truck – she had one spare tire, but not two. She had torn up the lawn when she'd driven off the driveway – she needed to see if that was visible from the road, or if they'd left any other signs of their passage.

Hades' head was up, his nose sampling the soft breeze; he was utterly silent, utterly alert. What she wouldn't give, for his superior senses right about now. Hades stopped to look at her, and as soon as his eyes met hers, Naomi's perspective shifted.

She staggered. Smells, so many smells, some of them accompanied by impressions – hot engine, burning tires, danger; her, Macy, horrible cat, wonderful Persephone, home; death, everywhere death, some old, some fresh, all of it sad, so sad...

"What the hell?" Naomi breathed. She blinked, shook her head, and the sensation dissipated as suddenly as it had begun. Naomi ran her hands over her face, scrubbed, and clutched at her hair for a moment. "Holy shit, Hades, what was that?"

Hades looked away, and his ears pricked. The buzzing sound was growing louder. Naomi retreated back behind the house with Hades at her side, listening until the sound grew faint again. Then she slipped and slid as fast as she could down the driveway, smoothed some loose gravel and dirt over the fresh skid marks marring the tarmac, and puffed back to the truck and Macy.

Macy was sleeping with Persephone in her arms. Seeing her so still and pale made Naomi's heart stutter in sudden terror, but Persephone lifted her head, and a wave of comfort and reassurance washed over her. Naomi leaned against the side of the truck, taking deep breath after deep breath.

They would hide here for the rest of the day, maybe overnight, to rest and regroup. Naomi needed to think through their options, plan, maybe scout out the area, maybe look for another vehicle. She looked down at

Hades, who was still scrutinizing their surroundings, and felt an echo of that bizarre, shared perception. She stroked his beautiful, blocky head and choked on a sound that was part hysterical giggle, part sob. Apparently, she also needed to give serious consideration to the possibility she was losing her mind.

ELEVEN
Grace and Quinn: On the Colorado Plains

Grace woke to a sky flushed deep, rosy pink and the lilting cacophony of the dawn chorus. Stretching in her warm sleeping bag, she sorted the birds out by the songs her grandmother had taught her: Chickadee, Meadowlark, Red-winged Blackbird. Snug and comfortable, she drifted between sleep and dream-like memories for a while, reliving cool early mornings in the garden with her grandma, picking beans or peas before the day's heat descended while grandma whistled her lessons: Sparrow, Goldfinch, and Grace's favorite, Robin, with his rain song.

Grandma had been gone for a few years now, her farm long since sold, and Grace was strangely glad about that. This way, she could keep those sweet and simple memories intact, separate from all the other memories she had to process and make sense of now. She couldn't think of her mother or Wayne, or little Benji, without remembering the horror of watching each of them drown slowly in their own blood, gurgling, clutching, gasping. Someday, she hoped, she'd be able to remember the sweetness, and forget those dark days.

A soft clatter made her turn her head. Quinn was crouched by the smoldering remains of their fire, coaxing it into life. They were camped in the shelter of a circular Cottonwood grove, and through the trees, she could see the horses picketed on the grassy slope that rose from the creek bed, both of them contentedly cropping grass. Quinn had already been down to the creek; his hair was damp, his face freshly washed, and he had filled a stock pot with water. Grace watched his practiced movements, marveling again at how different he seemed out here on the trail.

They had been riding for two days. After their disastrous trip into Limon, they had decided to take the horses cross-country, rather than risk the give-away noise of a vehicle. Grace had resisted the idea at first – she had been riding since she was small, but they were talking about a 100 mile trip, after all. Quinn had been unusually insistent.

"I've camped along the Big Sandy all my life," he had said quietly. "We'll be safer if we stay away from people." He had looked up into her eyes then, a rare gesture for him. All the Harris boys had inherited their father's thickly-lashed gray eyes, and for a moment, Grace was disoriented by how William-like his gaze was. Confident. Sure. "Please Gracie. I know what I'm doing. I can keep us safe."

They had spent a day preparing their scavenged food for travel – Grace had come up with some surprisingly edible "travel cakes" using beans, rice, eggs and various spices, and Quinn had cracked the remaining precious eggs into a chilled thermos, explaining that raw eggs would keep longer than boiled ones. As the day wore on and their preparations progressed, Grace was aware of a subtle shift in the balance of power between them.

Before, she had thought of Quinn as a little brother – helpful, but dependent on her for direction and reassurance. It reminded her of Benji, the way he just needed to be near her sometimes. He would haul whatever he was working on into her vicinity, then return to tinkering with a little motor, or repairing a piece of tack without saying a word. That day, however, he had been downright chatty, talking about why they should take this or that, or leave this or that behind. The closer they came to departure, the more excited he got, and the more terrified Grace felt.

She'd done her best to reason away her fear; she wasn't an indoor girl, after all. She'd grown up playing and working on her mother's ranch, and had camped out on numerous occasions. Those occasions, though, had included a ridiculous abundance of food – s'mores and hobo pies, popcorn popped over an open fire and rich with butter, and more than sufficient bottled water. By contrast, they were taking off with scanty, hobbled-together provisions for at least 6 days of steady riding, and just enough water to get them through their first day. Too heavy for the horses to carry more, Quinn had explained.

He had gone over the map with her every time she'd expressed doubt or worry, showing her how they could ride along the Big Sandy Creek, which was running full and on the surface, thanks to a wet spring. The creek roughly paralleled Highway 24, but would keep them out of sight of the road. People, Quinn insisted, were their biggest problem, and needed to be avoided. Grace was more worried about dying of starvation.

"You sound like a city girl," Quinn had teased, in a moment of rare levity for him. "There's tons of food out there, even this early in the season. Why, there's enough dandelions in the front yard for a week's worth of salad." He put on a thick, local-yokel accent that would have made his mother smack the back of his head for mockery. "Them's good eatin', Gracie!"

She hadn't been reassured then. Now, after two days on the trail with him, she was changing her tune. They hadn't seen another soul, though they had taken the time to sneak into Mattheson, Simla and Ramah. Those trips hadn't yielded any food, but they were still fairly well-provisioned. Quinn supplemented their supplies constantly with cattail roots and shoots, fish, young thistles, and the dandelions he had teased her about before. He talked more than she'd ever heard him talk, teaching, instructing, explaining, and for the first time, Grace saw the intelligence William had always insisted was there.

"Almost all wild plants are edible," he said. "Some just taste better than others. Look for new growth – that's your best bet. And stay away from mushrooms – they're just too risky, and they don't have hardly any nutritional value."

He'd taught her what to avoid - Larkspur, Death Camas, Water Hemlock – and what plants had medicinal or first-aid value – Burdock and Willow – and he waxed rhapsodic about the many uses of Yucca. The only time he slipped back into his shy self-consciousness was when Grace complimented him on his knowledge and expertise.

"Oh, no. It's nothing special." He looked down, rubbed at the saddle horn with his thumb. "I'm not like William. Or you. School never made sense to me. There was so much stuff to remember, and nothing to attach it to. Plants are easy – they're part of all this." He swept an arm around them, indicating the rustling cottonwoods, the chattering creek, the wind shushing through the swaying, rolling, spring-green grass on the prairie. "This makes sense. It all fits together."

Grace was intrigued. She knew Quinn had a learning disability, but she had never really thought about what that meant. She'd always assumed he was mildly mentally retarded, but he sure didn't seem slow to her now. "Didn't you have to memorize all the plants' names, and what their properties are? How did you learn all that?"

Quinn shrugged. "I didn't sit down with a book, if that's what you mean. My mom taught me a lot – she was a great gardener. And I took 4-H classes. Mr. Baker, he knows everything about every plant you can pick up. How to make medicine out of it, how to preserve it. I was supposed to take another class with him next fall." Without shame, Quinn wiped tears off his cheeks. He never tried to stifle the grief when it visited him. "I hope he made it. I hope I see him again – he was like me. No good in school, but really good with outdoor stuff."

She hadn't thought much about *thinking* before; she had been glad learning was easy for her, but she had completely taken it for granted. William used to say her mind was like a computer; she could process a lot of raw data swiftly and easily, organizing, categorizing and discarding until she had honed that data into a working hypothesis. To her, it felt like pieces of a puzzle clicking into place, each piece revealing more of the picture and hinting at the overall landscape. Often, when she had collected enough pieces, the whole puzzle would suddenly solve itself, like a painting suddenly sweeping, complete and beautiful, across a screen in her mind.

William had been smart, but not as smart as her, and they had both known it. Grace had harbored secret doubts about how they'd handle that, if they stayed together. Now, she'd never know. And, after the last two days, she was starting to seriously question who was better equipped to move forward in this awful new world – her, with her showy book smarts, or Quinn. His knowledge seemed to grow right out of the land like one of his beloved plants.

Grace stretched again, and tried to convince her lazy limbs to get up. She was a little stiff and sore after two solid days of riding, and it felt so good to just lie here, luxuriating in the peace of the moment. Quinn was sorting through their supplies, and he looked up at her movement.

"Do you want eggs or some of that homemade granola for breakfast?"

Grace sat up and scrubbed her hands over her face. "How many eggs do we have left?"

"Enough for one more meal."

"Whatever sounds good to you, Quinn – I'm not picky." She stood up and headed for the area they'd designated "the bathroom." "But maybe we could hold off on the dandelion greens until lunch? Salad for breakfast just doesn't hit the spot."

When she returned, he had the eggs sizzling in the small frying pan they had brought. "I thought we'd eat up the eggs. We should be north of Peyton by late afternoon, and we'll be in the suburbs of the Springs tomorrow. There'll be a lot more houses to check for food."

"Oh, goodie," Grace muttered. They both hated searching houses – the intrusion, the fear of meeting another person, and everywhere, the smell of death and the buzz of flies.

"There's always dandelions," Quinn said. He looked around. "You know, we could stay here for a few days. Rest. I could set up some snares, see if I could catch some rabbits."

He'd stay forever, Grace knew. He had agreed to go on this journey because they had to do something, but they both knew the likelihood of finding Grace's father still alive was very low. Now that she'd seen Quinn in his natural habitat, it was very, very tempting to agree to his suggestion.

"I think we should move on," she said finally. "While we still have some provisions. And while the weather holds. What was it, Mother's Day last year that we had snow? I'd hate to ride out a spring blizzard in that little tent we brought."

Quinn sighed, but didn't disagree. He scraped the cooked eggs onto two blue-speckled camp plates, and handed one to her. When they had eaten, Grace washed up the dishes they'd used while Quinn re-packed their supplies, then they went together to tack and load the horses.

Grace's horse, Buttons, had been Mrs. Harris', and she was as sweet and steady as her name implied. Mrs. Harris had adopted her through the Bureau of Land Management years ago, then had gentled and trained the sturdy little mustang herself. Quinn had decided on her as a mount for Grace for her sure-footedness and her wind, and Grace was already half in love with the little bay.

Quinn was riding his father's big sorrel quarter horse, Koda. It had broken his heart to leave Mitsy, his own quarter horse, behind, but she had a tendency to spook, and she didn't get along well with Buttons. He had considered bringing her along as an extra mount, but had decided against it in the end. She had been set loose along with William's horse; Grace liked to imagine they would soon join up with one of the free-ranging herds on the plains.

When the horses were ready, Quinn checked the campsite one last time, making sure the fire was dead. Then, they headed out. They rode without talking for a while, the silence between them filled with the creak of their saddles, the occasional blow or snort from one of the horses, and always, the soft swish of the wind in the prairie grass. Grace's body rocked easily with Buttons' gait, warm and relaxed in the soft morning sun. Her mind drifted and swayed as well, just as relaxed as her body; she hadn't felt this safe since the plague started.

Ahead of her, Quinn rode with the ease of second-nature. Grace watched his shoulders shift from side to side with Koda's movements, and found herself admiring the bulk there, the strength. His back made her think of the diagrams they'd been studying in anatomy class of the muscle and skeletal systems, and she reviewed as her eyes lazily coasted: Trapezius. Posterior Deltoid. And oh, yum, Latissimus Dorsi.

Grace's spine snapped straight. Yum? Had she seriously just thought *yum*? A deep flush started at her neck and swept up to her hairline. She pulled her hat low on her forehead, and dropped her head to hide behind the brim, mortified. Beneath her, Buttons shifted and nickered, picking up on her sudden tension, and Quinn looked back.

"Everything okay?"

She peeked out from under her hat. He was twisted to the side to look back at her, and the posture emphasized his heavy pectoral muscles, his tight, lean abdominals, and the solid curve of his bicep. His hands on the reins looked strong, tanned. Her body felt loose and tense, and strange, delicious tingles raced along the nape of her neck, down her spine, and settled low, low in her pelvis. She dropped her head again, hiding the even deeper flush she could feel on her face.

"I'm fine," she strangled out, but he didn't turn back around. Instead, he frowned.

"Your face is pretty red," he said. "Have you been drinking enough water? If you're too warm, we can stop and find some shade for a bit."

"I'm fine," Grace repeated, and fumbled to pull up her canteen. "I'll just take a drink. We can go on."

He watched her for a few more seconds, then mercifully turned back around. Grace drank from the canteen, then poured a little water in the palm of her hand and spread a thin layer of moisture over her forehead and cheeks. She shut her eyes.

Unbelievable. Was *this* what her friends had dithered on and on about? Was *this* desire? And she was feeling it for William's *brother*?

She would have liked to excuse her feelings as something else, as some sort of anomaly, but self-delusion had always struck her as a waste of time and effort. Best just to face facts, then figure out how to move ahead. Tears stung her eyes suddenly, and she blinked hard, struggling to hold them at bay.

She'd never felt desire for William, not the kind that made her tingle, or feel that low, embarrassing, exhilarating burn. She had liked it when they kissed, and she had felt a surging, thrilling power when he had made it clear how much he wanted her. But she'd never looked at him like she'd just looked at Quinn.

What an awful betrayal of William.

Grace frowned. But was it? Was it really? William surely wouldn't have wanted her love life to die with him. He would have wanted her to go on, to grow up, and fall in love, and make a life with someone. Maybe he would even have been happy to see her and Quinn together – they had never been competitive the way some brothers were...

Oh my God. Just *listen* to yourself, she thought. Rationalizing. Justifying. She stared hard at Quinn's back and forced herself to recite the facts: She was only 17. Quinn was just 16. They had been thrown together under extreme circumstances. He had not even hinted, by word or deed, to feelings for her that exceeded brotherly concern.

What she was feeling probably had more to do with the relief of momentarily surrendering the lead to him than with anything else. Out here, he was the alpha. She was probably experiencing a primordial desire to ingratiate herself to the leader, nothing more. It was rather fascinating, from a psychological perspective. The recitation left her feeling cold and clinical, which was exactly what she'd been shooting for.

And enough with staring at his backside. She kicked Buttons into a trot, then settled into a walk again when they were side-by-side with Koda and Quinn.

"You should teach me more about the plants," she said brusquely. "It's not like we can run down to the Food Mart and pick up a loaf of bread anymore. What could we store for the winter?"

Quinn had obliged her request, and had spent the next several hours pointing out plants, then having her spot them. He had talked about drying and preservation, roasting versus boiling, and by the time lunchtime rolled around, Grace had nearly put her earlier feelings out of her head.

They stopped near a ranch and watered the horses in a trough below a briskly creaking windmill. Grace eyed the ranch, looking for any sign of life, then looked over at Quinn. "Should we search it?"

He was studying the house and outbuildings as well. "Yeah. People out here usually have food put by. If they didn't make it, there might be something we could use."

They rode slowly up the drive towards the house. The horses were agitated, snorting and shying a little, which probably meant they were smelling what Grace and Quinn couldn't yet: death. They both dismounted, and Quinn handed Koda's reins to Grace.

"Wait here. I'll check it out."

He went in the back door, which was unlocked, calling out as soon as the door popped open with a loud creak. "Hello? Is anyone here? We don't mean any harm. Is anyone here?"

Grace heard an interior door open, and Quinn stumbled back outside a few moments later, his face grey-going-green. He leaned against the side of the house, shut his eyes and tipped his head back, swallowing over and over. Abruptly, he muttered, "I'm sorry," and leaned over to vomit up his breakfast.

Alarmed, Grace let the reins of both horses drop to the ground and hustled to his side. She rubbed his back as he heaved a few more times, then hurried back to Koda for his canteen when it looked like he was empty. Quinn took it from her, swished his mouth out with water, and spat. He kept his eyes closed the whole time.

"What was it? Were they dead? Can you tell me?"

Quinn shook his head. "I don't want to say. Let's just go on."

A morbid curiosity seized her. They had seen some terrible things. What on earth had shaken him so? "Did you look for food?"

"No. Let's just go on."

"Wait here." She ignored his protest, evaded his reaching hand, and stepped through the open doorway and into a mudroom. Another door was open to a kitchen beyond, and Grace immediately saw what had rattled Quinn so badly.

What was left of a man was seated at the kitchen table. Curled in his disintegrating lap was a tiny corpse dressed in a Hello Kitty nightgown and wrapped in a fuzzy yellow afghan. A shotgun lay along the man's chest, the barrel resting underneath his chin. Grace could see how he'd rigged it, using a forked stick to push the trigger and blow the top of his head and his brains all over the bright white kitchen cupboards.

A low buzz started in Grace's ears. Well, she'd insisted on seeing. Next time, she'd listen. She turned away from the table and spotted a walk-in pantry. Aware of every movement she made, she walked into the pantry and assessed the contents, taking a partial box of rice – why did people always have rice? – a bag of flour, a plastic container with a skiff of sugar in it and a box of powdered milk off the otherwise empty shelves. She walked back through the kitchen, and found Quinn waiting for her just outside the exterior door.

Without a word, she handed the supplies to him. She turned to walk back to Buttons, but her legs suddenly wobbled right out from under her and she went down to her hands and knees, feeling the world revolve around her sickeningly.

"Oh, Gracie." Quinn moved to shade her head, and his hand rubbed her back, just as she'd rubbed his. "I told you not to."

Sheer orneriness kept her from heaving up her breakfast as he'd done. "'I told you so' isn't really helping right now," she gasped. "Just give me a second. I'm alright."

When the world stopped spinning, she stood up, refusing his help. She stalked over to Buttons and hauled herself into the saddle. They rode away in silence, neither one saying a word about the lunch they hadn't eaten yet. Quinn led them back to the creek, and they rode on for another hour before he stopped and dismounted.

"The horses need rest, and we need to eat," he announced. Grace dismounted and led Buttons to the creek's edge, allowing her to drink. She heard Quinn rummaging around in his saddle bags, and swallowed hard, nauseated by the thought of food. She looped Button's reins around the saddle horn so they wouldn't trail in the water and went to sit beside him in the shade.

He had pulled out some of her improvised travel cakes, and he handed her one as she sat down. Though they tasted okay, they weren't the most appetizing things to look at – she'd plopped the brownish batter onto baking sheets, the result looking rather like a pile of...well, like a pile of vomit. She eyed the cake, swallowed again, then looked up to find him watching her. She smiled weakly, a peace offering and an apology for not listening to him.

"I don't suppose you have any dandelion greens instead?"

Quinn looked down at the cake, cocked his head to the side, then made a horrific retching sound and pretended to heave into his hand. He grinned and offered the cake to her, and all of a sudden they were both giggling like little kids.

"Gosh, that is so sweet of you – did you regurgitate that just for me?"

Quinn laughed even harder at her quip. He took a big bite of his travel cake and chewed with his mouth open, rolling his eyes and smacking his lips. "Mmmm," he crooned around his mouthful of food. "If you're not going to eat that, can I have it?"

Grace grinned, and took a big bite of her own cake, tasting cinnamon, ginger and cloves. Some of the horror and sorrow at what they'd seen uncoiled, lifted free of her body, and drifted away on the soft breeze. "Back off, pal. This is my lump of puke. Eat your own."

They relaxed in the shade, leaning against tree trunks as they finished their lunch, sipping water and watching the horses crop at the soft grass beside the creek. She was just thinking of suggesting a fifteen minute nap when Quinn surprised her.

"Gracie, have you ever thought about suicide?"

It was unlike him to introduce a topic of conversation, and such a serious one at that. He wouldn't look at her, focusing instead on the lines he was scraping in the dirt in front of him with a twig. She thought for a moment before she answered.

"I guess I haven't, at least not as something I'd do," she said. "When that girl, Angela, killed herself last year, I guess I thought about it. I wondered what made her hurt so much, that she thought dying was the only way out. Did you know her?"

Quinn nodded. "I did. We started kindergarten together. We weren't friends, but I knew her. People were saying her boyfriend broke up with her, and that was why she did it."

Grace had heard the same thing, and she felt ashamed of the contempt she'd felt at the time. She had a deeper understanding of pain and loss now. "Why did you ask? Have you thought about it?"

Quinn shook his head. "No. I can't imagine wanting to die." He slid a look sideways at her, then focused fiercely on his lines and his twig. "You didn't think about it, even when you found out William was dead?"

Grace's heart rate kicked up a notch, and she was suddenly as interested in the tuft of grass in front of her as Quinn was in his lines in the dirt. She started braiding the grass into a 4-strand plait while she scrambled for something to say.

"I cared about William a lot," she began, then faltered to a stop. She took a swig of water from her canteen to relieve her suddenly dry mouth. "I...don't really think about losing him. Or my mom, or Benji, or Wayne. I can't think about those things."

"You don't cry," Quinn said softly. She could feel him looking at her now, but she couldn't lift her head. "Why don't you cry?"

Ridiculous, that him pointing that out made her want to do just that: cry. Sob out loud like a child. Wail at the sky and pound her chest. "If I start," she said finally, "I'll never stop. I can't do that. I can't give in to that."

She rose to her feet and dusted off her seat, 100% aware that she was running away from this conversation. "Let's go. We've got some ground to cover if we want to make Peyton tonight."

They rode long and steady through the afternoon, stopping once to water the horses, stopping again to check out another ranch. A scruffy border collie came to the edge of the property before they got close to the house, barking and snarling, and Quinn shook his head, turning Koda away. "Someone's still there, I can feel it," he said. "Let's get out of here."

Grace didn't question his certainty. During the long hours in the saddle, she'd had plenty of time to think back over the confrontation with the men in Limon, how both she and Quinn had seemed to *know* things without explanation or reason. It stood to reason, she had concluded, that surviving the plague had gifted them both with a heightened awareness, an instinct for survival. It would be interesting to see if their perceptions returned to normal when life stabilized, or if the changes were permanent.

They reached the end of the Big Sandy Creek late that afternoon. Quinn guided them away from open country and led them down a dirt road, heading south towards Peyton. After days of riding across the prairie, Grace felt exposed and uncomfortable on the road; by the hunch in Quinn's shoulders, she was guessing he felt the same way. Their horses' hooves crunched loudly on the gravel, and clopped even louder when they transitioned to pavement. Quinn moved Koda to the grassy shoulder, and Grace followed suit.

They were starting to pass more and more houses, and the sensation of occasionally being watched was making Grace's skin crawl. She couldn't stop checking behind them. Buttons was tired, and Grace's tension was making her fractious. She shied at nothing once, then did it again, nearly unseating her. Quinn looked back, his face tight with the same tension she was feeling.

"I've got the hinks, Gracie. Something feels wrong. Let's find someplace to settle in for the night."

They found what they were looking for on a quiet knoll: a deserted horse property with a well, and a pump powered by a generator. Quinn winced at the noise when he fired up the generator, and they ran it just long enough to pump water for the horses and their own needs for the night. A fire seemed too risky – too easy to see and smell – so they spread out their sleeping bags on the ground underneath a big cottonwood beside the barn. The sun was just touching the top of the mountains when they finished setting up camp, and they sat watching it slide away as they munched on granola and dandelion greens.

Quinn pulled out the map to go over the route he had planned for the next day. From Peyton, they would travel southwest as the crow flew, angling north of Highway 24 and cutting across suburban neighborhoods when they left the plains. They would pick up 24 again where it headed up into the mountains outside of Manitou Springs.

"We'll be camping in the city tomorrow night," Quinn commented. "I figure if we make it west of Powers Boulevard, we'll be doing good. It'll be slower going if we're looking for food as we go, and water will probably be harder to find, so we'll take as much with us as we can. The horses are tired – I don't want to push them too hard before we start heading up in elevation."

They were both quiet for a while, neither one wanting to bring up what needed to be discussed. Finally, Grace dove in.

"What if we run into more people like the Weavers? People will be desperate – they may try to take what food we have, or take the horses."

"I've been thinking about that. If someone confronts us, I think we should run for it in opposite directions. It might surprise them long enough for us to both get away. How well do you know Colorado Springs?"

Just the thought of being alone in the city made her heart pound faster. "I know parts of it, I guess. The movie theater on Powers. Chapel Hills Mall. I can get to the zoo, and the World Arena. And Memorial Park – we always go to the Balloon Classic over Labor Day weekend."

"Okay, let's go with Memorial Park – it's just a few blocks south of Platte, which is what 24 turns into in the city. So if we get separated for any reason, we'll meet at Memorial Park, by the statue of the firefighter on the ladder."

Grace listened as he went on, talking about making sure they both carried food and water just in case, talking about other water sources he knew of in the city, talking about finding supplemental feed for the horses. She murmured her agreement occasionally, but mostly she drifted, not really paying attention to the content of what he was saying, comforted by the low rumble of his voice. Had it really been just this morning that she'd woken feeling safe, secure, almost happy? A deep foreboding chilled her, but it seemed selfish to mention it. They both had enough on their minds without sharing imaginary fears.

Before it was full dark, they both settled into their sleeping bags. The horses were tethered nearby – Quinn said they were better than watchdogs for letting them know if a threat was approaching – and the steady, soft whoosh of their breathing made Grace's eyes droop. She burrowed deeper into her sleeping bag, pulling it up around her head and burying her nose in the folds. She could smell Buttons and the familiar and comforting scent of her own skin, and she dropped into sleep like a stone.

Grace slept dreamlessly until just before dawn, when a shout from Quinn ripped her out of sleep. She sat up, wildly scraping her hair out of her face, hands scrabbling for a weapon, anything she could use as a weapon. The horses were snorting and yanking on their tethers, and Buttons shrilled briefly. Quinn shouted again, and Grace's eyes flew to him.

He was thrashing violently, and he looked to be sound asleep. "No, no, no, no, no!" He muttered, then another shout: "Gracie, no! No!"

"Quinn!" Grace hissed. She fought free of her sleeping bag and scuttled to his side, dodging his flailing arms to grasp his shoulders. She shook him hard. "Quinn, wake up! It's a dream! Just a dream!"

Quinn shot upright, and narrowly avoided slamming his forehead into Grace's. She lurched back, but he lunged at her. He grabbed her arms, and his eyes raced over her, over and over again. "Are you okay? Are you hurt?"

"I'm fine, for heaven's sake!" Now that her heart was slowing, she was not appreciative of being yanked out of sleep like that. "You must have had a nightmare."

Quinn let her go, and rubbed his hands over his face, then into his shaggy hair. "A bad one. Really bad." Before she could ask, he added, "I don't want to talk about it."

"Fine." Grace got up, stretched, then started to head around the barn to their designated "bathroom."

Quinn shot to his feet, nearly falling over in his frantic haste to get free of his sleeping bag. "Wait! Where are you going?"

Grace turned around and raised an eyebrow at him. "Do you really want the details?"

"No, I mean..." He hung his head, miserable, and the confident Quinn was gone, just like that. Uncertain, self-conscious Quinn was back. "Just don't go far. Be careful. That's all."

Grace turned back around, disappointed and unnerved, and just plain irritated by both feelings. "I'll pee very, very carefully, I promise."

They prepared breakfast in silence, and packed up camp the same way. The horses were picking up on the strange discord between them, and shifted uneasily as they were saddled and loaded. When they were mounted, Quinn sat silently for a moment, staring at the mountains. They were pink in the early dawn light, gilded along their crests with the rising sun. Quinn turned suddenly to Grace, his face tight with anxiety.

"Let's go back to the reservoir," he said in a rush. "I have a bad feeling about going on. Let's just...wait."

Grace just looked at him, while Buttons shifted underneath her. Finally, she asked, "Wait for what?"

Quinn sighed. "I knew you'd ask that. I don't know. Wait until it feels safer, I guess. It doesn't feel safe."

"Nothing feels safe anymore," Grace said quietly. She debated whether or not to tell him about her own misgivings, her own cold foreboding. Maybe it would be safer to wait.

But there was something unbearable about waiting. Delaying the inevitable just made the inevitable harder to bear – Grace knew that for certain. Better to forge ahead. "I think we need to just get it over with," she said. "Waiting won't change anything. Unless we want to go a long way north or a long way south, we've got to go through the city."

Quinn looked away again, back at the mountains, thinking. She knew for certain he was calculating the miles against their remaining supplies, and she saw the moment he capitulated to her authority. Without a word, he clucked Koda into motion, riding briskly towards the city.

Half-way between Peyton and Falcon, they crossed a north/south road that was blocked by a massive pile-up of vehicles. Impossible to tell what had caused the accident, but the chaos had stretched for hundreds of yards on either side of the road as people attempted to go around, only to become mired in the water-soaked ground. The same wet spring that had gifted Grace and Quinn with such abundant water on their journey had stranded these motorists.

They sat on the horses for a while, looking for any sign of movement or life. There were bodies slumped in many of the vehicles; others had clearly been looted. The line of cars, trucks and SUV's stretched as far as they could see in both directions.

"Where did they all go?" Grace whispered. "After they got stuck here, what happened to them? Did they continue on foot? Or did they walk back home?"

"We haven't seen anyone. Most of 'em headed home, I'd guess. That's human nature – they'd head back to what was familiar."

Human nature. Grace thought about that as they rode on, the good and the bad of it. People could be heroic under stress, or they could be monstrous, and there didn't seem to be any way to predict which way it would go. Never in a million years could she have guessed the little-league-coaching Mr. Weaver would shoot at them.

They stopped only briefly for lunch. By late afternoon, they had left the prairie behind and were riding through open spaces bordered by sprawling tracts of suburban housing. The quiet, which had been soothing on the plains, was haunting here. There was a still quality to the silence that kept the hair on Grace's neck prickling constantly.

The afternoon was aging into evening when they reached the junction of Powers and Woodmen. Both roads were jammed with vehicles, and Quinn led them onto the overpass, winding between the silent cars and trucks. On the far side of the overpass, he paused, reining Koda in and looking back at her.

"We should start looking for a place to stay," he said. "According to the map, there's a creek just west of Austin Bluffs and Woodmen, can't remember the name of it right now and I don't know if it runs on the surface, but..."

His voice trailed off, and he frowned. He looked all around them, his frown growing darker, cutting deep grooves into his face. Suddenly, his eyes flew wide, and he stared at her in horror and terror. "Gracie! Ride! Ride hard!" He leaned over and slapped Buttons sharply on the rump. "Go go go go!"

Buttons squealed and bolted, Grace clinging desperately as she tried to control her. "What the hell, Quinn!"

The world around them erupted. Booms and pops and men yelling. Buttons jerked, then jerked again and screamed, and her front legs folded. Grace flipped over the mustang's head and landed on her back, skidding along the gravel at the edge of the road. Buttons' momentum carried her into Grace, her head plowing into Grace's shoulder, and she struggled to sit up, struggled to breathe – why couldn't she breathe? – and finally fought up onto one arm. She stared down at Buttons and could not make sense of what she was seeing: blood coated Buttons' neck and chest, and her visible eye was white and rolling. She heaved a terrible, rattling groan just as Grace managed to suck in a breath of air. She did not breathe again.

"Quinn!" Grace screamed. She tugged frantically at Buttons' head, then ran a comforting hand down her neck and shoulder. Her palm came away coated with blood and she stared at it, not processing, not believing, not accepting. "Come on, girl, it was just a stumble, let's get you up..."

Something plowed into her from behind, sending her sprawling in the gravel again. It dug into her scalp, her cheek, her neck. Grace smelled smoke, and sweat, and rot. She struggled to get out from under the weight that was crushing her. A wet mouth landed on her temple, then slid to her ear.

"Hey there, honey."

Through the chaos, somehow, she heard Quinn. Heard him, exactly as she'd heard him this morning, in the throes of his nightmare. "Gracie, no! No!"

TWELVE
Jack and Layla: Woodland Park, CO

"Jack."

Jack looked up from his attempt to tie his shoes without suffering total exhaustion. Things were looking up; he'd made it through one whole shoe and wasn't even breathless yet. In the doorway, Layla was watching him analytically, her face wearing equal parts encouragement and concern. Jack puffed his chest out with mock pride and held out his sneakered left foot.

"Check it out: a 100% improvement over yesterday."

Layla chuckled. "I guess so. Yesterday, just the socks wore you out." She paused. "You don't have to do this. There's no rush. If people really need to see you, they can come here, so you can rest."

"We've been over this. If we're going to survive, we need to start building a sense of community, and it needs to happen yesterday. You said yourself that people are fearful and isolated, that they're not responding to yours or Rowan's requests to pull together."

He got his other shoe on, then paused for breath under the guise of looking at Layla earnestly. She wasn't fooled, he was sure. "I'm not saying I have the magic bullet. But if people are looking for spiritual solace, or if they're ticked at God and they need to get angry and yell at someone, that's a start. If nothing else, some of them will want to show up just to see a real live survivor. Maybe it'll give them hope for friends or family that are far away and out of touch."

They had put the word out that Jack would be at his old church this afternoon, in spite of Layla's misgivings. He had regained his senses less than a week ago, and had only been up and around for three days. Jack overrode her concerns with Rowan's backing, citing his need to reconnect with members of his church, but there was more to it than that for him. He needed to talk to other Christians, to ask them the questions he had asked Layla. He needed to comfort and be comforted by people of his faith, to be reassured that they hadn't, in fact, been left behind.

Layla stepped into the room and knelt at his feet, tying his remaining shoe for him. "Let's save your strength for the important stuff, shall we?"

When she was finished, she didn't get up right away. Instead, she settled onto her hip and looked up at him, her forehead wrinkled with care. Jack could feel both her need to speak and her reluctance to do so.

"What is it? Just say it."

"Okay, but you're not going to like hearing what you need to hear." She took a deep breath. "All I ask is that you hear me out before you go all outraged fire and brimstone on me."

Jack's lips twitched. "I'll keep my hellfire reined in until you signal you're ready for it."

"For a pastor, you're a real smart-ass." Before he could fire back, she rushed on. "People are different now, since the plague. Rowan has started cataloging the changes, with her brother's help." Layla paused, scrutinizing him, then went on. "I think you're different, too, though you may not know it yet."

Jack eyed her warily. He wasn't sure what she was talking about, but he had a feeling she'd been right – he really didn't want to hear this. "Well, I'd expect all of us to be different. We've all suffered terrible losses, the world as we know it is completely changed, our future is uncertain-"

"Stop."

He did, because there was *power* in her single word. Power that he didn't understand, and that roused an instinctive fear in him. She nodded slowly, never taking her eyes off him. "You felt it, didn't you?"

"You asked me to stop talking, so I stopped-"

"Jack." His softly-spoken name made him flinch like she'd slapped him across the face. "Don't waste time avoiding the new reality. You can either talk to me about this now, or you can go out there with no protection or shielding whatsoever, and be completely overwhelmed."

Weakened he might be, but not so weak that he couldn't work up a solid sneer. "Protection? Shielding? Those are New Age beliefs. I don't subscribe."

She had this way of just staring for several long seconds, her face calm and stern, her eyes cool and assessing; he was sure she'd used that stare to massive advantage as a teacher. "Fine. When you want to talk later, I'm going to be condescending and rub it in. Just so you know."

"Appreciate the forewarning." Jack slapped his thighs, and stood. "Let's get going."

He was ridiculously excited just to get outside. He'd spent a little time on Layla's tiny patio each day, and the sun on his face had been as invigorating as any spring tonic. Seeing other people would do him a world of good as well – he owed Layla and Rowan his life, and he would never forget that. Now, though, it was time for him to pick up the mantle that suited him best: counselor, comforter, spiritual leader. That, at least, hadn't changed. It would be so good to feel like his old self for a while.

In spite of himself, his thoughts returned to Layla's earlier caution. Her words recalled the cascade of impressions, sensations and feelings, all of them startlingly vivid, that he'd been trying to process during the last week. He'd noticed it most when Rowan or her brother Alder visited – it was as if he could *feel* what they were feeling, as if their emotions slid inside him to co-exist with his own. He had always been extremely empathetic, but this went beyond that. It was disorienting as the dickens.

He had assumed the shift in his perception could be attributed to his close brush with death – he had also been experiencing a sharp, increased enjoyment of everything. Food tasted better. Scents were richer. And a simple flower could move him to tears with its beauty. It seemed, though, that Layla was suggesting something different.

They stepped out the front door together and headed for Layla's jeep. They had been urging people to drive as little as possible, she had explained – every gas station in town was dry, and they would soon have to start siphoning gas out of abandoned vehicles. Their destination was far enough away, though, to justify the fuel usage.

Jack settled into the passenger seat, and pulled out a notebook and a pen. "I thought I'd start a list of our needs, and keep adding to it as we talk to people. Sometimes all people need is to know that their concerns are being heard to get them involved."

Layla nodded. "Good idea. Put 'Help for Rowan' at the top of the list, would you? As far as we know, she's the only person left here with any kind of medical training, and she is worn to the bone."

Jack wrote. "Done. What else?"

Layla slowed the vehicle, her mouth firming into a grim line. She nodded in the direction of the passenger window; they were creeping past a small cottage much like Layla's, where a man's body spilled out the front door, holding it open. He was face down, arms outflung, and his hands and skull had been cleaned down to the bone by predators of some kind.

Jack winced. He had wondered if he would see bodies, had tried to steel himself against it, but maybe that just wasn't possible. Maybe it wasn't even right. It should hurt, after all, it should horrify him, to see a body so neglected. He met Layla's eyes and nodded. "Care and burial of our dead," he said softly, as he wrote it on the list.

Layla reached out and rested her hand on his shoulder for a moment. A warm glow of comfort suffused him, a sensation like a hug, a backrub, a soft stroke on the brow. Jack heaved a deep sigh and shut his eyes. One of these days, he was probably going to have to ask her how she did that.

Layla removed her hand without fanfare. "You should probably add 'electricity and water' next, though I don't know how to get more specific than that. I'm embarrassed to admit I don't really know how they were supplied in the first place."

Jack grimaced. "I guess I'm pretty shaky on the specifics myself. Our electricity is supplied by Colorado Springs Utilities, but we have a water treatment facility here in town. Let's see what Alder can tell us, see if any of the surviving community members have useful knowledge."

He thought for a minute, then wrote on his list again. "In fact, I think that should be one of our top priorities. We need to understand what resources we have, and what we need to seek. We need to know not just what people's professions were, but what their hobbies are, what they might have learned to do as a kid or a teenager – that kind of thing."

Layla smiled. "I worked my way through college on my uncle's fishing boat in Florida. I don't suppose that'll help?"

"Well, other than the reservoir, we're kind of land-locked here." Jack looked over at her. "You never mentioned family. When you talked about your charms, for the people you'd lost. Is your family still in Florida? Have you heard from them?"

"I haven't been in touch with my family for years." Her tone was flat, without a trace of emotion. More than that, he couldn't sense a thing from her – she was like a concrete wall. Before he could ask her about it, she gave him a tight, controlled smile and turned into the church's parking lot. "We're here."

She parked the jeep, then sat for a moment, looking at the small group of people who had gathered in the spring sunshine outside the church's front doors. Rowan and Alder were among them; Layla smiled and raised a hand in greeting, then turned to Jack.

"Okay, I know you don't want to talk about this, but I can't send you in there blind. Just...be aware of what you're feeling, and what comes from other people. If you start to get confused or overwhelmed, let me know. I can help."

She was out of the vehicle before Jack could comment or question her, and he followed more slowly, giving himself a moment to process what she'd said. How could she have known what he had been experiencing? He certainly hadn't talked to her about it.

As soon as he neared the group, he was rushed. A woman he recognized as the mother of one of his youth group kids ran to him, arms outstretched, face contorted by grief. "My Jenny," she gasped as she collapsed into his arms. "My Jenny. My baby. Why? Why, why, why would God take her?"

Jack staggered both under the physical impact and the emotional one. Her grief flooded him, terrible and bottomless. As if Jenny had been his daughter, he experienced love for her, a love that had roots in her tiny newborn newness and had grown year after year into a rich and nuanced love, a love that recognized both human failings and the spark of the divine that had lived in Jenny's beautiful soul. Except now, where Jenny's living presence had been was an awful, gaping, void.

He looked up, nearly blinded by the tears flooding his eyes, and an onslaught of *feeling* hit him in wave, after wave, after wave. People were moving towards him, a few he recognized, many he didn't, all of them emanating *emotion*. Grief, rage, courage, determination, misery, despair, hope, and fear, fear, fear. He couldn't begin to sort it all out.

He would have gone to his knees if Alder hadn't shoved a shoulder under his armpit and wrapped an arm around his waist, while Layla gathered the sobbing woman into her own arms. He met Layla's gaze over the woman's head, unable to hide his shock. She shook her head, exasperated, muttering, "I tried to warn you about this. This is me being condescending. Here, Alder, can you help her? Let me talk to Jack for a second."

Alder traded burdens with her. Layla didn't try to hold him up physically, but when she locked eyes with him, he felt strength pour into him. She reached out and grasped both his hands, and the sensation intensified tenfold. It seemed as if a sound-proof curtain dropped around the two of them, but instead of noise, the curtain blocked out the *feelings* that had been bombarding him.

"Listen to me," she said in a low voice. "This is what I meant – things are different now. We don't have time for a discussion – I should have insisted we talk earlier – but for now, you need to get your shields up."

"Shields?" Jack's brain was spinning. "As in Star Trek? 'Shields are at maximum, captain?' Layla, what are you talking about?"

"I'm running interference for you now, but you're going to need to learn to do it for yourself. Close your eyes." He obeyed, too rattled to do otherwise. "Envision a cone of white light that starts above your head and cascades around your body, all the way to the ground."

He cracked open one eye. "You cannot be serious."

She squeezed his hands so hard he winced, and glared so fiercely he shut his eyes again. "The white light is your shield. It protects you. It allows in only what you allow it to. If you start feeling the emotions of others, you need to take a moment to re-envision the cone of light. Do you understand?"

Jack nodded; he really didn't know what else he could do. Layla let go of his hands, and instantly, Jack was buffeted by *feeling*. By *emotion*. It was weaker this time, but still there. Layla shook her head. "Your shields are like swiss cheese," she said. "Imagine the light brighter, stronger, and more complete."

Out of desperation, Jack did as she instructed. To his astonishment, he re-experienced the sound-proof curtain phenomenon. The buffering sensation was such a relief, his knees went watery. He stared at her, looked around, then stared at her again.

"Are you experiencing this, too? Are they? What's happened to us?"

"We're not sure," Layla answered. She linked her arm with his as she would with an invalid's, and started walking him towards the church. "Let's get inside. I'm sorry, I should have warned you, but I honestly wasn't sure what you'd experience. It seems to be different for all of us."

The group parted to allow them passage, then fell in behind them. Layla led them through the foyer and into the sanctuary. At the front of the church, she urged him into the front pew, then sat while people arranged themselves as they saw fit.

Rowan and her brother sat side by side on the steps to the pulpit. Jack knew Rowan was only a few years older than her brother – they were both in their late 20's – and he was struck by how much exhaustion had aged her. Her eyes were sunken and rimmed with darkness, and her normally vibrant skin looked dull and yellowish. She scanned the crowd constantly, her eyes lingering here and there, a frown of concern deepening the lines on her face. Jack wondered what she was seeing that worried her so. Beside her, Alder was scanning, too. Occasionally he would nod at the people trickling in, but he seemed to be looking for someone who had not yet arrived.

Jack waited until the rustling behind him had settled down, then shifted to sit sideways in the pew. Layla let go of his arm and scooted away from him, and the onslaught was immediate. *Feelings.* From everyone, coming from everywhere, a cacophony of emotion. He actually put his hands over his ears for a moment before he remembered the cone of light thing. He did a half-hearted visualization, experienced a little relief, then gritted his teeth and got serious. He closed his eyes and envisioned a blinding white cone of light, protective, strong, yet flexible. *Christ Light*, his mind whispered. *Think of it as the Light of God.*

Intense relief filled him. He kept his eyes closed, bowed his head, and said the most heart-felt prayer of thanks of his life without words, without conscious concepts – just a flood of gratitude to God for His protection, His comfort, His wisdom. When he opened his eyes and looked up, he was confronted by a group of 20 or so individuals of varying ages, all of them watching him.

"I had a plan," he began. "I had a notebook." He held it up and smiled wryly. "I even started to make a list. And the things on that list are very important – I still believe that – but first, we need to talk about us. About how we're different. I didn't want to listen to Layla."

He turned his head to look at her, nodded his head in apology, then turned back to the group. Most of them were leaning towards him now, some of them wearing expressions of urgency or eagerness. "We're different. I'm different – I can feel what you all are feeling. As if I'm you, and your feelings are mine. Is this happening to all of you?"

Hands shot up all over the room, but before he could point at someone, Alder spoke from behind him. "It's different for me. I understand mechanical devices, even ones I don't know anything about. I can *see* how the energy should move through them."

Jack turned around. "You couldn't do this before?"

"Not really. Not like now." Alder looked at his sister, and she nodded her encouragement. "I've always liked to tinker with electronic or mechanical things. But now I can just look at something and know how it should work, what parts aren't functioning or need to be replaced, that kind of thing." He nudged Rowan with his elbow. "You should say what you've observed, and what you can do."

Rowan stood up. "I started to see this emerging as the plague was burning itself out. People started asking me about strange experiences, things they were seeing or feeling that didn't make sense or that scared them. They *knew* things without being able to explain how, like what other people's thoughts or feelings were, or what their intentions were. Some people have talked about being able to detect when others are lying. Other people have an uncanny rapport with animals. Often, it's something they had flashes of before, but now it's more...permanent. More strong."

Jack looked around; some people were nodding excitedly, while others were frowning. Several were darting glances around the room, as if plotting the best escape route. He was tempted for a moment to lower his shield of light, but decided it would be foolish, given the evidence of strong emotion in the room. He turned back to Rowan.

"Do you have any theories as to why this is happening?"

Rowan looked at Layla and smiled crookedly. "At first, I thought you were all losing your freakin' minds." A smattering of laughter greeted her words. "Then, it started to happen to me. I can *see* what's wrong with people. Medically, I mean, disease states or malfunctions. Diabetes, heart disease, tumors. It started when I would touch a patient. Now, I just have to look at someone and...ask, I guess. Ask for the information. Layla's the one who came up with a working theory."

Jack turned to look at her, and didn't have to ask. She met his gaze steadily.

"I think it's intuition. I think those of us that survived are evolving, or have evolved. I think we're a new species of human, and that our brains have adapted to accommodate intuition as a true sixth sense."

Her words were met with dead silence and stillness, a collective holding-of-breath. Then, from the back of the sanctuary, a voice spat: "That is Satan talking! Evolution is a myth, and the Godly know better than to believe in it!"

Jack turned around. An older, graying man was on his feet, a younger woman with a pinched, hunted face beside him, and their joint emotions overrode his cloak of light. *Outrage, defensiveness, righteous and fanatical belief, and fear, fear, fear.* Without a word, Layla put her hand on his arm, and his feelings were once again his own.

From a place of calmness, Jack regarded them. Suddenly, he knew just what to say and how to say it. "This is frightening for all of us, and none of us know what to think. I'm afraid that Satan has a hand in it, too. But we have to put aside the fear so we can talk about all the possibilities. If we don't speak of things we fear, the fear grows worse, and the thing may take on greater significance than it deserves. We all know this."

He paused, focused on the man, and found the balance he sought between kindness and implacability. "We will listen to your concerns with respect. Will you listen to others with that same respect?"

The man blustered up, out of life-long habit. "I will not listen to blasphemy in silence! And shame on you for suggesting I do!"

"Then you must choose to go. We need everyone we can muster. There are so few of us left to rebuild. But we must begin as we mean to go on. We can't go forward stifled by fear. You're free to choose your course." Deliberately, he turned his back on the pair, and sought Layla's gaze. "Please, go on."

Her eyes flickered between him and the couple, then she squared her shoulders and looked around at the other congregants. "Some of us have already talked about this, which is how we started to form a theory. Intuition can be experienced in many different ways – some people get hunches, or see patterns; others feel the emotions of others; some people experience physical sensations like chills, or a certainty in their guts; and there are some rare souls who are spiritually attuned."

She looked around the room, then glanced back at Alder with her eyebrows raised in question. He shrugged in answer; clearly, they were looking for someone who wasn't here, perhaps someone who fit the latter description she'd offered. Then, she looked at Jack, and her chin tilted at a defiant angle.

"I've been privileged to meet a few true spiritual intuitives. They're some of the strongest and most fragile people I've ever met. Some of them can communicate with people who have passed beyond the veil." She looked around the room, and sorrow settled on her face, a mask that aged and burdened her. "I imagine it would be a very painful time to have that particular ability."

Every head in the room bowed, and Jack felt their collective loss like a tsunami. He did cover his ears this time, and squeezed his eyes shut, and focused on nothing but his cloak of God Light, the Light of Christ that surrounded and protected him. Layla's hand landed on his shoulder; he knew it was her because he didn't have to struggle any more. She was shielding them both, and she had been all along. He had no idea how to deal with that reality, how to incorporate it into his spiritual foundation.

Jack lifted his head and scanned the crowd again, noting the tears, the despair, the despondency. They needed to focus on action, not loss, at least for the time being. He stood up, and flipped open his notebook. "Alright, everyone, let's do this: We need to inventory two things – what people's experiences have been, and what their skills are. You've already started to talk to Rowan about your experiences, so let's keep on that way. I'll start talking to people about what they can do – hobbies, skills, jobs – all that. Before we go any farther, do any of you have medical training of any kind – first aid, CPR, anything?"

From the back of the sanctuary, a soft dreamy voice answered. "Well, I grow medicinal herbs, and I make tonics, tinctures and teas with them."

Jack squinted. A woman was walking up the center aisle, backlit by the brilliant sunshine coming through the windows in the foyer. He blinked a few times, and not for the first or the last time, wondered if he was losing his mind.

She looked like every clichéd, idealized depiction of an angel Jack had ever seen. Soft, pure blonde hair floated around petite shoulders. A face of delicate, otherworldly beauty was set in a serene expression. She was tiny in stature, and her small feet hardly seemed to touch the carpet as she glided towards them. Her hand fluttered to her cheek to brush back a wisp of hair, and she smiled gently as she came to a stop in the midst of the group.

"I also grow medical marijuana," she announced. "And to borrow a phrase, I see dead people. But please don't ask me to speak with your loved ones. If they want to communicate with you, they'll let me know."

She may as well have lit a string of fire crackers. The room buzzed and stirred around her like a rattlesnake disturbed from a nap. Jack looked to Layla, but she was looking at Alder, who looked grim. He left Rowan's side and bounded down the steps to their mysterious visitor. Escorting her back to the front of the sanctuary to rejoin his sister, he didn't hesitate to place his body between the woman and the group; protectiveness radiated off him like an aura.

Layla stood up again, "Everyone, this is Verity Brooks. She used to supply many of our area naturopaths and herbalists with their medicinal supplies. And as she so precipitously announced..." she glanced wryly at Alder and Verity, "...she has some other skills as well."

"Why would you do that?" Jenny's mother was on her feet, her face stricken. "Why would you tell us you can talk with people who have died, then tell us not to ask you about it? It's cruel!"

Verity blinked. "I'm so very sorry," she said slowly. "I wasn't trying to be cruel. I was just telling you the truth. The dead only communicate when they want or need to. It can't be forced or coerced."

Jenny's mother slid into the aisle, and started creeping forward. Hope and desperation fought on her face. "But you could tell me if Jenny was alright. You could tell me if she was with God, or..." Her voice trailed off, and she stopped walking, listing to the side, hands wringing.

Alder shifted his body in front of Verity, but she sidestepped him and walked to Jenny's mother with fairy-like grace. She reached her hands out and stilled the painful wringing. "Of course she's alright. All souls return to the Divine One, at least eventually." Her eyes went unfocused for a moment, and her face seemed to glow with ethereal light. "Your daughter didn't linger. She's at peace."

Jenny's mother started sobbing. "She's with Jesus? She's with the Savior?"

Verity reached up and touched the other woman's cheek with a hand so delicate, it looked transparent. "If that's what she expected in the Time outside of Time, that's what she's experiencing."

A commotion at the back of the church pulled Jack's attention away from the astonishing tableau. The older man and woman who had protested before had stood, and were shuffling hurriedly out of the pew they'd been seated in. The man glared at Jack.

"Did you hear that?" He hissed. "The 'Divine One' – not God! She claims she can speak with the dead – she's a demon! A tool of the Devil!" He seized the woman's arm as soon as they were in the aisle, and they both hustled out without a backward glance.

Jack was starting to feel like he was in a marathon episode of the Twilight Zone. He turned back to Jenny's mother and Verity. Jenny's mother had taken a step back, her face wrinkled in confusion, and she was looking back and forth between Verity and Jack.

"What does that mean? Those don't sound like Christian teachings."

Before Jack could form a stumbling reply, Verity answered. "The Time outside of Time transcends religious teachings. Christianity isn't wrong. It's just not all there is. We participate in our reality when we rejoin the Divine One, just as we participate in it on the Earthly plane."

Jenny's mother took another step back, then another. She was gazing at Jack now, her broken heart in her eyes. "I don't know what to think. I don't know what to believe." Her face crumpled, and she started to sob again. "Help me."

Jack looked around. Confusion. Anger. Fear. Weariness. He was losing this group, before it had even formed. There was just too much, too much for them to assimilate on top of their grief and the changes in the world. He closed his eyes and prayed, for guidance, for wisdom, for the right words. When he opened his eyes and lifted his head, Layla was standing in front of him. She looked as exhausted as he felt, but she reached out to rest a hand on his forearm, offering her help, her strength.

Jack knew, then, what he had to do.

He smiled at her and patted her hand. "Thank you." Then, he lifted her hand free and turned to face the people, many of whom were on their feet ready to flee, many of whom were crying quietly. He deliberately let his cone of God Light thin to near non-existence. Then, he began to talk, meeting the eyes of each person there one by one, letting their feelings guide his words.

He spoke of their fears, their doubts about finding the strength to go on. He spoke of their secret wishes for death, so they could rejoin the loved ones they were incomplete without. He spoke of hunger and deprivation, and the sure knowledge that worse was to come. He spoke of spiritual doubt, the fear that what they'd been taught had been wrong, that God had forsaken them.

Finally, he spoke of the guilt they were all feeling. "What if we've all been kept alive for a purpose? Why us, and not them? Are we supposed to feel special? Or is this penance, a terrible burden, punishment? I don't know. I don't."

Jack hung his head for a moment, thinking of all the beautiful souls who had left them, and struggled with his own unworthiness. Why, God, *why*? Why leave such an imperfect soul behind? Am I forsaken? *Am I?* He wanted to demand an answer from God, and wished he knew how.

Layla's hand, on his shoulder, again. He knew she could feel what he was feeling – she shared this skill, it made so much sense, explained so much – and he felt a flash of the most intense shame he'd ever experienced. For her, of all people, to witness his naked humiliation, his spiritual doubt.

Layla's hand fell away, and he dared a glance at her. She had bowed her head and shut her eyes, affording him the only privacy she could. He recognized the respect, but didn't know if he could forgive her for what she'd seen in the first place.

Shaking himself, Jack looked up, looked around at the faces that were all turned towards him, all waiting. They were poised on the fulcrum, prepared to take his direction. All he had to do was decide how to direct them. It struck him, then, the *power* he could wield if he chose.

Even he, who had never craved or sought authority, was tempted.

Another hand lighted on his opposite shoulder, a butterfly touch. Verity. She gazed up at him with eyes so blue, eyes that *saw*. He would have known that, would have sensed it, even in the time before the plague.

"The Archangels are arrayed with you," she said, her voice a soft, musical lilt pitched only for his ears. "Michael, who guides those seeking a new path. Raziel, who helps you know Divine guidance. Zadkiel, who helps you hold mercy and compassion towards yourself and others, and let go of judgments. They're here. Their wings are locked around you, right now."

Jack felt the hair on the back of his neck rise. With her touching him, he could almost see them, shimmering celestial beings of unspeakable power and beauty, encircling them both. "Do they have instructions for me?" he whispered. "A message?"

A grin of impish glee lit her features. "Yes! Well, it's from Raphael – he's here for Rowan – but he says," she dropped her voice to a lower register and intoned, "'With great power comes great responsibility.' He says he's not going to get into a debate about who said it, Stan Lee or Voltaire, because they were both paraphrasing Jesus anyway. But, yeah. There you go." She winked at him. "Raphael's a real joker."

Verity's hand fluttered away from his shoulder, and Jack blinked. He no longer had the impression he was surrounded by powerful angelic beings, but he wasn't sure he was completely back on the planet yet. The exchange between them had taken mere seconds, but everything felt different. At least for now, the path was clear.

The group in front of him was still poised, still waiting. Jack took a deep breath. "Here's what we have to do: Learn. Listen. Help each other." His eyes met Layla's. "Survive."

THIRTEEN
Naomi and Macy: Manitou Springs, CO

Naomi smoothed her hand over Macy's forehead and pulled the blanket up to snuggle it under her chin. She leaned to kiss her daughter's forehead. "Sleep and sleep, honey. Big day tomorrow."

Macy's eyes were already fluttering heavily. "Yup. Our big adventure. Love you, Mama."

Naomi brushed the silky skin of Macy's cheek with another nuzzling kiss and closed her eyes, breathing in her warm, familiar scent. Moments like these were an oasis of right in a world gone wrong. "Love you too, baby girl. I'll finish up and come to bed in a little while."

She could tell by Macy's breathing that she was asleep before she reached the door of the bedroom. Persephone jumped up on the bed and settled in to keep vigil – she rarely left Macy's side these days – so Naomi waited for Hades to follow her into the hallway, then pulled the door shut and headed into the living room with the big dog trailing behind her.

They had been hunkered down in this house for three days. Naomi had broken in to five houses in the vicinity of their disabled truck before she found one that was deserted, or rather, free of corpses. If anyone was left alive nearby, they weren't interested in making contact, which suited Naomi just fine. Several times a day they heard a motor bike, sometimes near, sometimes far. She couldn't be sure it was the same bike she'd heard the day they escaped the gang, she didn't know if those people would still be looking for them, but it was safer to assume both were true.

They had passed the days resting, re-grouping and on Naomi's part, reconnoitering. Two days ago, she had left Macy in the care of the dogs and had slid through neighborhoods until she reached the spot where Manitou Avenue joined Highway 24. From there on, there was only one way to Woodland Park: through the narrow pass with its steep, high canyon walls.

Not only was it blocked, it looked like a riot had occurred. Vehicles were piled on top of each other – several 4 wheel drive trucks had tried to crawl around or over the top of the jam – and many of the vehicles had been burned. Those that weren't damaged by fire had been looted. Worse, there were bodies everywhere, some still in the vehicles, some reduced to disintegrating piles of rags and putrefying flesh on the road.

Naomi hadn't seen anyone, but she had literally crept backwards until she was out of sight of the pile-up, so great was the threat she sensed. There was no way she could take Macy through that. They would have to find another way.

And they had.

Naomi stepped into the living room, and her eyes locked on the pile of supplies in the middle of the room. Sinking onto the couch, she wrapped her arms around herself, squeezed, and started to rock. Now that Macy was asleep, she could give in to the terror she had been trying to hide all day.

"I cannot do this. I can't. I can't I can't I can't I can't." It was such a relief to speak the words, to let her face twist and the burning tears fall. "I want to go home. I want Scott, and I want to go home, just want to go home…"

The plan they had settled on was extreme, but try as she might, Naomi couldn't think of something better: They were walking out; hiking, actually, over some of the toughest trails in the region. Macy had come up with the idea. They had hauled all the books they'd brought with them out of the back of the truck — Naomi hoped something familiar would comfort her daughter — and after a day spent reading, Macy had held up Piper's old trail book.

"We could hike out, Mama. We could take trails all the way into Cascade." Her delicate finger traced the route on the map. "We could start out on the Barr Trail, connect to the French Creek Trail, then the Heizer Trail, which goes right down into Cascade. I bet we could find a car to use there, to drive the rest of the way. Do you think that would take us past the traffic jam?"

Naomi examined the route Macy had pointed out, looking for a flaw in the plan, because…well, because back-country hiking was not part of her skill set. "It doesn't look like the French Creek Trail and the Heizer Trail actually intersect. I don't have enough experience to just wing it, honey. The few times I've hiked, I just followed the person I was with." And gasped and wheezed, and wondered why she had ever agreed to such madness.

"It says right here that you just follow the pink or orange ribbons on the trees to the Heizer trail."

Naomi took the book from her and read for a moment, then handed it back. "It also says that Barr Trail is one of the most difficult regional trails because of the elevation gain. It climbs 3,800 feet in the first three miles."

Macy stared at her for a few moments, then narrowed her eyes. "You're planning to go home."

"It's the only thing that makes sense, honey. We need to be somewhere safe, somewhere you can rest and recover."

"You promised daddy. You lied."

The accusation made Naomi's temper fray along the edges. "I did not lie. He couldn't have known what things would be like."

"He knew exactly what it would be like! I heard him talking to you – he said the city was the most dangerous place to be, that people would be looting houses and killing each other! Those people that tried to stop us – that lady – she wanted to take me. What if they find us?"

Her words dumped adrenalin into Naomi's bloodstream, but she managed to maintain a calm, rational tone. "Even if I had experience, neither one of us is physically prepared for a hike like that. I'm overweight and out of shape, and you're still terribly weak."

"It's only about ten miles. The book says people can walk about two miles an hour. We could get there in a day."

Naomi raised an eyebrow. "You carried two loads of supplies in here last night, then slept through your dinner. You really think you can walk for five hours, with that kind of elevation gain? Really?"

Macy had thrown herself back against the pillows of the couch, skinny arms folded across her skinny chest, tears flooding her eyes. "You lied to Daddy. And Piper will look for us at the cabin. You could at least think about it."

"I will," Naomi had soothed, sure she was lying again, and reconciled to that fact. "I'll think about it, honey, I promise."

But she'd kept her word, in spite of herself. The idea kept creeping back in, as she considered and discarded their other options. Rampart Range Road was out – she wouldn't risk taking them anywhere near where they'd been ambushed. Old Stage Road was equally problematic – too close to Fort Carson's refugee camps and NORAD, which surely had become a military stronghold with a patrolled perimeter. Besides, with the rains they'd been having, she couldn't be sure either of the precipitous dirt roads were still passable.

Then there was the problem of transportation. The truck had two flat tires. She was sure the spare was in good shape – Scott had maintained their vehicles meticulously – but she just had the one, and she'd never changed a tire in her life. Abandoned vehicles were everywhere, but if she didn't have a destination in mind, it didn't make sense to risk the noise a vehicle would make, the attention they would attract.

Piper was the clincher. Macy was right; if Piper was alive, she would look for them first at the cabin, Naomi was sure of it. If she didn't find them there, she would head for Colorado Springs, and run into the same dangers she and Macy were facing now.

She had capitulated late in the afternoon of the second day, and to her consternation, Macy had sobbed with relief. "Oh, Mama, I've been so scared you'd say no! We have to get to Woodland Park, and I have to get to the cabin. I just...have to."

Cold, cold, streaking down her spine and clenching her stomach in a fist of ice. Naomi ignored it. She was learning to ignore a lot of things, like anything she didn't have the resources to deal with in a given moment. Ominous pronouncements from her daughter. Bizarre mind-melds with her dog. She forced a light tone and ruffled Macy's hair. "Then I'll find a way to get you there."

A promise which had brought her to this point, sitting on a couch in some stranger's house, rocking and sobbing like a child while she stared at a pile of supplies she needed to carry into the mountains.

Hades whined softly and pressed up against her leg. She wrapped an arm around his chest but avoided looking directly at him; every time she made eye contact with one of the dogs, her perception shifted and wobbled. The sensation was weaker with Persephone, but still very real. Naomi snorted. As if she knew what "real" was these days. Surreal, she was becoming quite conversant with.

She pressed the heels of her hands to her eyes and heaved a few more deep, shuddering breaths. Then she swiped the tears off her cheeks and stood up.

"Miles to go before I sleep," she muttered. She had started talking to herself more and more lately, which didn't even worry her, given the weirdness with the dogs. She moved to the pile of supplies on the floor for one last winnowing before she started stuffing it all in a backpack.

She hoped they would make it in two days but was planning for four, packing nutrient-dense food and layers of clothing, a single sleeping bag for them to share, and the single-person pup tent. Macy was so tiny right now, they would both fit easily. She didn't think water would be a concern – they could replenish their supply at No Name Creek on the first day, French Creek the second day. They were still getting water out of the taps, but Naomi didn't know how water sanitation worked, so she had been using the water purification drops from Scott's camping supplies for the last several days. The first-aid kit, fire-starting materials, Scott's hunting knife, the hatchet, rope, her shotgun and the handgun. All the ammunition. Food for the dogs. The trail book, a compass and a map.

And that was it.

With the exception of the sleeping bag and the tent, she had gotten it all into a single pack. Macy wouldn't be carrying anything except an umbrella that could double as a walking stick. Naomi sat back on her heels and took deep breaths to ward off another crying jag. Such a huge pack when she thought about carrying it. Such a tiny pack when she thought about walking into the wilderness with her frail daughter and two animals who were completely dependent on her.

Marked trails or not, Naomi had no illusions about the danger of what they would be attempting. She had lived in Colorado all her life, and knew how quickly the unprepared could get into trouble, even on well-used, popular trails. Every year, search and rescue teams were called in to save someone who had tried to rock-climb wearing flip-flops, or summit Pikes Peak supplied with a camera, a granola bar and a bottle of water.

She had been reading the guidebook over and over, but all it did was terrify her more. So much to remember, and it was all alien to her. Scott and the girls were the campers – she had always sent them on their way with homemade cookies and a pot of Irish stew, then gone off to get a pedicure and meet girlfriends for lunch. Now their lives depended on her remembering to make noise while they walked to scare off bears, or how to identify edible plants if something went wrong and they ran out of food, or how to filter and disinfect water when the purification drops were gone.

A skittering thump at the sliding glass door and a low whuff from Hades startled a muffled shriek out of her. Ares was dangling by his claws halfway up the screen door. She hadn't seen him since they had arrived; he had huffed into the overgrown back yard to sulk, and when he didn't show up for food, she assumed he'd found good hunting as well. She met his green gaze without thinking, and the world shifted.

The room brightened immediately, but she was seeing it now in shades of black and white, enriched by deep blue and purple tones. There were three flies in the room - she could hardly rip her gaze away from their buzzing movements. Reflexively, she clapped her hands over her eyes; at the screen, Ares let out a startled yowl and dropped to the ground.

Naomi peeked at him using her peripheral vision. He was stalking back and forth in front of the door, every hair on his body bottle-brushed out, and when her face turned towards him, he hissed. He hadn't hissed at her since she brought him home from the shelter. Naomi approached the door warily and opened it for him. He stalked past her, took his usual swipe at Hades, then jumped up on the back of the couch.

Well. If she didn't fear she was losing her mind, this would be fascinating. Keeping her face averted, she gave Ares a stroke along his spine, then headed to the bedroom she was sharing with Macy, Hades a faithful shadow. Sleep seemed unlikely, but she needed all the rest she could get.

As if she'd set an alarm, Naomi opened her eyes when the sun was only a lighter gray color in the eastern sky. She roused Macy, and they dressed in the clothes Naomi had set out, whispering in the chill quiet. She fed the animals a generous breakfast, then braided Macy's hair while she ate. The tiny slice of familiar soothed them both. When she was done, she left Macy to finish eating and called Hades to her.

She had planned to rig a pack of sorts for him with the tent and the sleeping bag, using bungee cords to secure them on either side of his torso. To her relief, he seemed agreeable to carrying it, standing patiently while she fussed with the cords. Then she stood and shouldered her own pack, slinging her shotgun over her shoulder by the strap. The handgun was in a mesh side-pocket of her backpack; she could get to it fairly easily, though it wouldn't be a quick draw.

By the time she finished, Macy and Persephone were waiting by the slider, Macy carrying the umbrella and Persephone dancing her perky ready-ready-ready-to-go dance. And just like that, they were out the door.

Ares slunk out between their feet, and Naomi watched him go, wondering as she always did if they would ever see him again. She looked at Macy and forced a grin, in spite of her pounding heart and dry mouth. "Wagons west!"

They slipped through the neighborhoods quickly and silently, walking single-file with the dogs flanking them, using whatever cover was available. Naomi had warned Macy about the need for speed and silence on this part of the trip; they were in far more danger here in Manitou Springs than they would be when they were on the trails. And in spite of the soft, rosy light of dawn and the lilt of birdsong, a subtle menace pervaded the morning.

Naomi had estimated they were just under a mile from the trailhead, and she didn't want to stop until they got there. She scanned their surroundings constantly, using all of her senses to *feel* their way along. A few times, she was sure she felt eyes on them, and she hurried their pace until the feeling passed. They were just over what she guessed was the half-way mark when Hades trotted in front of her and stopped dead. He didn't growl, but he wouldn't move, and Naomi didn't hesitate.

She hustled Macy and Persephone up between two houses, while Hades brought up the rear. She hid Macy behind a shrub, then slid to the corner of one of the houses to look out. Hades moved to stand beside her, and that was when Naomi heard it. Faintly at first, then getting louder, the buzz of a small motor – the same one she'd heard a few days ago, she'd swear it.

She looked back at Macy, and put a finger to her lips. Then she returned her attention to the street, rested her hand on Hades' head, and allowed his perceptions to augment her own.

The buzzing was suddenly much louder, and the smell of death was overwhelming. There were people dead in both the houses they were standing between, she was sure of it. An involuntary shudder ripped down her spine, and she struggled against the urge to hurry Macy away. Ironically, Hades' instinct to stay and hide overrode her mother's instinct to distance her daughter from death.

The buzzing got even louder, and Naomi retreated back behind the shrub with Macy. She positioned her body in front of her daughter, and Hades lay down in front of them both. When the buzzing was nearly on top of them, Naomi looked down and shut her eyes, willing herself into invisible stillness.

She didn't see the little dirt bike flash past, but Hades did. She had a quick impression of noise, the stink of the bike, and a man riding it. Whether he was young or old, she couldn't begin to say, but the danger clinging to him was unmistakable. They stayed where they were until Hades stood up and looked back at her. She nodded, helped Macy to her feet, and they crept on their way.

It was so hard not to hurry, but Naomi forced them to maintain a slow, steady pace. She was winded already and they hadn't even left the city yet. Macy's energy seemed good, but she knew how quickly that could change. They were nearly at the trailhead when a sudden rustling from the underbrush beside another house startled all of them.

A small dog charged at them, barking wildly. A Brussels Griffon — Naomi automatically identified his breed. His desperation preceded him like a punch — his people were dead, he was hungry and alone for the first time in his life, and his mind was nearly unhinged by terror and loneliness. Naomi knelt down to shush him, heart pounding in response to both his fear and her own. They could not afford this kind of commotion.

The tiny dog wiggled against her, licking and whining. Hades was rumbling a low growl, and Persephone was rigid with disapproval, staring at the newcomer. Macy knelt too, and stroked the small, quivering dog.

"Mom. We have to take him with us. Look at him — he's so scared."

"No." The word barked out of her, part pain, part instinct. Naomi took a deep breath and softened her tone. "Honey, no. Feel his body – he's older than he looks, feel how frail his bones are. And..." She hesitated, not sure how to tell Macy what she *sensed* without starting a conversation she wasn't ready to have. "He's immature in temperament, too. He's been spoiled and pampered, and he's not trained. We can't take him. I'm sorry."

"But Mama-"

"No." Naomi stared into Macy's eyes, willing her to understand. "You used hard truth on me. You reminded me about my promise to Daddy, and about Piper meeting us at the cabin. This is hard truth. We can't rely on him. He'll endanger us."

Before Macy could reply, Hades' head lifted, and his body stiffened. Naomi lifted her head as well, and heard it: The buzzing motor bike. Coming closer. Fast.

She scooped up the little dog and hurried them all behind the house he'd come from. Sensing the increased level of excitement, he started wriggling and yipping, oblivious and eager to play. Naomi cupped her hand over his muzzle and tried to reach out to him with her mind, tried to calm him, to convey the danger they were in, but her attempt just confused and excited him more. His wriggling increased, and he started trying to nip at her quieting hand, his yips turning to sharp, agitated barks.

Sweat greased Naomi's forehead and coated her from her underarms to her waist. The buzzing motor bike was deafening – she couldn't tell if she was experiencing it through Hades, or if it was that close – and there was no time, no time.

She turned her back on Macy, closed her hands over the little dog's skull and around his neck, and twisted with all the sudden violence she could. A sudden yelp, a ripple of crunches, and his body jerked once. She felt his life lift like smoke through her hands.

She kept his limp corpse resting across her knees. Macy was crying silently behind her; she could feel her daughter's anguish as clearly as she could hear her hitching breaths. The buzzing motor bike was still close, but the danger seemed remote now, compared to what Naomi had just learned she could do.

She wanted to vomit, wanted to join Macy in tears, and would not permit herself either luxury. Those reactions belonged to the old Naomi. The soft-hearted Naomi, who had never touched another living creature in anger, not in her whole life. From one heartbeat to the next, she had become someone she no longer recognized.

The buzzing drifted farther and farther away, and finally retreated out of earshot altogether, and still they sat there. Naomi knew they needed to move, knew that the higher the sun climbed, the hotter the first part of the trail would be, but to move meant looking into Macy's eyes. What would she see there? Disapproval? Fear? Hate?

Macy's hand landed on her shoulder, soft and light as a bird. When her little arms slid around Naomi's neck, and her soft baby cheek, tacky with dried tears, pressed to her mother's, Naomi heaved a breath that seemed to fill her body all the way to her toes.

"Honey, I...I couldn't quiet him...I didn't know what else..." Naomi shut her eyes and heaved another enormous breath. "I'm so sorry," she whispered.

Macy's arms tightened for a moment, then she rose and slid around in front of her mother, lifting the little dog's body into her own arms. "Mama, I know. And he's okay. He really is. He's with his people now."

Naomi couldn't change the subject or pretend to misunderstand. Not anymore. "Are you sure?"

Macy held her gaze steadily. "Yes. They waited for him. And now they've all gone on together."

"You could see them. Like you see Daddy."

"Yes."

They regarded each other from this new place, in the bright light of day. Then Naomi took a deep breath and plunged. "I feel things. Like danger, or the right thing to do." Another deep breath. "And I can share senses with the animals. I can smell and see and sense things through them."

Macy's face bloomed into a delighted smile. "Seriously? Mama, that is so cool! Way better than seeing dead people!"

Her disgruntled expression made Naomi laugh, and the lift in her heart gave her the courage to take the next step on this awful journey. She reached out and lifted the little dog's corpse out of Macy's arms, and laid him gently on the ground. "I'm glad he's okay. I'm glad you could tell me that. Now we need to go."

It took two blocks for the wobble in her knees to steady, but by the time they finally reached the trailhead, she had refocused her attention on the next step in front of them, and the next. She didn't have time right now to wonder about this evolution of self, this woman who could kill with her bare hands to keep her daughter safe. Later, when they were safe, she might figure out how this new truth fit into the compassion and tenderness she had always thought of as her core.

At the Barr Trailhead, a sign provided them with dire warning just in case they weren't aware of what they were getting into. Naomi turned her back on it, and they sat in the shade to eat a quick snack and drink some water before they started on the trail. It had taken them longer to get here than Naomi had planned; the sun was searing, though it couldn't be more than 8:00 am.

In the parking lot, several abandoned vehicles stood, leaves and debris accumulated around their tires. For the first time, it occurred to her that other people might have hiked out this way, for the same reasons they were. What if they met them on the trail? She felt another spike of anxiety, then pressed her lips together hard.

Without making a big deal out of it, she took the handgun from the backpack, checked the safety, and put it in the pocket of the sweatshirt she had tied around her waist. Macy didn't comment, but when Naomi looked up, she was watching her with eyes that were just a little too big.

Half an hour ago, Macy had seemed otherworldly, wise, possessed of a mysterious knowledge that rendered her ageless. Now, she was just a little girl who was tired and sweaty, and overwhelmed by the changes in her mother.

The remedy for that was a taste of practical, bossy Mama. Naomi nudged Macy's half-eaten granola bar towards her mouth. "Come on, chop chop. Eat that up so we can get going." She poured some water into her cupped hands for the dogs, adjusted Hade's pack, and winced her way back into her own backpack. She was pretty sure the shoulder straps had rubbed her raw already.

By the time her preparations were complete, Macy was ready to go. Naomi gestured for her to take the lead – the better to keep watch for the signs that she needed to rest – and without looking back, they walked into the wilderness.

FOURTEEN
Grace: Colorado Springs, CO

Grace opened her eyes and found herself staring up at pipes and ductwork. A tiny, grimy window set high in a cement wall struggled to let in light. She blinked once, and before she had moved a single muscle other than her eyelids, her brain started outlining the situation and cataloging facts.

A basement. She didn't recognize it. The cement was crumbly, but the foundation wasn't stone, so an older home but probably not historic. Her nostrils flared; she could smell urine and feces, strong but not overwhelming, and under that, damp and mold.

The silence was absolute. She couldn't detect a single sound other than her own soft breathing. She would need to move to learn more, and slowly, cautiously, she turned her head away from the window.

The simple movement sent pain spiking through her neck and shoulders and ripping down her back. She shut her eyes for a moment, trying to breathe away the pain, but a sudden rustling and an unfamiliar voice popped her eyes wide again.

"Oh my god, you're finally awake. I thought they killed you."

A girl scooted out of the shadows towards her, and stopped a few feet away. She appeared to be a few years older than Grace, though it was hard to tell for certain – she was filthy, and it looked like she had been beaten. Bruises discolored both her cheeks, and one side of her mouth was swollen, giving her face a lopsided appearance. Her blonde hair hung in matted hanks around her face, and dried blood caked one ear and the side of her neck.

The girl slid closer, then wrapped her skinny arms around her knees and squeezed. "I'm Bri. That's short for Brianne – all my friends call me 'Bri.' I know we're not friends, but I've been sort of watching over you for the last two days, so I feel like I know you..." Bri shut her eyes and pressed her lips together for a moment. She took a deep, shuddering breath, and when her eyes opened, they were shiny with tears. "I'm talking too much. I do that. I really thought you were dead, but I was too afraid to check. You haven't moved in, like, hours and hours."

Grace scanned the room again. In a far corner, another girl was curled in the fetal position on a ragged comforter, knees drawn so close to her face, Grace couldn't see her mouth. Her eyes were open but blank, her face still, expressionless, serene. Bri followed her gaze and grimaced.

"That's Jen. She's...well, she's not okay. Not anymore. Back when she was talking, she said they got her a few days before they got me. I don't know how long ago that was. Maybe a month. It's easy to lose track of time."

Grace let her eyes complete the circuit of the room, noting a bucket in the farthest corner – probably the source of the smell she'd detected earlier – and a door in the wall behind Bri. She returned her gaze to Bri and tried to speak, but her throat felt like it had been glued together. She cleared it, tried again, and managed to croak, "I'm Grace."

Bri's smile was dazzling white in the dim room. "Grace. I'm so glad to finally know your name. Here, let me get you some water."

She scooted back into the shadows and returned with a milk jug half-filled with dingy water. "I know it looks gross, but it won't make you sick. At least it hasn't made me sick yet. I don't know where they get it – last I knew, nobody had running water. I'll help you sit up."

She put her arm under Grace's shoulders, the gentle contact so painful, Grace had to hold her breath against crying out. When she was finally upright, she released the pent-up breath on a whoosh of air and panted for a moment, watching stars dart behind her closed eyelids. Bri helped her tip the milk jug to her lips; the water tasted musty, but was so soothing against the tissues of her throat, she didn't care. When she was finished, she slowly and painfully pulled her legs into a crossed position and took stock.

Her jeans were filthy, and both knees were torn. Through the holes, she could see that her knees were scraped and had scabbed over. The front of her t-shirt was stiff with dried blood that had turned brown, and it looked like her arms and hands had been coated at one time, though much of it had flaked away. Her upper arms and wrists were black and swollen with bruises, though her questing fingers told her that her face was uninjured except for a scabby scrape on the right side. Worst of all, though, was her back; she felt like she'd been skinned from neck to heels.

Time to get some answers. She refocused her attention on Bri. "Who are 'they?' Who's keeping us here?"

Bri blinked, clearly a little startled by Grace's brusque tone. "Uh, I'm not really sure. I think they're kind of a gang – some of them talk like they're in the military. Do you want something to eat?"

"In a minute. Do you know where we are? Are we somewhere in Colorado Springs?"

Bri blinked again, then smiled at her sadly. "You think you can escape. Jen thought the same thing. And she ended up like that." She nodded her head in the other girl's direction. "It's better if you don't fight them. They don't hurt you so bad."

Okay. Grace took a deep breath. She needed to know, even though this line of questioning was likely to lead to a place she would not like. "What happened to her?"

"She fought them." Bri frowned. "She fought them, every time they came for her. At first, anyway. I tried to tell her, but she wouldn't listen. She said she'd rather die fighting than submit to them. I told her she should just try to make them happy. I figure if I make them..." Her face spasmed. "If I make them like me, maybe they'll let me out..."

She fell silent for a few moments, completely absorbed in picking at a scab on her elbow, and Grace stared at her. Was she really hearing what she thought she was hearing?

Bri sighed and looked back up. "Then Jen got tired, and I think they hurt her. Broke some ribs or something. So she tried reasoning with them. She was really smart. She said she could help them, help them figure out how to survive. They just laughed at her. They don't bother her anymore, now that she's like this. But they don't feed her either. I've been trying to get her to eat some of my food, but..."

The other girl's evasiveness – not to mention her habit of leaving sentences unfinished – was starting to drive Grace nuts. She needed hard facts, not euphemism. "When you say she fought them, and when you say 'they don't bother her anymore,' you mean they were raping her, but they're not doing that now that she's unresponsive."

"What?" Another series of blinks made Grace wonder if Bri wasn't too far from joining the other girl – Jen? – in catatonia. Either that, or she wasn't the brightest of bulbs. "Well...yeah."

"They have been raping you, too." She paused and took a deep breath. Then another. Surprising, how hard it was to ask. "And they raped me before they brought me here, didn't they?"

Bri's eyes slid away, and Grace could tell she was going to evade the question. She felt a surge of impatience and tried to control it. This was data she needed. The last thing she remembered was riding into the outskirts of the city with Quinn. After that, it was just flashes: fire, guns popping, dirt in her mouth, the smell of sweat.

"Look. Just tell me."

"You don't remember?"

"If I remembered," Grace gritted out, "I wouldn't be asking."

"Oh. Right. Well." Bri's eyes flitted to hers, touched briefly, then flitted away. "Yeah. They dumped you in here with your clothes, but you were, you know. Naked. I tried to clean you up – your back is all skinned up, I guess from the road – and then I dressed you."

"And you could tell they had raped me." It was easier to say this time around.

Bri nodded without looking at her. "Yeah. I...I cleaned you up. I could tell."

Grace didn't ask her to elaborate. It wasn't that she was afraid to know – it was just that the details were irrelevant. She was aware that her unemotional response wasn't necessarily healthy, but she needed to function right now, and emotions would only hinder her. She thought for a minute, then decided to try a different approach. "How did you end up here? What happened?"

Bri brightened and sat up straight. Like most survivors of trauma, she wanted, *needed*, to tell her story. "I was a freshman at UCCS – I lived in the dorms. When the plague hit and they quarantined the city, I just stayed there 'cause I didn't have anywhere else to go – my mom and dad live in Grand Junction." Pain flickered across her face, and her voice faltered. Then she took a deep breath and went on. "I haven't heard from them in a long time – my dad said they were going to come over and stay with my uncle in Denver, so they'd be ready to get me when they lifted the quarantine, but, well, you know. I don't know if they tried to come get me, or if..."

Bri looked away this time, throat working. She looked up at the ceiling and blinked rapidly to dry the tears that had welled in her eyes, and went on. "I left when we ran out of food – I was with a guy from my dorm, and we were going house to house. If everybody was-" She hesitated over the word, "- dead, we'd stay. Eat whatever food was left, then move on. We were working our way towards Fort Carson. Tyler – that's the guy I was with – had heard there was a refugee camp there. We never made it."

Grace leaned forward intensely. "Tyler. What happened to him?"

Bri's eyes dulled and lost focus. She turned her profile to Grace, and for long moments, she was silent, staring at nothing. She shuddered once, then turned back to Grace, eyes still lost to a scene Grace could not witness.

"They broke into the house where we were staying in the middle of the night – we had a fire going in the fireplace, and I guess they saw the light or smelled the smoke or something. One of them grabbed me. A couple other guys grabbed Tyler, and said he had 10 seconds to decide – join or die. Tyler tried to ask who they were, and before he even finished talking, one of the guys shot him, right in the head." Bri started rocking gently, arms clenched around her knees. "His brains blew all over the wall. They were laughing about it, and they took turns trying to say what the pattern looked like while the others took turns...with me..."

Her voice trailed off, and she shuddered again. For the first time, it occurred to Grace that she should pity this young woman. She hesitated, then reached out and rested her hand on Bri's forearm, squeezing to convey comfort, all the while aware that the gesture was calculated. The place in Grace where feeling lived was stone cold, a total black-out. But she needed Bri, needed her knowledge and possibly her cooperation.

"I'm sorry," she said, hoping she didn't sound as stiff and insincere to Bri as she did to herself. Bri swallowed repeatedly, fighting for control, then started sobbing, a soft, hiccupy sound. She slid closer to Grace, and pressed into her side, burrowing for comfort like a child. Grace put her arm around Bri's shoulders, rocking and patting, while her mind raced and calculated.

Apparently, she'd landed in the worst-case scenario of every post-apocalyptic movie she'd ever seen. They were being held by a group of military or wannabe-military men, being used for sex, discarded when they were no longer useful. If Quinn had been taken with her, it was likely he'd been killed – Grace couldn't imagine him capitulating without a fight. That thought made her heart beat heavily, a deep, uncomfortable thumping in her chest, but otherwise caused her no pain. She rubbed at her chest absently, and kept assembling the facts she had, working towards a big picture.

Fighting was out. She wasn't afraid to defend herself, but she wasn't a fool. She believed Bri was right – fighting would only make them hurt her more, and even a minor injury could be life-threatening under the circumstances. Not worth the risk.

She could pretend to be like Jen, pretend the trauma of the experience had unhinged her mind, curl up in the fetal position and drool until they ignored her. But that would require Bri's cooperation, and Grace wasn't sure she could trust the other girl to maintain the deception. And it wouldn't get her out of this room.

Grace did not like the option that was emerging.

Bri's sobs gradually subsided into ragged breathing, punctuated by the occasional wet sniff. Finally, she sat up, pushing back a hank of hair.

"I'm sorry," she said thickly, her stuffed-up nose making her little-girl voice sound even more pitiful. "Crying doesn't help, either, but sometimes..."

Grace twisted her face into an expression she hoped conveyed understanding. "It's okay." She counted to ten silently. "Look, I need your help. I need you to tell me what to do when they come for me."

Blink. "What do you mean?"

"I don't know what to do. I've never had sex." Well, that wasn't quite true now, was it? Grace pressed on. "I just want to know what to do, so they don't hurt me."

Bri didn't need to know the rest of her plan. The older girl might be right about the futility of fighting, but she was wrong about their chances of winning over their captors. The facts were clear: they had used Jen up, and weren't even attempting to keep her alive any longer. They would use Bri up, and unless she escaped, they would use Grace until she died as well.

Therefore, she had to get out of this room. To do that, she had to submit. Once out of this room, she could look for a way out, a hole, a weakness in their security. She had to be patient, had to bide her time, had to wait for opportunity, had to endure.

On some level, Grace knew she should be shocked at herself. She had always believed there were lines that shouldn't be crossed, even if you had to die defending those lines. Right at this moment, though, Grace couldn't think of a single thing she wouldn't do, if it meant getting out. Survival was everything.

She pressed on. "Look, I get the mechanics. I just don't know the specifics." When Bri continued to look blank, Grace felt her face heat, embarrassment brushing her with brief feeling. She stifled it, and sought for words to make the other girl understand. "How do I make them like me? What do they want me to do?"

"Oh!" Under the dirt, Bri's face bloomed pink, and she actually giggled. "It's pretty simple, really. I mean, it's just sex. You just go with the flow. And do what they tell you to do. They only rape you if you fight them."

Grace stared, trying to comprehend the way this girl had twisted what was happening to her. Was this how a breakdown began, a desperate rationalization to make unbearable circumstances bearable? Pity spiked through the buffer around her feelings, followed closely by guilt.

Bri was another human being, a young girl with a family to search for and a life to salvage out of this mess. She had taken care of Grace, had watched over her, yet Grace had no plans to help her. In fact, she would throw her under the bus if she had to. Grace took a deep breath and willed herself to coldness. Willed herself to feel nothing, and shut down that line of thought. Guilt would cripple her. Bri would cripple her.

Survive.

"Tell me what they will want me to do. Specifically." When Bri giggled again and started to turn away, Grace grabbed her hand, trying not to grate the other girl's bones together. "I'm serious." She gentled her tone. "Please. I need to know."

Blink. Blink. "Okay." Another giggle. "This is weird, but okay..."

Bri giggled almost constantly at first, using phrases like "You know what," and, "You know where," but as she warmed to her subject, her shyness dissipated. Before this, Grace deduced, she had been a young woman completely comfortable with her body and her sexuality. Another stab of pity threatened the numbness she'd wrapped herself in; she didn't doubt those days were long over for Bri.

By the time Bri wound down, Grace just wanted to curl up and sleep. She felt sick to her stomach. Part of it was hunger, she was sure. Mostly, though, she didn't know how she was going to bring herself to do the things Bri described. Her stomach heaved, and she moaned softly, sliding down to her side and closing her eyes.

"Oh!" Bri rubbed a hand down her arm. "You must be starving – I should have had you eat something before we started talking." She slid into the shadows and came back with a grimy Tupperware bowl. "It's beans – I think they mixed them with some kind of Hamburger Helper, but there's no meat. It's not good, but it will fill you up."

The contents of the bowl were stone cold, the beans caked with strange, congealed spices. Grace swallowed hard and forced herself to scoop some out with her fingers and take a tiny bite, forced herself to swallow, forced herself to not vomit it back up. One bite after another, she finished the bowl. As the nourishment brought her blood sugar back up, she became aware of Bri's repeated, nervous glances at the window. The angle of light had changed, probably indicating late evening.

Grace used her finger to clean the last of the spices out of the bowl. "What is it?"

Bri was rocking again, arms locked around her knees. "They'll come soon. They come every night about this time."

Grace's heart launched into a hard pounding, so hard it hurt her ribs. "Okay. Okay." She realized she was almost panting and tried to slow her breathing. "Anything else I need to know?"

Bri scooted close, and this time, Grace leaned into the comforting contact. "Just go away, if you can. Go somewhere in your mind. You need to listen at first, so you know what they want, but when they start... Just leave it behind." She smiled sadly. "I always go to Christmas morning, you know, before we open the gifts? So many pretty packages, and the smell of my mom's cinnamon rolls..."

Grace clung to Bri's descriptive ramblings as the minutes ticked by, listening as she segued into other holidays, trying not to listen for a sound at the door. When the rattle and scrape came, it was almost a relief. The door swung open. Grace jumped violently, then scrambled backwards. She hadn't intended to, and the part of her mind that was still capable of observation noted that fear could make you lose control of your body in so many ways.

A man stepped into the dirty yellow light coming from the window, and she almost laughed. Why, he wasn't so bad. He was just a man, not very tall, probably not much taller than her own 5'4". He had on digital army fatigues and a Broncos baseball cap, and when he smiled, his teeth were straight, white and even. Then Grace got a good look at his eyes.

Terror dried her mouth and made her heartbeat surge. There was nothing in his gaze that recognized her as human, as another person. His gaze swept over her, assessing, and Grace was reminded of the way the judges at the state fair had looked over her horses. She was nothing more than livestock to him.

"Well, well. Looks like the cowgirl finally woke up." He didn't even glance at Bri, though his next words were clearly directed at her. "Looks like you got her all fixed up for us, and fed her, too. You get the night off, just like I promised."

It took a minute for the import of his words to sink in, then Grace's eyes flew to Bri. The other girl was staring miserably at her kneecaps, rocking faster and faster, her face twisted with guilt. So. Kindness hadn't been Bri's motive for helping Grace. She was just desperate for someone to take her place.

Ironically, the betrayal calmed Grace. She was truly on her own now, no need to hinder herself with worry about Bri. She took a deep breath, and felt her brain shift into a kind of turbo mode she had never experienced before.

She locked in on every detail about the man, from his ramrod straight posture and the proud tilt of his chin, to the pristine cleanliness of his hands, to his almost dainty combat-boot-clad feet. In the space of several heartbeats, the pieces had fallen into place, the picture had formed in her mind, and she knew just how she needed to play this to make him think she wasn't a threat.

"Please." Her voice shook, and that suited her purposes just fine. She kept her tone high, almost childlike. *I'm dumb,* she willed him to believe. *I'm no threat, just a stupid girl.* She blinked at him, and silently, viciously thanked Bri for teaching her that trick. "I'll do whatever you say. Please just don't hurt me."

His smile broadened, and dimples appeared in his cheeks. "Well, cowgirl, I'm glad to hear you want to cooperate."

He walked over to Jen, and without any apparent malice, kicked her once, twice, right in the face. Her head cracked back into the cement wall, and she gave a gurgling sigh, but otherwise did not react. Blood began to pump from her flattened, crooked nose and her front teeth were gone, her mouth a scarlet and black gaping hole. The man looked back at Grace.

"This one fought all the time. Some of the guys like that, but I like 'em soft. Willing. You understand me?"

Grace clung to calculation by the wispiest of threads. The need to scream, vomit, run, cry, beg, anything anything anything to protect herself from the violence she had just witnessed came perilously close to overwhelming her. One question kept her on track: What did he want?

Again, she felt a shift, as if time slowed and facts clicked. He wanted to be big. He wanted her to be small. He wanted her to fear him, because to him fear was respect, and respect was everything. All of these things were so clear, in the tilt of his head, the twist of his mouth, the way he watched her for her reaction to what he had just done.

She gave him the reaction he expected, letting tears well up and flow. "I won't fight," she choked. "I promise."

And she didn't fight, not as he dragged her to her feet and out the door, pausing to lock it behind him. Details leaped out at her as he hauled her along: their room was part of a much larger, lavishly furnished basement – further proof of their lack of value to these men – clean, comfortable rooms were just a thin wall away. A daylight window caught her eye, overgrown with vines, but a possible escape route. At the top of the thickly carpeted stairs, another door opened into a kitchen. Grace had a brief impression of cheerful red apples as he pulled her through, then they were outside in the fading sunlight.

Grace could smell a fire on the soft breeze, smoke, meat roasting, and the faint scent of gasoline. Houses crowded closely around them, older, well kept, with mature landscaping and tall trees. They were in the city, she would guess, not one of the outlying suburbs, probably not far from the downtown area. Grace snuck a look over her shoulder to note the proximity of the mountains and her position relative to them.

The man yanked her along, walking swiftly through back yards and alleys, until they reached a spacious open area. Lake to the south, big bonfire already roaring near the shore, and an open area crowded with campers and tents. Grace swept the area again, squinting, and felt her stomach clutch.

Unbelievable. Memorial Park. Her eyes flew to the north, and picked out the statue of the firefighter in the near-dark. Even if Quinn had survived, their rendezvous was in the middle of a gang-controlled refugee camp.

The man hauled her across a street drifting with trash. In addition to the fire, she could smell people now, too many people, living too closely together, with inadequate sanitation. Here and there, a small fire flickered and a shadow moved, but for the most part, the camp was still. Not deserted, she realized, but hidden, crouched, a stillness that prayed not to be noticed. The people in this camp were afraid; she could feel it as clearly as she felt her own heart pounding in her chest.

The bonfire was their destination. Camp chairs circled the blaze, and outside of that, concentric circles of trash and debris told of the activities that went on here. Empty beer cans and liquor bottles, empty cartons of cigarettes, junk food wrappers, and bones. Lots and lots of bones, in various sizes, most of them charred. Grace recognized a cat's skull, and the beans in her stomach lurched and rolled.

Over the fire, the haunch and leg of something big was being turned on a spit by a boy about 9 or 10 years old. He stood as far away as he could get from the heat, shielding his face in the crook of the opposite elbow, and after a while he switched hands, rubbing and blowing on the hand that had turned the spit. Before he hid his face again, Grace saw that his eyebrows, eyelashes and the front of his hair had been singed away.

The man let go of Grace's arm and put his hand on her shoulder, pushing her to her knees. "Wait right here. If you move or try to run, I'll kill you. But first, I'll make you wish you'd never been born."

As threats went, it wasn't original, but it was effective. Grace dropped her head, nodding her acquiescence. She watched the man's little combat boots stride away and lifted her head the slightest bit, trying to take in everything that was going on around her.

Three men were sprawled in the camp chairs, one of them dozing, the other two staring into the flames. All of them were armed with multiple weapons – knives, pistols, and larger, complicated-looking firearms. Grace knew next to nothing about guns, but they looked like the military-style weapons she'd seen on TV or in the movies. The men did not speak to each other.

Her eyes slid to the activity on the other side of the fire. A semi truck trailer sat with its doors open about 20 feet beyond the flames, and in the back of the trailer, a man sat in a lawn chair. Two men stood on the ground on either side of him, fingers on the triggers of the guns they held, waving people forward one at a time from a line that snaked back into the darkness between the nearby campers.

The people – mostly men – that came forward were all carrying something: a handful of canned goods, a jumbo pack of toilet paper, an amber bottle of prescription medication. As they stepped up, another man would take whatever they had to offer, examine it, then either nod and set the offering in a pile at the seated man's feet, or shove it, with sharp words, back at the person who had brought it.

Some kind of barter system, Grace thought, and squinted at the seated man, trying to see him more clearly. That would make him the leader. Making sure he was visible, demonstrating his power, receiving his due. At this distance, it was impossible to make out his features, and Grace dropped her head back down, certain her curiosity would be noticed and discouraged if she kept her scrutiny up much longer.

Besides an older woman or two in the offering line, she hadn't seen any other women, and no children, other than the singed boy that tended the fire. She watched out of the corner of her eye as the line dwindled and finally petered out. The man in the back of the semi trailer stood, stretched, and leaped lightly to the ground. He said something that made the man who had been assessing the goods bark with laughter, and together, they swung the doors of the trailer shut, securing them with a heavy padlock.

Grace's heart stuttered into a faster rhythm as he strode towards the bonfire, trailed by his bean counter – the guy was actually carrying a clipboard, which struck Grace as exceedingly incongruous – and both the trigger-fingers. The little man returned to the circle of light, and sat down in the chair closest to her, leaning to give the side of her head a stinging swat.

"Behave." He said mildly, before he settled back with his dainty feet stretched out in front of him.

Grace could no longer control the shaking – her arms, her legs, her stomach – all jumping uncontrollably. Her vision started to dim, and she realized she had been holding her breath. She released the pent-up breath as quietly as she could and focused every bit of her considerable brain power on breathing.

In. Out. In, deeply, filling her lungs with oxygen and life. Out, completely, breathing out carbon dioxide and toxins. She sent her concentration then to her adrenals, little glands on top of her kidneys, and willed them to stop firing, willed her lower back to relax, willed herself away from fight-flight-or-freeze and back into observation. She could not afford to check out, could not afford to disassociate from this situation, as easy as it would be to let that happen. She needed to understand these men.

They were talking when she tuned back in, reporting in to the boss one by one. She listened fiercely, determined to remember every tiny detail. She had not fully assembled the big picture yet, so she had no way of knowing what information was relevant – best to just store it all.

The bean counter was in mid-report, consulting his clipboard, describing the goods they were most in need of: prescription medications, especially antibiotics, antidepressants and painkillers, water purification systems or chemicals, gasoline generators, and medical personnel. That last made Grace flinch; not a good sign, when human beings were discussed as goods to be procured.

The sleeping man roused around long enough to detail the surveillance measures he was in charge of, speaking of watchers at high points in the city and on the roofs of the buildings downtown, and of monitoring the activity of soldiers from Fort Carson. He finished his report and was already dozing back off before the man next to him began to speak.

In a voice so soft it was hard for Grace to hear, the giant with the huge shoulders and the shaved head spoke of keeping peace and solving disputes in the refugee camp. His efforts in organizing the creation of new latrines, as well as teams to clear the nearby houses of the dead were succinctly described before he concluded his brief report.

By contrast, the wiry, dark-haired man next to him couldn't shut up – talking in a rapid-fire mix of Spanish and English so heavily laden with military jargon, Grace didn't understand half of what he was saying. She thought he had something to do with explosives – he talked with great enthusiasm about taking out two Humvees from a convoy out of Fort Carson with a single IED – but the rest of what he said was beyond her.

When he finally wound down, the little man next to her began to speak, and it took Grace a few moments to realize he was talking about her. About the night she had been taken.

"The kid she was with rode off – Larry swears he winged him, but Larry swears that every time someone gets away. He probably ran back out on the plains where they came from, which is too bad." He gestured with his little foot at the haunch of meat turning over the fire. "This is the last of the horse the cowgirl was on – we could have used the meat."

When his words sank in, Grace couldn't help herself; she leaned over, and quietly vomited up every bit of food and water she had consumed. If the men noticed, none of them said anything. She couldn't stop the memories that had started flashing like a slideshow – blood, coating her hands; blood, coating Button's chest; her rattling, wheezing groan; her terrified, rolling eyes. And Quinn's hoarse scream.

Grace straightened back up when she was empty, and kept her eyes down, resolutely down, desperately down. She would not look at what was left of Buttons, roasting on that spit. She could not feel right now. To feel was to die, she was sure of it. Breathe. In. Out. Focus. Survive.

When the buzzing in her ears quieted, the little man was still talking. "Dumb bitch got the cowgirl here all fixed up, which was our deal – she gets the night off. And I don't know about ya'll, but I'm getting sick of her anyway. She tries too hard." He raised his voice to a falsetto. "Do you like that? Should I do it again? Just tell me what you want – I'll do anything." A few of the men chuckled, and the little man continued in his normal voice. "Anyway, the fighter should be dead in a day or two at the most – I helped her along, and we'll let her rot right where she's at. It'll keep the other two in the right mindset. And that's about it."

Attention turned to the boss. He hadn't spoken a word or asked a question while his generals reported in, and he sat now – still flanked by both of his silent thugs – hands templed by his mouth, lightly stroking back and forth across his lower lip. After a moment of silence, he spoke in a soft, southern drawl.

"Good. Let's get the show on the road, then."

All of the men rose. A couple of them disappeared into the shadows and came back carrying bottles of beer. The thugs set up a card table, and the boy deftly swung the haunch of roasting meat away from the fire. The little man came to stand beside her.

"Okay. Who's first?"

Everything inside Grace went still. This was it. She ticked through the key points Bri had told her, then discarded them. She'd heard what these men thought of the other girl. Trying to please them wouldn't help her. Grace kept her eyes down, panting, teetering precariously on the edge of self-control. Her original plan was no good, and she had no time to come up with another one.

The sleepy man yawned and stretched, then shuffled over. "I'm in. I like 'em fresh. Dumb bitch is gettin' skunky."

"I'm in, too." The loudmouth stepped forward, and ran his hand over Grace's ponytail, then down her cheek. "Pretty dark hair and eyes, just like I like."

She jerked away. She couldn't help it. The action earned her another glancing slap from the little man, and a satisfied snicker from the loudmouth, who reached to caress her again. This time, she forced herself to hold still, though every muscle in her body shook with the effort.

A coin flashed in the air, the loudmouth crowed in triumph, and Grace's mind went completely blank.

It happened, right there in front of God and everybody, only a few feet away from the bonfire. Worse than the attack, worse by far, was Grace's inability to control her own mind. The blankness came and went, interspersed with flashes of terrible clarity: The flinching, crawling of her skin as the man roughly tugged her clothes off. One side of her naked body freezing, the other crisping. The casual eyes watching, as men munched on roasted horse, laughed at each other's jokes and played cards. The smell of beer and spearmint on the loudmouth's breath, the tearing pain, the humiliation that permeated all but the deepest, steel core of who she was.

At the end, Grace turned her head away from the ridiculous, blissed-out contortion on the loudmouth's face, and her eyes focused on the boss.

He sat on the fringes, not taking part in any of the activities, not watching the rape, though his eyes brushed by occasionally. He was watching his men, listening to their byplay, analyzing their interactions and actions. His eyes lingered on the sleeper, sprawled out and open-mouthed in his camp chair, and those eyes narrowed slightly before moving on. Every once in a while, his gaze would sweep slowly around the darkness beyond the light of the bonfire before returning to his men.

Click. Click, click, click.

Grace's brain detached from what was happening to her body as the puzzle pieces snapped together.

This was just a show. This wasn't about lust or debauchery. This was a display of power, a method of maintaining control. She and Bri were just props – here's what'll happen to your women if you cause any trouble – just as the boy turning the spit was an example as well – look what we'll do to your children if you don't do what we say.

Before the next man took the loudmouth's place, Grace's realization had set her free.

Not entirely, not a retreat into the oblivion of disassociation, or the comfort of memories like Bri had advised, but she was able to leave all but the most rudimentary connection to her body behind. She moved her arm when it got too close to the fire, shifted her body when she was told to, but the bulk of her focus spread outward in concentric circles.

She memorized every word she heard. She noted which men lost at cards, which ones drank too much, and which ones just pretended to drink. She watched how they interacted with each other, noticed where there was camaraderie and where the joking stopped just short of disrespect. And she analyzed which of them took more than one turn with her, and which had to be goaded into it, which ones touched her with unnecessary roughness and which were covertly gentle.

By the time it ended in the wee hours of the morning, Grace had the beginnings of a plan.

FIFTEEN
Naomi and Macy: On the Heizer Trail

The early morning sun was glowing softly through the red walls of the tent when Naomi's eyes snapped open. The sound came again, a rasping swish, a rubbing along the side of the tent. Naomi propped herself up on an elbow, trying to listen past the thunder of her heart. Macy slept on, oblivious to the sound of something investigating the perimeter of their tiny, flimsy shelter, looking for a way in.

At their feet, Hades' head lifted, and a basso growl rumbled in his chest. Persephone's head rose as well, though she didn't growl. The rubbing stopped, and a moment later, a familiar, obnoxious "meow" made Naomi collapse onto her back, breath bursting from her chest in relief.

Macy stirred. "Was that Ares? Is he back?"

Naomi rolled on her side to face her daughter, eyes assessing, voice light. "Sure sounds like it. That was his 'I want breakfast NOW!' meow, I'm sure of it."

Macy giggled and stretched, speaking through a giant yawn. "Gosh, mom, he's going to be ticked when he finds out you didn't pack any kitty chow." Though she'd slept from early evening until well past dawn, her eyes were ringed with black and sunken. She cuddled close. "I'm not ready to get up yet. Let's pretend I'm a baby."

Naomi closed her eyes, resting her cheek on Macy's soft, bright hair, their bodies curled together like halves of a whole. She had played this game with both her girls – it was their way of saying they needed to be held close, to be cuddled and babied, just for a little while. Macy still asked to play at ten. Piper had rejected the game at six. So different, her girls.

As always, thoughts of Piper made her rub the center of her chest; where there had been connection, now there was just slicing pain. She wasn't gone, like Scott. But something was dangerously wrong.

Macy's voice was soft. "You're thinking of Piper, aren't you?"

Sensitive little soul. "Yes." Here in the tent, so far from anything resembling the "normal" she had known, it was safe to speak of it. She shifted to look at Macy's face. "Can you feel her, honey? I've tried, but she's...disconnected. I don't know what it means."

Macy's eyes were distant and peaceful. "She's locked deep inside," she said in a voice that didn't sound like her own. "She's being forged by the fire. She'll either burn or be made new."

The hair on Naomi's nape rose, but she was finished with avoiding the changes in both of them. It took too much effort, and it didn't make those changes go away.

"I wish I could feel her like you do. I wish I could *know* things, so I'd know if she's going to be okay."

Macy's eyes shifted to gaze at her steadily. "Nobody can know what will be, not for sure. I think I know what *could* be, sometimes. But that can change really fast." She was silent for a moment. "I miss Daddy. I can't see or feel him as well anymore."

"Any idea why that is? Do you think he's moving on, to the next place? How did you say it – stepping through the veil?"

"No. I still feel him with us, but I haven't seen him since we left home."

"Does it hurt him, staying here? Is it dangerous?"

"You mean, could he get stuck? Yeah. But I don't think he will."

Naomi twirled a strand of Macy's soft hair around and around her finger. Now that she wasn't freaked out, this was fascinating. "Why not?"

"Because he's not like the ones that are stuck."

"Do you see them a lot? Ghosts?"

"Now I do. Before everybody got sick, I couldn't see them, but I could feel them. I just didn't know what it was."

"Is it scary?" Naomi conjured a combination of *Poltergeist* and *Sixth Sense*, and she frowned. "They can't hurt you, can they?"

"No, they can't. Sometimes they startle me, but they're not really scary. Most of them are just moving on – they haven't stepped through yet. There have been a lot of them lately. I've seen a couple that were stuck though, and they're sad. They don't really understand what has happened to them."

"Wow." Naomi stared at the ceiling of the tent, thinking it all through. "So you've changed and I've changed, but in different ways. I wonder if other people are different, too? I wonder if Piper is?"

"She is." Macy looked up at her. "She's going to be really different when you see her again, Mama. You'll be different, too."

"It makes me sad, that you know these things." Naomi's throat tightened. "All I ever wanted was to give you a safe, happy, normal childhood. It's all I ever wanted for both you girls. I can't give safe or normal to you, not anytime soon."

"Mama. It'll be okay. I promise." Then Macy smiled her sly smile. "But if you want to make it up to me you could use your animal voodoo on a beautiful white Arabian horse and tell her she's mine forever."

Naomi laughed and relaxed again, curling around her daughter, closing her eyes, enjoying the warmth and relative comfort of their little tent world. Just a little while longer, and she'd get up and get them underway. Goodness knew, they could both use the rest.

They had been walking for two days. Macy tired so swiftly, even though she tried to hide it. The first day had been the worst. As advertised, the first section of Barr Trail was brutal, especially for a recovering invalid and a plump housewife. By the time they reached No Name Creek, they had been advancing in ten step increments: walk for ten steps, rest for a few minutes, then walk on.

Naomi would have stopped right there, but she didn't want to make camp next to a water source – who knew what animals might visit. They had spent the night in the ruins of the Fremont Experimental Forest, pitching their tent by the concrete foundation of a long-gone building. The manmade structure had comforted Naomi as she laid awake most of that night, starting at every sound and trying not to think about how easily they could die up here.

The second day had been better, thank goodness. The hike through Hurricane Canyon Natural area and behind Mount Manitou was so much easier, she had actually looked up once or twice to appreciate the spectacular beauty of their surroundings. It had been such a wet spring, the ripening summer was lush and full, right on the edge of blossoming into its full beauty. And quiet – Naomi had never known such quiet. Whenever they stopped to rest, the only sound was the soft hush-hush of wind and the trilling call of an occasional bird.

As the day wore on, the trail got faint and harder to follow. When they finally reached the sign marking the way to Heizer Trail, Naomi had used the last of her courage to hike from one faded pink or orange ribbon to the next. A hard scramble up a steep slope, and they were home free: at the top of the trail that would take them down into Cascade. Macy had fallen asleep in a patch of shade and Naomi had pitched the tent right there. Better another night in the wilderness than to press on and risk further weakening Macy. She figured they only had about three miles to go, most of it downhill

Today. They could be in Woodland Park and at the cabin today, if all went as planned. Naomi smiled. It might be a little early to feel triumphant, but she allowed herself the indulgence. Fat and inexperienced she might be, suffering from weeping blisters, raw chafing and a multitude of screaming muscles, but by thee gods, she would get them through this.

They drifted and dozed a while in silence. Every now and then Ares would yowl, but letting him in was out of the question – their little tent wouldn't survive a brawl between a Rottweiler and an exceptionally large, half-feral tomcat. After a while, Macy stirred and spoke again.

"I wish I could talk to the animals. I could get Hades to eat my vegetables."

Naomi yawned and tweaked her daughter's nose. "He'll eat just about anything – I don't think you need any special powers to pull that off. And I don't really talk with them, not in words. I feel what they feel, and sometimes I sense what they can sense."

"Can you do it on purpose?" Macy snapped her fingers and made a kissing sound, and Persephone left Hades' side to wriggle up between them, quivering with delight. She cuddled the little dog close, and Persephone licked her chin over and over in an ecstasy of love. "Can you tell what's she's sensing right now?"

Naomi titled her head to the side, considering. Why not? Now that she had accepted this as her new reality – if she was nuts, so be it – it could be incredibly useful to connect with the dogs at will. "I'll try."

Naomi focused on the little dog, stroking her golden butterfly ears, and immediately felt the shift. *Love, such love.* That she had been expecting, and protectiveness towards Macy. Persephone's head lifted, and she gazed into Naomi's eyes. *Anxiety.* As Naomi watched, Persephone repositioned herself, curling up against Macy's midriff. She met Naomi's eyes again and whined softly.

Anxiety. Separation. Fear.

Naomi frowned, trying to determine what was agitating the little dog. Gradually, she became aware of a scent, something...not right. It wasn't decay, nor was it dirt or filth of any kind. Naomi groped for a word to describe what she was perceiving. It was... imbalanced... toxic... dysfunctional.

Macy heaved a deep sigh, hugging Persephone closer, and Naomi stared at her in sudden, horrified comprehension. What she was smelling was *disease*. And it was coming from Macy.

She sucked in a huge breath, her mind scrabbling like a rat in a maze. Could the plague have damaged her body somehow? She had to get her to a doctor, get some tests run. Maybe she should just check her into a hospital until they figured out what was wrong–

The air left her lungs explosively as the reality of their situation kicked her in the chest. No doctors. No hospitals. No help.

"Mama." Macy's voice was soft and calm. "Mama, look at me."

Naomi met her gaze, and there was just no way she could hide her terror. With shaking hands, she caressed her daughter's hair, her soft face, her shoulder, everything she could reach. She could feel her face twisting as she tried to control her emotions, and pulled Macy close, sandwiching Persephone between them. Macy's body was warm, but so, so frail, and Naomi thought her heart would burst in an agony of fear.

"Baby girl. You need a doctor. We need to find a doctor. You just need some medicine and some time, and you'll be right as rain."

Macy leaned back and looked at her. She didn't ask "why," didn't question her mother's statements. She knew. She *knew*. "We'll be in Woodland Park today."

Naomi couldn't stop stroking her, frantic to reassure herself. Her little girl. She was here, and warm, and alive. She had survived the plague, she would survive this, too. Her baby. "Will there be a doctor there? Is that why you wanted to go so much?"

Macy smiled, but her eyes were solemn. "There will be people who can help us. I know that for sure."

Naomi shut her eyes. It was so hard to keep breathing. She forced herself to move, suddenly desperate to get underway. "Let's get our breakfast and go. I'll take care of the dogs while you go to the bathroom."

She crawled out of the tent, her movements stiff and jerky, a combination of overused muscles and terror. She understood, now, Persephone's unwillingness to leave Macy. The little dog never let Macy out of her sight. Even now, Persephone trotted on Macy's heels as she made her way to the area they'd designated "the bathroom." Naomi tilted her head back and glared up at the rich, blue sky.

"You listen to me," she hissed. "You listen, God. You will not take her from me. You will not. You will not."

The mantra ran non-stop through her head as they ate breakfast and packed up, and as they hiked through the morning. She managed what she hoped was some natural-sounding conversation with Macy, who was enchanted with the views – Pikes Peak, huge boulders, and when they reached the top of Cascade Mountain, the North Pole Amusement Park and the city of Cascade, far below.

You will not. You will not. She couldn't make it stop.

"Look, Mama." Macy was pointing. "That's 24, isn't it?"

"It is." *You will not.* She was terribly afraid she would start screaming it soon. She had to hold it together. "Looks like it's blocked heading down into Colorado Springs, but not going the other way. We'll know more when we get to Cascade."

She decided it was a good spot for a snack, a drink of water, and a rest. The dogs settled down in a patch of shade, and Macy curled up with them, feeding them little bites of the granola bar she was supposed to be eating. Naomi sat down heavily on a cool boulder and pretended not to notice, for the time being, that her daughter's snack disappeared a delicate bite at a time between the two dogs.

Ares had been slinking along with them since they broke camp, ghosting in and out of the woods, and he slid to Naomi's side now. He hadn't asked for affection since the night she had inadvertently joined her senses with his, and it pleased her to be back in his good graces. Purring, he brushed back and forth against her leg and stroking hand, a blessed distraction. For the moment, at least, the mantra in her mind quieted.

She didn't let them linger for long. After just a few days in the wilderness, it was disconcerting to see the road, the cars, the silent and deserted amusement park, the reminders of the plague. It was hard not to hurry down the steep, wide switchbacks, but as on each of the previous days, Macy's early morning strength had given way to exhaustion, and Naomi slowed their pace to a crawl. Her own strength was faltering; she could feel it in the constant tremor in her legs, the ease with which she stumbled. She knew she couldn't carry Macy very far, and had to put off that moment, if it came, as long as possible. They stopped twice more to rest, and to eat lunch, before they arrived at the last switchback leading down to the trailhead. From here they could see houses through the trees, but before they stepped out of the cover of the pines, Naomi stopped.

Torn between the urge to hurry, hurry, hurry and reluctance to go on, she hesitated, debating. Just like in Manitou Springs, a subtle menace permeated the air; there were predators here, desperate people, she could feel it. Hades moved to her side, taut and alert, and she didn't need to *join* with him to know he sensed it, too. She reached down to undo the straps that held his pack on, and led Macy over to a relatively flat, open spot just off the edge of the trail.

"Macy, I'm going to go down with Hades first. I want you to wait here with Persephone and our pack until I come for you. I'll find a vehicle and bring it back, but if you hear a car or a truck, stay out of sight. I'll come get you." She smoothed her hand over Macy's hair. "You can rest and get some more to eat and drink, okay? I won't be long."

Macy's face was pinched with exhaustion and anxiety, but she nodded. Even though it was a warm mid-May day, she was shivering here in the cool shade. Naomi spread the sleeping bag out on the thick pine needles which covered the ground, then settled Macy on it, setting up the pack as a backrest. She zipped Macy's hoodie up to her chin, then took off her own sweatshirt and wrapped it around her daughter. Persephone curled against Macy's side, and Naomi gave the little dog a stroke along with silent instructions. *Keep her safe. Protect her.*

She hugged Macy, forcing herself not to cling, then stood. "We'll be back soon. Eat a little if you can, and try to sleep."

She picked up the shotgun, and instead of slinging it over her shoulder by the strap, tucked it under her arm. The handgun, she slid into her back pocket. Then she and Hades headed down to the railroad tie steps that marked the trailhead, Ares slipping along beside them.

She could go left, and uphill, or right and downhill. She chose downhill. The first house they came to seemed deserted, but Naomi couldn't see any vehicles. She started up the driveway, but a low growl from Hades commanded her attention. He was staring at the house, rigid with tension. He broke off his growl, glanced at her, then focused on the house again and resumed his rumbling warning.

Danger. As before, it wasn't a word but a feeling, and it made Naomi's heart pound heavily.

"Well. I guess that's clear enough." She swiped her sweaty palms on her jeans and repositioned the shotgun. "Let's go."

The connection between her and the dog remained strong as they moved on, but wasn't as overwhelming as what Naomi had experienced in the past. Her hearing and sense of smell were heightened, but it wasn't the sensory onslaught of before. As they walked, Ares slid up and down the bank on the downhill side of the road, crouched and slinking. Every time he appeared, she felt an echo of Hades' loathing. Given the chance, the big dog would happily use the nasty kitty as a chew toy.

They passed a couple more houses on the steep uphill side of the road, but didn't investigate. Naomi was really hoping they would find a vehicle parked alongside the road, preferably with the keys dangling from the ignition. She'd been thinking this over for the past several days, and she realized her best chance of finding what she was looking for probably meant finding a body as well.

Quite a few people had died behind the wheel, she had observed, though she wasn't sure why. Maybe they hadn't realized how sick they were when they got behind the wheel. Maybe they'd been trying to find help. Maybe they'd been in denial – it was human nature to pretend the unthinkable wasn't true. Whatever the case, Naomi just needed to find one who had shut the engine off first.

They slowed as they approached a cluster of houses on the downhill side of the road. Several vehicles were parked in the vicinity, and Naomi looked over at Hades. He was alert, but not growling. Moving as quietly as she could, she side-stepped down the hill until she reached the clearing behind one of the small cottages. Hades stuck close to her side as they moved around to what appeared to be a parking area shared by several houses. Two pick-ups, a mini-van, a tiny subcompact and a brand new hybrid. Bodies in one of the pick-ups and the subcompact that she could see for sure. She moved to the mini-van.

No body, and unlocked. She popped the door open, wincing at the loud metal-on-metal screech of hinges that needed WD-40. No keys. She eyeballed the cottage the vehicle was parked in front of. Did she dare go in, look for a key rack or a purse? She left the door standing open and moved to the passenger side of the occupied pick-up.

The woman had died wearing a soft pink robe and matching fluffy slippers. She was slumped to the side and her face was turned towards the driver's side window. Her purse sat in the passenger seat. A shopping list lay beside it, written on the back of an envelope: Cough syrup, milk, diapers, animal crackers. Naomi shut her eyes and swallowed hard.

She opened them again and focused on the keys dangling in the ignition. Decision time. The pick-up was just a two-seater; it would be crowded with her, Macy, the dogs, and if they could convince him to join them, Ares. To go looking for the minivan keys, or remove this sad, dead mother and get back to Macy that much faster? Her stomach tightened at the thought of touching the woman, but–

Hades gave a short, sharp bark, and Naomi whirled around. A girl was standing about 20 feet away, staring at Hades with glassy eyes. She was perhaps a few years older than Macy, right on the edge of adolescence, and she was filthy, wearing stained jeans and a discolored Denver Broncos t-shirt. She took a hesitant step forward, then another.

"Your dog is big. Is he nice?"

Naomi had to swallow several times before she could speak. "He is. Are you alone here?"

The girl didn't answer. She took another step towards Hades, holding her hand out. "Nice doggy. Will you let me pet you? You're a sweet boy."

Hades radiated caution and watchfulness, but he wasn't sensing a threat from the slowly approaching girl. Naomi tried again. "Are your parents still alive? Is someone taking care of you?"

"Nice doggy. That's a good boy. Do you want a treat? Want a chewie?" The girl didn't seem to have heard Naomi's question; she was focused completely on Hades. Naomi had a moment to wonder if she was mentally unstable when Ares came out of nowhere.

With a banshee yowl, he darted between the girl and Hades, every hair on his body bottle-brushed out. He hissed, yowled, and hissed again, his green eyes narrowed to glowing slits as he glared at the girl. Both the girl and Hades started back, then the girl made a short dash at Ares.

"Get out of here! Scat! Go on!"

Ares batted at the air and stood his ground. Hades growled, barked, then his head snapped up and he stiffened. He trotted swiftly to Naomi's side, and barked sharply at something behind her. Naomi whirled.

The boy stepped around the corner of the nearest cottage holding a baseball bat. "We won't hurt you. We just want your dog."

"My dog?" This was getting stranger by the minute. "Why on Earth do you want my dog?"

The boy was maybe 15 or 16 years old, and like the girl, hadn't taken his eyes off Hades. His grip tightened on the baseball bat, flexing it slightly into the air. "We're hungry."

My God. Naomi looked back over her shoulder. Ares was pacing between them and the girl, emitting a low, feline growl. The girl's eyes were full of angry tears now, and there was a long kitchen knife in her hand. Where it had come from, Naomi didn't know.

It would be so easy to do. Dogs were conditioned to trust humans, and had been for millennia. You could lure them in with a gentle tone, commonly recognized words of praise, and kill them before they sensed a threat. Lucky for them, Ares was by nature far more suspicious.

Naomi lifted the shotgun to her shoulder, pointed it straight at the boy's chest and clicked the safety off. She looked over her shoulder at the girl, and then back at the boy. Her legs were trembling violently, but the shotgun was rock-steady.

The boy flexed the bat again and took a step forward. Naomi sighted in, mouth so dry she could scarcely speak. "I will shoot you." Her voice shook so badly, it sounded like she was crying. Maybe she was crying. "I don't want to, but I will. I won't let you have my dog."

The boy lowered the bat. "It's just an animal. We're people. We're starving. Our parents are dead, and we've cleaned out all the houses around here."

"I'm sorry for that. I am." God, should she try to take them with her? She couldn't just leave them here, could she? She glanced behind her at the girl, who hadn't once taken her hungry eyes off Hades. Then she thought of Macy. She tightened her grip on the shotgun, and her voice came out steadier. "I have to take care of something, but I'll try to come back for you. Can you hang on for a day, maybe two?"

The boy didn't answer for several long seconds. Then, sullenly: "I guess."

"Good. Okay." Naomi lowered the shotgun slightly and snapped the safety back on. She slid the handgun out of her back pocket and held it so the kids could see it, then slung the shotgun over her shoulder. "I'm going to get this woman out. Then I'm going to leave." She hesitated, feeling more than a little ridiculous. "If either of you move towards me or my animals, I will shoot you. I'm a crack shot. I almost never miss. I mean, I never miss. Never."

Babbling, she thought hysterically. Teenagers always made her nervous. She closed her trembling lips firmly, and moved around the pick-up. When she opened the door, the smell of corruption made her eyes water and her nose run. She sucked in a deep breath of air and held it, using her free hand to grasp the collar of the woman's robe and drag her out.

The corpse thumped wetly to the ground. Naomi dragged the body clear of the truck, leaving a wet trail on the ground, checking the position of the children every few seconds. She let the woman's body drop, then moved back to the truck, grimacing at the condition of the front seat. She checked the minivan, then the other pickup, keeping her handgun at the ready, looking for something to throw over the ruined seat. She finally found a space blanket in the subcompact.

The boy and the girl watched her every move in silence, not offering to help. Every once in a while, the girl would lift a hand to swipe at the now-flowing tears, but she didn't seem aware that she was crying. Hades and Ares stood together by the bumper of the pickup, united for the moment by a common threat. Naomi covered the seat with the space blanket, then snapped her fingers at the animals. "Hades. Ares. Come."

Both animals obeyed at once, leaping into the cab of the pickup at her gesture. Naomi slid the shotgun off her shoulder and tucked it firmly between the top of the seat and the back window, checking to make sure the safety was still on. Then she stood there, feeling as lost as she'd ever felt.

She had no idea what to say to them. A part of her couldn't believe she was going to just drive away and leave these babies on their own, starving, reduced to hunting pets for food. Another part of her shut that line of thought down cold. What was her guilt, when she weighed it against Macy's survival?

She ended up not saying anything at all. She climbed into the truck and set her handgun in her lap. It took two tries to start the engine, and when it finally roared to life, she glanced one last time at the children but avoided making eye contact. There was nothing to say. She would either be back for them or she wouldn't.

Naomi crept out of the parking area, keeping the children in her peripheral vision until they were out of sight. Once she was on the road, she rolled the driver's side window down, trying to dissipate the smell. She was painfully aware of the amount of noise the truck made – in such a silent world, the sound of an engine would attract trouble from miles away. She drove the short distance back up to the trailhead, then parked the truck, pocketed the keys and shoved the handgun in her back pocket.

Hades was right on her heels as she ran up the path to where she'd left Macy. Her daughter was curled up, sound asleep, but Persephone was wide awake, rigid with tension until she spotted them. She wiggled and pressed close as Naomi first shouldered the pack then scooped up her daughter, sleeping bag and all, and headed back down the hill.

Hurry, hurry, hurry, her mind chanted. The kids might have followed her. Other people might have heard the truck, and already be on their way to investigate. Feet sliding on the scree, she slipped and staggered back to the vehicle, tucked Macy into the passenger seat and buckled her seatbelt. Persephone jumped in and curled up on Macy's lap, who slept on. Naomi struggled out of the backpack and threw it in the bed of the pickup.

Hades followed her around to the driver's side, but didn't jump in when she asked him to. Instead, he turned to face back down the road, alternately whining and growling. The hair on Naomi's nape prickled painfully, and she sharpened her tone.

"Hades! Up! Let's go!"

He obeyed, finally, crowding close to Macy but refusing to sit on the bench seat. It was then Naomi realized Ares had disappeared. "Kitty, kitty, kitty! Ares! Come on, kitty, kitty, kitty!"

She waited an agonizing minute, then two, then three. Then, despairing, she slid in beside Hades and ended up with his rear in her face. She gave his hip a shove, but the normally obedient dog didn't budge. He stared out the back window, growling louder now. Macy stirred and sat up, blinking in confusion.

"Mama? What's going on? What's wrong?"

Naomi's hand was shaking so hard, she had to steady her wrist with her left hand to get the keys in the ignition. She had no idea what was upsetting Hades, but she shared his anxiety completely. "I'm not sure, honey. Hades is sensing something. Slide down low in the seat and hang onto Persephone."

"Where's Ares?"

"I don't know. He was here a minute ago." She turned the key, then put the truck in gear and took off, gaining momentum as they headed downhill, searching the sides of the road for a flash of grey. "He saved us, honey. We ran into some...not-so-nice people, and he figured it out before Hades and I did. He saved Hades' life, I'm sure of it."

"No way. Seriously?"

Macy's look was so filled with disbelief, Naomi found a shaky laugh. "Seriously! I couldn't believe it! One minute we were – oh my God! Macy, get down!"

Three people, ranged across the road, two holding shotguns, one holding a shovel. Men, women, Naomi didn't bother to analyze. She crouched behind the wheel, shoved Hades down with all her might, and floored it.

They stepped easily out of the way. One – a woman – raised her shotgun to her shoulder, but didn't fire. Naomi flew by them, waiting, waiting for the boom of the shotgun, but it didn't come. She watched the rearview mirror as much as she dared, saw when the other person – a man – waved the woman's gun down, watched until she nearly missed a curve in the road, the tires squealing wildly as she jammed on the brakes.

Hades thumped heavily into the dashboard and scrambled to regain his footing. Macy had slid right out of her seatbelt and was crouched on the floorboards, clutching Persephone. A terrible sense of déjà vu gripped Naomi: this was just like their desperate flight into Manitou Springs. How many people was she going to have to run down or threaten to shoot before they made it to safety?

She drove on as fast as she dared, trying to remember the way out of the neighborhood, and failing that, just guessing by the sun and the terrain. Hades settled onto the seat beside her, and Macy was still on the floor, head pillowed on her arms, face hidden. When they reached Highway 24, Naomi sobbed aloud in relief.

Macy lifted her head. Her color was terrible – somehow gray and yellow at the same time. "Mama? Are you okay?"

No, she was not okay. She was pretty sure she would never be okay, not ever. Is this what survival was going to be like? Children killing family pets for food? Violent strangers ready to shoot before they'd even talked to her and determined her intent? Shouldn't people be helping each other? So far, she didn't have any reason to believe they would ever be safe again.

But she didn't say these things. Instead, she nodded, and forced her face to smile. "I'm okay, baby girl. I'm just so relieved 24 is open. It's clear as far as I can see."

They turned onto the highway, and Naomi accelerated until it felt like they were flying. Wind pounded into the cab through the open window, but she was afraid the smell would overwhelm them if she rolled it up. She reached down and tucked the sleeping bag more securely around Macy.

"If you're comfortable enough, let's have you ride right there. It's safer, and it gives Hades some room. Okay?"

Macy nodded and burrowed into the sleeping bag, covering her head against the wind. Persephone wriggled free and curled up against Hades' side, but her eyes never left the lump that was Macy. Naomi thought of Ares, alone now and with little chance of finding them, and her eyes welled with tears.

He'd be okay, she was sure of it – he was too savvy and too darn mean to die. But they had lost so much, the thought of never seeing him again teetered on the edge of unbearable. She could feel his ornery presence in her heart, next to the strength that was Hades, the sweetness that was Persephone, the pain that was Piper, the emptiness that had been Scott, and the glowing everything that was Macy. She sent a pulse of love and gratitude through that connection, and prayed it wouldn't freak him out too much.

The wind had hardly dried the tears on her cheeks when they were pulling into the outskirts of Woodland Park. It was disorienting to say the least, having spent three days walking, to traverse the eight or nine miles between here and Cascade so quickly. Naomi slowed the truck, scanning for threats, *feeling* her way along. Long before they arrived at the blockade at the intersection at Baldwin Street and Highway 24, she *felt* it.

She crept along, her eyes moving ceaselessly, then came to a stop well short of the orange sawhorses that had been placed across the road. One man stood in front of the blockade in plain sight, holding a shotgun at the ready. Two more men stood on either side of the road, sheltered behind parked cars but making no effort to fully conceal themselves. She looked over at Hades, who was on his feet again, staring intently out the windshield.

"What do you think, buddy? I'm getting 'wary but not dangerous.' And I can't *feel* any but these three, not right here. What about you?"

Hades looked over at the sound of her voice, and just like that, his perceptions were hers. He whined softly – she could feel his worry, how badly the encounter with the children had shaken his confidence, but his read on this situation reinforced her own. She put the truck in park but left it running. Then she reached behind her and pulled the shotgun free.

She stepped out of the truck with her shotgun in one hand, holding both arms up high. She wanted them to see that she was armed, but also that she didn't intend harm. "Hades, come."

The men shifted nervously when the big dog bounded out of the cab. Naomi left the door of the truck open and walked slowly towards them, Hades prowling beside her so close his body brushed her leg.

"I don't want any trouble," she called. "I'm looking for a doctor, or someone with medical training. My daughter needs help."

All three men shifted their weapons to the ready. Naomi stopped walking, and Hades' aggressive growl ripped out of his chest so loudly, Naomi jumped.

"Stop right there," the man in front said. "Is she sick with the plague?"

"No. She survived it." She saw the men exchange glances, and willed them to believe her. "We're from Colorado Springs. She got sick April 7th, the day after my husband died. I don't know what the date is, but that has to have been over a month ago. No one survives that long with the plague. But it did something to her body. She's..." Naomi's throat closed, and she had to clear it several times before she could go on. "She needs help. Please. Please."

The man in front squinted at her for a long moment. Then, he lowered his weapon. "She's telling the truth." He spoke over his shoulder to the other men, but didn't look away from her. "At least, she believes she's telling the truth." Then, to Naomi: "We don't mean to seem uncaring, but the plague has pretty much burned out here, and we need to protect our own."

"I understand." Naomi brushed Hades' head with her fingertips and he stopped growling like she'd flipped a switch. "Can you take us to someone who can help?"

The man smiled. "We can."

SIXTEEN
Jack and Layla: Woodland Park, CO

"What about guided meditation?"

Jack ground his teeth. In the office adjoining his at the church, which Layla had taken over as her "work" space, Rowan and Layla were brainstorming. He'd been invited to join the conversation, but had politely declined. Now, he found himself alternately straining to listen and striving to ignore. It was maddening.

"Hmm." Rowan was skeptical – Jack could *feel* it. "I don't know. These are working folks – a lot of them are just desperate for something to *do*. I don't know if asking them to sit still and visualize something is the answer."

A worried Rowan had taken a break from her endless medical rounds this afternoon to talk to Layla. The people, she reported, were scared, and getting more so. Many of them were not coping with their losses – literally everyone had lost someone – and on top of that, they were dealing with profound, paradigm-shifting changes in themselves. An exponential increase in intuitive, "sixth-sense" experiences had been reported by the majority of the people Rowan spoke to. And some of the ones who denied such experiences, she was sure, were too scared to tell her the truth.

Grief-counseling, Jack could do. New Age woo-woo, he could not.

He had tried. Some of his surviving parishioners had come to him, desperate to talk about it, and he had truly tried to help them. But he'd come off as insincere, no matter what approach he used, and he knew it. It just wasn't his area of expertise, and he couldn't bring himself to parrot what he'd heard Layla say. It wasn't his Truth. He had ended up sending them to talk to Layla instead, and without exception, they had left her comforted, at peace.

She had been nothing short of amazing these last few days: calm, quietly authoritative, wise, and respectful of the beliefs of others as she helped the people of their community cope, survive, and take their first steps towards healing. And while she was busy being a paragon, she was simultaneously shielding Jack, protecting him from the worst of the emotional buffeting they were both enduring. He had tried to remove that burden from her, had tried to handle things on his own, but even small groups quickly overwhelmed his fledgling "shields." He always ended up hurrying back under her wing, never able to stifle a sigh of relief as he felt her protection fold around him like a warm quilt.

He was perilously close to hating her.

Jack dropped his face into his hands and scrubbed at the tense muscles of his cheeks, his forehead, his scalp. He felt like he'd been wearing a mask for days, trying to protect himself behind it, trying to keep his feelings private and respect the privacy of others. What Layla did so effortlessly was a constant strain for him. That was just item number one on the "Reasons to Hate Layla" list he'd been composing in his head. He knew it was childish, and didn't care. Like everyone else, he was doing what he had to do to cope.

The constant proximity wasn't helping. He wished he could justify moving back to his own house, but they were encouraging everyone to consolidate, to make the most of their finite resources. Layla's place already had a generator, and his didn't. End of story. For now, food and fuel were not issues; so many people had died so quickly, they were able to scavenge what they needed. But if the rest of the world had been hit by the plague as hard as Woodland Park, they wouldn't be able to count on supplies from the outside any time soon.

And if he was going to be of any assistance to his community at all, he had to stay near her as they worked on the endless list of issues the survivors now faced: Reestablishing communication with the outside world, especially urgent for those who had lost contact with distant family members; clean water, and how to get the municipal water treatment plant back up and running; medical care for the survivors, particularly those with chronic health conditions; and burial of the dead, which was a task no one wanted to deal with. Rowan warned constantly of the threat of disease, and it was their duty as survivors. But how to assign such a disheartening task, to an already disheartened people?

He and Layla had been trying to work out a rotating duty roster, but they were both reluctant to implement it. And they had barely scratched the surface. What to do about law breakers? What laws were still relevant? What about people hoarding their own food and supplies, who didn't want to participate in the collective society that was forming? Did they have that right? Jack's head spun with details, his shoulders sagged with responsibility, and his heart burned with resentment, all of it directed at Layla.

He knew his feelings weren't rational or just, but he hadn't had even a single waking moment to sort them out. He and Layla had been together day and night, non-stop. Even in their separate rooms of her little cottage, he was aware of her constant presence. He would bet he was getting on her nerves, too, but he lacked the courage to lower his "shields" – man, he hated that term – and *feel* what she was projecting. And even if he wanted to try, he was pretty sure she could control what she projected as well as what she received. So unlike the rest of them, her thoughts were still her own. Reason number two on the Hate List.

Layla spoke again, and her tone had Jack reconsidering that second item. Not only did she sound frustrated, he could *feel* her impatience without even trying. "I'm at a loss. The people that I've talked to seem to be handling the changes, but so many of them just want to isolate, to hide at home. We can't help people that just want to cower in fear."

Jack didn't care for the *contempt* that rolled off her. He didn't care for it at all. How dare she judge? He was considering calling her on it when Rowan spoke.

"Layla, what about that thing you do? That thing with your voice?"

Jack sat up straighter, and his heart started to pound. They hadn't spoken of this, and he'd been hoping he had imagined it.

"Rowan, I can't *make* people not be afraid."

"No, but you could encourage them to listen. With great persuasiveness."

Jack was on his feet and moving before Layla could answer. He stepped into the open doorway, and glared at them both. "I don't like what I'm hearing. Not at all. What is it you want her to do, Rowan?"

Rowan radiated *busted*. "I wouldn't have her force anyone to do anything they didn't want to do. But she can do this thing, with her voice, and I just thought..."

She trailed off miserably and Jack shifted his glare to Layla. "Why don't you explain exactly what it is you can do?"

Layla's nostrils flared and her eyes narrowed. She didn't like his tone – he could both *see* and *feel* that. "You didn't have to eavesdrop. You could have just joined us, like we asked you to in the first place."

He ignored the swipe and kept his eyes on the goal. "What is it Rowan wants you to do?"

Layla and Rowan looked at each other for a long moment, then Layla returned her gaze to him and lifted her chin. Her dark eyes were as inscrutable as her energy. He couldn't feel a thing coming from her now.

"I can command people to do things. I didn't realize I was doing it – have been doing it my whole life, I guess – until Alder was moving the generator into my house. He was starting to slide it out of the back of the pick-up, and he didn't see that the board he was using as a ramp had moved – I thought he was going to drop the generator. I told him to stop, and he froze. He says he literally couldn't move."

Chills of alarm raced up Jack's spine and prickled across his scalp. "Like that time you told me to 'stop.' In your living room, that first day we met with everyone at the church."

Layla nodded, and Jack's stomach tightened. He could see why she'd kept this a secret. Such power was not from God. It couldn't be. He kept his eyes on Layla, but spoke to Rowan. "Could you please leave us alone, Rowan? We have some things to sort out."

Rowan's *relief* wafted after her like a perfume as she zipped out the door and shut it behind her. For a long, long moment, Jack stared at Layla. Intellectually, he recognized her value and importance to their community. The smart thing to do would be to talk to her, gather more information, find out exactly what they were dealing with calmly and rationally, before leaping to condemn.

Instead, he cocked his head to the side, read every nuance of her posture and emotion he was able to, and calculated his words for maximum damage. "So. Were you saving that little parlor trick for a special occasion?

Waiting for a chance to show it off in front of a crowd? Pretty good strategy - bet it would give your little Tarot card racket quite a boost."

A flare of white-hot rage kicked off her before she locked it down behind that hateful wall of ice. "I won't even justify that with a reply." She rose from her seat and moved towards the door, head high. "When you're ready to talk about this instead of hurling ridiculous accusations..."

Jack moved to block the door. "You're not calling the shots right now, Layla, and you *will* talk about this. You and Rowan didn't give me much choice about assuming a leadership position here, and now you get to abide by that. It's one thing to accept that we can both read people's emotions. It's something entirely different to learn that you're capable of the kind of manipulative power Rowan described."

"You can do it, too."

Her soft words derailed him completely. He blinked at her, and decided he must have misheard. "Excuse me?"

"You can do it, too. I've seen you. Or rather, I've *heard* you do it. That first day, when you talked to the crowd. And every day since, whenever you need someone to do something you want."

An awful recognition teased the edges of his righteous anger. No, she could not be right about this. He didn't think he could take her being right about one more thing while he stumbled around on unfamiliar ground, trying to regain his footing. "I'm persuasive. There's a world of difference between that and *commanding* people to obey your will."

"They're not exactly the same, I'll give you that. I can use one-word commands to influence a person's immediate actions. Rowan and I have done a little experimenting, a very little, there just hasn't been time. But the effect is momentary only. What you can do lasts much longer."

His heart was pounding. No. "Layla, you're trying to deflect this, and it's not going to work. I offer my thoughts and opinions. Others are free – *free* – to make up their minds as to whether they agree or disagree, and then act accordingly. I don't use force or coercion of any kind."

"No, you don't. But you *read* people, and you're able to manipulate their thoughts and feelings. You choose just the right words, the exact, precise words. You're so good at it, people think your words are their own thoughts, their own opinions. I think you've always been able to do this, just like I have." She looked down, and a tiny vulnerable crack in her wall of ice appeared. "I thought I was just a good teacher with exceptional classroom-management skills. Turns out I probably had an unfair advantage."

He could *see*, through that crack, how to cut to the heart of her. How to make her doubt herself and her own integrity, how to wound her so deeply, she might never heal. That he was even considering using that knowledge was what stopped him.

He turned away from her and shut his eyes, searching for anything in his heart or mind that felt familiar. "I hate this. I hate feeling like I'm on an alien planet. I don't understand anything. I feel like I can't trust myself or anyone around me. I don't know what's real or imaginary anymore."

He turned back towards her and opened his eyes. She had returned to Remote Ice Queen mode, and he could not stop the sneer that lifted his lip. "Sometimes I hate you, too. I hate that you seem to understand all these changes, when I don't. I hate the words you use to talk about this – intuition and shields and cones of light. The words are so stupid, I can't even talk with you and Rowan about it."

He didn't give her a chance to reply, and took a step towards her. Now that the floodgates were open, he had to complete the purge. "I hate the way I feel when I'm around you. Awkward. Stiff. I've always felt this way, and it's worse now. I don't recognize myself when I'm around you, and I don't like myself. What the hell? Is that you or me?"

Again, he didn't give her a chance to respond, plowing forward. "But most of all, more than anything, I hate the way you can hide your feelings from me. Everyone else is an open book, but you've got that little two-way shield-thing going on, and it's driving me crazy. What makes your feelings so precious, so sacred, that you protect them like that? What are you hiding?"

And now he did shut up, because he wanted her to answer. Layla was just staring at him, eyes wide. She took a deep breath, then another. Her face tightened, then relaxed, and she dropped the wall.

Jack took one stumbling step back, then another, dumbfounded.

Love. Tenderness, exasperation, admiration, protectiveness, vulnerability and dear *God*, a whole-body stroke of lust that electrified the base of his spine and burned along every nerve ending he possessed. This is what she was hiding, this nuanced but fledgling love. And she felt it for *him*.

Jack shut his eyes. He would master himself before he responded, by God, he would. The silence between them stretched on and on. He *felt* her slip back behind her wall, and oh, the relief of it, the loneliness of it. He opened his eyes, and she smiled sadly.

"I guess we don't have the luxury of pretending there's not a pink elephant in the middle of the room anymore, huh?"

His brain wanted to scramble, but he controlled it. Question after question arose, and he discarded all of them but one: "Why?"

She actually laughed a little. "Well, it's not because of the sweet and courtly way you treat me, that's for sure." She paused, staring down at the ground between them without seeing it. "I don't know. I don't think I'm meant to know yet. There's a synchronicity between us that feels significant. It's not something I chose. It just is."

Now he was scrambling, and he couldn't control it. He had asked, she had been honest, and he owed her some kind of response. "Layla, I don't... I can't..."

He felt a sharp flare of humiliation from her before she held up her hand, her face mask-like, controlled. "Please. You don't need to say it, remember?"

They stared at each other, the moment stretching on in silent stillness, until Jack felt almost afraid to move. How to go on from here? How to return to the ordinary, the everyday? Another consequence of the world they were now inhabiting: gone were the days of hiding one's true feelings behind a polite façade. People were going to have to deal with each other in a whole new way. At least until they learned the idiotic shield thing.

Hurried footsteps in the hallway outside gave both of them permission to move, to look away. A brief knock, and the door popped open. Martin, one of the men who had been on sentry duty that day, stuck his head in. He glanced between the two of them, eyes narrowed, and cocked his head to the side.

"Ah. Am I interrupting?"

Five minutes earlier, Jack thought, and they could have been spared the awkwardness they were currently suffering.

Layla answered. "Not at all. What's wrong?"

"Nothing wrong, exactly." Martin was vibrating with excitement. "There's a woman here, with her daughter. She says they're from the Springs."

Jack and Layla moved together to follow him, the situation between them abruptly – blessedly – pushed to the back burner. As far as Jack was concerned, it could simmer there forever. Martin led the way, striding swiftly and talking just as fast in his excitement.

"She says they hiked out of Manitou Springs and down into Cascade, then found a vehicle. Highway 24 is blocked clear back into Colorado Springs, she says, and they were nearly caught in an ambush when they tried for Rampart Range Road. She didn't want to attempt Old Stage Road – she said it was too close to Fort Carson – they've got a refugee camp started there, and she didn't want to get sucked into that. Her daughter is sick."

Jack stopped walking, and caught Martin's arm in alarm. "Hold on – sick? Is it plague?"

Martin gave him an exasperated look. "Of course not. I know the protocol. She's a survivor, like you, but she doesn't look good."

"I know you know. I'm sorry. They're our first refugees, and I guess I'm just jumpy."

Martin nodded his acquiescence, and they hurried on. One of the questions that had arisen repeatedly over the last several days concerned the lack of refugees from Colorado Springs and other parts east. According to the survivalist types in their group, the cities would rapidly become unsafe, and survivors would head for more remote locations. Woodland Park was a scant 20 miles from the larger city, but other than a handful of people who had snuck out before the plague broke the boundaries, they hadn't seen a soul.

There were, however, a limited number of ways to approach Woodland Park, especially if Highway 24 was impassable. Rampart Range Road and Old Stage Road both provided alternate, if circuitous routes into the Woodland Park area, but both were dirt roads that had to be constantly maintained. Without that maintenance, they wouldn't remain passable for long, even in a four-wheel-drive vehicle. Getting someone to check the condition of both roads was on the endless to-do list. In the meantime, it looked like they might have an explanation for their isolation in spite of their proximity to a major metropolitan area.

Layla spoke. "You said her daughter's sick. Is Rowan with them?"

"Yes. I tried to ask if she had any other news, but once I introduced her to Rowan, that was it. She's pretty intense. Totally focused on her daughter. I don't even know her name. Oh, and I hope neither one of you are afraid of dogs."

Martin was desperate for news, particularly of Limon, where his daughter and son had been living with his ex-wife. He had lost his new wife and their infant son within hours of each other, and it had taken all of Jack's persuasive abilities to keep Martin from heading out to search for his children. The thought gave him pause now; had he given Martin a choice? Really? They needed every able-bodied person they had left to begin the rebuilding process, but that wouldn't justify imposing his will on another...

Jack shook his head and pushed that thought, too, to the back burner. Quite a collection of simmering pots he was accumulating back there. They arrived in the general purpose room, which Deb had been set up in anticipation of refugees, using the cots, bedding and supplies left over from the last time the church had housed evacuees from one of Colorado's infamous forest fires.

Rowan knelt by the cot nearest to the kitchen, bent over a little girl tucked under a soft peach blanket. She had set up an IV pole with a bag of clear liquid hanging from it, and was frowning in concentration as she inserted an IV needle into the crook of the little girl's arm. Beside them stood a woman, blonde hair held back in a disheveled pony tail, arms folded across her chest, face reddened by time spent in the wind and the sun. She glanced up at their approach, and both Jack and Layla stopped as if they'd hit a wall.

Desperation. She was frantic with fear, and it rolled off her in powerful waves. Her eyes returned to her daughter's face, and her emotions shifted to *love*, a mother's love, fierce, transcendent, limitless. There was nothing this woman would not do for the little girl on that cot.

"Holy shit."

Jack glanced at Layla, startled. It wasn't like her to swear – she claimed the habit made it too easy to slip up in front of her students. She met his gaze and grimaced. "That is some powerful juju she's putting out."

He raised his eyebrows. "'Juju?' Seriously?"

She rolled her eyes at him; he felt the amusement she didn't show. "It's a technical term." She took a deep breath, then held out her hand, not making eye contact with him. "Better do this together, I'm thinking."

He didn't let himself analyze or obsess, just joined his hand with hers. Instantly, he could manage the woman's emotions, keep them separate from his own. "Thank you," he murmured, and they started walking again, hand in hand.

They were only a few feet away when the big Rottweiler rose from the floor under the cot where he'd been lying. He didn't bark or growl, but it was clear they weren't getting any closer. At the foot of the cot, a tiny golden sprite of a dog also lifted its head, and the delicate growl that vibrated the air was no less intimidating than the Rottweiler's quiet watchfulness.

The blonde woman's head turned in their direction again. She glanced between Jack and Layla, her eyes measuring. Then, she nodded. Both dogs relaxed instantly. The little golden dog returned her gaze to the little girl's face while the Rottweiler moved to sit by the woman, pressed against her leg, panting. Jack and Layla exchanged a glance. Interesting.

Jack nodded at her. "Hello. I'm Jack, this is Layla, and Martin here is the one who brought you in. We're glad to be able to help you."

The woman hardly glanced at them. "I'm Naomi. This is Macy." To Rowan, "Is she unconscious or just sleeping? She spoke to me as we were leaving Cascade, but she was so limp when I took her out of the truck. She hasn't been eating or drinking – she sneaks her food to the dogs when she thinks I'm not looking."

Rowan's face was tight with concentration and concern. She lifted her hand to smooth it over the little girl's hair, which glowed incandescently, even in the dim light of the church basement, even through the evident trail dust. Jack didn't think he'd ever seen such a beautiful color, like a sunrise. Rowan lifted Macy's eyelids, peering at her pupils with a tiny flashlight, then glanced up at Naomi. "A little of both. She's dehydrated and exhausted. We'll get some IV fluids in her and let her rest, then I'll complete my exam."

She turned her face towards Jack and Layla, but didn't meet their eyes. Jack felt a flare of alarm; it wasn't like Rowan to be evasive unless the prognosis wasn't good. "In the meantime, I'll stay with her if you'd like to get something to eat, maybe use the bathroom and clean up. Jack and Layla can show you where everything is."

Naomi was already shaking her head. "No, I won't leave her. I can't. I can't let go. I can't ever let her go." Her voice rose with every word she spoke, and the animals mirrored her agitation. The little dog whined softly and the Rottweiler rose to his feet, shifting and pressing against Naomi's leg, his head turned up to her as if she were his whole world.

Jack groped for the right words to take her anxiety down a notch. "Your dogs probably need some care as well. Are they hungry? We can come up with something for them, I'm sure."

Naomi looked down, then bent to stroke both animals' heads. She didn't speak a word, but Jack had no doubt whatsoever that communication was taking place. Again, he and Layla exchanged a look. He hoped they could shift her focus long enough to answer a few more questions.

Naomi straightened. "They're alright for now, in terms of food, but Hades needs water."

Layla squeezed Jack's hand once to warn him, then let him go. It took everything Jack had learned about shields to keep Naomi's worry from overwhelming him. Serious juju indeed.

Layla stepped forward and rested a gentle hand on Naomi's shoulder. "Let's go get him some. I'm sure your daughter will rest better without us talking nearby, and she couldn't be in better hands. Rowan here pulled Jack through the plague. He's a survivor, like your daughter."

Naomi focused on him, analyzing him from head to toe with laser sharp eyes. "You survived? You're healthy now?"

Layla snorted as she gently steered Naomi away from her daughter's bedside and towards the kitchen. Hades stayed glued to Naomi's opposite side, though the other dog stayed where she was, attention never wavering from the little girl's still face. "He'd be a lot more healthy if he would slow down, rest more, and eat more. But will he listen?"

A tiny smile touched Naomi's lips. "Of course not. Typical man." Then, her terrible sorrow permeated the space around all of them. "My husband was like that, too. He died April 6th, the day before Macy got sick. Do you know what the date is today?"

Jack, trailing behind with Martin, answered. "May 14th. I'm told I fell ill on April 10th, but I don't remember much of anything until about 10 days ago. Rowan and

Layla pulled me through. We only know of a few other survivors."

"May 14th," Naomi murmured. "It seems like so much longer, like years have passed."

They entered the kitchen, and Naomi situated herself so she could watch her daughter's cot as she leaned against a stainless steel worktable. Layla filled a large bowl with water and set it on the floor for Hades, who lapped eagerly. Then she went to their generator-powered fridge and started rummaging. "We've got some vegetable beef soup – does that sound good?"

"Wonderful." Naomi heaved a sigh that seemed to go all the way to her toes. "I'm so grateful for your help. Everyone else we've met has been so hostile. Oh – I almost forgot – I ran into some kids in Cascade that need help. I told them I'd send someone, if I could. I would have brought them with me, but Macy needed immediate attention and they were, well..." She fell silent for a moment, the expression on her face conveying how deeply she was disturbed. "They weren't right. Maybe not totally sane." She glanced down at Hades, and reached to stroke his blocky head. "Then again, maybe none of us are sane anymore."

Jack looked at Martin. "Can you organize some folks to go down and get those kids? If possible, I'd like it if you were one of them. Just to be sure they're on the up and up."

Martin didn't bother to conceal his impatience. "I'd like to find out if she has news first." He didn't wait for permission, speaking to Naomi. "My kids were in

Limon – have you heard anything? Any information at all? Or do you know of a survivor in one of the eastern ranching communities? It's a small, close-knit group, even though it's spread out. Maybe..."

He trailed off, face grim, when Naomi started shaking her head. "I'm so sorry, there's nothing I can tell you. I picked up an automated radio station a few weeks ago – April 28th, the announcement said – but it just summarized the progress of the plague world-wide. It was really bad. 99-100% fatality rates in some places." Her eyes returned to Macy's cot, and she rubbed the center of her chest. "I've lost contact with my oldest daughter, Piper. She was at UNC. That's why we came to Woodland Park – she'll meet us at our cabin, up at Carrol Lakes. She may be there already."

They were all silent, then, the only sound the quiet metal clink of the spoon in the pot Layla was heating soup in. No reason to voice what they all feared, that Martin's children were likely dead. That Noami's older daughter was likely dead as well. Finally, Martin took a deep breath.

"Okay, then. We'll go get those kids. I'll bring them here as soon as we've got them." He nodded brusquely at Naomi and strode out without saying goodbye.

Layla dished up a bowl of hot soup for Naomi, and Jack waited until she'd savored a few bites before speaking. "Do you intend to stay in the area, then?"

Naomi nodded, hesitated, then shrugged. "It all depends on whether or not Piper has reached the cabin yet.

I haven't thought much beyond that, to be honest. I've just been trying to get us here in one piece."

"I understand that. There are just over 100 of us still alive in the immediate area, as near as we can tell. We've started talking about how to go forward, and our chances of surviving are better if we all work together. Do you think you might be interested in being a part of our community?"

Again, Naomi shrugged. She took another bite of soup, and smiled sadly. "I was president of the PTA, and served on just about every school committee you can think of. I like to join, to help. But right now, I've got to get Macy well. And I've got to find Piper." Her voice caught, and she had to swallow several times before she could continue. When she looked up, her eyes were bright with tears she fought to keep from falling. "My girls are everything. The whole world. Without them, I'm not...anything."

Oh, but you are, Jack wanted to argue. But it wasn't the time. "We'll do anything we can do to help you with both goals. In the meantime, do you have any work skills or hobbies that we might be able to ruthlessly exploit?" He smiled engagingly, and was rewarded by Naomi's rusty chuckle.

"Well, I bake some mean cookies." Her face fell, and she looked down again. *Shame, inadequacy, embarrassment.* "I don't have any skills, really. I was just a housewife, before. I didn't work. I just took care of my family."

Layla stepped towards her, and ducked until she was looking into Naomi's face. "You walked out of Colorado Springs with your daughter, two dogs and only what you could carry. You got all of you here safely. Are you seriously going to stand there and tell us you're unskilled?" She shook her head, her eyes openly admiring. "I hope you stay. We need someone as strong and resourceful as you."

Jack *felt* Layla's words sink into Naomi, felt their balm and comfort. Naomi smiled shyly at Layla. "Thank you. I guess I'm used to people dismissing what I do as unimportant. Oh!" She brightened. "I can shoot! I forgot that. I've never hunted, but I almost never miss when we shoot skeet." She looked thoughtful. "I'm not sure if I could hunt, to tell you the truth. I've always had such a rapport with animals. But I could teach others, I'm sure of it."

"That's excellent – exactly the kind of thing we're looking for." Jack paused, and judged the moment was right. "This may sound strange, and I don't want to alarm you, but can I also ask if you've experienced anything unusual, any unusual perceptions or feelings?"

Naomi looked up, startled, the spoon halfway between the bowl and her mouth. She glanced briefly at Hades and hedged. "Ah, I'm not sure what you mean."

Jack smiled his reassurance. "Since the plague, we've had a lot of people talking about unusual experiences – they know things, but they're not sure how, or they have really strong hunches or intuitions, so strong they're sure they're true. Anything like that?"

Again, Naomi glanced at Hades. "Hmm. Well." She took a deep breath. "Yes. I guess you could say that. I can, well, you see..." She laughed, and blew out a breath of air. "Geez, this is hard to talk about with anyone but Macy! I can communicate with the dogs," she said in a nervous rush. "And my cat, sort of. I'm not sure about other animals. Have other people talked about that? Being able to share senses with their animals?"

Layla spoke. "We heard there's a horse rancher on the west side of the city who can communicate with animals. We haven't met him yet. Rowan's working theory is that this is an evolution of the human species, brought on by stress." She shot a glance at Jack and folded her arms across her chest. "I agree, though my take on it is a little different. I do readings at metaphysical fairs, and those of us who work in the field have seen this shift coming for a long time. It's just that none of us expected it to happen so fast, or to so many people at once. I think the plague accelerated the shift in consciousness for many of the survivors."

Naomi tipped her head back and shut her eyes for a moment. *Relief.* "I was afraid I had lost my mind. Macy said no, that lots of people had changed, but I wasn't sure..." Her voice trailed off. *Guilt.*

"You weren't sure if you should believe her," Jack said gently. "I felt the same way. Layla and I can both sense what others are feeling, but I didn't want to believe it at first. I had to get run over and wrung out before I took it seriously." He paused and let her think about that, forgive herself. "What about Macy? Has she changed as well?"

"Oh, yes." Naomi's face was grim. "She *knows* things. About her sister, and about the world. It's frightening, to tell you the truth. It feels like she knows too much. She can also, well..." Again, Naomi trailed into silence, her eyes shifting between Jack and Layla. She folded her lips firmly for a moment, then went on. "Well, she has some other interesting...talents."

She was hiding something about her daughter, that was clear. Before Jack could probe further, Rowan appeared in the doorway, an expression on her face that was equal parts wonder and trepidation. Her eyes found Naomi.

"Your daughter is awake," she announced, then shifted her gaze to Layla and Jack. "And she's asking for Verity."

SEVENTEEN
Naomi and Macy: Woodland Park, CO

Naomi set her soup bowl down with a clatter and hustled toward the kitchen door, Hades tight on her heels. "Is there some plain broth that can be heated up for her? I know you've got the IV going, but I really need her to eat something."

She turned when Rowan didn't follow her, and found all three of them staring at each other in silence. A cool snake of alarm writhed down her spine. "Who is this Verity she's asking for? Is there someone here by that name?"

The charming young pastor answered with obvious reluctance. "Yes. We have a woman named Verity here..."

Naomi craned to look out the doorway. Macy was accepting adoring chin-kisses from Persephone, smiling and stroking the tiny dog, and looked okay for the moment. She turned back to face the three of them fully. She didn't have time to tiptoe around this. "Why is this making all of you so uncomfortable? I told you Macy *knows* things. She told me there would be people here in

Woodland Park that could help us, and there were. What is it about this Verity?"

"Well," a soft voice floated from the doorway on the far side of the kitchen, "It might be that I grow marijuana."

Naomi looked up to find an angel made manifest, and didn't even feel surprised. "Verity, I presume?"

"I am." The woman's smile was a glory to behold. "I love timing an entrance perfectly. It truly is one of my finest talents." She brushed back her darling angel-blonde curls. "I also have a habit of saying what everyone is thinking but no one wants said. It's off-putting, I'm told. Oh, and I communicate with the dead, which is why Macy wants to see me. May I go introduce myself?"

"I suspect introductions won't be necessary," Naomi said dryly, though her heart was pounding. Why would Macy have asked for this woman by name? Why not Rowan? "Let's go."

She plodded after the delicate, floating Verity, and watched what could only be called a reunion. Verity knelt by Macy's cot, and the two gazed at each other in wordless delight for a long moment, hands twining together. Then Macy reached her arms up for a hug. "I dreamed of you. I'm so happy to meet you face to face at last."

"And I you, little sister." Verity leaned back from the embrace, and curled one of Macy's strawberry curls around her finger. Her expression was tender. "You made it just in time."

"I know." Macy's gaze flickered to Naomi. "Mama, I could eat some soup. Would you bring me some?"

There was something terrifying moving under the surface of this exchange. Naomi raised her eyebrows and tried for a light tone. "You don't want soup. You just want to get rid of me."

Verity's laughter rang like Christmas bells. "She's right, little sister. Say what you mean. Always."

Macy looked chagrined for a heartbeat, then sighed. "Okay. Mama, would you please let me talk to Verity alone for a while?"

Naomi knelt on the other side of the cot, searching her daughter's eyes. "Why? Why can't I hear what you have to say to her?"

Macy glanced at Verity, who nodded. Her eyes returned to Naomi, shuttered and unreadable. "I need to talk to her about some things I'm not ready to talk to you about yet. About Daddy and Piper, and some other things."

Naomi stroked the soft curve of her cheek, and traced a finger down her little nose. For this moment, she would allow herself to believe Macy. She would go heat some soup, and pretend that it would help. She could feel a division forming in her mind, a barrier between what was, and what could not be. What must not be. "Will you tell me? When you're ready?"

"I promise."

Naomi rose and headed for the kitchen, ruthlessly focusing her attention on her footsteps and not on the soft murmur of voices behind her. Beside her, Hades was whining, low and constant, expressing her own anxiety. She dropped her hand to his head, sent his heart a pulse of comfort, and kept on walking.

In the kitchen, conversation hushed the minute she stepped into the doorway. Jack, Layla and Rowan all stared at her from wary, pitying eyes. From out of nowhere, rage boiled up, red-hot and uncontrollable. "Oh, for pity's sake," Naomi snapped. "As if I didn't know you were talking about us! It doesn't take supernatural ability to figure that out!"

Her eyes lasered in on Rowan. "Tell me. All of it. I can't help her if I don't know."

Rowan tilted her head respectfully. "Okay. Your daughter survived the pneumonic version of the plague, but the bacteria multiplied in her blood, resulting in septicemia. Her organs are failing."

A high-pitched buzzing started in Naomi's ears and bright lights darted and swooped in front of her eyes. She took a deep breath and forced, *forced* herself to stay calm, to keep questioning, to find solutions. "Is there a surgeon here? I can donate a kidney, and I've read that I can donate part of my liver and still survive."

Rowan shook her head. "She's bleeding internally, and has been for days. Even if we had someone capable of performing such a specialized surgery, she wouldn't survive the procedure." Her gaze didn't waver from Naomi's even though she was delivering the worst possible news, the most unthinkable news. "Her body is shutting down. It's just a matter of time."

The high-pitched buzz became a hollow roar, and Naomi's vision shrank to a pinpoint. Her head felt so strange – tight and too hot and tingly. She blinked over and over, and found herself sitting in a chair with Jack and Layla hovering at her shoulders, Rowan kneeling in front of her.

Rowan grasped her hands tightly. "Let us move Macy to Layla and Jack's cottage. I can keep her comfortable, and we'll be there to support you. After."

Naomi stared into her eyes, searching for even a trace of uncertainty. "They said the same thing about the plague. That no one would survive. My husband died, but Macy didn't. She didn't. She beat the odds once, she could do it again. You could be wrong."

Rowan's eyes were tortured with sorrow and knowledge. She shook her head again. "Naomi, it's not just an educated guess. I *see*. Do you understand? I can *see* people from a medical perspective. I knew Jack would live. And I know Macy won't." She squeezed Naomi's hands so tightly, their bones grated together. "I'm not sure why she's alive now. Please. Let us help you both."

Jack's hand came to rest gently on her shoulder. "She's right, Naomi. Please let us help. Are you a person of faith? We'll pray with you–"

Naomi surged to her feet so fast she knocked the chair over. She glared at each of them in turn, then fixed her gaze on Jack. "Your God," she hissed, "Is not here. He has left us, if he was ever here at all. What kind of God could let such a sweet, beautiful, little girl die? To have survived so much, just to die now? How is that fair? How is that right?"

Tears slid steadily from the corners of Layla's eyes. "I don't have words for how sorry I am," she said brokenly. "I wish there was some way you would let us help you."

Jack's voice, too, was rough with barely-controlled emotion. "If you'll allow it, we'll hold vigil with you, and be with you in your time of grief. I know you're angry at God, but I believe He sent you to us for a purpose."

"What purpose could any of this have?" Everything that had been building and growing in her, all the anger, uncertainty and fear that she'd been hiding from both Macy and herself, burst free. "What possible 'reason' could there be for a plague that wipes out mankind, except that God is finished with us? There's nothing of God in this – it's natural law! We poisoned our own nest. Animals that foul their nests are doomed. In just a few weeks, our children are reduced to hunting pets for food. What's next? Hunting each other? I don't want to live in a world like this. I *won't* live in a world without-"

She broke off and turned her back on them, taking her bowl and spoon to the sink, an automatic gesture that gave her shaking hands something to do. Standing there, she closed her eyes, groping her way forward. There had to be another answer. Had to be.

A preternatural calm settled around her. She turned to face the three of them, her face frozen, her eyes burning and dry as dust. "If there's nothing more you can do for her, Macy and I will head to the cabin this afternoon. Piper is probably already there."

They exchanged glances again, Rowan's lips parted to speak, and Naomi let slip control of what was raging inside her.

"Don't," she snarled. Jack and Layla both took a staggering step back. Beside her, Hades seemed to expand, bristling to his full height, his broad chest ripping with a growl that pitched and rolled with violence. She reveled in her fury, in his fury, in the power of it to hold back the grief that would stop her heart. "Don't say a word, any of you. It's done."

She left the kitchen on numb legs, the only spot of feeling in her body the bright flame of rage that consumed her chest. Verity looked up at her approach. She stood, still holding Macy's hand.

"Thank you for letting us talk. Your daughter will be fine." She reached out and laced her fingers with Naomi's. "You'll both be fine."

Naomi blinked in shock. For just a moment, it seemed as if they were surrounded by beings so beautiful, they hurt her eyes to look at. Verity released her hand, she blinked again, and the impression was gone.

An impish smile, a brush of her fingertips on Macy's cheek, and Verity turned and headed for the exit. She stopped a few steps shy of the door and turned back. "Oh, I almost forgot! Scott says the duct tape was perfect."

She could not have heard that correctly. "Excuse me?"

"Scott. He loved the duct tape. It made him laugh, and he says he knew then that you would do whatever you had to do, improvise however you had to, in order to survive." Verity beamed at her. "He's so very proud of you."

Naomi's legs went out from under her. She collapsed on the end of Macy's cot, deaf and blind to everything around her. Old, rational thought processes kicked in first: How could she possibly have known that? No one knew about the duct tape she'd used to secure Scott's makeshift shroud, no one but her. Well, and Scott. And now Verity.

He was proud of her. Why that, of all things, should break her wide open, she could not say. She curled up next to Macy and sobbed. So afraid, she'd been so afraid she was inadequate to the task, doing the wrong things, failing to protect her daughter, failing at everything in this new world she was so ill-equipped to navigate. Scott was proud of her. Validation from beyond the grave. Her sobs dissolved into hiccupping laughter. He had promised her, over and over, that he'd always be there for her. The man certainly knew how to keep a promise.

Gradually, her sobs subsided and she returned to awareness to feel Macy stroking her hair, Hades curled in the curve of her legs, Persephone tucked against her chest. She drifted in a twilight between sleep and wakefulness for a long time, resting deeply, permitting her mind to float on the soft, surface currents of silence and physical comfort. Occasionally she was aware of a muffled noise from the kitchen, but Jack and Layla kept their distance, and Rowan intruded only to change Macy's IV bag.

Hours had passed when she was roused by a need for the bathroom. Macy was sleeping again, and Naomi scrutinized her in the dim light. She looked better. She really did. Her skin was less gray, and her eyes didn't seem as sunken. Moving as gently as her stiff joints would allow, she extricated herself from her softly snoring dogs and shuffled to the bathroom, taking a moment when she was finished to wash her face with deliciously warm water and restore some order to her crooked ponytail.

When she returned, Macy was awake and Rowan was at her side. They both looked up at Naomi's approach, and Macy made a disgusted face. "She had me use a bedpan, Mama! So gross!"

Naomi was sure her face cracked when she forced it to smile. "Gross for you? What about Rowan?"

"Just part of my glamorous job." Rowan stood up, holding said bedpan with a towel draped over it. "I'll go take care of this. When I come back, we'll take out the IV. That she's urinating tells us we've brought her body back to a hydrated state."

Naomi's head came up, and she searched Rowan's eyes for some encouragement, some hope. Rowan met her gaze steadily, and shook her head.

Well. She was entitled to her opinion, but medical professionals could be wrong. Macy had proved that already. Naomi knelt by her side.

"When Rowan's done, we'll get around and head to the cabin. I'd like to get there before dark." She licked her thumb and gently rubbed Macy's grubby cheek. "You can take a bath in the tub by the fireplace, if you're feeling up to it. I'll bet Piper's already there, waiting for us."

Macy gazed at her, something deep and unknowable moving in her eyes. "Okay, Mama. I'm ready."

She left both dogs with Macy, silently commanding them to *stay*. While they had all slept, Martin had returned with the kids from Cascade. They were both asleep on cots at the far end of the multi-purpose room, an older woman Naomi hadn't met seated between them, reading. She looked up when Naomi stopped in front of her, and nodded a greeting.

"I see Martin found them," Naomi said. "Are they okay?"

The woman reached out and brushed a lock of hair out of the girl's face. "No. They're not."

Naomi swallowed. "I wish I could have helped them."

"No one could have. Their bodies will recover – other than being hungry and dehydrated, they're both fine. But her mind is broken. I don't know about the boy yet."

Naomi looked at the woman more closely. "You can *see* that? Like Rowan?"

"Not exactly like Rowan, no. She sees medical conditions. I see...a path. I can see the way a person is likely to go forward. I'm not always right, but most of the time." She smoothed the girl's hair again, tucking a greasy strand behind a grimy ear with great tenderness. "This one will always be like a child, I'm afraid. She's gone back in her mind to a time that was safe, and I don't think she'll leave it. Her brother, well, as I said I just don't know. He loves animals, and what they were doing to survive broke his heart. We'll just have to see how he mends."

She looked across the room then, at Macy. "Your daughter is beautiful. Such lovely hair."

"Thank you." The woman's eyes returned to Naomi, and in them, she saw knowledge and empathy. Naomi held up her hand, warding off her words. "No," she said softly. "Some paths can be changed."

"Yes. They can." But the woman looked down, and Naomi could *hear* the certainty and sorrow in her voice. "Go with God on your journey. We'll be here, when you need us."

Naomi found Jack, Layla and Martin in the church parking lot, standing next to the little pick-up Naomi had driven from Cascade and a dusty black late-model SUV. Jack gestured to the newer vehicle as Naomi walked up.

"If it's okay, we moved your gear to the SUV. It's full of gas, and it's...well...cleaner."

In other words, someone hadn't died in it. Naomi nodded. "I appreciate it very much. I'll return it as soon as I'm able."

"No need." Martin spoke this time. "It was my wife's. She doesn't need it anymore."

Naomi bent her head. "I'm sorry for your loss." She could *feel* Martin's discomfort with her sympathy, and pressed on. "Thank you for getting the kids in Cascade. It's a relief to my mind."

"It was no trouble." He kept his eyes on his scuffing feet, his voice gruff. "I just hope someone is helping my kids, if they need it."

Naomi nodded at Jack and Layla then, keeping her expression polite and remote. "I am very grateful for your help."

Layla stepped forward. "I know you said your cabin was stocked with supplies, but if you need anything, please don't hesitate. We're here." She reached for Naomi's hand and tucked a small bag into it. "And it would mean a lot to me if you would take this."

"What is it?"

"A protective charm." Layla seemed uncomfortable for a moment, her eyes darting to Jack. Then she lifted her chin. "You can think of it as a prayer made physical, for you and Macy. It holds some elements that I hope will bring healing and peace to you both. Yarrow. Angelica. A piece of chrysoprase."

Naomi closed her hand around the small blue velvet bag, and to her surprise, felt a warmth that was distinctly "Layla." She nodded her gratitude. "I don't know anything about charms, but I appreciate the thought behind it."

Silence, then, filled with things no one wanted said.

Naomi left them standing there and hurried back to Macy. She'd been so glad to find other people, and now she didn't know how much longer she could stand the pressure of their unspoken words. Rowan, too, was silent as Naomi gathered her daughter in her arms, trailing behind her as she carried her out of the church basement and into the late-afternoon sunshine.

Martin opened the back door of the SUV, and both dogs leaped in obediently. Naomi settled Macy in the front passenger seat, fastened the seat belt around her, then turned for a final goodbye.

Verity stood in the center of the group now, the sun on her head and shoulders somehow brighter than on the others. She smiled at Naomi, her face infused at once with wisdom, mischief and sorrow. "Don't wander too long in the ghostlands, Naomi. You're needed elsewhere."

Oh, how she wanted to get in the SUV and drive, to pretend she hadn't heard. But her feet were rooted to the spot, and a reply forced its way through her stiff lips. "I don't know what you mean."

"Nostalgia can comfort, but the past belongs to the dead. Visions of the future can urge us on, but it's a place with no substance. Your power is needed in the here and now."

"My power." Naomi shook her head. "I suppose you're going to tell me God has a plan for me, too? Well how about this? What if God *does* have a plan, and it's to wash his hands of us? You know, like a loving parent would do with a grown kid who just can't stop screwing up – you've got to stop enabling them, right? What if this intuitive evolution or whatever is a parting gift? What if it's God's way of saying, 'You're on your own. Good luck. I'm out of here.'"

Jack looked pained, but Verity's smile was transcendent. "What an amazing idea!" She cocked her head to the side for a moment as if listening, then grinned. "Raphael says he thinks you're on to something."

Naomi stared. What could she possibly say to that? She shook her head, and was still shaking it as she got behind the wheel of the SUV, started the engine, and drove out of the parking lot without looking again at any of them.

Beside her, Macy stared out the side window in what appeared to be a half-doze. Naomi didn't know if she had heard Verity's words, and she had no intention of asking. She reached out and tucked the soft blanket Rowan had given them more closely under her chin. "How're you doing, baby? Are you warm enough?"

Macy's head rolled towards her, and she blinked a few times. Her little forehead wrinkled in confusion. "Mama? Where are we?"

Naomi's palms went greasy on the steering wheel. "We're headed to the cabin, remember? To meet Piper?"

"Oh." She thought about it for a few seconds. "I remember now." Her eyes drifted shut, and her head rolled back towards the window. "So sleepy."

Naomi stopped the SUV in the middle of the road – no traffic to worry about – and reached across Macy to recline her seat. Macy murmured, but didn't open her eyes. Naomi stared at her for a minute, then two, and finally forced herself to put the vehicle in motion again.

They cruised along without incident, Naomi analyzing their surroundings constantly for trouble to be avoided. Martin had assured her that their route should be safe, but nothing was certain. When they passed the water treatment facility and turned to wind up Rampart Range Road, she felt some of her terrible tension begin to uncoil.

The road twisted through dark pines and past huge, rounded boulders. After making sure the blanket was still warmly tucked around Macy, Naomi cracked her window and lifted her nose to the soft spring breeze. She loved the smell of the air up here. She had been coming to this cabin over half her life, since she and Scott started dating, and she never failed to appreciate the beauty and peace of this place. Even now, even under these circumstances, she could feel the muscles in her neck and shoulders loosen, feel her stomach relax.

The road lifted them into high mountain meadows, interspersed with thick stands of pine and aspen. Though it seemed remote, this was actually a well-traveled area. To the southeast, Rampart Reservoir was a popular camping and recreational area. Not many people, though, were even aware of the string of eight man-made lakes so close by. The people who lived and played on Carrol Lakes preferred it that way.

Scott used to call this place his "true north." He had inherited the cabin from his father, who had inherited it from his father, who had built it in the 1920's. Scott had proposed to her here, on a paddle boat in the middle of the lake. Would he be here? Would Macy be able to *see* him once again, instead of just feeling his presence?

Naomi reached over to fuss with the blanket and Macy startled, sucking in a sudden breath of air, but not waking. She seemed to hold the breath for a long, long time, releasing it slowly, and Naomi frowned. She switched her gaze back and forth between the road and

Macy, until she finally sucked in another deep breath, only to release it in slow increments again.

Naomi resisted the urge to step on the accelerator; these dirt roads were tricky under the best of circumstances, and she was in an unfamiliar vehicle. All she wanted to do was tuck Macy safely into the soft little trundle she always slept on when they stayed here, to surround her with the familiar and the comfortable, to begin the process of nursing her back to health.

It hardly seemed real when they finally pulled in at the cabin, the evening orange, pink and still warm with the lowering sun. Naomi put the SUV in park, then sat there with it running for a moment, making sure all looked and *felt* as it should, running her eyes along the familiar, whimsical lines of the little cabin. Home. *Home* at last, after the longest of journeys.

She shut off the ignition and popped the back door open for the dogs. They bounded out, both of them energized with the joy she was feeling. Then she went around the SUV to get Macy. She unbuckled the seatbelt from around her daughter, then shook her shoulder gently.

"Macy, honey, we're here! We're home!"

Macy's eyes fluttered. She stared at Naomi, confused again, then a little smile lifted her lips. "I was having the nicest dream." Her words slurred together, and a stab of alarm cut through Naomi's euphoria. "There were horses..."

Her voice trailed off, and Naomi bent to lift her with arms that were suddenly shaking. "You can tell me all about it while I get a fire started. You're so cold, honey, why didn't you say something?"

She hurried toward the cabin, Macy light as dust in her arms. They were almost to the porch when Macy's body twitched. She drew in another deep breath, but this one rattled. Her head lolled back, and her eyes met Naomi's, wide with terror. "Mama! Mama, I'm scared!"

"Shh, baby, shh. I've got you." She sank to her knees, curling around her daughter, trying to use her own body to shelter, to warm, to protect, to bind. "We're almost home. We're almost there, my baby."

The fear seeped out of Macy's eyes. She blinked, once. Twice. Then her face lit with a smile of such beauty, Naomi would see it every time she closed her eyes for the rest of her life. Macy exhaled, gazing over Naomi's shoulder, and on that exhale, greeted her father.

"Daddy."

She didn't inhale again. Naomi stared at her daughter's still face and shook her, gently at first, then with more force. "Macy! Macy, answer me, God damn it! Macy!"

But Macy was no longer inhabiting those glazed eyes. Something tore free in Naomi's chest and lifted out of her body, taking with it light, life, meaning, joy. She clutched Macy to her and huddled around the emptiness, the husk that had been her baby girl. Distantly, she heard the dogs howling, Hades' deep and broken voice sliced by Persephone's higher-pitched wails. A scream was jammed in her own chest, but she couldn't draw enough air to release it. Then, she heard Scott.

"Honey, for pity's sake, be careful! Let me help you up – are you okay? Is the baby okay?"

Naomi lifted her head, and there he was. His hands were full of balloons, flowers and gift bags, and he was scowling at her. The sun bouncing off the snow and ice surrounding him was so bright, it nearly blinded her.

She looked down, resettling Macy in her arms, making sure her tiny face was covered and protected from the biting cold. Icy moisture seeped through the knees of the maternity jeans she wore. It irked her to be back in them, but she had to admit they were warmer than the cheerful sundress she had packed. That's what she got for packing her hospital bag on an optimistically warm spring day. A late-season blizzard had surprised even the weather forecasters, so instead of the adorable, Easter-egg-plaid going-home outfit she'd bought for Macy, the baby was layered in long-sleeved hospital onesies and jury-rigged receiving blankets. Behind her, she heard the front door burst open.

"You're home!" Piper slipped and skidded down the front steps. She helped Naomi to her feet with uncharacteristic gentleness, then reached out to touch the blanket covering her new baby sister. Her face glowed with delight. "Can I hold her when we get inside? Oh, and we don't have any power. I started a fire in the wood-burner."

"Fantastic." Scott joined them and took Naomi's elbow firmly. They shuffled along, Naomi feeling both awkward and nimble, still trying to adapt to the abrupt gravity-shift that went with giving birth. Piper bounded up the steps ahead of them and slipped in the door.

"I'll make sure the dogs don't take you out, Mom. They missed you."

Once they were inside, Naomi closed her eyes and inhaled. *Home.* Even with the chill in the air, the warmth of it folded around her. She made her way to the keeping room, Scott trailing behind her, shedding packages and parcels as he went.

Persephone danced around her feet, while Zeus bounded back and forth between her and Scott, never able to decide who he was happier to see. Naomi looked around for a moment, wondering where Hades was, but the thought fluttered away as quickly as it had come.

As promised, Piper had built a fire in the wood-burning stove. She had also dragged in a mattress – probably from the daybed in the guest room – and made up a neat and cozy bed close to the fire. A pot simmered on top of the stove – by the smell, she was heating some of the turkey soup Naomi had made then frozen at Christmas time. Piper fussed with the pillows on the bed, then gestured to the pot.

"I thought you'd be hungry. And this is the only place that's warm, until the electricity comes back on."

Naomi opened her mouth to thank her, but before she could speak, Piper pointed at her, shaking her head.

"Don't say anything!" Her expression was equal parts embarrassment and pride. "Just because I *don't* embrace 'Martha Stewart' doesn't mean I *can't.*"

Naomi walked right past her daughter's prickles, cupped the back of her huffy head, and pulled her in for a smacking kiss. "I *will* say 'thank you.' You're so thoughtful, honey. I appreciate you." Then she held out the baby. "Do you want to hold your little sister?"

Piper slid her arms under Macy and cuddled her close, eyes locked on the baby's tiny, smushed, red face. "Oh," she breathed. "Look how perfect she is. Look how beautiful."

Scott moved a rocking chair close to the fire, and Piper sank into it, never taking her eyes off her sister's face. Naomi watched, heart-full, as her oldest daughter fell in love with her youngest. Scott slid an arm around her shoulders and squeezed.

"What am I going to do with all these pretty girls?" He murmured. "If only my high school buddies could see me now. Scott the Nerd, surrounded by cute chicks." They smiled into each other's eyes, enjoying their history and these new moments, as their family re-formed into something wondrous and new. Then he let her go and started his characteristic bustling.

"This settles it, honey. We're getting a generator, just as soon as I can get to the store and buy one." He left the room, and puffed back in a few minutes later with another mattress. "No reason we can't all be comfortable. If the power doesn't come back on, we'll end up sleeping here anyway. Have a seat, honey, and I'll dish us up some soup."

They spent the rest of the afternoon and the evening cocooned in the warmth of that room, admiring the baby and playing games, smiling as the dogs approached with cautious sniffs, laughing at Ares' haughty disdain for the tiny new interloper. The power wouldn't come back on until the following morning, a fact Naomi would always remember with profound gratitude.

She lay in the stillness late that night, nursing the baby, listening to the soft pop and hiss of the fire, and reveling in the perfection of this slice of time. Piper was burrowed deep in the covers, only her eyes and forehead showing, as usual. Scott was curved around her back, his big body warm, strong, familiar. And this tiny new person, sweet little mouth tugging at her breast, little body curved with the intensity of a nursing newborn, a whole new adventure spreading out before them. She drifted to sleep knowing in her bones that this moment, *this exact moment*, was the happiest moment of her life.

Naomi opened her eyes. She was lying on the floor in front of the cold fireplace in the cabin. Hades was pressed against her back, from her nape to her knees, and Persephone was curled under her chin, against her chest.

Between her and the fireplace, wrapped in the soft, peach blanket so that only her hair showed, lay Macy. In the grey light of early morning, her hair glowed with life. Surely something that vibrant was alive?

Naomi lifted her hand, knowing, before she laid it on Macy's body, what she would feel. Stillness. Stiffness. A deep breath shuddered into her lungs, her first breath on the first morning without her daughter in it, and she howled.

EIGHTEEN
Piper: Walden, CO

Piper's eyes snapped open in the grey stillness before dawn. In the bed beside her, tuned to her every move whether he was awake or asleep, Brody tensed with sudden alertness. His hand closed around her wrist.

"What is it?" His voice was a hoarse grate in her ear.

She strained to listen. The silence was so complete, she could hear blood shushing in her ears. After several long moments, she finally answered. "Someone was screaming."

Brody rose from the bed naked, oblivious to the chill, and ghosted to the window. His face was sharp-edged in the soft gray light, his cold blue eyes quick and analytical as they scanned the area outside the cabin. Piper watched him, rubbing at the center of her chest, which ached unbearably. She felt like she'd been kicked by a mule.

For the first time in the longest time, she thought of her family. Of her brilliant and funny father, and sweet little Macy, and her maddening, tender mother. They would be at the cabin by now, surely, with a menagerie of animals in tow. She tried to picture them there, at this exact moment, using memory to create the image. Her folks would be sleeping. Macy might be awake, especially if Ares wanted his breakfast...

Brody slid back into bed beside her. "I didn't hear anything. You must have been dreaming."

Piper stared at the ceiling. "I must have been."

Brody reached out and picked up a piece of her sleep-mussed hair, stroking it straight before winding it slowly around his hand. He loved her hair, loved running his fingers through it, brushing it, and using it to make her do things she would never be able to speak of.

"What are you thinking?"

She knew better than to say "nothing" by now. "I was thinking about what Max taught me yesterday. Edible plants."

Brody grunted, and without another word, moved on top of her. Piper put her arms around him – she had learned that, too – and shifted her body to accommodate his. Tensing her muscles only made it hurt, and going limp was not tolerated, so she concentrated on a state that hovered somewhere in-between. When she achieved the proper tension in her arms and legs, she focused on the knotty pine ceiling, tracing shapes with her eyes and naming them: Owl. Ghost. Comet. Edvard Munch's *The Scream*.

Like using the bathroom or brushing his teeth, this was just something Brody did in the mornings. He finished in total silence, as always, and rolled off her. She waited until he shut the bathroom door behind him before she rose and dressed quickly. She never let him see her naked, if she could help it. She sat at the tiny kitchen table, waiting for her turn in the bathroom, and her thoughts turned again to her family.

She didn't want to think of them. Hurt too much. What would her father think of his little girl now? He had always been so proud of her, so proud to claim her as his own. And Macy idolized her – would she still, if she could see the depths to which Piper had sunk? She saw their faces in her mind's eye and cringed. She didn't know what to call what she'd become – whore or victim – but she couldn't imagine revealing her current circumstances to either of the people she most adored in this world. The ache in her chest blossomed into a throbbing burn that made it hard to breathe. She squeezed her eyes shut and hummed a little repetitive tune, rocking to the rhythm of it in her chair. Drown it out. Don't think about it. *Don't think about it.*

She had felt this sensation once before, that first morning, when she woke up naked, bloody and alone in Brody's cabin. He had tied her to the bed before he left, ankles and wrists. Her chest had ached then, too, something deeper than her injuries, something missing, an emptiness. She hadn't spent much time puzzling over it; more urgent was the need to free herself, which of course, had proved impossible.

Brody had returned to find that she'd twisted her skin off in the attempt. She had tried talking to him, that first morning. He didn't respond to a word she had to say. Nor did he acknowledge her involuntary cries when he used her torn body again. When he was finished, he untied her and tossed some clothes at her.

"Clean up and get dressed. There's a situation with the others that needs to be handled."

She had done as he told her – the first of many times. On the way to the mess hall, he had outlined the rules: Do not talk with the others, except to communicate necessities. Do not hint or suggest that this situation is not of your choosing. Do not cry or show any other signs of distress. The consequences of violating the rules were simple: People would die.

She hadn't believed him. She'd actually thought he was being melodramatic. She had nodded her acquiescence, but had pulled the sleeves of her sweatshirt up so the others would see her raw wrists, had held her head high and pushed back her hair, so they'd see the bruising on her face and throat. Some of the other men had been trying to romance her; she hated to stoop to it, but she would use that if she had to. This group valued strength and self-sufficiency. They were rough, often crude, and she suspected all of them were capable of brutality. But surely they wouldn't allow this. Surely they wouldn't just abandon her to this.

When they had walked into the mess hall, she had learned just how badly she'd misjudged the situation.

She hardly recognized Levi when he charged at her, didn't even have time to lift her hand to deflect the blow. She was on the ground before she registered the pain, the right side of her face a red explosion, a deafening ringing in her ears. She looked up at the hatred twisting his face, at the tears shining in trails down his cheeks, and didn't even see him draw back his foot. He kicked her savagely in the ribs twice before Brody stepped in front of her.

She curled into a ball, trying to wheeze in air, and heard him say, "Enough. She made her choice. It's not her fault he couldn't handle it."

Piper's head came up. She squinted at Brody, at Levi, at the others, trying to make sense of what was happening. That was when she saw Noah.

He was stretched out on one of the mess hall tables. His skin was the strangest shade of gray she had ever seen. His bloodshot eyes were open and filmy, his features frozen in a grotesque expression, tongue protruding from his wide-open mouth. Around his neck, she could see where the rope had been, a deep, bruised indentation. His sister Jenny was sitting beside him, humming softly and so, so carefully smoothing his hair, straightening his clothes, adjusting his hands. Her face was serene and empty.

Behind her, Jenny's husband was holding their only surviving child, his face as frozen as Jenny's while their son sobbed. The others were ranged about the room, grouped according to their alliances, and not one of them was making eye contact with her.

She looked at Noah's face again, and the ache in her chest expanded. She understood the emptiness now. The connection that had been her friendship with Noah had been severed, leaving her with the raw, amputated stump of it. She looked up at Levi and opened her mouth, but all the things she wanted to say were wrong: I didn't... We weren't... It's not...

Help me.

Finally, she managed, "I'm sorry."

She thought Levi's eyes would burst from his skull. He tried to lunge past Brody, who blocked him smoothly. "You're sorry? Sorry? You worthless, god-damned bitch!" He shook a piece of paper at her, spit flying as he raged. "Did you think this wouldn't crush him? 'Staying with Brody. Take care.' You're a fucking whore, and you didn't even have the decency to-" He choked on his words, crumpled the paper and threw it at her. "I want her out of here. Now. I won't have her here."

Piper caught the paper reflexively, and her eyes flew around the room. No one would look at her. She looked up at Brody. He was staring down at her, his eyes as arctic as ever, but a tiny smile played around his mouth. She had known then, *known,* and the depth of his ruthlessness had stunned her.

He had planned this. All of it. From what he had said to Levi the night before in the mess hall, to the note he had made her write, to the death of a good and kind young man. Noah never had a chance. He had been dead as soon as Brody decided on this course of action.

The only person in the group who knew her well, or cared enough to look past the surface, had been eliminated. Levi hadn't liked her from the start, and now he had even less reason to believe her, much less help her. She had been keeping a cool distance from the rest of the men, per Levi's instructions. And she hadn't had a chance – or the desire, to be honest – to connect with the other women. Jenny was drowning in grief, and Ruth wasn't exactly approachable. Piper looked around the room one last desperate time, calculating. He couldn't kill them all. If she told them all the truth –

Brody knelt beside her on the pretense of helping her up, speaking so that only she could hear. "I can see what you're thinking. I wouldn't recommend it." He inclined his head towards young Caden, weeping inconsolably in his father's arms. "He's next. Then Jenny. I'll make it look like they couldn't handle the grief of Noah's death, and that will come back on you." He helped her stand on watery legs, keeping his back to the group. "At best, they all think you're fickle or an opportunist. At worst, they'll throw you out of the group, on your own, with no supplies. They won't believe you, and if you do get someone to listen to you, you'll be causing more death. It's on you."

He had put an arm around her shoulders, steering her towards the door and speaking over his shoulder to the group. "We'll talk about this later."

She had dared one last look, and this time, they had all been staring at her. Emotions had ranged from disapproval to hatred, but their eyes had all conveyed the

334 | Kathy Miner

same message: Your fault. They all believed it. And from that moment on, she did, too.

For three days, Brody had kept her separated from the group. In that time, Piper had reasoned, empathized, wept, mocked, raged, begged and then screamed, screamed, screamed when Brody meted out his retribution. The first time she forced herself to obey him, it had shamed her. By the end of those three days, she was no longer capable of feeling shame. In fact, she didn't feel anything at all.

Since then, Piper had learned so much. She had learned to follow the rules, to the letter. She had learned to pretend so convincingly, she nearly fooled herself. She had learned to be silent. No matter what she thought or felt, the words stayed in her throat, frozen and still. These days, it took a concentrated effort to talk at all.

She had also learned how to insulate herself from the outside world. She could stare at nothing indefinitely, watch the tops of trees sway for hours, lose herself watching an ant struggle along under a crumb three times his size. Numb. Blank. In these ways, she made it from one breath to the next.

Outside the cabin window, the forest was warming to pink with the rising sun. Birds flitted from the tree tops to the forest floor and back again. Piper tried to attach her mind to their movements, to achieve the drifting, moment-to-moment trance that had been her refuge, but couldn't. She shifted in her chair, uncomfortably aware of her skin. She felt electrically alive this morning, unbearably awake.

She rubbed again at the ache in the center of her chest and frowned. "What the hell?"

Her mother's face bloomed in her mind – plump and soft, filled with love and intelligence. It was the intelligence that had always pissed Piper off – how could she choose such a mundane life? Where was the desire to better herself, to be *something* other than a housewife? Since she was 12, her mother had been a source of embarrassment and irritation.

But in spite of their strained relationship, Piper had been aware of a connection to her mother since the start of the plague, an awareness that felt like a homing beacon. Like she could close her eyes and start walking, and she'd end up with her mom. At first it had irritated her, but she'd gotten over that in a hurry. Funny, what a 99% death rate could do for even the most troubled of relationships.

Before Brody, she had longed to rejoin her family. Josh, their communications specialist, had tried every day to raise someone in the Colorado Springs area on his short-wave radio, hoping they could locate her family and come up with a plan to reunite them. Since Brody, she had thought of her family as little as possible.

Until today. The screaming she had awakened to echoed in her head. She felt like she was standing with her toes on the edge of a cliff.

The bathroom door opened, and Piper smoothed the frown off her face. She let her eyes go soft-focus and turned towards the window as Brody moved around the cabin. He tended to leave her alone when she was still and blank like this, and usually it wasn't an act. In the movements of birds, there was no Brody. Today, though, her mind was stuttering to life under her zombie façade, whether she liked it or not.

As clearly as if he were sitting beside her, her father's voice sounded in her ear. "Make a choice, honey."

Piper started, then threw a furtive glance at Brody. He was emptying his day bag so he could organize and refill it, the way he did every morning, and he didn't look up. First the screaming, now this. Looked like she was officially hearing things.

"Don't just drift, Piper. Decide what you want, analyze, and choose a course of action."

How many times had her dad given her that advice, especially in her party-till-you-puke college years? Hearing his beloved voice, even if it was a stress-induced hallucination, brought tears to her eyes. She blinked fast and kept her face turned towards the window.

So easy, to keep drifting. So hard, to wake up. Waking up meant thinking. Thinking meant feeling. Thinking and feeling would mean acting. Even in zombie mode, she knew that.

Brody was suddenly there, his hand encircling her wrist again. "What are you thinking?"

Shit. Shit! Usually she had some benign phrase ready for these "tests," but her mind was completely blank. "Ah, I, ah..."

Her head snapped to the side, her hair flying across her face to stick in her eyes and mouth. It never failed to shock her, no matter how many times he hit.

Until now, there had been no violence in her world. He could hit so fast and so hard, while barely seeming to move.

"Don't lie to me. What are you thinking?"

Piper righted herself slowly and swallowed the coppery taste in her mouth. "Birds," she said as evenly as she could manage. "I was watching a bird, and I can't remember the name. The big black and white one."

He stared at her, on and on and on. He always did this, and usually it terrified her. This morning, though, the theme song to "Jeopardy" popped into her head. She nearly started singing it. She dug her nails into the palm of her free hand and concentrated with all her might on looking blank and scared.

Finally, he released her wrist with a flick. "Magpie. Go use the bathroom. We need to get going."

Ducking her head, she scurried to collect clean clothes before shutting the bathroom door behind her. She used the toilet first, as fast as she could. Her time in the bathroom was carefully monitored; Brody checked on her frequently, regardless of how private a function she was performing. When she was finished, she stripped out of the sweats and t-shirt she had slept in and slid into her clean clothes, sighing in relief when the door didn't pop open while she was naked. She scraped her hair back into a low ponytail without bothering to comb it, then brushed her teeth gingerly. She spat in the basin and went still, staring down at the bright red streaks mixed with the foamy toothpaste. Then she did something she hadn't done in a long time.

She looked in the mirror.

The red mark on her cheek was layered over yesterday's deepening bruise, and a yellow smudge from the one a few days before that. Her skin was sickly pale and her face was thin to the point of gauntness. Now that she thought about it, her jeans were looser than normal, too. She pulled her sweatshirt to the side, staring at the black outline of Brody's fingers on her prominent collarbone.

Were the others blind? Did they think she liked her sex rough? Did they tell themselves she was losing weight because she was too madly in love to eat? She looked into her own eyes, and out of the deep box-inside-a-box where she'd stuffed it, rage bubbled up. She leaned towards the mirror, teeth bared.

"Choose!" she hissed at herself. "Analyze! Choose a course!"

Brody's sharp rap on the door nearly sent her scurrying back into her zombie cage. "Move it, Piper. Two minutes, or I'll help you finish."

She watched her own face pinch with fear. "I'm hurrying," she answered. She ran water in the basin, but her eyes never left her own in the mirror.

She would die like this, eventually. She was sure of it. She would either lose the will to live, or he'd kill her. A slow death either way. From the same place she'd stuffed the rage, a fierce desire to live surged through her. She leaned close to the mirror once more, smiling with red-stained teeth and touching her reflection-self tenderly on the cheek.

"I'd rather die quick, wouldn't you?"

She left the bathroom with exactly 15 seconds to spare, wearing the vague, obedient expression she had spent the last minute and 10 seconds practicing.

Analysis had begun.

They walked to the mess hall like always, Piper trailing slightly behind. Brody had defeated her at every turn so far by planning, as simple as that. He had anticipated every possible response she might have to the events he had set in motion, and had been ready with a ruthless counterattack. He was a brilliant tactician, she had to give him that.

Well, Brody might know tactics, but Piper knew people. She'd been studying them all her life. She had never questioned what she'd major in at college, not from the moment she learned what the study of people and social behavior was called. Under her blank mask, she smirked with ironic delight. How many people had informed her that sociology was a great major if you wanted to wait tables? Looked like some of those college classes might have some real-world applications after all.

Brody spoke without looking at her. "Who do you have left to do a rotation with?"

One of Levi's many objections to Piper's continued presence in the group had been her lack of any practical skills. To appease him, Brody had agreed to allow her to spend time with some of the others, to see if she had an aptitude for a particular discipline or skill set. So far, she had proven herself to be an abysmal cook and disinclined towards wilderness survival.

She had already thought this through and knew exactly how she would respond, but she waited a heartbeat. Then two. "Uhm. I was with Max yesterday."

"Yeah." Brody gave her a derisive glance. "He said you could live off the land just dandy, as long as the land was a fully stocked Walmart."

She didn't respond. He would lead her through this. His consistency was her advantage.

"Levi won't have you." He never missed a chance to tell her that. "And I doubt you'd be able to handle any kind of firearm, anyway."

Another smirk behind the mask, like a jewel in a hidden treasure chest. He couldn't know she was the daughter of Annie Oakley reincarnated, and had inherited at least a measure of her mother's aptitude. This time, she did answer. "I don't want to learn to shoot. Guns scare me."

She felt Brody's sharp eyes on her and plodded on placidly, her own eyes drifting between the path ahead and the tops of the swaying trees. Even now, they soothed her.

After a few moments, he spoke again. "You'll need to learn, eventually. It's a skill everyone in the group needs to have."

Score another one for her. "I haven't been with Ruth. Or Josh." She gave her voice just a little more animation. "I'd like to learn what Josh does. Communications was my major in college."

Brody shot her a disgusted look. "It's not the same thing. Idiot," he muttered under his breath, and Piper's heart beat a triumphant tattoo.

Her goal was simple: Escape from Brody, and reunite with her family. Something was wrong there, she was sure of it, but dwelling on it would cripple her. Above all, she needed to control her emotions so she could make quick, clean decisions. She had a single advantage: Brody thought she was cowed and more than a little stupid. Making sure he continued to believe that was her top priority.

Priority two: She needed to alter her position in the social network of the group. She couldn't survive on her own, at least not yet. Right now, she had no social capital whatsoever, no value, and no connections other than Brody. Her relationship with him was blatantly asymmetrical and as such, damaged her standing even more. This was a warrior culture, and she was chattel. She needed to re-cast herself without tipping her hand to Brody, and she knew just how to do it: Work.

This group was more formal than most, in that it had assigned specific tasks to its members in order to achieve a specific goal. She needed them to trust her enough to assign her a task. When she had been given that task, she needed to do it brilliantly, diligently, without complaint or fanfare. She needed to be noticed by everybody but Brody. This was the trickiest part of her plan, and she would have to negotiate every step with the caution of a tightrope walker.

"If she'll have you, you'll be with Ruth today. We should have more than one medic, and someone who passed a couple years of college should be able to learn basic first aid."

Piper wrung her hands. "I'm not very good with blood," she began, and as she'd known he would, Brody stopped and spun to face her, crowding his body close to hers, using his bulk to intimidate and subdue. He cupped her face in his hand, forcing her to look at him, thumb and fingers biting into her cheeks.

"Are you questioning me?"

"No! No, I'm not, really, it's just I get sick when I see blood, and I didn't want that to be a problem, and –"

"Shut up. You were questioning me, and you'll pay a penalty for it later." How he loved to promise future violence, then follow through. "Until then, you'll spend the day with Ruth. Do you understand?"

"Yes."

"Yes what?"

Everyone else called him "Sanders," but he insisted she call him "Brody." Over and over. It was a potential chink in his armor that she needed to analyze. "Yes, Brody."

"Good." He stayed where he was, gazing down at her, eyes narrowed. For just a moment, his hand softened on her face, nearly a caress. His eyes drifted to her hair, and he frowned. "Your hair needs attention," he said huskily. "I'll take care of it tonight."

He dropped his hand, turned and walked away, and Piper added another element to her analysis.

That first night, he had asked her to submit to him willingly. "I don't want it to be rape," he had said. Since then, he had not repeated those words. He used her whenever he wished, but he never tried to caress or arouse her. Occasionally, though, a moment would pass between them where he was almost tender. Occasionally, she caught him looking at her with what she could only describe as "longing."

Growing up, Piper's mother had tried to instill compassion in her girls. "Those who are heartless," she would say, "Once cared too much. How badly must they be hurting inside, if hurting others is the only thing that makes them feel better?"

Piper supposed her mother hadn't intended the lesson to be used as a weapon, but that's just what she planned to do. If Brody had a tender underbelly, she was going to find it. When she did, she would disembowel him.

They arrived at the mess hall. Brody held the door open for her, and she stepped in ahead of him. Most everyone was already seated at one of the long tables, the low buzz of conversation punctuated by occasional laughter. As always, her presence triggered a momentary silence. Then, as a single entity, they shifted their bodies, angling away from her, shutting her out.

She served herself from the kitchen and headed back out to the main area. Brody always sat with Levi and Tyler, and he didn't expect her to join them – part of his "everything's fine" camouflage. Jenny, her husband Aaron, and Caden kept to themselves. Josh, Ethan and Adam could usually be found together – the others had started calling them Things 1, 2 and 3 – but Piper only sat near them if either Ruth or Max was already there.

Being the oldest members of the group, Ruth and Max tended to stick together. They were also the only ones who appeared interested in increasing social cohesion in the group by rotating their seating choices. Most frequently, they could both be found sitting with the Things, but often one or both of them would join Jenny's family. Occasionally, Max would join Brody's group, though Ruth never did.

Piper had analyzed these connections without conscious thought. Up until now, she had chosen the seat least likely to earn her a reprimand later, then had concentrated on pushing her food around to form pleasing artistic patterns. This morning, though, she was glad to see Ruth and Max seated with the Things. They were definitely more prone to levity than Jenny's family. And she was hungry.

She sat down near the group, at the exact distance she had calculated to be "close but not intrusive." Aware of Brody's eyes on her, she stuck with the pattern she had already established, pushing the food around in a lackluster manner, eating only an occasional bite until he was fully engaged in conversation with Adam. Then, keeping her eyes on him, she shoveled eggs in as fast as she could. He looked up once, and she let her eyes go unfocused, let them drift up to the ceiling, and stopped chewing altogether, until he looked away again. Then she crammed half a piece of toast in her mouth.

She glanced at the group beside her and found Ruth staring at her, eyes narrowed. Shit, Piper thought. She let her eyes slide vacantly away, and put the rest of the toast back on her plate. She stared into space, face slack, berating herself. She needed to keep her behavior consistent in front of everyone, not just Brody, until she had properly set her plan in motion. One person on her side did her no good – they would just be eliminated. She needed to shift the entire group. Hungry as she still was, she left the rest of the food on her plate. To distract herself, she tuned in to the group's conversation.

Max was speaking, his voice animated. "We tested it out – just used a deck of cards and had them guess the suit, so a 25% chance of being right. The government used to do this same kind of experiment, years ago." Max leaned forward, nodding down the table. "Our boy Ethan here guessed right 55% of the time – 55%! That's crazy! And Tyler was right nearly 60% of the time!" He leaned back, shaking his head, laughing in wonder. "I won't play cards with either one of 'em ever again, you can bet on that!"

Josh looked uncomfortable. "Christ, Max, what are you saying? That the plague made people psychic? How's that work? They didn't get it – they were just exposed, like the rest of us. And if you're right, why aren't all of us mind-readers now?"

Ruth cut in. "It's not really mind-reading. It's an intuitive hunch – like when you know who's on the phone before you look at the name? Or you know when the Daily Double is going to come up on Jeopardy, just before it does? Stuff like that?" Josh just stared at her blankly, and she snorted. "Okay. Never mind. We don't think everyone is experiencing it, and certainly not at the level Tyler and Ethan are. And we're not sure how it's related to the plague. People change as a result of stress — it could be as simple as that. An evolution."

"We haven't talked to everyone about it. Jenny and her family have other things on their minds. And others, well..." Max glanced in Piper's direction, and she quickly looked away. "We think it's different for different people, too. Ruth says she's had 'gut feelings' all her life, but they're much stronger now. I haven't noticed any change, but I'm still hoping." He chuckled. "I will be so pissed if this passes me by — I read every book on psychic phenomenon I could get my hands on when I was a kid."

Josh still looked uncomfortable, his fingers rubbing over the small cross he always wore around his neck. "Yeah, well, some of us don't buy into that evolution bullshit. Ya'll can believe you're hairless apes if you want to, but I am a Created man." He stood, eyeing Ethan suspiciously. "Far as I'm concerned, you can keep your mind-reading shit to yourself. That is tool-of-Satan stuff, man."

"No problem." Ever easy-going, Ethan stood, collecting his plate and silverware then nodding to the others. "Off to do the Devil's work. Have a good day."

Laughter followed him, and Piper's mind raced. What was this? What had Ruth said? Evolution? As in evolution of the *species*? Piper searched her experiences, looking for evidence to support this extraordinary hypothesis, but quickly let that line of inquiry drop. She'd been so out of it, people could have grown tails and she wouldn't have noticed.

Brody finished eating, took his plate to the kitchen, then approached Ruth. Piper resumed her blank stare, heard Brody ask and Ruth accept, and kept right on staring. She jumped when Brody's hand landed on her shoulder.

"Ruth has agreed to spend the day with you. Try to keep your head out of the clouds and pay attention." He wrapped his hand around her ponytail as he spoke to her, just tight enough to sting her scalp. Using his hold on her hair, he twisted her face up to him. "I'm going out on patrol with Levi and Adam. We'll be back late this afternoon."

"Okay." She was aware of everyone's eyes on them, and kept her face still, though her eyes wanted to smart with tears.

He squeezed his fist once, hard, making her gasp, then dropped her ponytail and walked away. Piper waited until Ruth rose from the table, then picked up her plate and utensils and hurried after her.

Ruth had set up a clinic in a room off the kitchen. She had also commandeered one of the nearby cabins as a quarantine facility, though no one had been sick with the plague since Jenny's youngest son died. Ruth gave her a tour, explaining where supplies were kept and how they needed to be handled, as well as what she felt it would be most important for Piper to learn.

"I need someone to back me up for basic first aid, and simple procedures like stitches." As she talked, Ruth started setting out the supplies she would need for Piper's first lesson. "If this suits you, I can give you more extensive training. Someone else should know how to assess more serious injuries and illnesses, to be able to decide whether or not to use the pharmaceuticals we have on hand. Noah was really good with triage."

Piper couldn't suppress a flinch. It was the first time she'd heard Noah's name spoken aloud since the day of his death. She had not grieved him. She had not dared. Of all the things she had done in the last weeks, neglecting the memory of her friend shamed her the most. She looked up to find Ruth watching her. After a moment, the older woman shook her head.

"Quite a pickle you've got yourself in, little girl."

Piper kept her face still and returned Ruth's steady gaze, though her heart was pounding. She was fairly certain Ruth was offering an alliance, but she needed to stick to the plan. When it was apparent Piper didn't intend to answer, Ruth sighed and resumed her instruction.

They worked together all morning, took a brief break for lunch, and went right back at it in the afternoon. It was bliss to use her mind again, to concentrate and learn. She had maneuvered for this opportunity because it offered tactical advantages – people were grateful when you helped them, when you stopped their pain – but she hadn't expected to find it so interesting. By the end of the afternoon, Ruth was shaking her head in wonder.

"I've never seen someone learn as fast as you," she said. "I say it once, and you've got it. Maybe this is how you're manifesting psychic talent, like we were talking about at breakfast. What was it you were studying at college?"

"Sociology," Piper said, and Ruth snorted.

"Well, you were wasting your time, if you ask me. You've got an aptitude for the medical field. I think we can tell Sanders we've found your skill set. I'll have you trained in no time." She shot Piper a sideways look. "And here I thought you were a dimwit."

Oh, this wouldn't do. Brody wouldn't buy this sudden brilliance after she had failed so miserably before. He couldn't know she was awake and functional. On impulse, she put her hand out, resting it on Ruth's forearm. She had to play this just right. "I'm sure I'll forget it all as soon as I walk out of this room," she said, gazing at Ruth steadily. "And you'll need to repeat it all tomorrow. Every bit of it."

Ruth cocked her head to the side and just looked at her in silence for a few moments. Then she nodded slowly. "I see. Yes, I see what you mean. You have potential, but you need a lot of repetition."

"Yes." Piper didn't try to hide her relief. "Exactly."

In the outer room, there was the sudden sound of multiple pairs of boots on the wooden floor, as well as multiple male voices. Brody, Levi and Adam were back from their patrol, and it sounded like the Things had arrived in the mess hall in anticipation of dinner as well. Brody had told Piper to stay with Ruth until he came to get her, so she settled into a chair to wait. She took several deep breaths, searching for the still, blank place she had been inhabiting, and schooled her face to vacancy, but oh, it was hard. She was *alive* again, and she didn't want to go back in the box.

Ruth moved to stand close beside her, and Piper looked up, startled. Ruth frowned, and reached out to touch Piper's bruised cheek. She shifted her hand to lightly stroke Piper's messy ponytail, her expression troubled. Her mouth opened to speak, but she reconsidered, shutting it again. Then, a smile of evil joy transformed her face.

Ten minutes later, when Brody appeared in the doorway, Piper was covered from the neck down with a plastic sheet, and her hair was lying on the floor around her. Ruth was spreading mayonnaise liberally on her closely shorn scalp.

"Lice!" she barked at him. "She can't work here with lice! And-" She pointed her mayo-covered spatula at him. "She *will* be working here. I need the help, and she did okay today. She can learn this stuff – it'll just take her a while."

Perfect, Piper thought. She kept her head down and her eyes closed as Ruth swathed her head with plastic wrap, muttering her disgust. "You would think somebody would have thought to bring a nit comb and some of that fancy shampoo, but no. This'll have to do." She gave Piper's head a crinkly pat. "There. You leave that on overnight. When you come back in the morning, we'll rinse it out and hit you with the vinegar."

Piper rose from the chair, and she and Ruth worked together to collect and discard every strand of her hair. Only when they were finished did she dare a peek at Brody.

He was staring at her, unnaturally still, and she couldn't begin to analyze the expression on his face. Horror? Rage? Regret? Pretty big emotions, for someone else's hair. She stored the information away for future use.

Ruth shooed her along. "You go get those plastic bags and take care of your bedding, like I told you. Jenny can show you where the extra linens are." Brody moved to take her arm and escort her out the door, but Ruth's voice cracked out, whip-like.

"Where do you think you're going, Sanders?" She held up her spatula and jar of mayo, and gestured at the chair. "You're next."

Piper hustled out and headed for the storeroom, then reversed and slipped silently back down the hall to hover outside the doorway. She heard the rustle of plastic as Ruth prepped Brody for the homemade treatment, heard the buzz of the hair clippers, and all the while, Ruth talked, talked, talked.

Yep, sure enough, he was infested – had he been itching? No? Must have a thick hide. She'd have to check the others, damn it all. That Piper, she'd do as a helper – she tried hard, though she was none too bright. Had a gentle touch, but the technical terms confused her. Better than no help at all. Squalled like a baby when I told her we needed to shave her head, but no way could I get all that hair clean, not without a nit comb, no way. Some women sure put a store by their hair.

Piper heaved a silent sigh of relief and slid away, satisfied that Ruth wouldn't betray her. She headed once more for the storeroom, adapting her plan as she went.

She had an ally, whether she'd wanted one or not, and though it was riskier, it was good to know she wasn't alone.

One by one, she would build connections and alter her standing. Climbin' the social ladder, she thought, and smiled. Ruth was wrong; medicine wasn't her supernatural talent. People were.

All her life, she'd been reading the people around her, and when it suited her purposes, manipulating them. She was reading this group accurately, she *knew* it. They needed another medic, so she'd be the second-best medic they'd ever seen – outshining Ruth was just bad strategy - right up until the day she took over as tactician.

Because that was her end game: When she had achieved the status she needed, it would be time to kill Brody, and take his place as leader of this group. These people were going to pay her back for their blindness, their lack of judgment, and their failure to protect her from Brody's abuse, by conveying her safely to her family.

What she thought of as the mom-bond pulsed in her chest. Piper closed her eyes for a moment and put her hand over her heart. "I'll get there as fast as I can, Mom," she whispered. "I'm on my way."

NINETEEN
Grace: Colorado Springs, CO

Nineteen days. That was how long it took Grace to identify an opportunity and make use of it.

Jen, the catatonic girl, was long since dead. As promised, Little Man had left her body to rot as an "object lesson" for Bri and Grace. Bri had gone downhill swiftly after that, refusing to eat or drink, huddling as far away from Jen's corpse as she could get. Grace had found her dead five days later, slumped over on the floor, a peaceful expression on her young face.

Little Man had removed both corpses the next day, and since then, three other girls had come and gone. Grace had never learned the name of the first one. Little Man had shoved her in the room, then swiftly shut the door, leaving Grace to deal with her panicked, endless circuits around the room. The girl moaned as she half-ran half-crawled, clawing at every crack and crevice in the wall or around the door, until her fingertips were shredded. By the end of the day, Grace had been near-crazy herself. She ended up sitting cross-legged in the middle of the room, fingers in her ears, humming to block out the girl's incessant, low whining. Little Man took the girl away as the sun went down, and he never brought her back.

Two other girls had followed shortly after, sisters whose names Grace never asked for. They were 12 and 14, and their presence offered Grace a few days of respite as the men amused themselves with what Little Man called "sister games." The younger one made a break for it one night, and never recovered consciousness following the beating she received. She died in her sister's arms three days later. When the older sister finished keening, she had started growling, the animal-like sound making the hairs on the back of Grace's neck prickle.

As soon as Little Man opened the door that evening, she attacked like a berserker. No matter how many times he hit or kicked her, she came back, biting, clawing, flailing, screaming. She died fighting, something Grace both admired and disdained. She had gone out like a warrior, but she was, after all, dead. Grace knew she should feel bad about the girl's death, but she didn't. Maybe she couldn't. Didn't matter. Feeling bad wouldn't get her out of this room.

Take the next step, she reminded herself. Planning and executing the next step had kept her alive through the plague, and it would keep her alive beyond this room. She had identified a pattern she believed she could use.

Among other things, Little Man was responsible for procuring the girls the men used, and she had deduced that he preferred to have no less than two at any given time. Grace had memorized every word of the men's nightly reports, amassing a staggering catalog of information, which she repeated over and over to herself during the days when she couldn't sleep, and during the nights when her body was being used. According to Little Man, they had long since exhausted the supply of young women in the refugee camp, and he and his men were forced to range farther afield.

Twice, he had been absent from the nightly revelry by the bonfire. Both times, he had returned with girls the next day. And both times, there had been a time, just before dawn, where the remaining men were exhausted or otherwise occupied. Distracted. Their lusts had been spent, their minds dulled by whatever substance they were using and exhaustion.

Little Man never took his eyes off "his girls," not for an instant. But the others did. Grace had been alone for two days now. If the pattern held, Little Man would be gone this night or the next. Then, she could make her move.

She rested as much as possible that day, and ate every bit of the cold, congealed mystery food they brought her, washing it down with murky water. They never brought quite enough to eat or drink, and she could feel the lack dragging her body down into ever greater weakness. If this escape attempt didn't work, she would soon face a choice: Either go out like Bri via starvation and dehydration, or try to leave Little Man with a mark to remember her by. Alone in her stinking prison, Grace bared her teeth and a soft growl vibrated in her throat. That choice was already made.

When the sun had nearly set, and the lock on the door rattled, she was ready. And when Giant entered instead of Little Man, she felt a smile lift the stiff muscles of her face for the first time in weeks. She ducked her head to hide the expression and followed him docilely.

She knelt by the fire while the men gave their reports, repeating every word they said in her head and committing it to memory, adding to the mental picture she had been creating of conditions in the city.

Bean Counter was the first to speak, as always. "Drugs, people," he said, and the rest of the men groaned. "Yeah, yeah. I know you're sick of hearing about it. I'm sick of hearing about it, too. I got people begging every day, especially for anti-depressants and painkillers. Withdrawal's a bitch. Seems like everybody was on some kind of pharmaceutical, legal or otherwise, and now they're all dying without. So keep your people looking, keep your ear to the ground, all that. And while you're looking, we need seeds, and people who have gardening or farming experience. It's the end of May. Winter's nearly here."

His words induced a moment of stillness. Then Loudmouth jumped in, his voice blaring. Grace figured he'd been around a few too many explosions. "Haven't seen a patrol leave Fort Carson for three days." He fist-bumped the man next to him and cackled. "Guess they finally got sick of losing Humvees."

"Soldiers being soldiers, though, we shouldn't expect that to last." Bean Counter's observation made Loudmouth roll his eyes. There was no love lost there. "They know we're here, and they're hard-wired to either bring us in or take us out. We've got a man inside. Word is, they're having trouble feeding their refugees, which means they're having trouble keeping the peace. People are trying to leave, forming delegations, demanding the right to self-govern – all kinds of civil-disobedience shit."

"Desperate people are disobedient." Giant's voice was a low rumble. "We feed ours enough, keep 'em safe enough, keep this show up every night." Grace felt multiple eyes touch her and kept her head down. "People who got nothing to lose fight back. People who are scared but are getting their basic needs met will do anything to keep it that way."

"Damn straight!" Loudmouth crowed. He leaned forward, grabbing Grace's breast and giving it a groping twist. "Feed 'em and fuck 'em – that's how you keep 'em in line!"

Laughter sprang up around the circle. Grace heard Bean Counter sigh, and didn't need to look up to know Giant would just be waiting patiently to continue. Of all the men in the group, the participation of these two men in what went on every night bothered her the most. It wasn't just that they were obviously smart – all these men were smart, in their areas of expertise. It was that they thought about things, as evidenced by their observations.

When the laughter died down, Giant went on. "Camp's quiet. We haven't seen new survivors for 10 days. By now, they're either here, on Fort Carson, or they're laying low and staying hid. For now, we're not going to bother with them – we got enough to feed, and we'll leave the forced relocation to Carson."

Sleeper was kicked awake, and he sat up nodding. He heard everything, Grace had figured out, even when he seemed to be unconscious. "My spotters have seen some smoke, small trails here and there. If it ain't bigger than a bread box, we don't check it out. Figure it's people's cookfires." He turned to Bean Counter, yawning hugely as he spoke. "Have your people finished their sweep of the homes along the foothills? Fire season's here."

Bean Counter nodded. "We started there – didn't want to lose our chance if there's another Waldo Canyon fire. We've cleared from Mountain Shadows down to Manitou, more or less. South of 24, we're starting to step on Carson's toes. No need for that yet."

"Good." Sleeper nodded as well. "We finally found the hideout of that group that was poaching Highway 24 up in Manitou. It was a different group than the one controlling Rampart Range Road, trickier, but we control access to both roads now. Fort Carson still controls Old Stage Road, and they're welcome to it. Probably washed out anyway, what with all the rain."

Sleeper fell silent, and for a few moments, the only sound was the crackle of the fire. Then Giant spoke again, looking directly at The Boss, something the men rarely did. "For now, our location is secure, but it's not defensible. I recommend we look for another site, something with greater tactical advantage. Carson's not going to stay locked down for long. We should think about Manitou Springs, or somewhere in the mountains, like Woodland Park."

For a moment, Grace went light-headed with distress. She had plans and contingency plans following her escape, but all of them centered on Woodland Park. She didn't hold out much hope that her dad had survived, but she had to know, one way or another. Now, a layer of urgency reinforced her plans. If there were any decent people left in Woodland Park, any survivors at all, they needed to know what was headed their way.

Flanked by his two Trigger Fingers, The Boss nodded. "So advised." He looked around the circle of men. "And have any more incidents of psychic activity been reported or observed?"

Grace risked a peek out of the corners of her eyes, watching and analyzing the men's reactions. The Boss had started asking this question a little over a week ago, after Giant had reported an increasing number of problems and complaints connected to what could only be called supernatural experiences. People knew things they shouldn't. People predicted things, had unnatural luck at cards, or knew when someone was lying to them. It was, apparently, causing even more fear among the already frightened refugees.

As soon as Giant had started describing the situation, Grace had recognized the phenomena as what she and Quinn had been experiencing – a *knowing* that couldn't be explained. And the men's reactions to this question were telling – she was pretty sure she could identify which of them were and which of them weren't experiencing a heightened sense of *knowing* themselves. Not one of them, though, had admitted it.

Sleeper spoke up with obvious reluctance. "One of my guys is pissing off the whole crew by finishing jokes – he jumps in with the punchline, even though he says he's never heard the jokes before."

The Boss' facial expression didn't change, but Grace could sense his increased interest. "Where is he now?"

"Bunked down with the crew."

"Bring him to me tomorrow, and pick a man to replace him."

Sleeper nodded, and The Boss' eyes probed around the circle. Grace was sure he was analyzing the men's reactions, just as she was. She had yet to figure out the source of The Boss' power. She had never seen him engage in a violent act, had never even heard him raise his voice, yet every man here feared and respected him, in that order. She had begun to suspect his power rose from the supernatural arena the men were so uncomfortable discussing.

"Anyone else?" After a long silence, The Boss nodded one last time. "Let's get the show on the road."

He said the same thing every night. Usually, his words triggered Grace to start her internal recitation while her body was stripped, argued over and abused. Tonight, though, she couldn't afford the luxury. She had to implement her plan.

With every rape, she scooted closer to the edge of light cast by the bonfire, dragging her clothes with her. Hour after interminable hour went by; she tried to doze in the lulls between the attacks, to get as much rest as possible. Finally, finally, after Loudmouth's second time, they lost interest.

Dawn wasn't even a lighter color in the sky yet. Bean Counter, both Trigger Fingers and Giant were exchanging half-hearted insults over a poker table. Loudmouth was alternating between snorting lines of something off a dinner plate and collapsing back in his chair with a whoop. Sleeper and The Boss were bent over a half dozen maps layered on a card table. A motley collection of electric lights had been brought in to surround the table, powered by a gas generator that buzzed on the far side of the semi-trailer.

Grace fisted her hand in her clothes and rolled once. She lay still, counting to 100. She rolled again, counted again. Twice more, and she was under the semi-trailer. She dressed in swift silence, counting on her clothes, dark with filth, to contribute to her camouflage. Then she curled up behind one of the tires, tucking herself into a tiny ball and hiding her face against her knees. Her heart was pounding so hard, it made her whole body shake.

Three minutes later, Loudmouth raised the hue. "Hey! Where'd the cowgirl go?"

There was a moment of total silence, and Grace shut her eyes, willing herself beyond invisibility, into non-existence. This was it. If she'd miscalculated, she was about to die. Then, The Boss spoke.

"Spread out and find her. She can't be far. Let people know if they try to help her, they'll take her place."

Grace nearly sobbed her relief. They would expect her to run, not hide under their noses. She didn't move so much as an inch for an hour, listening as the men circled back and checked in, swearing with increasing frustration and exhaustion. Usually, they headed for their beds at dawn. The descriptions of what they'd do to her when they found her got increasingly creative and violent as the sun rose higher.

Finally, they gave up. Before they dispersed, The Boss gave a final order: "When she's found, she'll be executed. Publicly and painfully." His mild tone rendered his words all the more chilling. "It's been a while since we've made an example. Now go get some rest."

The area around the trailer grew quiet. Grace could hear activity in other parts of the camp now, could smell the scent of smoke and cooking food, and still she stayed put. She had a plan – find other clothes, preferably something with disguising bulk and a hood, move with confidence, don't run or sneak, watch where other people moved and move with them, lose herself in the neighborhoods surrounding the park at the earliest opportunity – but she couldn't make herself roll out from under the trailer.

Another hour passed. Finally, a desperate need to urinate got her moving. She scooted to the far side of the trailer, took two deep breaths, and rolled into the open. She stood up and steadied herself for a moment, blinking to adapt her vision, and found herself staring straight at Quinn.

Several things happened at once: Her bladder let go, her legs wobbled out from under her, and the world started to revolve sickeningly. She slumped against the side of the trailer, gaping, as Quinn strode towards her. Without a word, he zipped her into a dark brown sweatshirt three sizes too big for her, tucking her hair under the hood. Grace looked down, plucking at the grungy fabric.

"Huh. This is just what I was hoping to find," she said. Her voice sounded slurred, which struck her as strange in a distant sort of way. She squinted up at Quinn's face. "You're supposed to be dead."

Quinn didn't answer. He cast a look over his shoulder, then looped an arm around Grace's waist. "Can you walk? It'll look weird if I carry you."

Grace took a shaky step, then another. "Let's go."

They moved through the camp at a leisurely pace, leaning into each other like young lovers. In no time at all, they had slipped into the neighborhoods surrounding the park, and still they kept moving. Quinn seemed to be following a path known to him, mostly through abandoned yards, always under cover, always moving to the northwest. Neither one spoke a word.

Grace guessed they had walked for half an hour when they stopped, tucked under a sagging pergola in someone's overgrown back yard. Quinn disappeared around the side of the house and returned a moment later with a plastic-wrapped bundle, which he held out to Grace. "Clean clothes and some water I stashed here earlier. I didn't pack any food – I was afraid an animal would get after the bag."

"Thank you." But Grace just stood there, arms hanging at her sides. She could not wrap her mind around this, couldn't adapt any of her carefully made plans to this. Quinn was not dead. Tears started into her eyes, which surprised her, because all she could say she was feeling was shock. She gazed up at him, feeling the tears slide free one by one. "I don't know what to do now."

Quinn opened the bag, showing her the carefully folded jeans, t-shirt, underwear, socks, even a pair of tennis-shoes that looked to be her size. He had yet to meet her eyes. "See? Everything you need." He rummaged in the bottom of the bag, pulled out several bottles of water and a washcloth. "I thought it would make you feel better. You can have a real bath later. I'll turn around. You can get rid of your old clothes and put on the new ones." He took her hand, looped the handles of the bag around it. "Just take the next step. That's what you always said to me."

He turned around, and she felt her face contort, ruined, wrecked, leveled by his kindness. She started to undress, moving faster and faster as she freed herself of the clothes that had started to rot on her body, clothes that smelled like all the men she had endured and that awful room. Naked, she had to sit down on the edge of the picnic table because the world was spinning again. She picked up the first bottle of water and the washcloth.

She wet the cloth and ran it over her face, wet it again, and ran it down her arms and over her torso. She was caked with grime, the creases of her elbows and wrists black with it. Her thighs were chapped where her jeans had been wet with urine, and she patted them gingerly with the cloth, hissing at the stinging pain. Then she stopped.

There, above each knee, were black marks that wouldn't wash off. Her hands started to shake so violently, she accidentally dumped the rest of the water on the ground. She scrubbed, scrubbed harder and harder, and still they wouldn't budge. Bruises. Handprints. She heaved a huge, hiccupping sob and scrubbed with all her strength.

"Gracie, shh, Gracie, it's okay." Quinn was kneeling beside her, taking the washcloth away. He opened a fresh bottle of water, wet the cloth again, then smoothed it over her face. His voice was a constant low murmur of instructions and comfort, but it was shaking, like he was crying, too. "You'll feel better after a real bath and some food, let's get you dressed so we can get going, let me help you, it's okay, it's okay..."

She couldn't stop sobbing as he slid her into the clean clothes, even tying her shoes for her. And she couldn't for the life of her figure out why. She didn't feel sad, or angry, or even embarrassed. She didn't feel anything at all. It was like her body had decided it was time to cry, and she was just along for the ride.

Quinn coaxed her into drinking the remaining water bottle, then helped her to her feet. He still hadn't looked her in the eye. "I found a place a ways from here where we can hide, maybe five miles as the crow flies. It takes a couple hours to walk it. Are you okay to go on?"

Grace nodded, still not in control of her voice, and Quinn led them on their way. She just followed, not thinking, hurrying when he told her to, hiding when he said. They stopped to rest a few times, and the sun was high when Quinn led them out of a neighborhood and into an area Grace recognized.

Tears had plagued her on and off throughout their journey; her throat was raw and her eyes burned. She had to swallow several times before she could speak. "Quinn? Are we at Garden of the Gods?"

"Sort of." Quinn had been checking endlessly over his shoulder – his neck had to be stiff by now. They paused at the edge of an open meadow so he could take a long look around, then he hurried them down a dirt path. The path curved, they passed a windbreak of trees, and the modern world dropped away. "Didn't you ever visit Rock Ledge Ranch when you were in school?"

"Well, yeah..." Grace stared around her, flummoxed. They were approaching an old stone ranch house, and a little valley spread out in front of them, green and lovely as a picture. "What in the world made you think of this?"

"I needed somewhere to keep Koda that was safe, a place where he could graze. There's a stable here, and a fenced pasture, and water." Quinn's voice got more enthusiastic as he talked. "They did those historical demonstrations here, so a lot of stuff actually works. It was still a working ranch."

Grace stopped dead in her tracks. Sure enough, there was Koda, grazing in the pasture. And beyond him – "Buttons! Quinn, how did you get Buttons?"

Quinn looked down at the ground, scuffing his boot in the dirt. He didn't answer for long minutes, and when he did, his voice was hoarse. "That's not Buttons. Her name's Kava, at least that's the sign on the stall she goes to." He looked up, squinting at the towering red rocks of Garden of the Gods to the northwest. "I think there were more horses, but the fence was broken when we got here. She was the only one left. She kept her distance for a few days, then came right up to me one morning."

Of course. How silly. She didn't look anything like Buttons, now that Grace really looked at her. The tears started again, but Grace ignored them. "How long have you been here?"

Quinn's head went down again, and he scuffed the ground harder. "Since five days after they took you." He was quiet for a moment, then continued with obviously forced enthusiasm. "Oh, I almost forgot - someone started the garden, before the plague hit. It's weedy, but we'll have food."

Food. Plants, and probably more seeds where those came from. Bean Counter would love to know about this place. And Quinn was just the kind of person he was looking for – a talented and knowledgeable gardener. "There's no one else here? Surely someone else thought of this."

Quinn shook his head. "I heard people talking in camp – the gang has already made a pass through this area. They killed a lot of people – people who were weak, or old, or who didn't want to join them. Pretty near emptied the area out. I haven't seen a single person anywhere nearby."

For now, Grace thought, with a chill of foreboding. Neither one of them spoke, then, standing there in the mid-afternoon heat, the air around them alive with the sounds of insects and birds. The fledgling apple orchard was in bloom, and the soft sweet scent of apple blossoms drifted to them on the breeze. Grace closed her eyes and lifted her face to the sun.

It was so quiet here, so steeped in peace. She opened her eyes again, and swept them around the little valley, noting the big white Victorian house, two more modern buildings, the big white barn, and the log-walled general store. A few chickens were strutting around, and some sheep were grazing in the open space to the east of the pasture, near the thriving garden Quinn had mentioned.

The plague hadn't touched this idyllic place. It was so clean. So safe.

She looked up at Quinn. "Can we stay?" Her voice sounded tiny, young, even to her. "Can we please stay? Just for a while?"

He turned to face her, but looked at her left shoulder. "We can stay as long as you want. Whatever you need, Gracie."

He turned her then, and led her up the porch steps and into the ranch house, taking her back to the kitchen.

"Are you hungry? I've got some canned soup – I can heat you up a bowl, then you can have that bath..."

Grace sat at the table, letting him fuss and care for her. After those first moments, nothing about her escape had gone as planned, yet here she was. Free. Safe. Suddenly, Woodland Park seemed very far away, the journey too long and dangerous. Eventually, they would have to make the trip, if for no other reason than to warn any survivors... Grace let her mind drift away from that train of thought, and looked around the homey, old-timey kitchen. It was so cozy here.

After she'd eaten, she soaked in the big galvanized steel washtub Quinn had hauled into the kitchen area and filled with water he'd heated on the stove. When she was done, the water was grey, and she was nearly asleep. She crawled into the soft t-shirt and sweatpants he'd set out for her, and went to find him. Her eyes were so heavy she could scarcely keep them open.

Quinn was on the front porch, rocking in an old bentwood rocker, gazing out over the valley. Grace glanced to the southwest, noting the thunderheads building over the mountains, as they so often did this time of day. Looked like they were in for an evening shower.

"Is there a place I could lie down? I really need to sleep."

Quinn nodded and they went back in the house. She could see where he'd been moving aside the historic artifacts to create living space in the dining and living areas. He led her to a second floor bedroom, where the walls were bright with yellow-flowered wallpaper, and a soft breeze stirred lace curtains at the window.

"I made the bed up fresh, with sheets and blankets I found at another house," he said, gesturing at the bed. "The ones on it were antique, just for show. They smelled musty. And the mattress isn't too comfortable."

She thought about sleeping on a cement floor for the last few weeks, then pushed the thought away, let it drift right away on the breeze. She yawned until her jaw cracked and crawled into the bed, curling on her side, already drifting.

Quinn moved around the room for a while, and she watched through slitted eyes as he straightened up and folded clothes. Obviously, this was where he'd been sleeping. She turned her face into the pillow, and sure enough, there was his scent. Just his scent, no one else's. On that thought, she slept.

Hours later, the low rumble of thunder nudged her from sleep. It was dark, and she didn't know where she was at first. Lightning flickered, lighting the room like a strobe, and memory returned. Rain drummed in uneven surges against the roof as the storm gathered strength, until a particularly strong gust of wind spattered Grace with raindrops from the nearby window. Probably ought to shut it. She sighed, stretched, and swung her feet to the floor.

Quinn woke from where he'd been sleeping on a pallet beside the bed, all surging, violent motion. He lunged across the floor, knocking over a table, and Grace heard glass break. He crashed into the wall, then swung around. In the flash of lightning, she saw his wild eyes and twisted face.

"Run!" he gasped. "Gracie, run! Run!"

Grace huddled against the headboard, clutching the covers so hard her hands cramped, heart pounding. "Quinn, what's wrong?" Was he awake? Should she run? "Quinn, tell me what's wrong!"

She could hear his labored breathing. Lightning flashed again, showing her he was now leaning back against the wall with his eyes closed. A few minutes later, she heard him start to move around. He struck a match, and she shielded her eyes from the sudden brightness. When she looked up again, he had lit a hurricane lamp. He picked it up and carried it to the table beside the bed, then sat down cross-legged on his pallet. Finally, he heaved a deep breath.

"It was a nightmare. I'm sorry."

She couldn't figure out why he looked so miserable. "It's okay. It happens."

"No. You don't understand." He sat with his arms looped around his legs, and wouldn't lift his eyes from his knees. "It's the same dream. The same one I had the night before you were taken. I have it over and over."

She remembered suddenly, the nightmare that had sent him lunging from his sleeping bag, and her irritation, from what seemed like a thousand years ago. "What are you saying? That you had a premonition or something?"

"Yes. I dreamed it, just like it happened. Exactly."

Grace frowned. "Do you do that often? Dream something that happens?"

"No. Never before that, anyway."

"Then how could you know that time was different? Quinn, it wasn't your fault-"

"Don't say that!" He bellowed the words at her.

Grace started back, filled with sudden terror. He was looking at her, finally, and she wished he'd look away. His eyes were agonized. Something inside him was broken.

"I should have warned you, and stopped it from happening! Why else would I dream that? I failed you, and they-" He broke off, staring at her, chest heaving. Then he reached for the hem of his t-shirt and pulled it off.

Dozens and dozens of tiny cuts marched up and down his ribs, some healed to pink lines, some scabbed over, some still oozing and angry. "Every time they touched you," he whispered, "I made a cut. It was the only way I could stand it. I was given a warning, and I ignored it. I watched, every night, every single night I watched, so I'd be ready to help you. I knew you'd find a way out, and you did."

Grace shut her eyes. She would never stop seeing those cuts. So many. She swallowed hard, feeling bile push its way up her throat. "You watched?" Her voice was a feeble trickle of sound. "You saw?"

She heard the rustle as he pulled his t-shirt back on, but kept her eyes closed. In that place of filth and pain, she'd felt no shame. Survival was everything, survival was all. Here, in this sweet, old-fashioned bedroom, shame closed over her head, a flood that would never recede.

How could she ever look into his eyes again, knowing what they'd seen?

She heard him scoot closer, felt his warm hands close over her knotted fists. "Grace, open your eyes. Look at me."

She shook her head, but her closed lids couldn't hold back the rush of tears. "No," she choked. "You shouldn't have watched. I can't stand it."

"I had to," he said, and she could tell by his voice he was crying, too. "Gracie, I know you'll never be able to forgive me. We were a team, and I failed. I didn't show you those cuts to make you feel bad. I showed you so you would know you were never alone, not ever. I stayed with you the whole time. I couldn't help you, but I didn't leave you. I never will."

Grace took a huge breath and opened her eyes. "If you pity me, I'll kill you."

Quinn barked out a laughing sob, swiping at his tears and runny nose with the back of his hand. "I don't pity you, Gracie. You were so brave."

Her eyes slammed shut again. "I wasn't brave. I didn't fight them, not even once."

His fingers landed on her cheek, soft as down. "Fighting would have been stupid. It just would have gotten you hurt. I could see you thinking the whole time, working out a plan, like you do." Grace's eyes cracked open, and Quinn smiled crookedly. "I pitied them. I knew you'd make fools of them, eventually."

His words made alarm dance down her spine. She *had* made fools of them, and they wouldn't forget it. She stared into Quinn's eyes, knowing she should share her concern, knowing they should talk about leaving as soon as possible, knowing she should tell him about everything she'd heard, but she couldn't make her lips form the words.

Was it so selfish, to want some time to heal? Wasn't she entitled to some safety and some peace? This place was magical, and she didn't want to leave.

Grace closed her eyes, and leaned to rest her head on Quinn's shoulder, comforted by his warmth and closeness. During the long hours with nothing to do but think, she'd realized that she might never want to be close to another person again, especially a man. But this was Quinn. He was, simply, her home.

"It's over," she said sleepily. "It's over, and we both survived, and we never have to think about it or talk about it again."

She felt Quinn stiffen, and stopped him before his protest could begin. "There's no reason to. It happened. It's done. That's all."

He pushed her back so he could look at her face, his eyes troubled. "If that's what you want, Gracie."

"It is." She curled back up on her side, burrowing under the covers. The storm had subsided to an occasional rumble of thunder and a steady patter of rain. "Will you hold my hand, while I sleep? It's so good to not be alone..."

Quinn blew out the lamp, then stretched out on his pallet and reached up to twine his fingers with hers. Their hands were still joined when she woke up the next morning to bright sunshine and birdsong.

For a few days, she was content just to eat and sleep. Quinn left her only for brief forays into the adjoining neighborhood in search of supplies, and to care for the animals he'd adopted. Two sheep were left, and half a dozen chickens, along with the two horses. As her strength returned, Grace began to join Quinn as he worked, weeding in the garden and exploring the other buildings on the grounds. Anything they could use, they brought back to the ranch house – books, games, cooking utensils. Slowly, they stopped feeling like they were living in a museum that needed to be preserved, and adapted the house to suit their needs.

Grace drifted along, quietly content, a state she could never remember inhabiting before. She thought about the task that was under her hands, nothing more. There was so much to learn, and so much work to be done, there wasn't time to remember lost families or nights of horror. No time to worry about the future, about violent men with expansion plans. On those rare occasions when dark thoughts snapped at her heels, she would close her eyes and recite something – the periodic table of elements, a poem she'd learned for a long-ago English class, anything. Memorizing had always come easily to her. Now, she learned it was just as easy to forget.

Occasionally, they spoke of the extraordinary changes it appeared people were going through; Quinn's gift with plants had grown to a whole new level. All he had to do was touch a plant, and somehow, he *knew* what its medicinal qualities were, how it was best used, how to propagate it and so on.

"It doesn't feel like a new thing, though," he explained as he hoed swiftly down a row of carrots. "More like something that's always been in me that I've grown into." He snickered, and for a moment, sounded like the teenage boy he was. "Kinda like puberty. Before that, you think girls are pretty, but then puberty hits and you *feel* how pretty they are. Know what I mean?"

Grace gave him her best eye roll. She listened when he talked about this, but didn't share what she'd overheard the men in the gang discuss. She didn't speak of her time with the men, not ever. Nor did she offer her own thoughts or comments. Though she sensed in herself a growing potential, for her it remained a step yet to be taken.

Days slid quietly into weeks. The valley vibrated with the life of high summer, and they were starting to have trouble keeping up with the bounty of their garden. Grace had found a book on canning and preserving, and they'd scraped together supplies from every kitchen they had access to.

Quinn sat at the table shelling peas one hot, close afternoon, while Grace washed canning jars. She had about ten seconds to register that she wasn't feeling all that well before she hit the floor. She came back to herself a few moments later, took one look at Quinn's frantic face hovering over her, then promptly rolled over and vomited her lunch onto the kitchen floor.

She was fine half an hour later, and they brushed it off as a touch of summer 'flu, or maybe something she'd

eaten that was off. Until it happened the next
And again the next.

Quinn was wild with worry. He disappeared the next morning, returning a few hours later with his arms full of medical books. "I saw these in one of the houses up on the ridge," he explained as he piled them on the table in the dining area. "I think the guy must have been a doctor. They're all pretty old, but maybe..."

He trailed off, running his fingers down the spine of one book, then another, frowning. He darted a look at her from under his eyebrows. "I'm not much good with books, but I can try to help. You know. I can try to help find out what's..." Again, his voice stuttered to a halt. Then, he burst out. "What if it's the plague? What if you've finally caught it?"

"I don't think so. The symptoms are different." Grace frowned in concentration, processing all the information she had stored on the plague. "Do you know what the date is?"

"June something, towards the middle."

"Based on the course they thought it would follow, the plague should burn itself out by the end of June. Why would I catch it now? We've only seen each other – who would I have caught it from? No, it's not the plague." She patted the medical books. "I'll take a look at them later, when I have time. I feel fine now, so I'll see what I can find for our lunch."

The next afternoon, she didn't have time to read because she was teaching herself to use the treadle sewing machine they'd found. And the next afternoon, she couldn't put off weeding the green beans one more day. And the next afternoon, it was something else. Quinn was perplexed, then exasperated with her. In desperation, he cracked the books open himself, nagging at her to describe her symptoms in greater detail so he could play medical detective.

"I'm tired!" she snapped at him. "All the time. This is dumb, Quinn. There's nothing to worry about."

He ignored her, and continued doggedly turning pages. "What else?"

Grace started huffing around the kitchen, putting away the dishes she'd washed earlier that day. "This is embarrassing," she groused. "I think I might have a urinary tract infection." She felt her face heat. "It burns when I go. And I have to go a lot."

Quinn flipped to the index, found the section he was looking for, then painstakingly read for a while, his lips moving with the effort. He sighed. "That wouldn't explain the fainting. Or the vomiting. Are you running a fever? Waking up at night in a sweat?"

"No."

"It's probably not an infection, then. What else?"

Grace crossed her arms over her chest and glared at him. "My boobs are killing me."

She saw Quinn's Adams apple bob as he gulped. "Okay," he said in a strangled voice. "We'll add that to the list. Can you think of anything else?"

"No." She returned to putting dishes away. "I told you, it's just a passing bug. I got run down. Maybe I'm missing a vitamin or mineral or something. I'll get some extra rest, and I'll be fine."

She looked up, and Quinn was just staring at her. His face had blanched to a ghastly milky shade. "What?" she said, alarmed. "Are you feeling sick, too? What's wrong?"

"Sit down, Grace."

When she hesitated, he stood up and took her arm, steering her into the other chair. He sat down as well, and scooted close to her. He gripped her hands so hard it hurt, his eyes sharp and intense as they roved over her face.

"When was the last time you had a period?"

She slapped his arm reflexively. "Ugh, Quinn! Guys don't ask that stuff!"

"When, Grace?"

Her heart started to pound. No. No. She had gotten so good at burying it deep, at pushing it away, she could go days without remembering. "I had some cramping not long after you brought me here, and I thought it would start. But I didn't... There wasn't any..." She started to pant. "There was no blood. Just the cramping. No, Quinn. No."

"Grace. Gracie, it'll be okay. I'll take care of you."

She exploded out of the chair, ripping her hands away from his. "No. No!" She screamed the word at him. "I won't do it! I won't go through with it! There has to be a way to get rid of it! It'll be a monster, Quinn! They were monsters, killers, all of them! You saw! You saw what they did, what they were!"

"I don't know anything about that, Gracie. About how to get rid of a baby safely. You could die, if we do something wrong."

"I'd rather die than..." She gulped back tears, too angry to give in to them. "Fucking hell, Quinn! Why? Why? I was a virgin! I never did anything bad, not even with William, and I loved him!"

Quinn was crying now, tears tracking steadily down his face. "Tell me what to do. I'll do anything. But I won't agree if it means you'll be in danger. You've made it through so much, I've been so proud of you." He sobbed, once, then fought himself back under control. "You're all I've got, Gracie. All I've got in the world. I can't lose you."

"Then help me get rid of this." She was thinking furiously, picking through the puzzle pieces and discarding them when they wouldn't form the picture she wanted. Quinn was right about one thing; she would be good and god-damned if she'd survived this much, only to die trying to kill the horror growing inside her.

She started pacing back and forth, muttering. "There's got to be a safe way to do this. I'm too far along for the morning after pill, based on what I learned in health class. Probably couldn't find any drugs anyway – Bean Counter was always talking about that. What about herbs?" She stopped and fixed her gaze on Quinn. "Do we have a book on herbs?"

"If there's not one here, I'll find you one." Quinn stood up. He stared down at the table top, and once again, Grace caught sight of the old man he'd be one day, if he lived that long, in the lines of weariness and despair on his face.

"I thought it would be me," he finally said in a choked voice. "I thought in a few years, when we were older and had found somewhere safe, we could be a family. Have a family. You and me."

Grace recoiled; she couldn't help it. "Why on Earth would you want to? Why would you want to bring a baby into this world, so she can be raped and raped and raped?" She backed away from him, shaking her head. "I'm sorry you thought that. I'm sorry, if I let you think it. I'll never be a mother, Quinn. Never. And I'll never be with a man again." She looked down at the table, unable to bear the misery in his eyes. "Better you know now."

Silence fell between them. Grace could hear the low rustle of the fire in the stove, the constant drone of insects outside, birdsong, and the occasional bleat of a sheep. None of these familiar sounds could bring her comfort.

A tiny sip of bliss, and now more hell. This was her penance for seizing some moments of happiness, her wake-up call. She had been a fool to think they could hide here, be safe here. Reality was back, with a vengeance. Bitterness twisted in her heart and rose in her throat.

She choked words out past it. "We need to make plans to go. Other people will think of this place, and they'll tell Bean Counter about it. We've stayed too long already."

"Whatever you think, Gracie." Quinn didn't question her abrupt change of subject. He moved towards the door, stopped, then came back. He took her hand, and ducked down until he was eye to eye with her. There was something older in his gaze, disillusioned, resigned. Nothing was left of the innocent boy she'd left Limon with. It made her unbearably sad.

"It doesn't matter," he said. "What you do or don't feel for me, it doesn't make a difference. I love you. I always will. You don't need to think or do anything about it. It just is."

She shook her head at him slowly. "Not a good plan, Quinn. You should just let it go. There'll be other girls. Lots of them."

"Not for me." He squeezed her hand, then headed for the door again. "Besides, I'm not the one with the plans. That's you." He turned and tried to smile, but failed. "I just keep taking the next step."

TWENTY
Naomi: The Cabin on Carrol Lakes, CO

Keeping the baby warm – that was Naomi's top priority. Night and day, the fire had to stay lit. If it burned low, even for an instant, little Macy got so very cold.

She was aware, sometimes, that she was well and truly lost. The needs of the dogs kept her connected to reality by the thinnest of threads. They were in constant physical contact with her as she sat by the ever-roaring fire, never leaving her alone. They took turns slipping out through the dog door Scott had installed, or eating a few bites of food from the bag Naomi had torn open and dumped on the floor. When she slept, they pressed against her. When she cried, howled, screamed her grief, Persephone would press tiny licking kisses along her jaw, and Hades would rest his massive head on her shoulder. Their love was her only tether to a world without her baby in it.

She had washed Macy's body carefully, then wrapped her in a soft sheet so that only her hair showed. She changed the sheet when it became soiled, turning and tending her daughter's slowly desiccating corpse. She understood the process Macy's body was going through, the gradual mummification, and there was nothing to be repelled or disgusted by in it. This was her daughter. Naomi had been caring for her since the day of her birth, and it gave her great comfort to continue caring for her now. Not for a moment did she consider digging a hole in the cold, dark, suffocating earth and putting her baby in it.

And when she couldn't bear the empty loneliness any longer, she fled, into the ghostlands Verity had warned her about. Backwards and forwards in time she traveled, between dreams and memory. Macy's wedding day, when a white veil would frost her glorious hair. Macy's toddler days, when she ran everywhere on chubby legs and gave smacking kisses to complete strangers. On to her teenage years – would she go to the prom? They could sew her formal dress together – wouldn't that be fun? Back again to those first days, to the power outage and the warm cocoon of family. Naomi visited there again and again.

She drank water when the tissues of her throat stuck together. She used the bathroom when great need drove her to it. In the years that would follow, on the rare occasions she would speak of this time, she would say, "I wasn't trying to die. But I wasn't trying to live, either." And then she would laugh, sadly, and say, "Saved by the most obnoxious of cats. I don't think Hades ever got over it."

He strolled in one morning as if he'd just been out carousing, King of All He Surveyed, God of War himself. Hades barked and charged, then spun away with a sharp yelp, his sliced nose already dripping blood on the floor.

Naomi gasped and staggered to her feet. "Ares!"

Her legs shook, then collapsed from under her. She tried again to stand, and was shocked when she couldn't. When had she gotten so weak? She crawled first to Hades, to press the hem of her shirt to his nose. Then she glared over her shoulder at Ares. "Well, that's a fine 'Hello' you damn cat! We missed you, too!"

Then she started to sob, filled with joy to see him, filled with guilt for feeling joy. Ares yowled and stalked to her side. She leaned down and his purr rumbled into the room as he butted her head repeatedly with his. With her free hand, she stroked him over and over while Hades emitted a constant, grumbling growl. Ares' body was thin but strong, rising under her hand.

"I can't believe you found us. How on Earth did you make it so far? How did you know the way?"

Ares prowled to the spill of dog food on the floor, sniffed at it, then loudly voiced his disdain. Persephone gave an excited bark of greeting, her little tail a wagging blur, and bounded to touch noses with the cat. They sniffed each other for a few moments, then Ares yowled again and glared at Naomi. She felt a wobble and a shift as she was invited into his perception.

Miles and miles and miles, and sore paws. Stray dogs, fights, coyotes, and a very close call with a hawk. Naomi. The bond between them, pulling him home. Hungry, always hungry, hungry NOW.

Amazing. Naomi swiped at her tears, then checked Hades' nose; it was still oozing, but the worst of the bleeding had stopped. She gave him a comforting stroke, then crawled across the floor to the food cupboard, not trusting her legs. "Let's see what we've got for the prodigal son."

Ares wound and twisted around her as she dragged out a bag of dry cat food, rubbing and purring and radiating approval. She tried to tear the bag open and couldn't, which told her just how run down she'd become. Just sawing it open with a kitchen knife exhausted her. She filled a bowl for Ares, then crawled back to the cupboard and grabbed a box of granola bars. Seated once again by the fire and Macy, she made herself eat one, washing it down with little sips of water.

Had she eaten since they'd arrived here? She couldn't remember. She looked down at her clothes. She hadn't bathed or changed her clothes, of that she was certain. Now that she was thinking about it, she couldn't even say how long they'd been here. Weeks? A month? Longer?

So tempting, to curl up by Macy and sleep, to slip back into dream and memory. But Hades was whining softly beside her, not so much from the pain in his nose as from jealousy and hurt feelings, and he needed some reassurance. Persephone was a mess, her golden coat matted and filthy – Naomi was probably going to have to cut a lot of it off. And Ares was intent on his food, crunching enthusiastically, but when he finished, she needed to check him over for any wounds that might need tending...

She heaved a huge breath that hitched and caught, looking around at the animals and recognizing the choice she'd just made without realizing she was standing on the brink of it. Tears seeped from the corners of her eyes – she didn't think the flow would ever stop. She was overwhelmed by the idea of breaking free of her cocoon of grief. Of standing up, of taking steps to survive, of going on without Macy.

But Ares' return felt like nothing short of a sign. He had survived, had made it back to her, against all odds. As if her thoughts had summoned him, he looked up from his food, then slid to her side and into her lap. Naomi closed her eyes, held him close for comfort and courage, and for the first time since Macy's death, allowed her heart to open beyond this space, beyond the cabin.

"Piper!" she gasped. There her girl was, vibrating with life and oh! Angry! Right there in her heart. Naomi's face lifted in a smile of delight and recognition and relief, then just as quickly twisted in pain. No Macy. No baby girl. Her shoulders curved around the hollowness. She made herself breathe steadily for a few minutes, then explored the altered terrain.

It wasn't that Macy and Scott had left her heart. Rather, their presence was static, still, a love that was memory. They had gone on together, Naomi was sure of it. She had tried so hard to believe they were both still here, just in another form, but she knew it wasn't true.

Piper, by contrast, felt like a roaring fire in her chest, living, changing, shifting, raging. Her temper had always run hot, but this definitely felt like more than a tantrum. Whatever had enraged her girl, she was grateful for it; the connection between them was alive again.

Determination to find her warrior girl surged anew, and she closed her eyes in gratitude. The needs of the living kept grief from killing. She couldn't follow Macy into death, not while Piper lived.

It took her almost a week to regain enough strength to move easily around the cabin, and another few days beyond that to find the strength and courage to step out the door, to walk down to the lake with the dogs and leave Macy alone for a few minutes.

She stood on the shore as the dogs played in the shallows, scanning the lakeshore for signs of other people. She had thought, the other day, that she'd heard a motor off in the distance, but whether it was a vehicle or a boat, she couldn't say. She needed to get out and check the lakes one by one, but she was reluctant to use the SUV to do so. So much depended on the nature of the people she might find. The sound of a vehicle was so rare these days, it would be too easy to track and locate.

No, she needed to walk it. It was only a few miles, after all, though some of it was rough terrain. The dogs bounded out of the water, shaking and spraying, and she turned to head back up the hill to the cottage. She had to pause halfway to rest, and she laughed a little at herself.

"Sure. You're going to hike around the lakes. Better make it up the hill first."

She went out every day after that, trying to get farther and farther each day. She'd never enjoyed exercise, but she began to find the rhythm of hiking soothing. Her mind emptied and went still, and she could enjoy just being outside, watching the dogs range around her sniffing and exploring, the feel of the sun on her face, the soft tug of the wind in her hair.

They didn't encounter any humans, but ran into plenty of animal neighbors: mule deer, rabbits, squirrels, the occasional fox and once, a pair of coyotes. Birds were everywhere, too, only a few of which she could name. Scott had kept an identification book by the window in the cabin; he and Macy had spent hours with that book and their binoculars.

There was one bird she was coming to recognize though, a huge raven that seemed to be waiting high in a tree every time she stepped outside. Usually, he would glide from the branch and fly off when she appeared, his croaking calls echoing back to her, but this morning he stayed for a moment. He cocked his head to the side, examining her, and just for an instant, she thought she felt the brush of his awareness: curiosity and a surprising intelligence. He flew off before she could explore the connection, but she would be on the lookout for him tomorrow.

She adjusted the straps of her day pack and her shotgun, then took a deep breath of cool morning air, and looked down at the dogs. Hades was seated by her side, his beautiful, strong head tilted up to her as if she were his sun. When she made eye contact with him, his mouth opened in a doggy grin, and his stump of a tail wiggled with happiness. He adored these walks, and as he became more secure and settled at the cabin, the silly, clownish side of his personality was starting to emerge.

Persephone was dancing around them both, butterfly ears perked and quivering in anticipation as they started down the road running along the west side of Rainbow Lake. The little dog was proving herself to be a ruthless hunter, reinforcing Naomi's belief that she carried terrier heritage under that soft golden coat. The first time she'd emerged from a burrow with a rabbit dangling from her mouth, her pretty face scuffed and triumphant, Naomi's instinct had been to take it away from her. She'd stifled that urge; it wasn't as if she could buy more dog food when her current supply ran out.

She had kept her face averted as the dogs worried and tore at the rabbit that day, trying to figure out how to get through fur to blood and meat. At the time, neither one had been overly hungry, as they'd already been fed; their interest in the rabbit had been more about novelty than food. Since then, Naomi had waited to feed them until after they returned from the day's hike – if Persephone could hunt up their breakfast, all the better. With practice, they were getting better at consuming what she caught.

Hades was attempting to hunt as well, though his tendency to bulldoze through the forest hindered his efforts. In the clear, without a lot of underbrush to give him away, he had come close, but he'd yet to make a kill. Naomi knew she was going to have to figure something out before too much longer; Hades was a big dog, and needed a lot of fuel. If possible, she needed to conserve the dog food for emergencies, or for the coming winter.

As near as she could figure, it was the first or second week of July. She had never been able to reconstruct the weeks following Macy's death, and she had stopped trying. What did it matter? Other than keeping track of the seasons so she'd be prepared for the weather, what did the calendar mean anymore?

She had hardly begun to wrap her mind around the changes in the world, and what they would mean. She had a single objective – find Piper – but she knew from her short trip here to the cabin that such a journey wouldn't be easy. She couldn't just hop in a vehicle and drive up to UNC on the impossible chance Piper was still hanging out in her dorm room. She had racked her brain for any detail she might have forgotten, any information Piper might have shared about the friend she had mentioned, the one with a home in the mountains, but had come up with nothing.

All she had to go on was the *feeling*, strong and steady as a compass needle, that Piper was somewhere to the northwest, fairly far away. When Naomi closed her eyes and reached out, she could feel the thread connecting them like a thrumming guitar string. All she knew to do at this point was follow it.

So that was her plan, in its entirety. It was almost as simplistic as her plan to come here, to the cabin, but far less naïve.

First of all, she would wait, until the following spring. Piper could very well be on her way to the cabin, and unlike her mother, she knew where she was going. Besides, Naomi would need that time to prepare, physically and mentally. A great deal of the journey might be on foot, and she needed to be fit. She'd lost weight, an awful lot of it, but it had been the kind of weight loss that debilitated rather than strengthened. She could walk for a couple of hours now, but she had a long way to go.

She also needed to learn how to read a topographical map and use a compass, as well as learn some survival skills. Scott had kept a few area maps here at the cabin, and she had brought his compass with her, but she didn't know where to begin. Gaining those skills was going to involve a visit to the Woodland Park community, in the hopes that someone there could teach her.

She was fairly certain she was the only person left on Rainbow Lake. She thought there might be some people on Aspen Lake – she'd been down that way a couple of times and had seen a thin trail of smoke once – but she hadn't found anyone. As far as she knew, she was the only one left in the area, and she couldn't teach herself the skills she needed. She knew she should make the trip to Woodland Park sooner rather than later, but she hated to leave Macy for more than a couple of hours.

And if she was honest, there was more to it than that. She'd thought about them, about Jack and Layla, Martin and that bizarre Verity, during her walks. She wasn't sure she could take their pity. And while she'd liked Layla well enough, she wasn't sure about Jack – if he started in on Macy's death being God's will, well, she didn't know what she would do or say. Just the thought made her heart pound with rage. Martin, she'd understood – he was desperate to find his kids, and she got that. Why he hadn't left yet she couldn't figure, but that was his business.

It was Verity that kept her away. What would she say? What wouldn't she say? A few months ago, Naomi would have dismissed her as a crackpot charlatan. Now, she envied and feared her entrée to a world beyond what most of them could see.

They stopped to rest where the road veered back to the west. From here, they could hike cross-country along the shore of Gem Lake, and on to Columbine Lake to the south, or they could circle around and cross Rainbow Dam before heading home. Naomi opted for the lakeshore; she had to keep increasing her comfort level with stepping off the road. She couldn't get lost if she stuck to the lakeshore then retraced her steps.

Hades flushed a pair of quail, and, giving a great, athletic leap into the air, caught one. His shocked expression made Naomi laugh out loud; then, the bird fluttered, and his hunting instinct kicked in. A crunch of his powerful jaws and it was over. He dropped the bird on the ground, and Persephone joined him in sniffing it. They hadn't eaten a bird yet, and neither one seemed to know what to do with the feathers. Naomi watched them poke and prod in confusion, then knelt down between them.

"Here." It was hard to touch the bird, still pliable and warm with life, but what wasn't hard these days? She swallowed and persevered, holding the bird with one hand and pulling a handful of feathers free from its breast with the other. She kept at it until she'd cleared a small patch of breast down to the skin, then put the bird back down between the dogs. "Now you try."

She sent them both a mental image of pulling the feathers out with their teeth, and Persephone was the first to respond. She fell to the task with bloodthirsty enthusiasm, and was rewarded with the first bite of warm, raw quail. Hades whined softly, and looked up at her. *Hungry.*

"Well, get in there, silly. It's your bird." She stroked his head, pictured him gently nudging Persephone aside, and that's just what he did. She left them to work it out and wandered to the far side of the clearing.

Her communication with the animals didn't feel strange or surprising anymore. It was a part of her now, like breathing, or her sense of smell, or sight. She reached out and brushed against Ares' awareness – he came and went as he pleased, and had slipped out early this morning to hunt. She picked up an impression of dozing in the sun back at the cabin, along with a distinct *leave me alone* sensation that lifted her lips in amusement.

A flash of blue at the base of a pile of boulders caught her eye, and she hurried over to kneel beside a clump of delicate wildflowers. "Colorado Blue Columbine! We don't have this one yet – Macy will be so tickled..."

She thudded over onto her hip, curling around the slicing pain in her heart. God, how she hated the moments when she forgot. And then remembered. She keened softly, and didn't fight the tears. Her baby, her sweet girl. Never to finish the pressed wildflower books they'd started together. The list of things Macy would never do stretched on forever, to a grey, empty horizon.

Hades was there in an instant, pressing against her back, and Persephone nuzzled into her lap, daintily licking her muzzle clean of blood. Naomi closed her eyes and absorbed the comfort they offered, rocking Persephone gently in her embrace while Hades leaned against her, shifting with the rhythm of her movements.

She let the tears run their course, then wiped her eyes and gently set Persephone back on the ground. The little dog returned to worry at the bird, but Hades stayed beside her. Before she stood up, she plucked two perfect blooms from the plant, one for her book, and one for Macy's. There was no reason she couldn't finish it for her.

When the dogs finished with the quail, they headed back to the cabin where, sure enough, Ares was dozing in a shaft of sunshine. Naomi hurried to Macy's side, confirming that all was as it should be before she turned her attention to building the fire back up to a blaze. She hadn't needed to wrap a new sheet around Macy's body in almost a week, and she knew the time had come to make a decision as to Macy's final resting place.

She was no more inclined now than she had been before to dig a grave and bury her. But she wanted the matter settled before she left to visit Woodland Park, a task she felt she should complete in the next day or two. She pondered it that afternoon, as she set their Columbines to press and dry between sheets of wax paper in the giant old dictionary, and as she fixed herself a simple dinner of canned soup and fruit.   Finally, with the sun sinking towards the horizon, she made her decision.

The north bedroom where Piper usually slept was cool, and the air smelled stale when Naomi opened the door. Macy had always coveted this room for her own, and it felt right, fitting, to be able to finally grant her wish. Naomi didn't allow herself to think as she made the bed up with fresh sheets and turned down the covers. One of the secrets to surviving, she had learned, was to concentrate completely on the task at hand.   Life was now.   She couldn't stand to imagine a lifetime without Macy, but she could tuck in this blanket and take the next breath.

Macy's body was stiff and light when Naomi lifted her from the pallet in front of the fire. The dogs trailed behind as she carried her baby to her new room and tucked her between the covers. When she had Macy situated, she lit a hurricane lamp, then pulled a chair up to the side of the bed. The dogs settled beside her, curled up on the rag rug that brightened the floor, Persephone snuggled in the curve of Hades' big body.

"There you go, honey. Tucked in all safe and sound." Naomi reached out to smooth Macy's bright hair. "I'll stay here with you tonight. I've got to go to Woodland Park tomorrow, and I wanted you settled before I go."

She plaited Macy's hair into a row of soft braids as she talked, telling her about the day, about the Columbines, about Hades' first successful hunt. When she ran out of things to say, she read aloud for a while. She had read a Harry Potter book to Macy every summer since she turned seven, and they had just started *Harry Potter and the Goblet of Fire*. When her voice was reduced to a hoarse whisper and her eyes were drooping, she set the book aside, blew out the lamp, and leaned to rest her head beside Macy's body on the bed.

Just for tonight, she told herself. Tomorrow, she'd sleep in the master bed, but she needed this transition. She had not slept a single night without Macy beside her since the beginning of the plague.

In the dark silence of the cabin, she let her mind drift back to the time before, to the two friends she had known who had lost children. Lara had lost a baby boy shortly after he was born, and Sandy's daughter, a classmate of Piper's, had committed suicide the summer before her freshman year of college.

Both times, Naomi had done what people do: She'd made banana bread and lasagna, had shown up with cleaning supplies to run a load of laundry and keep the practical, day-to-day necessities of life going. She had taken Lara for coffee, had gone for walks with Sandy, had listened and held their hands as they cried. At the time, she'd felt like she was being a good friend. Now, she knew she'd done something unforgivable: She had told them that they would be okay.

There was no "okay." Not ever again. She knew that now. There was no return to the Naomi she used to be. She felt like everything soft and feminine, everything frivolous or indulgent or weak had been burned away, leaving her with the thin, hard core of a woman she barely recognized. Inside, she was mutilated, disfigured by an ugly, gaping wound she knew would never completely heal.

A soft thump on the bed startled her out of her thoughts. Ares settled in against her head and shoulder to snuggle, and after a moment, he started to purr. Naomi found a smile in the darkness, and focused on this moment. The soft blanket under her cheek. The faint whistling snore from Hades. Ares' contented purr. And she slept.

She woke at dawn the next morning, stiff from slumping over so awkwardly, but otherwise rested. She fed the dogs and put together a day pack with enough food and water to hold them until the next day if necessary. If all went well, she could drive down to Woodland Park and be there in under half an hour, but she no longer assumed things would go as she planned. She loaded the dogs, checked once again that the door to Macy's room was securely closed, locked the cabin, and they were off.

She kept her attention focused outward as they traveled, *feeling* for any threat or danger, detecting none. Little had changed, she noted, as she entered the outskirts of the city. Here and there she noticed a garden being cultivated. She didn't see any people, but she could *feel* eyes on them, and the curiosity that followed their passage.

In no time at all, she was pulling into the church parking lot. She shut the engine off, listening to it tick as it cooled for a moment. "No thinking," she reminded herself, and hopped out of the SUV. She let the dogs out of the back seat, quietly commanded them to "heel," and headed for the front door.

It popped open when she was still 10 feet away, and Verity floated out, her grin broad and triumphant. Martin was right behind her, his expression disgruntled.

"That is the last damn time I bet against you," he said to Verity, loud enough for Naomi to hear. "You cheat."

"I do not cheat," Verity sniffed. "I'm just more conversant with the subtleties of Woo Woo." She took both of Naomi's hands in hers by way of greeting. "Martin and I both knew someone would be coming this morning. I said it would be you. Martin said no, it didn't *feel* like you, not like he remembered." Verity squeezed her hands and spoke softly. "But you're not that person anymore, are you?"

"No." Naomi had dreaded this moment, but now that it was here, she had just one question. And it wasn't really a question; she knew the answer. "They've moved on, haven't they? Both of them."

"Yes. They're together in the Light."

Naomi nodded but couldn't speak. She wouldn't want it any other way, but the confirmation hurt just the same. She felt alone and adrift; if she wasn't a wife and mother, she had no idea who she was. Hades leaned against her leg, and she leaned back, anchoring herself. Verity shifted to her other side, looping her arm through Naomi's and walking them towards the front door.

"Jack and Layla will want to see you. Layla refused to take sides, but I'm sure she thought I was right." This was said with a quick smirk over her shoulder at Martin. "Jack, of course, would rather just pretend this stuff doesn't exist – he only talks about it when you corner him. And he's got so many other things to worry about, it's easy for him to avoid."

"Well, aren't you just a little sweetheart?"

Naomi turned to find Martin gently scratching Persephone's head between her ears. As she watched, Persephone flopped over on her back, offering her fluffy tummy for rubbing. Martin chuckled and glanced up at Naomi. "Can I pick her up?"

"Sure." She watched as Martin scooped the little dog into the crook of his arm like a baby, rubbing her chest and tummy with gentle knuckles. Intrigued, Naomi touched her senses to Persephone's, noting her complete trust as well as the beginnings of adoration for this man she barely knew. Hades, too, weighed in with *trust*, though he was considerably more reserved on the adoration part.

The inside of the church was humming with activity. There were a lot more people here then when she had visited before, all of them milling around the lobby as if waiting for something. Before she could ask what was going on, Jack strode to the front of the room.

"Thank you all for coming," he said, looking around, making eye contact, nodding at people as he recognized them. Even before his eyes reached her, Naomi could *feel* the strength of his persuasive charisma. He might not want to discuss it, but his power had grown considerably since the last time she'd seen him. When his eyes landed on her, she felt that power tenfold.

"Naomi. It's good to see you again." His eyes noted the dogs, searched for Macy, then returned to hers. He placed a hand over his heart, and Naomi felt his compassion for her like a warm blanket wrapped around her shoulders. He didn't say a word about her loss, and she appreciated the privacy. Instead he just said, simply, "Welcome."

Naomi inclined her head in acknowledgement. When his attention returned to the crowd, she glanced sideways at Verity and Martin. "He *feels* different, too. Stronger."

Verity just hummed, a noncommittal sound. Martin, however, frowned, and his face stayed set in troubled lines as the three of them listened to Jack give instructions.

"I've organized you all into groups – we need to start a methodical search of the city. You're looking for anything that might prove useful, with food and medical supplies highest on the list." He paused, and looked around. "You also need to be on the lookout for bodies that had been left exposed to the elements. If possible, these bodies need to be buried, or at the very least, moved inside where they'll be protected from the weather and further degradation."

The crowd shifted uneasily at this last directive, and Jack paused again, looking around, his eyes probing. "I know it's disturbing," he said in a quiet voice that somehow carried to each person's ear as if he were speaking to them alone. "So many of us never saw death up close before the plague. But it's about more than the threat of further disease. These are our friends and neighbors. They deserve better."

Jack's persuasive *power* settled over the crowd like oil on turbulent water. As if they were one organism, they settled, the restlessness dissipating. Naomi didn't know whether to be impressed or disturbed. Her own intuitive sense was humming a soft alert, sending unease tickling down her spine.

Instructions received, the crowd broke up in purposeful knots and swiftly exited the lobby of the church. Jack spoke to a few people, shook a few hands, then headed towards them. Hades took two steps forward to angle his body in front of Naomi's. He didn't growl, but his still watchfulness reinforced Naomi's unease. Something wasn't quite right.

Jack didn't miss Hades' body language. He stopped a few feet away, eyes on the big dog. "I'm sure he doesn't remember me."

"He does." Up close, Naomi could see the lines of strain and tension aging Jack's face. He looked tired, like a man regularly pushed beyond his resources. She remembered that he too had survived the plague and was probably still recovering. "His breed is naturally reserved and cautious, and very protective. You shouldn't take it personally."

"I'll try not to." Jack met her gaze. "I'm sorry for your loss. Truly. She was a lovely young lady."

Naomi's throat tightened on words of thanks, so she just nodded. Jack turned his body slightly, angling his thumb towards the office area. "Layla will want to see you. Will you stay for a while and talk with us?"

Naomi nodded again, and the whole group followed Jack down the hallway, Verity's step so light she hardly seemed to touch the ground, Martin bringing up the rear with Persephone still cradled in his arms. When Naomi glanced back at them, he gave her a broken smile and unselfconsciously shrugged a shoulder to wipe at the escaping tears.

"It's comforting, to hold her, isn't it?" He smoothed a finger between Persephone's eyes and around a perky ear, and the little dog's eyes drifted shut in bliss. "She feels like a baby, warm and solid. I bet it helped a lot, having her, when your little Macy passed."

Naomi nodded, dropping her hand to Hades' head. "They kept me alive."

Martin gazed down at Persephone. "I'm glad you had them. When my son..." He pressed his lips together, swallowed, then looked up at her, his eyes liquid with the same bottomless sorrow she stared into each day. "My son."

"I'm so sorry." Naomi stopped walking and touched his forearm. "With my whole heart, I'm sorry. Parents should never outlive their children. We shouldn't have to figure out how to keep breathing without our babies." On impulse, she sent his heart a pulse of comfort, just like she did with the animals. Martin started, then laughed a little.

"Wow. That's pretty cool."

Naomi dropped her hand, and her shoulders rose self-consciously. "It's just something I do with the animals. I wasn't sure people could feel it. I'm sorry if I...intruded, or over-stepped."

"It's okay. We're all trying to figure out what the new boundaries are. It's a strange new world."

"Very."

They started walking again. Jack and Verity were waiting for them in a doorway at the end of the hallway, he frowning, she beaming. Both expressions gave Naomi pause, but she didn't have time to puzzle either out before they were stepping into the room. Layla rose from where she'd been seated in a leather wing chair. She looked as wrung-out as Jack.

"Naomi, I'm so happy to see you again." Like Verity, Layla stepped forward to take both her hands. "I *felt* it when your Macy crossed." She squeezed Naomi's hands. "I hope you're not offended, but I cast for you, a spell to strengthen and comfort you in your sorrow, and of remembrance for your daughter. There's nothing evil in what I do," she added, her eyes sliding briefly to Jack. Naomi sensed the divide between them on this, as well as Layla's steady defense of her position. "No Satan, no devil-worship. It's just a different way of approaching the Divine, to ask for blessings on your behalf."

"It's fine with me." Naomi squeezed back, feeling her throat tighten yet again. She forced words out past the knot. "Thank you. For caring. And most of all, for remembering her."

They settled around the room, and Naomi spoke. "Is Rowan here? I wanted to thank her. For trying to help."

Layla answered. "She's out on her rounds. She never stops." She looked down. "We're starting to lose more people. Some of them to disease – not plague, but dysentery. Some of them to suicide. Rowan *feels* every death, but the suicides hurt her the worst. She *knows* when people are going to make the attempt, but nothing any of us has tried so far has prevented someone from following through."

"Now that the worst of the plague is over, people are facing what the world has become," Jack added. "Some of them don't want to go on. They feel they have nothing left to live for, and the new world just seems too hard."

Naomi swallowed and glanced at Martin. "I understand that," she said softly. "It hurts to live. Dying looks so peaceful and painless." She cleared her throat and spoke with more strength. "But I can't leave my older daughter. Piper. I need to find her. I know she's still alive – I can *feel* her. She's in trouble, and she's angry, but I know for certain she's alive."

"You don't need to convince us," Martin said with a wry smile. "Strange new world, remember?"

Naomi smiled back, then swept her gaze around the group. "Piper may be on her way to the cabin – that was our plan - so I need to wait before I go looking for her. At least until next spring. In the meantime, I need to prepare." She outlined what she needed; when she finished, Layla nodded.

"We'll help you gather the resources you need." She looked at Martin. "You have some survival skills, don't you?"

"I would need to brush up, but yes, I do." To Naomi. "I'm retired military. Marine. Where will you start looking?"

"I'm not sure. Logically, I should go to UNC first – that's the last place I know for sure she was. She might have left a message for me there. She told her dad about a friend who had a place to go in the mountains, but nothing was ever confirmed and I don't have any information about this friend at all." She pressed her hand to her chest and closed her eyes, feeling stupid, but knowing that she would be believed. "I *feel* her in that direction." She pointed to the northwest. "Fairly far away, maybe a few hundred miles – I'm terrible with estimating distances. But I can find her. I know it."

Martin leaned forward, radiating excitement and purpose. "My older kids are in Limon, with my ex-wife. That's only 100 miles or so from Greeley, as the crow flies." He smiled. "I'm very good at estimating distances. We could team up. Look for them together." He set Persephone on the ground, then snagged a piece of paper and a pen off the desk, bending to draw a quick sketch. "Okay, here's Limon and here's Greeley. You definitely want to avoid Denver, so-"

"Hold on." Jack's voice was weary, with an edgy frustration underneath. "Martin, we've talked about this. About the importance of community, and each person doing their part. You're the only person we have with military experience, and one of the only people who knows how to operate a firearm. We need you."

"My kids need me." But Martin sat back down, abandoning his map.

"Martin, you know how sorry I am to say this, but the likelihood that they're still alive is so slim..." Jack's voice trailed into silence for a moment as Martin absorbed the words Naomi was certain he'd heard before. Jack went on. "Is it worth abandoning this community that needs you, this new family, on such a remote chance?"

Martin didn't reply, but slumped back in his chair, arms folded across his chest, expression stormy. If not for the liberal silver in his dark hair, he would have looked for all the world like a sullen teen. Naomi's eyes bounced back and forth between the two men, and she frowned in confusion.

Martin was older, and radiated a natural authority. Somehow, though, Jack had tapped into something that reversed their logical roles. Again, Naomi's intuition pinged a warning. She folded her lips tightly against the urge to speak up on Martin's behalf, even though a partner on her search would increase her chances of success exponentially. Martin was a big boy. It wasn't her place to interfere.

Verity sidled up to perch beside her. "Fascinating, isn't it?" Naomi glanced at her, and Verity nodded encouragingly. "Well, go on, then. Jump in there. I've been wondering how this would play out."

Her place be damned. Instinct gave Naomi the words. She leaned forward, ducking her head until she met Martin's troubled gaze. "He's not your father, you know." Martin's eyes narrowed angrily, but she plunged on. "You can tell when people are lying, right? You can *hear* truth. And what he's saying is true, logically speaking, so you listen." She leaned forward. "But what's *your* truth? What are your instincts telling you to do?"

"Naomi." Jack's voice was gentle, but not for a moment did she miss the anger simmering under the softness. "With respect, this isn't your business. You're not part of this community yet, and though we'd love to have you join us, I would ask that you stay out of this discussion. Martin and I have talked this over, at length, and we made an agreement."

Naomi straightened her spine and raised an eyebrow. She hadn't just survived Piper's turbulent teens; she'd learned a thing or two. Her daughter's ability to twist words and use emotions to manipulate had been second to none. Until she'd witnessed Jack in motion, that is.

"I will consider being a permanent part of this community," she said, holding Jack's gaze, "When I have found my daughter and brought her safely home. I am asking for some help, it's true, to learn the skills I'll need in order to do that. In exchange, I can share what surplus supplies I have. And I can teach people how to shoot and to properly care for their firearms. I'm not a hunter, so I can't teach those skills, but I can help you arm more of your people."

She paused, then went on with the same honesty and authority she had finally learned to use with Piper.

"But I won't be manipulated into staying, Jack. You can't use guilt or obligation to get me to stay, like you have with Martin. This is something I have to do. You don't have to agree with it, but you must respect my decision."

She stopped talking, and the silence in the room was absolute. Beside her, she could *feel* the slowly growing boil of Martin's anger as her words sank into the place in him that knew *truth*. He stood abruptly, glaring at Jack, then shifted his fierce gaze to her.

"I can teach you some of what you need to know. I know a rancher outside of town that can teach you more. When you're ready to start, let Layla know and she'll get in touch with me."

Without another glance at anyone, he strode out of the room, leaving strained silence in his wake. Naomi felt a spurt of social discomfort, and almost laughed aloud at herself. Such feelings were a thing of the past, and a waste of time. She'd set this in motion, and she couldn't be sorry. She sensed that Jack was essentially a good man, but he didn't seem to be using the best judgment when it came to the new *power* he possessed.

Layla must have been thinking the same thing. She leaned forward, speaking in a voice that both comforted and confronted. "Jack, Naomi is right. We can't coerce people into doing what we want. We can only invite them, ask them, then let them make their own choices."

"Oh, really? Is that what 'we' should do? Say what you mean, Layla – *I* need to stop manipulating people, isn't that right?" Jack glared around the room, at Verity, then at Naomi, then returned his gaze to Layla. Even though it wasn't directed at her, Naomi felt the force of his frustration and fear like a punch. Layla gasped and put a hand over her heart, and Jack sneered. "Whoops, sorry, didn't warn you in time to get your shields up, did I? My bad. Sometimes I forget that we live in the Land of Oz now, and it would appear I've been elected Wizard, whether I want to be or not."

"Jack, you don't need to-"

"Stop!" Jack shot to his feet. "Stop telling me what I do or don't need to do! I didn't ask for this, I never asked to lead these people. You and Rowan decided that for me, and now you think you can tell me how to go about it?"

He whirled on Naomi. "Do you know how many of us are left? Eighty-seven. Eighty-seven people, not counting you, and we need every single one. We need people who can work together, not just to produce food and shelter to keep us all alive, but for protection." He rubbed his temples, then scrubbed a hand roughly across his forehead. "Something is coming. Something bad. I...dream about it."

He returned his glare to Layla. "So do you. I hear you in the night, when you wake up terrified and cry out. Your shields are down and I can feel what you feel – you know what's headed our way as well as I do. So don't tell me what I can and cannot do. Don't tell me I can't manipulate people, to make them do what we need them to. Do you hear me, Layla? What we *need* them to do.

This isn't about what I want. It's about keeping this community safe."

Their gazes were locked; Jack's chest was heaving, and Layla's eyes glittered with tears. Verity leaned over to stage-whisper to Naomi.

"Gosh, if this was a movie he'd kiss her right now, don't you think?" Then, to Jack: "If you're not going to kiss her, you ought to storm out dramatically. After a speech like that, it's just called for."

Jack heaved a breath, and when he released it, he seemed smaller. Deflated. He shook his head wearily at Verity, too exhausted to even try to hide his hurt. "Thanks, Verity. Mockery was the only thing missing from this debacle, and you've supplied it." He headed for the door, paused, then spoke over his shoulder to Naomi. "I'm sorry for all this. We'll help you with whatever you need, and accept your help gratefully. Please excuse me."

Naomi just nodded. In the wake of his departure, Layla turned to gaze at Verity. "Why would you say those things?" she asked softly, her voice tender and exasperated. "I know you intended no harm – I could *feel* that. And yet you managed to cut him to the bone. Why?"

Verity shrugged; she appeared contrite for the moment, but the imp lurked in her eyes, ready to re-take control of her features. "I'll apologize," she said in a subdued tone. "I just thought the moment called for the distance and perspective that levity provides."

"Distance and perspective." Layla shook her head. "I wish I could disagree, but I think that's just what he needs. That, and maybe a solid whack upside the head."

She stood, and moved to rest a hand on Naomi's shoulder. "I need to see if I can get him to go home and rest – he's exhausted. Will you stay until I come back?"

"I will." Naomi rested her hand over Layla's and sent her a pulse of comfort, just as she had with Martin. "Please pass that on to him, would you?"

Layla's smile was both delighted and startlingly beautiful. "How lovely! I'll try, though he's a lot more comfortable doling out comfort than receiving it."

She left then, and Naomi turned to Verity. They gazed at each other in silence for long moments. Then Naomi narrowed her eyes.

"You planned this," she accused. "You wanted to talk to me alone, so you engineered this whole thing."

Verity's laughter chimed softly. "Boy, there is no fooling those mom instincts of yours. 'Planned' isn't really the right word. More like I nudged forces that were already in motion, and happily, everything turned out just as I hoped."

"Why? What is it you couldn't say in front of the others?" Naomi's heart started to pound and her voice dropped to a hoarse, excited whisper. "Do you have a message for me? From Scott or Macy?"

"Naomi." Verity gathered both her hands, then brought them to her lips, kissing first one then the other. From her, the gesture didn't even seem strange. "You were right the first time. They moved on together to join the One."

Disappointment slowed Naomi's speeding heart. She dropped her head for a moment, fighting not to cry. She was so very, very weary of crying. "Then what is it?"

"Your Macy didn't just see the dead. She saw possibilities, what might be, what could be, if conditions were right. That's what she wanted to talk to me about, when you were here before. She didn't have time to grow into her gift, to detach from the Earthly plane and learn what we all must learn to survive with such knowledge: That no path is written. That no future is better or worse than another. There is simply the path, which is created as people choose it."

"I'm not sure I understand," Naomi said slowly. "Are you telling me that Macy was trying to use her gift to control the future?"

"In a word, yes. She saw an outcome she desperately wanted for you, and for her sister. She wanted me to help you, to ensure that outcome."

Naomi gazed at Verity for a long moment, then shook her head. Once again, her question was not a question. "You're not going to do that, are you."

Verity stood, and floated to the window. She gazed out at the bright sunshine, and was silent for so long, Naomi thought she wouldn't answer. Finally, she turned back. Her face was aglow with a light that could only be called holy, her eyes faceted with knowledge, wisdom, sorrow, and joy.

"We are travelers together, in the time between what no longer is and what has not yet come to be. This is a time of chaos – change is almost never neat and tidy –

and mankind is transforming. That transformation will occur, no matter what path you choose." She paused, as if considering, then nodded. "I will tell you this: I saw Macy's path for you, and for Piper. It's a Hero's Path. If you choose it, your names will be remembered."

"I don't care about that. A Hero's Path?" Naomi shook her head, bewildered. "I don't know what you and Macy saw, but all I want is to find my daughter, to bring her home and keep her safe. You can keep your chaos and transformation – I don't want any part of it."

Verity's eyes lit with glee. "Ah, but that's not yours to decide. 'All we have to decide is what to do with the time that is given us.'" She chortled – actually chortled. "Tolkien, via Gandalf. Gosh, I have always wanted to use that quote – never thought I'd get the chance."

She sobered once more. "You can deny the task, Naomi, but not the call. I can mentor you as you travel across this space, but I can't decide for you. Always, always, the choice is yours."

Naomi felt like her fingertips were just starting to brush the edges of Verity's meaning. "What am I choosing between?"

Verity didn't hesitate. "Fear and love."

"Fear and love," Naomi repeated softly, and something inside her resonated. She could feel those opposing forces in her heart and mind, the push-and-pull of them. Fear would keep her at the cabin, reading to Macy's corpse and completing a wildflower book for a little girl who was as vibrant and dead as the blossoms preserved in its pages.

Fear was safety and security. It was prudence, caution, suspicion, defense. And love was...everything else. The whole wide world.

She looked up at Verity, speaking softly, shyly. "So, fear is limitation. It's the plan you make when you take into account your weaknesses." Verity nodded eagerly, and Naomi continued, groping towards understanding. "And love is a free-fall off a cliff. With only your courage for a parachute."

"Yes!" Verity shrieked the word, making Naomi jump. She fist-pumped and strutted around the room in a hip-wiggling victory dance. Naomi squinted, then knuckled her eyes like a tired five-year-old and squinted again. Surrounding Verity, like something seen from the corner of one's eye, was she seeing...angels? And were they...dancing?

Verity pirouetted to seize Naomi's hands. Her eyes were incandescent. "What an adventure!" She sighed happily. "Welcome to the Path."

Made in the USA
Lexington, KY
23 June 2015